In Loving Memory

of

Dianne Price

(1933 – 2013)

Broken Wings

Dianne Price

**BOOK ONE OF
THE THISTLE SERIES**

Ashberry Lane

© 2013
Ashberry Lane

All rights reserved. No part of this publication may be reproduced, stored in a retrieval system, or transmitted in any form or by any means without the prior written permission of the publisher. The only exception is brief quotations in printed reviews.

Published in association with Terry Burns of Hartline Literary Agency, LLC.

ISBN 978-0-9893967-2-1

Edited by Christina Tarabochia
Cover design by Miller Media Solutions
Cover images by Ashlee Murr Photography and iStock.com

Use of the Gaelic Biblical Texts by kind permission of the Scottish Bible Society.

Scripture used in this book, whether quoted or paraphrased by the characters, is taken from the English Revised Version of the Bible, Oxford Press, 1885. Used by permission.

Map © 2013 Mary Elizabeth Hall

Ach iadsan a dh'fheitheas air an
But they that wait upon the LORD
Tighearna gheibh iad spionnadh nuadh;
Shall renew their strength; they shall
eiridh iad suas mar iolair air a sgiathaibh;
Mount up with wings as eagles;
ruithidh iad agus cha bhi iad sgith,
They shall run, and not be weary;
siubhlaidh iad agus cha'n fhas iad fann.
They shall walk and not faint.
~Isaiah 40:31

Fuirich gu foighidneach ri Dia,
Wait on the LORD:
glac thugad misneach mhòr,
Be strong, and let thine heart take courage;
Is bheir e spionnadh cridhe dhut:
Yea, wait thou
fuirich ri Dia na glòir.
On the LORD.
~Psalms 27:14

"The selkie and her crofter were merrit in the kirk and lived on their wee island in the sea forever, and ever, and ever."
~The Selkie Tale—Scots folklore

Faith is deliberate confidence in the character of God whose ways you may not understand at the time.
~Oswald Chambers, Scottish Theologian, 1874-1917

Never, never, never give up.
~Sir Winston Churchill, 1874-1965

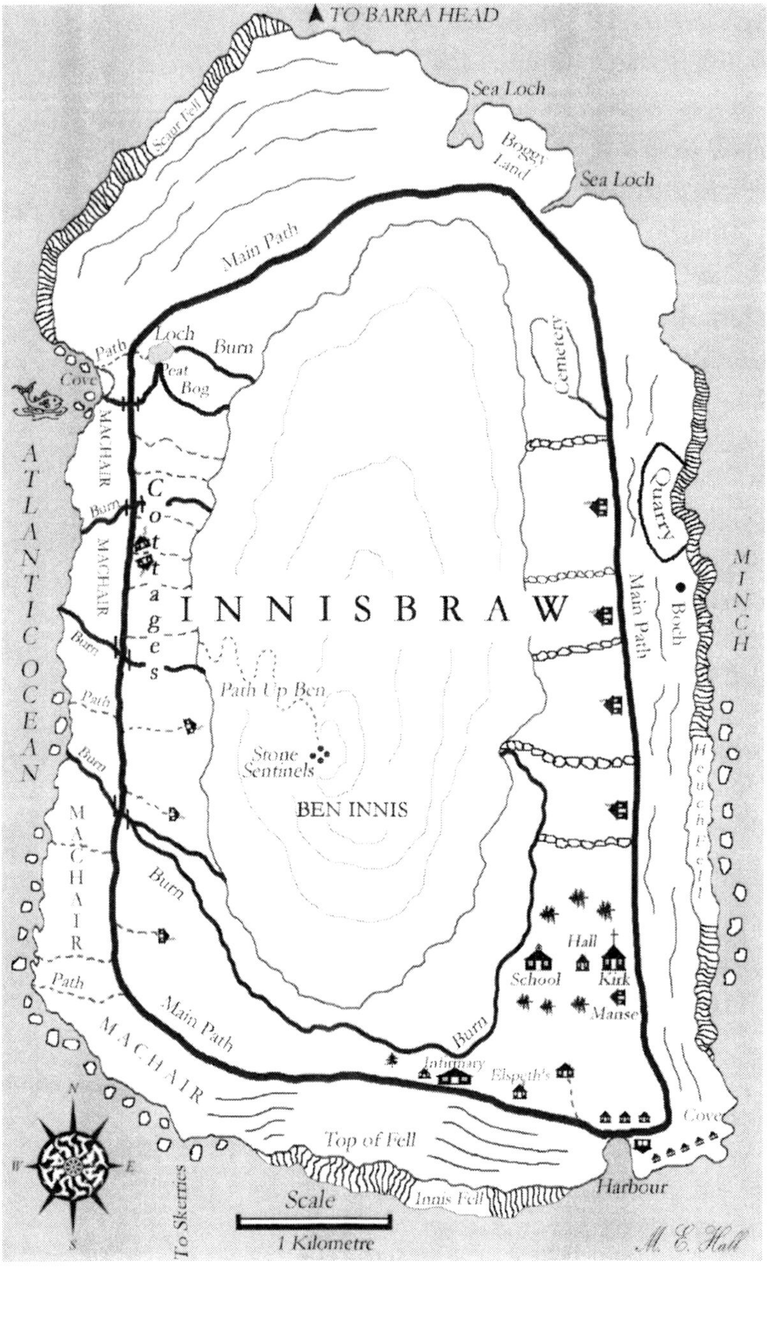
TO BARRA HEAD
Sea Loch
Scaur Fell
Boggy Land
Sea Loch
Main Path
Loch
Path
Burn
Cove
Peat Bog
Cemetery
MACHAIR
ATLANTIC OCEAN
Burn
Cottages
Quarry
MACHAIR
MINCH
INNISBRAW
Main Path
Bothy
Burn
Path
Path Up Ben
Burn
Stone Sentinels
BEN INNIS
MACHAIR
Burn
Hall
School
Kirk
Path
Main Path
Manse
MACHAIR
Burn
Infirmary
Elspeth's
Cove
Top of Fell
N
W
E
S
To Skerries
Scale
Innis Fell
Harbour
1 Kilometre
M. E. Hall

Dedication

Foremost, to the glory of my Lord and Savior, Jesus Christ. And for my husband and best friend, True, who always wore the "Colonel's cap" in our family, but only with calm Christian dedication, love, and compassion. See you in Heaven, my luve!

In Loving Memory

Dianne was granted her wish. A mere week before the release date of this book, she joined her beloved Savior and her husband in Heaven. She is probably dancing a Scots reel even as you read this.

Prologue

Isle of Innisbraw, Outer Hebrides, Scotland
August, 1938

Stay! Don't go! Maggie McGrath struggled to ignore the words screaming in her mind. She tucked a tissue-wrapped sprig of heather into a fold in her battered traveling bag. Too dry for the fragrance to linger, but she'd put it in a drawer. When the longing for home shredded her heart, she'd hold the fragile, purple buds close to her nose and imagine the sweet scent perfuming the air every summer.

Her fingers trembled as she fastened the bag and looked around the wee bedroom she'd shared with her younger brother, Calum, for over half of her life. His box-bed unmade, sheets and bed plaid in a muddle. A ragged sweater and pair of soiled trousers crumpled on the floor. Tears burned her eyes. Typical of a nine-year-old lad who lived for the day he would be old enough to crew a fishing trawler. Och, she would miss him so terribly.

Heedless of those words still torturing her mind, she pulled the sides of her waist-length black hair into a celluloid clip at the top of her head and dragged her bag into the cramped room that served as the cottage's living quarters and kitchen.

Her father stood at the small, deep-set window above the sink, his face toward the morning sun colouring the cloudless blue sky with a soft blush of orange.

The bump of her bag over the rough stone-flagged floor seemed to rouse him. He placed his cup of tea on the scarred table and walked toward her, arms outstretched. "Ready are you to be off then, lass?" He enveloped her in a hug, the tweed of his jacket scratchy, yet so familiar, against her cheek.

The soft cadence of the Scots he spoke threatened to crack her resolve. She'd hear only English in Edinburgh. *I cannot stay. I have to go.* A sigh. "Aye, as ready as can be."

"I know 'tis hard." He stepped back and wiped a tear from her cheek. "But in a bit over twa months I'll join you in Edinburgh."

She wanted him to beg her to stay, to refuse her opportunity to study at the Edinburgh Royal Infirmary's Nursing School. But why would he? It was her dream, the culmination of everything she had studied for, including four years at a boarding academy on the Isle of Harris where she had learned to speak English as fluently as her father. Hard years, those. Painful raps on her knuckles when she spoke Scots, followed by humiliating mockery from the English-speaking students.

His warm hand rested on her shoulder. "On you come, lass. I've a pottle of strong tea waiting." He poured tea into her mother's treasured china cup. The burden in her heart lifted a wee bit. It seemed only fitting she embark on her journey into womanhood after drinking from her mother's legacy. If Elizabeth McGrath had survived the birth of her laddie, Calum, she would have been proud of her daughter.

Maggie added heather honey and milk to her tea and stood in front of the glowing peat fire, shivering from an inner chill no flame could warm. It was already gone 0530. In less than half an hour she would be saying "guid-by" to all she held dear. And how would Calum fare? "Are you certain Calum will be all right staying with Morag and Alec when you leave?"

"Och, the lad's spent most of every winter with the MacDonalds since you started academy." Her father settled into his rocker with a grunt of satisfaction. "And he'll have a bed to himself now, what with their Graham going off to school."

A few strands of grey invaded his dark brown hair and short beard. When had that happened? It seemed only yesterday he'd rocked her in his lap and sung silly ditties in Scots or the Gaelic to soothe away her tears from a skinned knee or bad dream. That had all changed ever-so-gradually over the years. There was no question he loved her and Calum. But as head of Orthopaedics at the Royal Infirmary, he now spent most of his time in Edinburgh. Only one short three-month visit beginning in August and a weekly radio call the rest of the year to fill the aching void in their hearts.

Her heart cried out to recapture those carefree childhood days when her life revolved around family and friends, this wee stone cottage with its thatched roof, and her beloved green island. But she would be eighteen in a few months—old enough to fall in love, marry, and have her own bairns to rock.

And old enough to voice the one subject she'd never dared broach aloud. "Are you never coming home to open your infirmary permanently?" Maggie choked out the words. "I know what you do is important, but Calum needs a faither, no' just fishermen who have their own lads."

He stroked his beard, avoiding her gaze. Was he considering an excuse—perhaps something familiar, that he told himself every day to assuage his guilt?

She shouldn't allow such words to ruin her last moments at home. Leaving her untasted tea on the table, she dashed to the door, pulling it open with a jerk. Even the pervasive scent of the heather covering the towering slopes of Ben Innis and tumbling in purple splashes down braes and over hillocks brought no solace as she raced to the low, dry-stone wall separating their croft from the path which ran across the high, flat top of Innis Fell.

Tears pooled in her eyes, blurring the harbour below and the Minch stretching to the horizon, its waves capped with white horses whipped to a gallop by the brisk morning breeze. What if the rumors of an imminent war with Germany came true? Everyone on the island was talking about Hitler's invasion of Austria. Would he be satisfied to stop there or would he want more and more until all of Europe erupted into flames the way it had in the last Great War? Calum was too young to serve, but what about Graham MacDonald, Mark Ferguson, and the other lads on Innisbraw? Their ruddy-cheeked, innocent faces swam before her eyes. How many would die? How many would never come home to take up sheep or cow crofting or fishing with their fathers?

Her father came behind her and his strong arms pulled her against his chest. He rocked her back and forth for a moment before speaking. "I canna leave my work yet, Maggie. I'm on the brink of perfecting a new technique for repairing compound fractures. Mebbe when you've finished your training we'll come back together. I'll need a nurse at our infirmary, and in the meantime, Elspeth and Hugh have promised to write often." He squeezed her shoulders before his steps faded away on the scudding breeze.

Maggie bit her lip to keep from weeping aloud. She couldn't bear to hear the names of her two dearest friends when she wouldn't see them for at least two years. Elspeth NicAllister had been her surrogate mother since Calum's birth. Hugh MacEwan, the island's minister and other anchor in her life, had never been too busy to offer words of encouragement or scriptures to give her guidance.

Och, Heavenly Faither, please help me be strong, for You planted the need to help others in my heart. Help me remember the honey-sweet scent of the heather, the sound of the sea sooking on the shore, the tumbling burns and shaded glens, even the plomping rain and skailing winds of winter. But most of all, give me the faith that I'll come home to Innisbraw someday.

Chapter One

Edenoaks Air Base, England
Early May, 1942

"You gotta have a death wish."

Colonel Rob Savage steeled himself against the pleading eyes of Major Dennis Anderson, his second-in-command. "The mission's set. It's a go whether you approve or not." Rob untangled his long legs from the barstool, waved at the fug of cigarette smoke clouding the teeming officer's club, and shrugged into his A-2 bomber jacket. "I'm going to catch some shut-eye. Wheels-up at 0400."

Den snagged his sleeve. "Let me fly cover for you. A single-plane strike over Metz is suicide."

Arguments flew through Rob's mind, each as hollow as his bones. Suicide? No way. Pushing the odds against surviving the war? Yeah, he'd give Den that, but he'd never dodged his commitment, no matter the risk. Every bomb dropped on German-occupied territory brought them closer to victory. He shot Den a thumbs-up. "I'm counting on you to lead the group to that alternate target tomorrow."

Den returned the good-luck gesture. "Somebody needs to watch your back. At least I tried."

Rob grunted. Knowing Den, he hadn't given up. He'd be at the *Liberty Belle's* hardstand in the morning, trying to talk his way into flying right seat. "See you at Interrogation tomorrow. That cot's calling my name."

A grin split Den's flushed face. He leaned closer, Old Spice shaving lotion marking his territory like a feral tomcat on the prowl. "Who needs cot-time when there are enough nurses here to make a man drool?" He smacked his lips and exchanged winks with a nurse carrying two beers away from the bar. "Or are you going to spend the rest of your life married to an airplane?"

Not again. When would Den stop trying to set him up with a date? Sure, he wanted a family to replace the one he'd lost so long ago. But a world torn apart by war had a nasty way of putting the kibosh on most dreams, and his awkward attempts at social conversation were harder work than planning strikes and flying lead.

He reached for his beer and took a swig, gaze sweeping the officer's club. From the radio, a band belted out "Chattanooga Choo Choo," while loud, boisterous officers packed the Nissen hut, drinking beer, sucking on cigarettes, and openly ogling the nurses sitting at their own crowded table. Was it always this noisy?

It'd been a mistake to hope to relax before hitting the sack. The morning's bombing strike had him so tied in knots he'd be lucky to clock a couple of hours sleep before briefing his crew.

His crew. Nine good men—like family—whose survival depended on him. *Oh, God, don't let me fail them.* Den's poke in the ribs interrupted his dark thoughts.

"Dare you to dance with that teensy bee-u-tiful nurse in the RAF uniform." The redhead rocked back on his barstool. "That's what I call a babe."

Rob drained his pint. "Then you dance with her. The gossip mill's busy enough without adding the base commander to the mix."

"But she's just your type, Bucko. You know, serious looking, kind of uncomfortable, sitting on the edge of her seat like she's about to run—just like you at every dance at the Point."

Frowning, Rob turned to look. And froze. The lieutenant's black hair, pulled into a bun above her gray-blue uniform collar, caught the overhead lights and sparkled like raindrops on wet tarmac. His fingers itched to loosen the pins and watch it spill down her slim back. Pale skin, delicate nose—and the bluest eyes he'd ever seen. He'd signed the papers placing her on-loan from the RAF, yet he couldn't recall seeing her around the base hospital. A yearning he'd thought long buried threatened to weaken his resolve, and a bitter taste flooded his mouth as he looked away.

Den waggled his eyebrows and flapped his arms. "Chicken. I double-dare you."

"Enough." Rob growled. Refusing a double-dare would deal Rob a crushing defeat in their ongoing game of one-upmanship.

Besides, she might get his mind off that bombing strike.

He stood, unzipped his A-2, loosened his tie, and wove his way between the tables. Mouth dry as an empty fuel tank, he tapped her shoulder. "Care to dance?"

She stiffened and turned, gaze darting to the silver eagles on his shoulders.

He never fraternized with someone under his command. What if she refused? Then he'd get what he deserved—a red face and another foot added to that stone wall he'd built around himself.

"Och, no, but ... thank you," she stammered, cheeks flushing.

One of the nurses nudged her. "What's the matter, Maggie? You Scots only dance with men wearing skirts?"

She hesitated.

He tried a smile, nearly succeeded. "Well?"

A brief nod.

He pulled her to her feet and led her silently to the crowded dance floor. She really was tiny. At six-five, he was accustomed to towering over women, but the top of her head didn't even reach his shoulder. He turned and placed his arm around her, hoping his tense body didn't reveal his unease. Hard as it would be, he'd have to initiate the conversation. "So, um ... Leftenant Maggie, how do you like being here at Edenoaks?"

She averted her eyes. "'Tis very interesting."

That tickled his funny bone. Must have been around Den too long. "Interesting? That's not much of an endorsement." Emboldened, he stooped over and said into her ear, "What's the matter? Find us Yanks a little hard to stomach?"

She recoiled. "Och, no, Colonel."

"Rob, please."

"Rob."

He opened his mouth to comment on her charming burr when she spoke up.

"I ... I'd best be going. I've drawn an early shift and I—"

"I'm only teasing, Leftenant."

How stupid could he be? She'd offered him a perfect out and he'd thrown it away. Why could he conduct a briefing and argue bombing strategy with two-and-three-star generals, yet fail to untie his knotted tongue when talking to a woman?

Those blue eyes met his. "Only teasing, were you?"

The unspoken challenge in her slight smile dissolved the icy splinters of fear in his chest. He clasped her hand tighter as their feet moved to the slow love song, "The Nearness of You." The softly crooned words washed against the stony shore of his heart. The scent of warm honey dislodged another stone. He leaned closer, his chin brushing her forehead. "Your hair smells sweet."

"'Tis heather. A friend at home makes the soap and sends it to me."

Her voice, soft and warm, reminded him of a breath of summer air in an open cockpit. "And home is ... where?"

"Innisbraw. I'm certain you've never heard of it."

He tasted the word. Innisbraw, a fitting name for a village folded into the heart of mist-shrouded hills. "You're right. But it has to be somewhere in Scotland where the heather blooms wild and a good friend makes you soap." His labored breathing eased.

The nearness of you.

"Aye, 'tis a wee island. That's where the *Innis* comes from. 'Tis one of the Gaelic words for island and *braw* is Scotssag for fine, even beautiful, in a rugged sort of way."

"And what's the word for 'fine and beautiful,' in a more refined way?"

"Bonnie." Her shy whisper and downturned eyes brought a frisson of hope. Did she long for someone too?

The lilting Scots rolled effortlessly from his tongue. "Then, 'tis bonnie you are, Maggie, lass."

The music crescendoed, faded, and died.

She looked up at him, those blue eyes with their violet depths calling him to dive in.

Could he muster the courage to seek her out later? Perhaps—if he survived the mission. He squeezed her hand before leading her back to her table. One last touch to treasure.

The nearness of you.

"Thank you, bonnie Maggie, for the dance. I hope to see you again. Soon."

Chapter Two

Maggie McGrath rushed to the ambulance as the doors were thrown open. Medics unloaded the stretcher and thrust a plasma bottle at her. Holding it high, she ran beside the stretcher. "Operating room one," she shouted. "They're standing by."

Nurses and orderlies hugged the walls of the corridor as they rushed the stretcher into the OR.

Major Larson, the flight surgeon, stood at the foot of the operating table, already masked and gowned. "Hop to it! This is our base commander. We need to be on our toes."

Maggie swallowed a gasp. She looked down as she supported the patient's head during the transfer from the stretcher to the operating table. It *was* Rob Savage! Time froze as she recalled the warmth of his huge hand clasping hers, the brush of his chin on her forehead when he leaned closer to inhale the fragrance of heather on her hair, and how her heart melted when he spoke the lilting dialect like a native Scotsman. She'd even dreamed that he might be the one she'd been waiting for, the one she'd take home to her wee green island.

"What's he doing in here so early?" the scrub nurse asked. "The group woke me taking off at 0600. They shouldn't be back for another two hours at least."

"He must have aborted and got caught alone by the Luftwaffe," the anaesthesiologist said, hooking up the gas and oxygen tanks.

"From what I've heard, the colonel wouldn't abort unless his plane was shot out from under—"

"Major Hirsh called me from the flight tower," Major Larson interrupted the assistant surgeon's comment. "The colonel came in on one engine and crash-landed after a single-plane bombing mission over Metz. No more chatter, people. Get busy."

Broken Wings

The bright lights and noise of the operating room brought Maggie out of her shock. She willed her hands to stop shaking and quickly took a blood pressure reading. It was so low, she took it again, heart hammering in her chest.

Major Larson studied her over his mask. "You're pale, McGrath. I know you've worked a double. Do you need a replacement?"

She cleared her tear-clogged throat. "No, Doctor. I'm fine."

"What's his pressure?"

"Fifty over twenty-five."

"Let's get his flight suit off and find out where all this blood is coming from. I expected bruises or broken bones from that crash landing but he might have picked up a bullet or flak. We'll need some pictures—and open that saline drip to full."

As they cut off Savage's heavy flight suit, Maggie drew upon her extensive OR experience. She could not help the colonel if she allowed her emotions to run wild.

Ten minutes later, the team finished stripping Savage and turned him over onto his belly while Major Larson studied the X-rays. "He's taken several pieces of shrapnel in his lower back." He inserted a probe into the largest wound. "Don't like the looks of this one. Too close to the spine. Put him all the way under, Phelps. Jenkins, start a whole blood. And pray we don't need much. We're low on AB Positive."

As the operation began, Maggie's hands worked automatically. She slapped each instrument into the doctor's waiting palm. Incisions were made and widened, wounds probed, and jagged pieces of shrapnel removed.

After two hours, Major Larson looked up. "That's it."

Stunned, Maggie said, "But that large wound ..."

Larson glared at her. "They couldn't pay me enough to touch that one. It's pressing against the spinal cord. I'm sure he's already paralyzed." He snapped off his rubber gloves. "Put a drain in, Captain Clark, and close. There's no more we can do here." He left the OR.

Maggie watched while the assistant surgeon flushed the gaping wound with saline and anchored the drain in place with two small sutures.

"Poor devil," he muttered beneath his breath. "Wonder how he'll feel when he wakes up and finds he can't move his legs—if he lives that long." He stitched the other four incisions and dusted everything liberally with sulfa powder. "Light dressings, McGrath," Clark said. "He'll have to lie on that drain, but he's better off on his back."

She applied the dressings.

The captain helped ease the colonel over and removed the tube from his throat. "Start another saline, and take him into critical care. He'll need round-the-clock from here on."

Maggie nodded, unable to speak.

"Keep an eye on that pressure," Clark added. "If he gets shocky, he may need more blood. And keep a sharp eye out for sepsis. We're lucky to have a few ampoules of penicillin if it's needed. But go easy on the morphine. Give him two-point-five milligrams and only when it looks like he can't tolerate any more pain. It's not much, but more could kill him."

"Yes, Doctor." The captain was right. Morphine would depress the colonel's already dangerously low blood pressure and accelerate his heart rate. But what about the pain he would suffer when the anaesthetic wore off? She should have accepted that replacement. She had never been acquainted with a patient before.

Some of the nurses actually dated pilots. How could they do it, knowing the men they danced with and embraced and kissed could be wounded—or even killed?

They transferred him to a bed and she walked beside him into an empty critical care room. It was only when the orderlies left that her frayed emotions betrayed her and tears pooled in her eyes.

'Tis bonnie you are, Maggie lass. I hope to see you again, soon. The memory of his last words was so vivid she looked down to see if he had spoken.

She studied his ashen face, the half-moons his lashes made on his pale cheeks, his full lips, now so still, and remembered the extremely tall, strong man who had danced with her and gently teased her less than twenty-four hours before. She couldn't leave him now.

She checked to make sure the blood pressure cuff was properly placed around his upper arm, and hung a new bag of saline and set the drip rate, praying she wouldn't have a need to use the penicillin. "You'll have to fight, you will," she whispered, leaning over him. "But something tells me you're a fighter. And I swear I'll do everything I can to help you through this." She checked his pulse and respirations before sitting beside him, taking his limp hand in hers.

She had heard countless rumors of the commander's icy demeanor, his demand for perfection, and his constant battles with the American 8th Army Air Forces Wing Command.

Yet, she had nursed many of the wounded men who were under his command and they seemed devoted to the "old man." They told her proudly that no other group commander insisted upon leading their "A" Squadron on only the most dangerous bombing runs. They also said that it wasn't exactly true that he never loosened up with anyone other than fellow officers. He had been seen many times during off-duty hours at one of Edenoak's pubs with two of his own crewmen on the *Liberty Belle*, Sergeants Rich Florey and "Gunny" Hastings, enjoying a game of darts or quietly talking over bottles of the local ale.

She had seen him at the hospital of course, when he came to visit his wounded men, which he did every day even if he had led a mission. But she had been too distracted by her duties to notice how young he looked. His deep voice was distinctive and easily overheard as he tried to bolster their spirits, and he never left without offering to do anything he could to help them, whether it was seeing that a nurse wrote a letter to a loved one or hand-delivering something special to eat from a nearby pub.

It was his demeanor after spending time with the most critically injured men that puzzled her. Instead of sorrow or even concern, the moment the door of the critical care rooms closed behind his stiff back, his face became a mask of cold, hard indifference. The other nurses referred to him as "that gorgeous cold fish."

He moaned.

She squeezed his hand. "'Tis all right. You're no' alone."

His eyelids fluttered.

Rob Savage tried to open his eyes. *That voice. So familiar.* His back ached. Hard to breathe. *So much noise. Bail out, bail out. Oh, Lord, it hurts. Not going to make it.*

The sweet smell of heather swept over him.

Know that smell. Sweet. Like her. Maggie, help me. It hurts, it hurts. Please, please talk to me, Maggie. Hurts so bad ...

Maggie took his blood pressure and noted it on his vitals chart before sitting beside him again. His hand was so cold she placed it between her warm palms. "Go back to sleep," she said. "A nice long sleep is just what you need."

Pray God he would wake up.

Chapter Three

The colonel suddenly coughed and cried out.

She held him down when he coughed again.

"Hurts," he moaned. The inevitable pain had come full blown.

He thrashed and she held him harder. "Don't move, Rob, it only makes it worse." She instantly regretted calling him Rob. "Colonel Savage, you must lie still. That is an order!"

His body quieted, but his moans did not. The pain from the other wounds would be bad enough; but the remaining shrapnel could be causing excruciating pain. She inflated the blood pressure cuff. Still dangerously low, but how much agony could he endure? She reached for a syringe and withdrew a small dose from the vial of morphine.

He started thrashing again the moment her arms were no longer restraining him.

She administered the injection and put her arms around him until he stopped moving.

"Hurts," he moaned again.

"Shush, go to sleep. I've given you some morphine. Give it time to work."

She stayed with him through the long night, dismissing her replacement with a curt command, alternating between holding him down when the pain was at its peak and crooning soft Scots lullabies when he quieted.

By dawn, she had been on duty for twenty-four hours and was physically and emotionally exhausted.

Major Larson came in two hours later to check on Savage. "I'm surprised to find you still on duty. Get some rest, Leftenant, and that's an order. I don't want to see you back here—" he checked his watch "— before 1800 hours. Lieutenant Hawn is quite capable of taking over here."

Reluctantly, Maggie dragged herself back to her quarters. Lieutenant Hawn was the senior nurse and very efficient, but would she take the time to calm Rob when he was in the throes of such terrible suffering? She drew a shallow bath and almost fell asleep in the water before rousing herself, hastily drying off, and collapsing onto her cot.

Major Den Anderson eyed the charge nurse, who adjusted her bottle-bottom glasses, and leafed through a stack of charts. Rob's aide, Hank Hirsch, had watched the crash from the flight tower and told Den what he'd seen: only one prop spooling, the landing gear clipping the security fence, the Fort slamming into the ground and sluing off the runway, scattering a wide swath of shattered metal, torn rubber, and strips of aluminum underbelly. He had to see Rob.

The nurse slapped a chart on the counter and began reading. She looked up, myopic gaze finally zeroing in on the tip of his nose, frowning like she'd found a spot of dirt on her perfect white shoes. "No visitors, Major. Doctor's orders."

He straightened his crush cap. "I'm the colonel's second-in-command, Lieutenant. I demand to see him.

She tapped her pencil on the chart and glared at him through thick glasses. "Demands won't get you into that room. No visitors. None."

Not a spot of dirt—a stinking cow pie. What rock had she crawled out from under?

A long game of "stare-down." She didn't blink. Even once.

He grabbed her pencil, broke it in two, and threw the pieces on the counter. But even slamming the hospital door behind him did nothing to stem his anger. "Doctor's orders," he mimicked in a whining falsetto.

He'd show that fish-eyed, starched warden. They couldn't watch Rob's room 24/7. He'd see his best friend if he had to break down the door.

Maggie slept for eight hours, but awoke with a start, staring at the ceiling, trying to recall what had awakened her. When the memory of the day before came, she leaped off her cot and threw on her robe before racing for the phone in the hall.

Her thoughts in a jumble, she could hardly remember the number when the base switchboard operator asked for it. Her hands shook as she waited for the various connections to be made and the reverse charges accepted.

"Doctor McGrath speaking."

"Faither, I'm so relieved you're in your office."

"Maggie, lass, how are you? Is something wrong?"

"No, I'm fine." She bit back tears. "'Tis just ... I have a favor to ask of you." She paused, composing herself. "I need you to look at some X-rays of a patient at the hospital. I want you to tell me if you can help him."

"Maggie, have you got the smit?"

"Och, Faither, I'm no' in love. 'Tis just that this lad—" she swallowed "—was wounded so badly, and the flight surgeon says there's nothing more they can do for him."

"Perhaps he's right."

"But we don't know that. If I send you his X-rays, will you at least look at them? You may be able to help him. You're always coming up with new surgical techniques."

"And how are you going to acquire these X-rays to send me?"

She caught her lower lip between her teeth. "I'll steal them if I have to."

"You'll do no such thing. You could jeopardize your career with a daft stunt like that."

"What's a career worth when a man's life is at stake?"

He sighed. "Well, I have a better idea. You give me the patient's name and doctor's name and telephone numbers and I'll see how far a wee bit of professional courtesy can go with a fellow doctor—an American, aye—but we've quite a few of their lads being treated here at our infirmary."

She gave him the necessary information as she paced up and down the hallway, hampered by a telephone cord that was much too short.

"So, give me a few hours. I'll see what I can do. But, Maggie, if this Major Larson proves uncooperative, promise me one thing."

"Anything."

He slipped back into the familiar Scots vernacular. "Be verra, verra careful nipping those films. I dinna want to be visiting my only daughter in an English jile."

"I promise."

"Guid, lass. I'll let you know as soon as I've any news. Guid-bye, Maggie, luve."

She returned to her room. It was barely gone 1600 hours. Almost two hours to go. How could she bear wondering if—no, she would not think that. God was in this with her, and she needed to allow Him time to act. She knelt beside her bed and prayed.

At exactly 1800 hours, she padded down the polished, dark gray concrete floors of the hospital corridor toward critical care. Hushed voices bounced off the stark white walls, which were marred only by scrapes from gurney rails. Her heart pounded in her throat. *Please, please, Heavenly Faither, let him be better, or at the verra least, no worse.*

The colonel thrashed wildly in bed while Lieutenant Hawn attempted to administer an injection.

This time, her prayer appeared to be answered with a resounding *No*.

"McGrath, sit on him, will you? I can't get him to hold still long enough to give him his morphine."

Maggie leaned over and held his arms down. "Hush, 'tis all right, Colonel. Lie still, 'tis all right." To her amazement, he instantly quieted.

"Hurts," he groaned.

She tightened her grip. "Give it a wee bit of time and you'll feel better."

The injection administered, Lieutenant Hawn threw the syringe on the tray and heaved a sigh. "Well, lotsa luck, McGrath, you'll need it. He's a wild man every time the morphine wears off."

Maggie wanted to shout recriminations at Lieutenant Hawn's

retreating back, but all she could do was look at Rob's waxen face and vow to do everything she could for him. "We'll get along fine." She choked the words out.

The soft Scots burr penetrated Savage's stream of consciousness. His Maggie was here. Her sweet scent soothed him, easing the sharp pain. Why didn't she talk or sing to keep his mind focused on her instead of how much he hurt? Her palm rested on his forehead. Soft. Warm. Like her voice. *Talk to me, Maggie. Please talk to me.*

That night passed much the same as the first. Maggie changed his dressings, held, cajoled, crooned, and did everything she could to keep the colonel alive and in the least pain possible. Around midnight, she gave him another injection of morphine and held him tightly until the medication took effect. Her repertoire of lullabies exhausted, she began to tell the tale of the Selkie, a magical seal that turned into a beautiful woman the moment she touched shore. She told of the Selkie's fair, pale skin, her silken, black hair which fell to below her waist, her slim legs and tiny feet, only afterwards realizing she could have been describing herself.

He calmed immediately and, though his eyes were closed and his breathing steady, she was certain a part of his mind absorbed her words.

She held his hand in one of hers as she gently stroked his cheek, taking care to avoid the livid bruise on his cheekbone. "Chased by fishermen who feared she was an evil Selkie, no' a good one, and sought to kill her, the Selkie took refuge in a crofter's cottage. When the young crofter returned from tending his sheep, he clothed her in garments that had belonged to his dead sister. Together, they fled the cottage and took refuge in a cave at the edge of the shore."

"So, how is the colonel doing?" Major Lawson had slipped into the room.

She leaped to her feet. "Oh, sir, I was just ... just ..."

"As you were, Leftenant. The patient seems to be comfortable now. Let's keep him that way."

"Yes, Doctor." She sat again, hands clasped tightly together in her lap. "There's no major improvement to report, but he is holding steady."

He pulled the chart from its holder. "Yes, I see. Hmm, his vitals have improved slightly from this afternoon."

"Yes, they have that."

"Do you usually tell fairy tales to your patients?"

She felt her face flush. "Once in a while. It gives the lads something to concentrate on, other than the pain."

"I see." His eyes narrowed. "Well, whatever it is, it seems to be doing the trick. We'll want to stabilize him before his trip to Edinburgh."

"Edinburgh?" Maggie's joy was so great, she had to restrain herself from leaping to her feet to give the major a hug.

"Someone in this facility, and I'm assuming it was you because I know he's your father, contacted Doctor John McGrath, probably the world's foremost orthopedic surgeon, on behalf of Colonel Savage. You should have reminded me about him instead of calling him yourself. But I've gone through channels and cleared the colonel's transfer to the Royal Infirmary in Edinburgh. I've been told that many of our wounded GIs are sent there for medical treatments beyond the ordinary, and General Wells at Wing agrees wholeheartedly with the decision." He stifled a yawn. "A quick flight to Edinburgh and back is exhausting. Keep up the good work. I've assured Doctor McGrath that the moment the colonel is stable enough for travel, he'll be on his way."

"Och, thank you so much."

He turned to go, then paused. "By the way, Doctor McGrath has filed a formal request with your commanding officer that you accompany Colonel Savage on his journey. It's come to my attention that he responds well to your particular manner of nursing. Though we need you here, he is the group commander and we want to do all we can to see that he survives."

Maggie nodded, too relieved to speak.

He fidgeted. "I want you to know I'm not some hard-hearted monster, McGrath. I admire Colonel Savage greatly. He's formed the 396th into a well-disciplined, well-trained unit, and he goes to exceptional lengths to take care of his men. That's an enormous piece of shrapnel and I'm simply not trained to perform such surgery. There is one excellent Air Force orthopod, but he's stuck someplace in North Africa and I've been unable to find a qualified surgeon in the area."

"I understand, Doctor."

"Then, good-night."

Maggie almost collapsed. Her father had agreed to help. She grasped Savage's hand. "Did you hear that Rob ... Colonel? You're getting your chance."

"Heard, Maggie."

He responded! She leaned over, smoothing a lock of brown hair back from his forehead.

When he opened his eyes, though his pupils were dilated, his gaze focused on her. "Thank you," he whispered.

A day later, his condition had not improved, but it also had not deteriorated. Major Larson stooped and eyed the bottle of fluid beneath the bed, collecting blood from the drain in the colonel's back. "I'd like to see his blood pressure higher, but I'm afraid we're running out of time. Sepsis could set in at any time, and once that happens, nothing can save him."

"Then he's going to be transferred immediately?" Maggie asked.

The doctor straightened, kneading the small of his back. "I've made arrangements to have him occupy the new medical car the Flying Scotsman has added to its train."

"But, isn't that too slow? I should think he would be flown to Edinburgh."

"I decided against it. Though it is much faster, his comfort would be greatly compromised by the cold, rough ride in a transport plane."

"Train."

"Did he say, 'train'?" Major Larson asked. "Is he communicating with you?"

Maggie hurried to the colonel's side. Though his eyes were closed, she sensed he was awake. "A little," she replied. "It's on his chart."

"I thought you meant incoherent ramblings." He joined Maggie. "Colonel Savage, can you hear me?"

No response.

"Well, at any rate," Larson said, "we'll transport him by ambulance to King's Cross Station at 0900 hours tomorrow. Pack whatever you need: drugs, dressings, IVs, and any other medical supplies you may require for the trip. All the railroad provides is a car with stretcher accommodations."

"Of course, Doctor."

"And pack adequately for yourself. Your transfer orders have come through. For the indefinite future, you're to stay with Colonel Savage as primary caregiver until—" he glanced down at the colonel "—until he has recovered sufficiently to no longer need your care."

"Thank you, sir." The flight surgeon's hesitation made it clear he did not expect the colonel to survive.

"I'll be back in the morning to check him over before you leave"

The moment Major Larson quit the room, Maggie took Rob's hand. "Can you hear me, Colonel?"

He nodded.

"Why didn't you answer Major Larson?"

"Coward," he whispered. He groaned loudly. "Talk, please talk."

Maggie took his hand. "He's certainly no coward. He doesn't feel qualified to do the operation you need."

"Who?"

"Do you mean who is qualified?"

"Who?" he repeated.

"Doctor John McGrath."

"Scots?"

"My father."

When the pain took over, Maggie held him until it was time for his morphine injection. As soon as the medication took effect, she continued the Selkie tale. "At the start of gloaming, the Selkie walked out of the cave and up to her knees in the sea just as the sun cast its dying light on the crests of the waves. She looked out at the darkening sea, tilting her head as she listened to the sad, plaintive notes of her Selkie lover, who sang of his heartbreak. The crofter, hearing only the barking of a seal, raced into the water and pulled her back into the cave."

Maggie watched the rhythmic rise and fall of Rob's chest. Asleep at last.

Savage slept fitfully. He cried out once, "Lord, help me! Not going to make it!" His body stiffened and he shook with pain from spasming muscles.

Maggie bathed his face with a cold, wet face flannel. The time would come when she couldn't keep him from knowing his condition, but he was much too weak to face that now, so she crooned softly, trying to bring him awake enough to escape the horrible nightmare he was in, but not conscious enough to realize only his upper body was moving.

"Maggie," he groaned. "Maggie, help me."

She grasped his shoulders and pulled him close. "I'm here, Rob. I'm right here. 'Tis all right. Only a bad dream."

"Can't move, Maggie," he choked. He broke out in a sweat and his teeth chattered. He clutched for her, pulling her closer. "Help me with the rudders," he pleaded. "Please, Maggie, help me."

She sat on the bed and grasped both of his flailing arms. "Rob, you're on the ground. Listen to me. You're in hospital."

His chest heaved as he gasped for air. His groans turned to dry sobs and he suddenly stopped fighting her. "Can't work the rudders," he groaned. "My legs won't move."

He still seemed to be caught in the throes of his nightmare, but would reality be any kinder? She freed one arm, dipped the flannel into cold water, wrung it out and bathed his forehead again. Despite all she'd seen at her RAF hospital postings, she'd never become conditioned to such terrible suffering.

His eyelids fluttered, but he didn't appear to awaken. She hummed some of the old hymns she'd learned in kirk. When she had run through every hymn she could remember, she sang some old Scots folksongs in the Gaelic, the ancient language of Scotland.

At last, his breathing deepened and he slept.

The loud growl of B-17 engines rumbled and whined. The group was lining up on the runway for another mission. The overhead light rocked and bottles juddered together on the medicament shelf as they began their take-offs. "Godspeed," she whispered.

She rose and tiptoed to the basin, staring at her own image in the mirror. "Och, you look like a souching wind caught you up." She wrung out a cloth and scrubbed her face, then quickly re-pinned her hair into a neat bun. Only one more night, and they would be on their way to Edinburgh. *Heavenly Faither, if it be Your will, help Rob survive the journey tomorrow. And please, please heal his body and spirit.*

Two hours later, as she dozed beside him, she jerked upright.

He was looking at her.

"Och, you're awake. Would you like me to wet your lips?"

He nodded.

She did not like the look in his eyes—dull brown, almost lifeless. She forced a smile as she wet a flannel and carefully moistened his lips.

He reached unsteadily for her hand. "Maggie," he whispered. "Need the truth."

Her heart pounded. "And what do you need the truth about?"

"You know."

She caught her lower lip between her teeth to keep the tears at bay. She was not ready for this.

"No games. Want truth from you, bonnie Maggie."

An image of him in his uniform flashed through her mind. This man was an adult and the commander of over a thousand men and women; he deserved more than her resolve to save him from reality. She took a deep breath and raised her chin. "You cannot move your legs."

He closed his eyes and nodded.

"Is that the truth you want from me?"

He shook his head.

"Then what?"

"Is it forever?"

Tears gathered in her eyes.

He turned his face away.

"Don't!" she cried, catching his face between her palms and gently turning his head. "Rob, I need you to hear something. Please listen to me. I don't think the damage is permanent. When that piece of shrapnel is removed and the pressure is no longer there, you should recover."

He stared up at her.

"I'll always be truthful with you, and I'm telling you the truth now."

His eyelids fluttered, then closed. "A chance."

"Aye, a very good chance you'll recover completely." She took his hand in hers. "My father's the best surgeon in Scotland. You couldn't find anyone better in the world."

"Those r's," he said softly. "Love them."

Her cheeks burned.

His hand gripped hers. "Selkie again, please."

"Do you remember what you last heard?"

"Crofter ... pulled her into cave."

He remembered that? But she'd thought he'd fallen asleep.

She laced her fingers through his, smoothing his forehead with her other palm. "The next morning, the crofter warned the Selkie no' to leave the cave and sneaked back to his cottage. He herded his sheep onto fresh graze and gathered jugs of water, a piece of cheese and a loaf of oatbread, wrapping them in the course linen bedsheet from his sleeping pallet. Taking care not to be seen, he returned to the cave."

Early the next morning, Maggie took a brief respite and went to her quarters to bathe and pack, leaving Rob in the care of Lieutenant Baxter, a soft-spoken nurse with a gentle manner. When she returned, she found a redheaded major pacing the corridor outside of Colonel Savage's room. Though he looked familiar, she couldn't put a name to the face.

He caught her elbow as she tried to open the door. "Lieutenant," he said, "how is he? Please tell me. I have to know."

"'Tis Leftenant, and I'm in a terrible hurry, Major. You should see Major Larson for that kind of information."

He blocked the doorway with his body. "I don't want to hear the usual medical doubletalk. I checked and you've been with him almost constantly since they brought him in. I have to know how he really is."

The agony in his eyes tore at her heart. "Are you a friend of his, Major ...?"

"Anderson, Den Anderson. I've known Rob since we were plebes at the Point together. I love him like a brother. Is he going to ... make it?"

So this was Rob's friend and second-in-command. "We're doing everything we can to see that he lives. He's being transferred to the Royal Infirmary in Edinburgh today for surgery on his back. If everything turns out as expected, he should regain the use of his legs, though it will take months of rehabilitation."

Anderson recoiled. "The use of his legs? What do you mean? It has to be a mistake. Everybody on base has been talking about how only Rob could have brought that Fort back on one engine, and it wasn't even torn up that bad in the crash. He'd have aced that landing if his landing gear hadn't caught the top of the fence at the end of the runway."

"He has a large piece of shrapnel pressing against his spinal cord. He has no feeling or movement from his hips down."

The major reeled for a moment and grabbed the wall. "You mean he ... that's why he didn't bail out with his crew? Oh, please, not Rob."

His florid face had turned so pale she feared he might faint.

"Why don't you sit down over there?" She indicated a chair down the hallway.

"No. I'll be all right. I want to see him. I've got to see him before he goes. Please, Leftenant."

His tears broke her resolve. She removed a handkerchief from her white hospital dress pocket and handed it to him. "Then wipe your eyes. And you'll have to be very, very quiet. I'll not allow you to upset him. Do you understand?"

He mopped at his face, nodding. "Thank you."

She opened the door and motioned to the major to follow.

He took off his crush cap, tucked it between his upper arm and body, and tiptoed into the room.

Maggie studied the vitals chart Lieutenant Baxter offered. "Has he awakened at all?"

"No. He's been moaning a lot, but he's at least two hours from another morphine injection."

"Thank you for everything, Lieutenant. You may go now."

The major walked quietly over to the bed and looked down at his friend, his hands clenched, and his chest rising and falling rapidly. He laid his hand on Rob's. "I'll be thinking about you. You keep fighting, you hear? Don't give up, Rob, please don't give up." He straightened, studying Rob's face for a moment. "You should have let me fly right-seat like I asked. Ciao, Bucko," he said, voice breaking.

Maggie watched him shamble from the room, shoulders slumped.

※

Major Anderson careened outside and looked anxiously around for somewhere to be alone. He stumbled to a vacant place where he had seen ambulances parked when there was an overflow. He leaned against the side of the building, fingers clenching the security fence next to him. He couldn't draw a deep breath and his stomach cramped as if someone had punched him in the belly.

Paralyzed. Rob's legs were paralyzed.

How often he had teased his pal about his long legs and how hard it was to keep up with him when he was in a hurry?—which was most of the time. Now, he'd never have the opportunity again.

Anderson leaned over and vomited, clutching his belly. When the spasms passed, he wiped his mouth with his handkerchief and leaned his head back against the wall, looking up at the sky. "Where were You when he needed You?" he shouted. "I was right all along. I told Rob there is no God!"

Chapter Four

Maggie timed Rob's morphine injection for half an hour before they moved him from bed to stretcher but even so, he cried out when they lifted the drawsheet beneath him for the transfer.

In the ambulance, she rode next to him, trying to ignore the snide remarks about her Scots "burr" from the attendants who were sitting in the front. Didn't they know Scotland had pioneered modern medicine, including the new wonder drug penicillin? That the very care they gave patients had its beginnings at the Edinburgh School of Medicine, starting as early as the mid 1700s? She held her tongue. All that mattered was Rob surviving the journey.

The throngs of people in King's Cross Station readily parted for the patient. Pitying looks and stifled gasps followed as other travelers looked at the pale, inert man on the stretcher, the Royal Air Force nurse in her grey-blue uniform walking at his side, holding a bottle of saline. A few uniformed men saluted, while others turned away as though afraid they might be catching a glimpse of their own destiny. Many of the civilians turned pasty after one glance at the jar of cloudy, red fluid another attendant carried.

The moment Rob was settled in the medical car with the white cross on its side and all of their bags had been loaded, Maggie quickly unpacked and arranged the things she would need.

When the train lurched forward, Rob groaned.

She took his hand. "We're on our way to Edinburgh, Rob. You must be strong."

Though he didn't respond, his groans subsided and he fell into a deep sleep, undoubtedly aided by the gentle rocking of the train.

Thank the Lord there were no other patients in the car. Having to make small talk with other nurses would have been intolerable; she needed to focus on Rob only. She yawned. For the past twenty-four hours she'd only dozed beside his bed for a few minutes at a time. She grabbed one of the extra blankets and curled up on a seat at his side. As soon as she closed her eyes, the door burst open.

"Oh, good!" a woman exclaimed. "Look at all the room. Come in, my little lovelies. In. In."

Maggie stared aghast as three young girls crowded into the car, laughing shrilly, and threw their traveling bags onto the shelves reserved for medical supplies. "Stop," she demanded. "This is a medical car. You cannot stay here."

The woman waved a hand. "Oh, we don't mind, do we, darlings? There's ever so much more room in here than any of the compartments in the car behind."

Rob groaned.

Maggie leaped to her feet. "It's all right, Colonel, I'll take care of it." She held his hand and turned to face the woman. "You'll have to leave. And take those—"

"Oh, look, Auntie, I've a seat all to myself." One of the girls squealed, jumping up and down on the seat. "This is ever so much fun."

Rob moaned and thrashed about.

Maggie eyed the stout woman who outweighed her tiny, slender frame by a good six or seven stone. "I insist you leave this instant or I'm going to pull that cord right there and stop the train. You may have to walk to the next station."

Rob groaned yet again.

"Oh, ugh, what's that awful red goo," another girl squealed. "It looks like blood. I think I'm going to be sick!"

"Edith, control yourself," her aunt shrilled. She bent over and eyed the bottle. "It'll not spill now, will it?"

"Only if one of you knocks it over," Maggie answered with a glare. "This patient is in critical condition. If he dies, I'm going to charge you with his murder."

The woman's doughy face flushed and she fanned her cheeks. "You don't have to be so nasty about it. My nieces and me are going to Fife to stay with friends. The constant bombing, you know and every compartment is so full. We need more room to stretch our legs and get away from that dreadful cigarette smoke."

"Find room elsewhere."

Rob was shaking so hard Maggie feared he would pull out his IV needle.

She had no choice. She braced her body against his.

The door opened again as her fingers closed over the emergency cord. The conductor, waving his ticket punch, rushed into the car. "I thought I saw you four leave the other car." He eyed the interlopers, his face contorted with anger. "Oot, oot!" he cried, grabbing their bags and tossing them out into the vestibule.

Maggie dropped the cord and held Rob's shoulders down. "Please remove them immediately. The colonel's in terrible pain. All this noise could kill him."

"Don't upset yourself, lass, they'll be gone before you can blink." He corralled the three protesting girls and herded them out before returning for their auntie who stared, open-mouthed, at the colonel.

"The poor devil's really dying?" she gasped. "Why didn't you say so?"

The conductor followed her out into the vestibule where he berated her in an exaggerated whisper. "Did you no' see the white cross, Missus? That means stay oot!" He closed the door firmly behind him, only to open it a second later. "It will no' happen again. You have my apologies."

How could people be so uncaring and selfish? Maggie clutched Rob's shoulders as tears slipped down her cheeks.

"Don't cry, Maggie." Though he trembled, he smiled.

"I ... I'm sorry" she choked. "I didn't ever think—"

"Who would?" He raised a hand and tried to touch her cheek, but it fell short and he dropped it with a grunt. "Don't cry, please."

She swiped at the tears and grasped his hand, squeezing it. "I always cry when I'm angry—or happy, or sad, or very tired. Father says I put the winter rains to shame."

He closed his eyes and mumbled something unintelligible.

"Try to rest," she soothed, stroking his forehead. "We've several more stops coming up and I don't want you bothered by all the juddering from stopping and starting."

"Selkie."

"Again?"

He gave a slight nod. How much had he heard the last time? She'd have to start at the beginning. She leaned closer. "There once was a verra—"

"Beautiful seal."

She smiled down at him. "Aye, a verra beautiful seal ..."

The eight-hour journey seemed much longer. When the train made its last stop in Newcastle, England, she had to give Rob more morphine than usual.

Agitated, he trembled almost constantly.

She bathed his face and hands with cool water, then checked the drainage bottle, relieved to find that the contents were not any murkier than usual—nor was there any odor of sepsis. At least she wouldn't have to use the one ampoule of penicillin she'd been allowed to bring. She rubbed her cheeks briskly. Not much longer and they would be in Edinburgh.

The ambulance driver in Edinburgh avoided sudden turns or stops. Another attendant rode in the back with Maggie and Rob. The trip from Haymarket Train Station to the Royal Infirmary was only a few kilometres. Rob was taken inside. This time, as he was transferred to a bed, he didn't cry out in pain.

Her father hurried into the room. His hair and short beard were more white than brown now but he still wore his usual white lab coat over tweeds. His large, dark brown eyes were warm with welcome as he threw out his arms. "Maggie, lass."

"Faither." She collapsed against him.

He embraced her and scanned her face. "You look spent, lass."

"I'm fine. I'm so relieved to be here at last."

"Let's see how your patient's faring after that long train ride." He listened to the colonel's heart and lungs before studying the vitals chart Maggie handed him. He leaned over Rob. "Can you hear me, Colonel Savage?"

Rob opened his eyes.

"Good. Then let me introduce myself. I'm Doctor John McGrath. Now, we're not going to waste any more time. We'll be taking a few X-rays, and then the anaesthesiologist is going to come in and give you a shot to make you sleepy before we take you to the operating theatre. Do you understand?"

"Yes."

"Any questions?"

Rob trembled. "Will it ... help me?" he whispered.

Her father patted his shoulder. "There are never any guarantees, Colonel. It would have been better if I had seen you immediately after your crash, but I want to assure you this operation has proven very successful in the past."

"Thank you."

"You're very welcome." He turned to Maggie. "Say good-bye to the colonel for now, lass, and then I'll see you outside."

When he left the room, Maggie leaned over Rob. "I'll be praying. Don't be afraid." She squeezed his fingers when he groped for her hand. "Our Heavenly Father will be at your side throughout the entire operation and I'll be with you when you wake up."

"Bonnie Maggie. Will you really pray for me?"

"Of course, and I won't be the only one. Father always prays for guidance when he operates. Your guardian angels will be at your side, along with our Lord." She withdrew her hand and pressed a quick kiss to his forehead.

Her father paced the corridor. He looked worried as he embraced her. "Och, lass, you're ready to collapse. I've had a room in the student nurses' wing prepared for you. A guid sleep, some hot tea, and a meal will do wonders."

Maggie rested her cheek against his shoulder and closed her smarting eyes. "Will he live, Faither? Can you really save him and help him walk again?"

"As I told him, there are no guarantees." He smoothed wisps of hair back from her forehead. "I was surprised to find from the records Doctor Larson brought that the colonel is only twenty-eight. That's young for a colonel and a base commander, at that. But he does look fit. Pray God guides my mind and hands, the same prayer I'll be saying."

"You'll wake me the minute he's taken into recovery?"

"Of course. I've seen the miracles your nursing skills can bring about."

"I can't thank you enough for agreeing to treat him. They were just going to let him suffer and die while they tried to find a qualified surgeon."

"He has you to thank if he recovers. You're worn out, lass. On you come, I'll show you to your room."

As he walked away from Maggie's room, Doctor McGrath was aware he hadn't voiced his real concern. Was his daughter emotionally involved with this American colonel? He hoped not. Maggie was only twenty-two. His precious daughter should meet some fine, young Scots lad and settle down on Innisbraw to raise a croftful of bonnie children. Och, this war.

McGrath put together the finest from the Royal Infirmary: an anaesthesiologist, neurologist, another orthopaedic surgeon, and the most experienced operating room nurses.

The operation got underway almost an hour later. The anaesthesiologist administered nitrous oxide and oxygen, keeping a keen eye on the patient's vital signs. Each team member took an active part. When the piece of shrapnel was removed, Doctor McGrath held it up in his gloved hand so everyone could see.

Unlike the nurses, McGrath didn't gasp aloud, despite being amazed by its size and the sharpness of every edge. *Och, Heavenly Faither, only you could have kept this from slashing completely through that lad's spine.*

"We've got a run-away bleeder," the other orthopaedist said, voice urgent.

The head operating room nurse slapped a clamp into McGrath's hand as he tossed the shrapnel onto a tray and reached for the cauterizer.

Before they could stop the bleeding, another vein flooded the wound-site with blood.

"Keep the whole blood coming." McGrath opened another clamp and slid it into place. "He's losing it faster than we can replace it."

He and the other two doctors worked quickly, but another bleeder added to the gravity of the situation. Six hands coordinated, clamping and tying off bleeders or using the cauterizer when possible.

No one spoke.

Nurses slapped sponges or pre-sutured needles into the doctors' hands while the anaesthesiologist kept a close eye on the patient's plummeting blood pressure.

The crisis lasted an hour. When the last bleeder had been tended to, McGrath flushed the wound and stood back, studying it carefully.

"How's his pressure?"

The anaesthesiologist answered, "Still very low, but starting to rise."

"We'll need a drain inserted, then we should start closing."

Doctor McGrath left the operating theatre with a lighter step than he thought possible after such a grueling surgery. Though the colonel's spinal cord was bruised and swollen, no major nerves had been severed, only traumatized. The neurologist concurred that under the right circumstances and given time—and with a great deal of physical therapy—the lad should walk again. Of course, it all depended on the patient's will and determination to endure the weeks and possibly months of tedious and painful exercises and seemingly cruel regimen such a recovery required. Only time would tell.

He opened the door to Maggie's tiny room. She lay curled on her side with her hands still folded in prayer, long black hair fanned out over the pillow like a spate of dark, rushing water. How he loved this bonnie lass, the image of her dead mother, heart good and as pure as any he had ever known. She always cared about every wee hurt anyone endured around her.

Without her, he never would have made it through those lonely years after he'd lost his beloved Elizabeth in childbirth. Maggie had been his strength, a pillar of goodness keeping him focused on the positives life had to offer. From the age of eight, she had been both companion to him and mother to her younger brother, Calum.

Maggie twitched and opened her eyes. "Faither." She sat up. "Are you finished? How's Rob? Was the operation successful?"

He smiled and sat on the bed next to her, drawing her into his arms. "Aye, it is over, and he's doing as well as can be expected. I'm as certain as I can be at this point that he will make a complete recovery. Doctor MacMillan, our neurologist, also expects the paralysis to be only temporary." He looked into her shining face. "You didn't get much sleep."

"I feel wonderful." She pulled away. "Wait outside. I'll do up my hair, put on my hospital whites, and be right out."

"Slow down, lass. You can get dressed, and then we're going to have some strong hot tea and something to eat. Your colonel will not be awake for some time. How long has it been since you last ate?"

"Forever." She laughed. "And my stomach's growling. Out you go then. I'll catch you right up."

Maggie pushed away her empty plate and sipped her tea. "You can't know how I've missed guid Scots food. It's been forever since I've had neeps. You ask for them at Edenoaks and they look at you like you're daft, even when you explain it's only turnips."

"You're forgetting how much time I spend traveling. I know exactly what you mean."

"Of course you do. Shall we go? I can't wait to see Rob ... the colonel."

He reached across the table and took her hands in his. "Lass, there's something I must ask you."

Her cheeks burned and she steeled herself. "What?"

"Are you feeling more for this colonel than just the usual concern you would feel for any other patient? I mean, are you—"

"Of course no'."

How could she allow him to question her feelings when she

wasn't even sure of them herself?

"I do know that when I'm with Rob I feel truly alive, but you know how I am when I have a patient who needs me. All the nurses I work with are always saying I give too much of myself to my patients, telling them Scots fairytales and singing them songs. But how can I allow them to suffer without offering a bit of comfort?" She spoke too fast, her words tumbling out like water from a broken spigot.

He gently squeezed her hands.

She inhaled deeply. "I'm certain all Rob and I will ever be is friends. After all, he is the base commander. But I'd be most fortunate to count him a friend. He's a fine man, verra well thought of by his men and everyone else at Edenoaks." Unable to bear the suspense another minute, she pushed her chair back and jumped to her feet. "On we go. I want to see his vitals."

"Don't expect a miraculous change, lass. He's been through a trying ordeal. The pain alone would have killed a weaker man. We came close to losing him when he haemorrhaged. We stopped it just in time."

She gripped the back of her chair, legs wobbling like the bones had turned to jelly pudding. "Why didn't you tell me before?"

"Twa extra units of blood pulled him through. I only want you to understand it's going to take time before he recovers his strength, and he'll need blood until the drain is removed."

Maggie tiptoed into the recovery room, pulled aside the curtain and went to Rob's side, dismissing the nurse who had just finished taking his vitals. She plucked the chart from its holder and studied it carefully. His blood pressure was slightly higher than it had been at Edenoaks and his pulse and respirations were what could be expected so soon after such a grueling surgery. She read a note at the bottom of the page, obviously scrawled by a tired anaesthesiologist. "Patient responded verbally after endotracheal tube removed and oxygen administered in theatre. Transferred to recovery room at 2300 hours."

She checked the drip-rates on the bottles of saline and blood hanging by his bed before studying the slow rise and fall of his chest. He was still sleeping off the effects of the nitrous oxide. The bruise high on his cheekbone, though beginning to fade, stood out against his pale, drawn face. "Wake up, Rob," she said, taking his hand. "The operation's over." When he didn't respond, she patted his cheek. "On you come. Wake up."

His eyelids fluttered and he moaned.

"Are you in pain? I'm sure Father told you there would be some pain after the surgery. Wake up, Rob. It's Maggie."

His eyes opened and he squinted up at her. "My Selkie?"

Och, his mind was still jumbled. "Your Maggie."

"How'd it go?" he mumbled.

"Exactly as planned."

His eyes closed, and opened again. "Truth?"

"Truth." She sat on the side of the bed. "I know you'll no' remember this later and I'll have to be telling it to you again and again, but I'm going to do it anyway. There will be a lot of work to do before you can walk like you did before. But if you do everything you're told, that day will come."

"Mmm." He closed his eyes and slept.

She checked the drainage bottle beneath the bed. Not as cloudy as it had been. It was unfortunate he had to lie on that uncomfortable tube for a while longer and the stitches they used to keep the drain in place within the wound surely pulled every time he was moved, but it had to drain for a few days.

When his vital signs stabilized, she held his hand as two orderlies pushed his bed out into the corridor. "Father wants you to concentrate on healing. No visiting, so you'll no' be going to a ward," she said, smiling. "They're transferring you to your own private room, and that's quite a rare occurrence."

His hand tightened on hers. "Don't go."

"I'm no' about to leave you now, after all the time and effort it's taken to get you here."

"Promise?"

"I promise."

Chapter Five

Rob slept, fearing the moments when he woke and could only moan as the pain escalated. When he did not hear Maggie's voice asking him if he wanted something for pain or offering to wet his lips, he experienced a moment of panic before once again spiraling down, down, into blessed oblivion.

Early the third morning, he awakened suddenly, stricken with terror. He lay close to a steep cliff, sliding faster and faster toward the drop at the edge. He flailed his arms frantically, clutching for something to grab onto.

Firm hands grasped his and he gave a sob of relief. "Steady, Colonel, steady you go," a man's voice said. "I'm only turning you onto your back."

"Maggie," Rob mumbled.

"I'm here now, Rob."

The familiar voice slowed his thudding heart as Maggie's face swam into view. He blinked and tried to focus as she leaned closer.

"I'll be with you all the day." Her fingers brushed his cheek. "So you can let go of Ian's hands now before you break them."

As Rob loosened his grip and drifted off to sleep again, the orderly straightened, massaging his fingers. "It's grand to see you here early. I've been turning him every four hours from before the turn o' the night and it never startled him like that."

"It's the morphine making him hallucinate," she said. "Don't worry about it. Go have a strong cup of tea and take yourself off home. I've already signed in."

He left, shoulders stooped with fatigue.

Maggie shook her head. The orderly was too old to be doing this sort of work, but he was caring and competent and the war had taken all the young lads.

Rob grew more aware and alert as his morphine slowly decreased. But with the awareness came memories—and fear. He couldn't respond to Maggie's questions with anything but grunts, never allowed himself to meet her gaze directly and spent hours unmoving, eyes closed. She seemed to sense the emotional battle he was fighting and stroked his cheek or arm while telling him stories or singing softly in that strange, lilting language. His dreams were dark and filled with fragmented mind-pictures of his last flight, so vivid and jumbled he spent a great deal of time fighting to stay awake, hiding his panic by feigning sleep. One thought ran through his mind over and over like a damaged record with the needle stuck in one groove.

I'll never fly again.

Though he fought his drug-dazed memory to recall in detail that last fateful meeting with Wing Commander Wells, the pain medication made accurate recall impossible. He only remembered insisting he take out that airplane factory in Metz with a single bomber—his own *Liberty Belle*.

The fifth evening after his surgery, Doctor McGrath and Maggie used the draw sheet to turn Rob on his side.

"I'm going to remove the drain from your back," McGrath said, laying sterile gauze and tape on the bedside table. "I'm warning you now, it's going to be painful. The tube's buried deeply and scar tissue builds up around it very quickly. Hold onto something. I don't want you jerking away."

Maggie moved to Rob's side and gripped his hand.

Rob bit his lip and concentrated on the grey wall opposite his bed. How did they get the plaster so smooth? And why wasn't it white? Sweat beaded his forehead as the doctor pulled out the tube, inch by inch.

"That's it," the doctor said. "Maggie will cover that small gap with gauze and tape it into place before she removes the IV providing you blood."

"Wasn't as bad as I imagined." Rob wiped his forehead with his palm. "Thanks."

"You might not be thanking me when you learn you'll have your last shot of morphine tonight. Starting tomorrow, we'll manage your pain with aspirin."

"You mean no more bad dreams?"

McGrath pulled off his gloves. "You've been through a very traumatic experience, so you may still have an occasional bad dream, but it won't be drug-induced." He gathered up the drain and container of fluid and left the room.

Rob awakened early, and for the first time, felt good enough to return Maggie's smile of greeting.

"So you finally decided to leave the "land of Willie Winkie," as our bairns—children—call sleep." She took his blood pressure before checking his pulse. "Verra guid. How are you feeling this mornin?"

"It's great not having that garden hose under me, and at least one arm's free." He winced when he moved his shoulder too quickly.

"Then how about a wee bit of broth? If I can get enough liquid into you, you'll soon have both arms free."

"Good. I'm starving." His rapid reply surprised even himself, but it was true.

She washed his face and hands with a warm, wet face flannel and blotted them dry. "Now I'll go order you some tattie bree and a bottle of Lucozade."

What was tattie bree—and Lucozade? He'd heard somewhere that the Scots ate weird things, like oatmeal and liver stuffed into a sheep's stomach and everything that came from the sea, even slimy creatures without scales or fins. "Maggie, use English," he said more gruffly than intended. "I get so frustrated when I can't understand you."

"I'm trying my verra best no' to frustrate you, Colonel." Her sharp tone got his attention. She was so beautiful with her chin raised and her large, dark blue eyes sparking with indignation.

"So it's 'Colonel' now, is it? I must have put a burr under your saddle."

"Rob!"

He was sure she hadn't understood the American idiom, but it had surprised her out of her snit. He couldn't suppress a grin. "That's better. I don't like it when you're mad at me, bonnie Maggie."

She rolled her eyes. "For your information, tattie bree is a thick potato broth. They make it here in the kitchen and it's verra guid. And Lucozade is a nourishing drink made with glucose syrup. You'll find it all over Scotland, no' just in infirmaries."

"Why didn't you say so in the first place?"

"Because I'm back in Scotland now and I keep forgetting you don't understand Scots."

He reached for her hand, needing the comfort of her touch. "Did anyone ever tell you your eyes turn dark blue when you're angry?"

"Och, you're skiting—fooling—with me."

"I mean it. Right now, they're a sort of violet blue, but when your dander's up, they turn almost navy." He squeezed her hand. "Let your hair down, please. I've been trying to imagine all that black hair spilling around your shoulders and down your back."

She drew back with a gasp. "I cannot. It's against Regulations."

"Forget the Regs—just this once."

"Absolutely no'."

"I'm talking too much and that's a first. People usually accuse me of being a real bore."

"You don't like to talk?"

He wanted to tell her the truth—that until he'd met her he had never been able to talk to a young woman without mangling his words until he was so embarrassed he stopped talking completely—but he never shared his past with anyone. "Not idle chatter."

"I hadn't noticed."

"I guess I've never been around someone I wanted to pass the time with. Please bring me some of that 'guid' tattie bree before I starve to death."

She returned with a tray minutes later.

He ate a large bowl of the thick broth and choked down a bottle of Lucozade, squirming when the pain in his back began to escalate. He didn't want to ask for APCs this early. "I know you have things to do, but could you tell the Selkie story again?" he asked as she straightened his covers.

"The Selkie again?"

"I want to hear it when I'm not full of morphine." His thoughts did not stop there. *And I want to hear your soft voice that takes away the pain and fear.*

"We shouldn't spend that much time. I need to bathe and shave you."

"The crofter returned to the cave with food and water," he prompted.

"You've remembered. Verra guid."

He stifled a groan and tried to smile. "What happened next? I need to find out if she stayed on the island."

"Och, all right, but we don't have time for the ending now—'tis too important to hurry through." She pulled up a chair and sat beside him, accepting the hand he held out.

The story wove on and on as the two evaded the fishermen by hiding in caves or abandoned cottages, huddling together for warmth, eating what little the crofter could find in the fields. "It didn't take long for the crofter to fall in love with this bonnie lass with her rosy cheeks and lips and her silken, white skin. Of course, he couldn't believe she was really a Selkie, you understand." She continued by relating how the crofter's gentle, tender nature slowly won the trust of the Selkie. "After a week, she no longer waded out into the sea when the strange, haunting voice of her Selkie-lover crested the waves with the dying sun." Maggie laid his hand on the bed and leaped up. "Now, 'tis bathing time."

"You can't stop now."

"I can and will."

Rob awakened in the middle of the night, chest heaving, body covered with sweat. What a dreadful nightmare. He wiped his face on a corner of the sheet, trying to recall what he had dreamed. He could only remember a grinding, tearing, screeching sound, flashing lights and then—nothing.

So he hadn't made it over the security fence, after all. No wonder he had so many aches and bruises. If he could have used the rudders, he might not have lost so much altitude before he reached the base.

Used the rudders.

He tucked his hand beneath the covers and moved it down to his thigh. He pinched the flesh. Nothing. No pain, absolutely nothing. His breath caught in a ragged sob. The surgery hadn't worked after all.

If only he hadn't been so set on using a single bomber. If only Wells had refused to allow it. If only ... "Stop it!" he hissed. But he couldn't stop wondering if there had been another approach he could have taken. He closed his eyes. Maybe if he tried to recall the meeting with Wing, he could discover his mistake.

There was no bomber's moon that night. It was raining—no, pouring buckets more like. He was so tired it was hard to think and he nearly scalped himself hurrying through the doorway of the four-hundred-year-old mansion which had been taken over by the American 8th Army Air Forces for one of its Wing headquarters. At a little over six-five, Rob experienced this often in Europe, but it only fueled his anger at being called to Edenoaks Hall for another battle with General Wells over a poorly planned bombing strike.

The pungent odor of wet wool and stale cigarette smoke stung his nose and eyes as he nimbly avoided crowded desks and busy personnel and passed the flaming logs in the fireplace, the only source of heat in the defaced, once-elegant drawing room.

General Wells waited against the far wall, back stiff, face grim, in front of a large wall map with a red ribbon marking the flight path to the target.

Rob argued for what seemed like hours against the wing commander's plan to send the entire 396th Group to take out a target that a single uncorroborated French informer insisted was a new

Luftwaffe fighter factory located in Metz, France.

Wells, a smug, haughty, brigadier general with no flight experience, just the "Book" he had obviously memorized, never seemed to consider the loss of planes, or their ten-member crews, of strategic importance.

When Rob pointed out that this target was too small to produce fighter planes and was located in a congested industrial area, too far to taxi completed planes to an airfield, Wells began to bluster, a sure sign his argument was weakening.

That was when Rob offered his own plan: one B-17 only, his own *Liberty Belle*, crewed by volunteers, taking off from Edenoaks two hours early to surprise the German anti-aircraft gunners. They would drop their load of bombs down the smoke-stack and scoot for home.

But it wasn't until he pulled a tattered piece of paper from his blouse pocket and laid it out on the table that Wells finally capitulated.

"One of these days, I'm going to sign that reassignment form, Savage," the General growled, "and you'll have your wish. I'm sure you'll find leading your 'A' Squadron a very large step down from commanding the entire group."

Rob swallowed a grin. He had won.

Chapter Six

The first blush of dawn softened the darkly bruised sky to dove-gray. Maggie had parted the blackout curtain and closed the door to the corridor on Rob's request when she left late the night before.

Rob sighed. If he could do it all over, he wouldn't change a word he'd said to Wells. The opportunity to save possibly fifty or more lives had to be taken, even if it meant sacrificing his future.

Please, God, I'm not sure you have the time to hear me, with the war and all, but I'm not asking anything for myself, only that the factory was a decoy. I can't bear to imagine how many of my men were lost in a group raid if it wasn't.

If only he could hear Maggie's voice or feel her tender touch. A simple "guid-mornin" in her soothing burr would be enough to banish the dark thoughts from his mind. And her tale of the Selkie sparked his imagination, took him to a time and place where he could lose himself in a world of primitive, natural beauty, and care about the future of a magical, beautiful woman and her gentle crofter.

Selfish thinking. After all the time Maggie spent seeing to his needs, she was lucky to get five or six hours of sleep a night.

He stared out the window. Why had he never taken the time to appreciate the simple things in life, like being able to turn over in bed without help or stepping outside to feel the sun's warmth on his face at the dawn of another day?

Rob held out his arm and wiggled the saline IV. "Can this go?"

Doctor McGrath instructed Maggie to remove it. "He's hydrated enough to go without it." After completing a thorough upper-body examination, he asked Rob, "How are the bruises and sore muscles? Any better?"

"A lot better if I'm careful."

"Then let's see how your legs are doing." He pricked Rob's thigh with a pin. "Feel anything?"

"It didn't hurt, but I felt the pressure."

"Good, good." He went down the leg.

More pressure, but still no prick. The results were the same with the other leg.

Rob forced himself to speak. "Not so good after all, huh, Doc?"

"You young lads are all alike. You want instant gratification. Of course it's good. You're only a little over a week out of surgery and already feeling the pressure of a strong prick on your skin. Give it time, lad."

"You mean that's what you expected?"

"Exactly. It's the first sign of nerves responding to stimulation. Without that, you'd have felt nothing at all."

Rob took a deep breath. So there was still hope. But patience had never been one of his virtues. "When can I at least sit up?"

"Right now."

He could do more than lie on a bed? "That's what I call good."

The doctor cranked up the head of the bed. "Maggie, you position his legs while I pull him upright."

They worked in unison, Maggie moving Rob's legs and the doctor lifting him into a sitting position.

Once his legs dangled from the side of the bed, he slumped against Doctor McGrath's arms. "Whew ... I'm dizzy."

"Sit still. It will pass. Any pain?"

"A little. Not bad."

Concern cloaked Maggie's face. "Do you need something?"

"Not now." He forced himself to smile. "You really are a wee little thing, aren't you?"

Her cheeks flushed. "I'm no' so wee. You're tall as a giant."

His grin widened. "I'm six-five but you can't be much over five feet tall, so I still say you're a wee little thing."

"Quit your blethering. You're weaving about like a fisherman setting foot on dry land after months at sea."

"That's considered an insult to an Air Forces man. I'm more

like a rookie pilot attempting his first take-off."

"While drouthie—drunk."

McGrath cleared his throat. "It's time to lie back down. We don't want to tire you too much the first time."

※

John berated himself as he made his way to the next patient. The colonel would have enjoyed sitting up longer, but the easy rapport between Maggie and the American unsettled him and he hadn't trusted himself not to say something rash. Maggie had been away at the academy, nursing school, or at one RAF base or another since she'd matured. He'd never seen her interacting with a lad.

Would he rather she and the colonel not be so friendly? They obviously liked one another, and that would only hasten the patient's recovery, not hinder it. But what about Maggie? Would this American aviator break her heart?

Maybe it was time to separate them.

He decided to sleep on it. Nothing good came from hasty decisions.

※

Though Rob pestered Maggie all day about a trip outside in the wheelchair, she was adamant. "When you can sit on the edge of the bed for fifteen minutes without reeling from side to side. No' a minute sooner."

"Then, help me sit up."

"You're so impatient. Let me finish massaging your calf muscles. Next, we'll go through your exercises and then I'll help you sit up."

"I wish I could feel more than pressure. I've never had a massage by a wee, bonnie lass before. How long do you think it will be before I can feel your hands?"

He sounds like a hurt, wee laddie, wondering when everything will be all better. "I don't know, but I do know you don't want these muscles to atrophy. We have to keep them elastic so they will work properly when you're ready to walk." She raised his right leg as far as it would go. "Tell me if the pain is too sharp."

He didn't signal her to stop until that leg had been raised four inches. But he gasped when his left was only three inches off the bed.

"Are you telling me soon enough?" she asked as she lowered his leg. "Remember, it won't help if it causes sharp pain."

He wiped his forehead on the sleeve of his gown. "Here you are, doing all the heavy work, and I'm the one sweating."

"That's all we'll do for now. I've a feeling you're hiding your pain to get outside. Would twa aspirin help?"

"Twa?"

She held up two fingers.

"Twa aspirin sounds fine."

After the aspirin had time to take the edge off his pain, she cranked up the head of his bed. "All right, you wanted to sit up and dangle, but this time, with no one here to help, you'll have to manoeuver your body while I move your legs over."

"Don't know if I can."

"Use both arms to push up, and turn slowly while I swing your legs."

"My shoulder's still sore as blazes. Maybe if you put your arm around me, I'll have something to pull against."

Maggie slid an arm under his good shoulder. "Don't pull too hard. You'll put my back out and we'll both be in a muddle."

"I'll be careful."

She slipped her other arm beneath his legs, bracing her knees against the side of the bed. He pulled against her as she moved him toward the side.

He leaned over and touched his lips to her cheek.

She jerked away, nearly dropping him. "Don't do that."

"Why?"

She swallowed and looked away. "Because ..."

"Because you enjoyed it?"

She pulled him into position. If she removed her arm, he might pitch forward onto the floor. "Can you sit alone now?"

"Don't want to."

"Och, if you don't stop this, I'll call an orderly to put you back down."

"What's the matter? Does one little peck on the cheek constitute a breach of those Regs you're so determined to follow?"

"This isn't something to be treated lightly. I'm doing all I can to help you and you're playing ... playing games."

"It's no game, Maggie."

His soft voice cut through her sharper than a shout. Her cheeks flamed.

"I didn't mean to make you uncomfortable."

His husky voice brought shivers up and down her arms.

"I've wanted to kiss you for days. In fact, a kiss from you on my cheek might be exactly what I need to help my recovery."

"Is that so?"

"Yes, I think it—"

She turned, leaned over, and pressed her lips to his cheek.

He moved his head, catching her lips with his own.

Soft, so soft. Despite her resolve to pull away, her own lips responded. Something inside melted as she returned his kiss. His fingers caressed her cheek before pulling her face closer. He moaned and she felt her knees weaken as she relaxed against his chest. The scent of the heather soap she had used to shave him that morning was so familiar and comforting, yet her body felt strange—hot and tingly—and she could scarcely breathe. She had never been kissed like this.

"Excuse me." Doctor McGrath's voice cut between them.

They instantly drew apart, Maggie's cheeks aflame.

"I can come back another time."

Maggie smoothed her hair back from her forehead. "Come in, Faither. We just finished his exercises and Rob needed a wee bit of help sitting up and—"

"And I'm completely responsible for what happened," Rob said.

"Nonsense," she exclaimed. "It wasn't planned. It just happened. What do you want this time of day, Faither?"

"Making early rounds. I have a conference this evening."

Maggie recognized that tone. His words sounded strangled and his jaws knotted with tension.

Broken Wings

"I'm here, ready to be pricked and probed," Rob said.

There was an edge to his voice she had never heard before.

"No, no, you two seem to be doing fine. I'll just take a look at your chart."

"I insist." Again that sharp edge.

Maggie wanted only to escape. "If you'll hold him, Faither, I'll step outside for a breath of fresh air."

Rob's fingers brushed her cheek. "Sounds like a good idea."

She waited until her father had hold of Rob's shoulders and fled from the room.

※

"Have your say before you explode," Rob demanded as the door closed behind Maggie.

"We need to talk," the doctor said. He eased Rob back against the raised pillow and moved his legs onto the bed.

"So, talk. But before you do, I want you to know it was only an innocent kiss, nothing more."

"I don't want you taking advantage of my Maggie."

"Advantage?" Rob exhaled loudly. "Why would I do that? You've both been responsible for saving my life." He closed his eyes for a moment before looking at the doctor. "So that's it. You think I'm playing with Maggie's feelings and when I'm tired of her, I'll just say 'thanks' and 'it's been nice?'"

"Something like that."

"So what do you want, Doc? Ask anything of me, only don't take Maggie away. Without her I'll never be able to ...." He bit off the words, unable to voice his fears. "She's the only bright thing in my life right now." *And I can't bear the thought of losing her forever.*

The doctor sat on the edge of the bed. "And in mine."

Rob eyed him closely. "You're in the driver's seat. What do you want me to do?"

"Do you love Maggie?" Doctor McGrath picked at a minuscule stain on his lab coat. "Because, if you don't, you'll break her heart. She's led a sheltered life."

He'd only known Maggie for a few days. Who would ask such

a premature question?

The answer leaped into his mind.

A father.

"Love's a strong word. I've never had any women friends. Never had the time, or to be frank, the social skills."

Doctor McGrath humphed. "That surprises me."

"Look, commanding the 396th plus flying lead on so many missions took all my time and concentration. Maggie's just so easy to be around, I don't feel like I have to prove anything to her."

"Of course you don't. After all, you're an officer and, therefore, a gentleman."

"But you prefer a *gentle man* for your daughter."

"I do. This war will be over some day. I don't want to lose her to anyone who would take her far away from the only home she's ever known, the home she loves with every fibre of her being."

"Innisbraw."

"Yes, Innisbraw."

"She's a grown woman. How about what she wants?"

"She shouldn't be torn between her love for a man and her love for her home."

Though Rob was exhausted, his fear of losing Maggie would not allow him to quit now. "I asked you before, but I'll do it again. What do you want me to do?"

John McGrath tugged at his beard. If he had Maggie reassigned back to an RAF airfield hospital in England, she'd never forgive him for meddling in her life, to say nothing of the negative impact that could have on the colonel's recovery. But Savage couldn't stay at the Royal Infirmary for his prolonged therapy. Beds were always in short supply, especially in private rooms. The colonel said he did not love Maggie and he didn't appear to be lying. Maybe the answer lay in a bold but possibly dangerous alternative. He made up his mind quickly, praying it was not a terrible mistake. "It seems there may be a solution to this muddle after all."

"Like what?"

"I'll be leaving on a teaching tour of military hospitals in three weeks. You'll need intensive therapy for several months, at least. I have a small infirmary on Innisbraw with a rehab room."

"And you want me to go there? What about Maggie?"

He stared directly into the colonel's eyes. "She'll go with you."

"After all you've said, you seem to be putting a lot of trust in me. Why?"

"I'm taking you at your word, Colonel. I don't want my Maggie hurt."

"Neither do I." Rob slumped back against the pillow. "In other words, you're telling me to keep it strictly a patient-nurse relationship."

"That's the only way to ensure she doesn't get hurt. I'm not certain you're capable of doing it. If you aren't, tell me now and I'll try to come up with another answer."

"I may be a Yank, but I know how to behave, and I'm no liar," Rob said, his voice slurred, most likely from exhaustion. "I'll be a gentleman, that's a promise."

"I wouldn't even suggest it unless I believed that to be true."

Chapter Seven

Maggie brushed her long hair and twisted it up into her usual bun. Something had changed between Rob and her. The easy banter that had defined their relationship in the days since his surgery had been replaced during the past two weeks by a stilted politeness on his part and an ever-deepening distress on hers. Had her father said something to him about being too friendly?

He never smiled. When she caught him looking at her, his eyes had lost their green flecks and held that same sadness she had seen when he bid her good-bye the night they danced. He still worked hard but had become so unresponsive, she found it difficult to treat him with the same gentle cheerfulness she used with all her patients.

He never pressed her for the ending to the Selkie tale, and his appetite had dropped, though much of his weight loss could be the result of his aversion to the Scots food they served at the infirmary. He could now drink the Lucozade without making a face, and she always ordered oat porridge for his breakfast, never kippers, knowing an American would find the salted, smoked fish unpalatable. He refused to even taste the tripe, sweetbreads, or creamed calves' heads that regularly appeared on the supper trays. He toyed with the boiled cabbage and neeps, though he did seem to enjoy tattie bree, baked rabbit, and mashed tatties.

Desperate to assuage his craving for something sweet when sugar was so tightly rationed, Maggie had asked her father's head nurse to put out the word. The pantry down the hall from Rob's room now held several jars of honey and bramble jelly gleaned from the staff's own cupboards.

She spent hours every night praying for guidance, but nothing she tried broke through his reluctance to talk. Some of it was her fault. Why had she kissed his cheek? She had never been so unprofessional with a patient before. Every time she remembered how soft his lips felt against hers and that moan deep within his throat, she tingled all over, no matter how hard she fought against it. If only she had more experience with lads.

But Rob wasn't a lad. He was a man, and though his maturity and high military rank sometimes intimidated her, she had thought they were becoming friends. Why had he changed?

She buttoned her hospital dress and pinched her cheeks. Too little sleep had left her looking pale. Even her eyes had lost their usual sparkle. She left her room and plodded down the hall. How could she face another day of such unhappiness?

When she reached Rob's room, she forced a smile and opened the door. "Guid morning," she said with feigned brightness. "How did you sleep?"

He lay flat on his back, arm over his eyes. "Lousy."

She sat down on the bed and pulled his arm away from his face. "We have to talk."

"Not now, I have a headache."

"I'll get you some APCs." She left the room and returned in a few minutes with the aspirin and a glass of water, but when she attempted to place her arm beneath his shoulders to help him sit up, he pulled away.

"Just crank up the bed. Don't want you hurting your back." His hand shook as he reached for the glass.

"Is your headache that bad, then?"

"No. I need to learn to do things for myself. I can't expect you to be around forever, doing everything for me."

She was too shocked to say a word.

He glanced at her and quickly looked away. "Please forgive me, Maggie, I didn't mean that the way it sounded."

"But you did." She fought her rising panic. "And you're right, for I'll no' always be at your side. Father has received transfer papers from your commander, but mine was no' so understanding. I've only been given until the end of August before I have to report back to London and it's my duty to see that you ... that you. . ." Tears filled her eyes. She turned toward the door.

"Don't go." His hoarse whisper stopped her. "Please, Maggie, I didn't mean to hurt you."

She wouldn't let him see how much his cold words had upset her. "I'm going for your wheelchair."

"Maggie!" he called to her retreating back.

She ran outside and huddled on a bench in the center of the infirmary garden. She had been so terribly mistaken. His coolness the past two weeks had been his way of telling her he only wanted a nurse, not a friend. How could she face him again, let alone continue to be his nurse? As hard as it would be to leave his recuperation to others, perhaps she should ask for a transfer back to an RAF base.

Doctor McGrath spent several sleepless nights going over and over his conversation with the colonel about not hurting Maggie. His entire approach seemed to have caused nothing but pain. Not only had he hurt his precious lass, he had set back the lad's recovery, evidenced by his drop in weight. "You're an auld fool," he muttered to himself as he walked toward Rob's room. "You've been so afraid of losing Maggie you've forgotten how fine a happy relationship between a lad and lass can be."

He hesitated outside in the corridor. *Och, help me, Heavenly Faither. Give me the words I need to undo my foolishness.* He pushed the door open and peeked inside.

Guid, the lad was alone. He walked in and pulled up a chair, clearing his throat. "Well, how are the exercises coming?"

The colonel faced the other way. "All right."

"Are you able to endure the pain?" John rested his hand on Savage's shoulder.

"Of course."

He grasped the colonel's shoulders and turned him until they were facing one another. The lad's eyes showed no expression except, perhaps, indifference. "I've made a very big mistake."

Savage's expression did not change, though a dark shadow bloomed in the depths of his eyes. "I'll never walk or fly again? What's taken you so long to tell me?"

McGrath reared back. "Och, nae, lad!" he exclaimed, so startled he used Scots. "This has nowt—och, nothing—to do with your physical progress which is coming along very well. I'm talking about you and Maggie."

A flicker of pain crossed Savage's face as he turned to face the wall again. "You've had my promise, Doctor McGrath," he said, voice ragged. "If my behavior still isn't proper enough to satisfy you, then perhaps it would be kinder to Maggie if you ..." He swallowed. "If you assigned her to another patient."

"But why? You begged me not to take Maggie away."

"You've taken away everything but her body. Every minute she spends in this room is agony for her. She never laughs, never hums while she's shaving me. She's sad—not the happy, optimistic girl with the quick smile and teasing words."

McGrath leaned back in his chair, frowning. "It isn't me lying in that bed. It's you. If she's unhappy, then it's you who's causing it."

"You got what you asked for," the colonel said in a husky whisper. "I'm a perfect gentleman. I never touch her, don't ask for special favors like the stories she used to tell or the songs she sang to put me to sleep, or the scones she often sneaked me late at night. I'm only a patient in need of her care, nothing more." He winced as though in pain. "My life has been filled with losing those I care about and all I can do is face the fact that she's another one."

John bowed his head. "Then perhaps you and I need a new agreement, for it's obvious you've completely misunderstood the first one."

"I'm tired, Doctor. Maybe another time."

"All I wanted from you was a promise that you wouldn't lead my Maggie on, that you wouldn't promise her true love when that's not what you feel for her. I didn't mean you couldn't be friends." He leaned forward, praying for the right words. "My Maggie is young. She's never had any sort of lasting relationship with a lad. But there's nothing wrong with having a good laugh or her singing to you or telling you stories. She has a keen sense of humour and loves to sing. Can't you allow her that without promising her something you're in no position to promise?"

The colonel turned his head. "What can I promise a woman? A walk in a garden or along the beach? Maybe a bike ride through a park? To someday provide her with a home or give her children? Those are only some of the things I can't promise any woman."

"I mean a lifelong commitment of love—true love, forever and ever."

Trolley wheels clattered by in the hallway outside and nurses and orderlies chatted, their occasional laughter muting the sounds of squeaking rubber soles and the rustle of starched uniforms.

The colonel closed his eyes, silent for a moment. "I've told you before, I'm not in love with Maggie. For one thing, I haven't known her long enough, and I'm in no position to allow it even if I had. I care for her a lot and being around her makes me feel like someday, if I do all those exercises, I'll be able to ..." He rubbed his hands over his face.

John leaned close. "Be her friend again. Someone she can share a laugh with, someone who can greet her in the morning with a smile even if you've had a terrible night. Just be yourself."

Savage's laugh was short and harsh. "You don't know me or you wouldn't say that. Even I don't know what that means."

"But you know how to laugh and you know how to tease, for I've seen you do both." Sighing, John got up and turned to leave. "Remember this. I know you say you don't love Maggie now, but if that should change, the only promises I expect you to make and keep are that you won't commit yourself to her until you know deep within that you intend to keep that commitment for the rest of your life, that you will not hurt her, and that you will never, ever take her away from Innisbraw. I cannot allow that."

He walked from the room, his heart burdened. Being the father of a grown-up lass without the gentle guidance of her mother was proving much harder than he had ever anticipated. He had a lot of praying to do.

Maggie sighed and tucked a tendril of hair behind her ear as she looked out at the garden surrounding her. Spent daffodils wilted on their stems, overpowered by red and yellow tulips just coming into bloom. She had acted like a daft young schoolgirl with no brains and even less common sense when she kissed Rob's cheek. And the kiss they shared had been only that, a kiss, nothing more. She rubbed her burning cheeks with her palms. No more acting like a foolish schoolgirl, and no running off to another post to escape an uncomfortable muddle of her own making.

If Rob wanted to reply with grunts, that was his privilege. But if he no longer wanted to hear her sing or tell stories, that was just too bad. She'd be herself and treat him the same way she treated every patient—and expect nothing in return.

*

Rob wrestled his demons. Though the thought of never again seeing Maggie's tender smile or hearing her soft, comforting voice was agonizing, he couldn't continue to hurt her. He groaned. He didn't have the slightest idea how to treat a woman. If he acted cold or indifferent, her violet-blue eyes turned dark with distress, but he could not, would not, allow himself to mislead her. He should never have kissed her, no matter how much he wanted to. She was too kind, too tenderhearted to use and then discard if he found himself tied to a wheelchair for the rest of his life.

Could he somehow return to the light bantering they had once shared without stepping over the boundaries set by her father? He repressed another groan. Over three months was a long time to ignore how much he wanted to kiss her again.

*

Maggie spent several minutes in the bathroom, splashing her burning cheeks with cold water and re-pinning her hair, praying to God to ease the leaden feeling in her chest and guide her actions and thoughts.

Ready at last, she retrieved a wheelchair from its nook by the nurse's station and, smiling brightly, entered Rob's room. "Are you ready for your outing? The overcast is lifting."

He bit his lower lip.

"Is your headache no better? Is your back hurting?"

"The headache's gone and my back's the same."

"Something's wrong."

"I'd like to start the morning all over again. Can we?"

Her shoulders relaxed. "We can try."

"Will you come and sit here on the bed?"

She hesitated.

"Please. I haven't told anyone else. It's something I just discovered."

He was actually speaking in sentences. She sat on the bed beside him. "Well?"

"I have something to show you."

"Show me? I thought you had something to tell me."

"Both. Pull the sheet down, please."

Her curiosity piqued, she drew the sheet off of his legs.

"Watch." He clenched his tongue between his lips and closed his eyes. The toes of both feet moved.

She leaped up. "Och, how can you call that a wee thing? You can move your toes! That's wonderful. Do it again."

"Wait a minute, I have to concentrate." A moment later, his toes moved again and those delightful dimples danced beside his lips with the breadth of his smile. "Well? Surprised?"

"Of course I'm surprised. More than surprised. I'm so happy, I could dance."

He patted the side of the bed. "Now, I've something to say."

She fought an internal battle for control, forcing a smile when she sat beside him. "Whatever can you say to top that?"

He reached for her hand. "I never could have done it without you, Maggie. I—"

"Och, no—"

"Don't interrupt. I need to say this." He brought his other hand over hers. "I was out of line the other day. I had no right to ... to ..."

"Kiss me?"

"To kiss you. Not that I didn't want to," he added quickly. "I did, more than you'll ever know."

"And?"

"And I never stopped to think about ... about ... Oh, Maggie, I wouldn't hurt you for anything in the world."

He clasped her hand so tightly, she squirmed.

"Sorry." He measured her palm against his. "Look at that. I can close my fingers completely over yours, that's how much smaller your hands are."

"But you have verra, verra large hands."

"And they can cover yours."

"What are you trying to say?"

"I don't know, exactly." He sighed. "I guess I'm trying to apologize for how I've been acting. I'm just not good at conversation. Like I'm lacking in something important, that I don't know how to relate to people."

"I haven't seen that in you."

"You have a kind heart. You wouldn't."

"Nonsense. I've heard about your famous battles with Wing Command. You seem very capable of defending your men."

"You mean my infamous battles. Look, I can give concise orders and I can argue like mad for what I believe in, but until I met you, I don't think I ever spoke a complete sentence to a woman. Put me in a social setting and I'll end up with my foot in my mouth every time."

She stifled a laugh. "With the size of your feet, that must be quite an accomplishment."

"Touché." He looked at her for a long time, as though memorizing every feature. "Can we start over again, Maggie, please? I'll try to do better."

"Only if you promise you'll do your exercises without complaining."

"I promise."

She leaped to her feet. "Then I'll ring for an orderly. Your first exercise today is a ride in the garden."

※

Maggie knew Rob regretted his promise many times over the following days. The exercises were grueling and painful, yet he never complained. The movement in his feet and legs improved. In time, he moved his ankles and knees a few centimetres apart without any assistance. He even began eating more.

He also kept his word about trying to learn what he called "chit-chat." She carried the burden of most conversations, though he teased her when she used too much Scots. When he spoke, it concerned the present, never the past or future. Many of the paralyzed lads she nursed could not face the unknowns this early in their recuperation and naturally avoided the future.

But why not his past? Had he been ignored or never allowed to speak as a bairn? Chilled by the thought, she told him silly stories and sang humorous songs, treasuring the smiles that made his dimples dance

A few days before they were to leave for Innisbraw, Rob's nightmares returned. First, one early-morning dream filled with brief images of his crew's faces as he announced the target for the day and Rich Florey, his tail gunner, gave him a crooked grin and flashed him a thumbs-up.

He woke feeling restless and uneasy. He had picked up some flak in his back and crashed trying to land on the runway. The question that had been at the back of his mind for weeks finally pushed its way forward. What had happened to his crew?

No one here would know. He could ask Doctor McGrath to find out, but he wanted to hear the answer himself.

Though it upset Maggie, he found it hard to respond to her questions that day. He could only choke down a few bites of food. Even the scone with honey, a treat he looked forward to every night, had no taste.

"Are you in pain, Rob?" Maggie turned off the light and pushed aside the blackout curtains. "You left most of your plate and you didn't even finish your coffee."

"No pain," he said. "Tired, I guess."

"Are you certain your back's no' hurting?"

"I'm fine. Go to bed, Maggie. You've been on your feet all day."

When she reluctantly left his room for the night, he fought to stay awake, so desperate not to doze off, he resorted to pinching his arms and face.

He succumbed to the inevitable around 0330.

He was instantly caught up in a horrible, graphic, noisy nightmare. The flak surrounding the *Liberty Belle* looked thick enough to walk on and his ears rang from the constant staccato of machine-gun fire and the warning shouts of his crew over the interphone as wave after wave of Fw 190s filled the windscreen.

"Florey's dead, blasted Krauts got him!"

"Pilot to crew, bail out, bail out!"

"Florey's dead, blasted Krauts got him! Florey's dead, blasted—"

He woke, fighting the sheets tangled around his shoulders and arms, breath coming in strident gasps. Rich was dead. How could he have forgotten that? His eyes burned with tears that refused to fall. He inhaled deeply and struggled out of his soaked pajama top. If only he could open the window and feel the fresh air on his face.

The pounding of his heart subsided. Had thoughts about never walking again overwhelmed all memories of that last flight, burying them beneath unrelenting layers of fear? Guilt brought a bitter taste to his mouth.

Rich was dead, but there were eight other men still on that plane. Had he waited too long to order a bailout?

He closed his eyes and put his arm over his forehead. Maybe if he could recall the details of that strike he could discover if he had made an error in judgment.

Chapter Eight

His last flight with the *Liberty Belle*.

Dark shadows obscured corners as Colonel Savage entered his OP's office at 0300 and made his way toward the front of the room. "At ease," he said before pulling the drape back from an easel holding a large map adorned with red ribbons marking the mission route. He took a pointer and tapped a name circled in red. "Today's target is Metz."

He studied the faces of the nine men settling onto benches in front of him, feeling both pride and deep concern. To a man, his own crew had volunteered for this risky mission. "Before we have the weather, I want to make something perfectly clear. When I asked for volunteers, I didn't expect my own crew to step forward. This mission is no milk run. We'll be going in alone, no fighter cover. Now's the time to slip out of here, no questions asked, absolutely no repercussions." He smiled grimly. "If I had a choice, I'd beat you to the door."

He waited for a few chuckles to die out, briefed them on the weather, and handed his bombardier and navigator their flak and route charts, reminding them all to pick up bailout and survival packets before dismissing them. As he watched them file out, he prayed their trust in him to bring them back safely was not misplaced.

Den Anderson intercepted him as he was leaving for the hardstands. "Rob, I want to fly right seat on this strike."

"Jack Spears is my co-pilot. I'm counting on you to fly lead on that alternate target later this morning." He clapped the major's shoulder. "See you as soon as you're wheels down."

Den flashed him a thumbs-up. "Good luck, Bucko," he said as the colonel's jeep began to move.

Broken Wings

The green "go" flare lit up the dark sky at exactly 0400 and Wright cyclone engines roared as the B-17 rumbled down the runway. By 0530 they were cruising at twenty thousand feet on oxygen and deep into German-occupied territory.

Savage scanned the cloudy sky. Looked good so far; no bandits in sight. He pressed his throat mike. "Pilot to navigator. How are we doing, Loomis?"

"On time and on target, sir."

"Roger that. Listen up, crew. It won't be long before one of their HS-126 spotter planes picks us up. Let's hope they think we're a reconnaissance plane. No unnecessary chatter."

By 0710, the cloud cover dissipated and they encountered their first enemy aircraft. Savage saw the telltale spots through the windscreen and pressed his throat mike. "Bandits at 3 o'clock high." Seconds later, the loud clatter of machine gun fire filled the air as enemy planes screamed toward the B-17.

Why were so many fighters coming after a single bomber? Had his decision been faulty? But he had seen the same Intel report General Wells had referred to: only one French Underground uncorroborated report from a single informant. In his judgment, all these fighters could mean one of two things: either the factory was the real thing or they didn't want their decoy revealed until the entire group was involved.

"Got another one climbing our tail," Rich Florey shouted over the interphone, his two tail guns firing sustained bursts.

"Coming right at us!" the turret gunner shouted. Savage and Jack Spears instinctively ducked as an F.W.-190, the yellow circles painted around its engines glaring in the rising sun, streaked by within a few feet of the cockpit canopy before taking a direct hit from the turret gunner and exploding behind them.

"Pilot to turret," Savage radioed. "Good going, Gil, but next time, don't wait 'til you can see the whites of his eyes." He ignored the excited chatter in his ears and pressed his throat mike again. "Pilot to navigator. How long to the initial point?"

"Three minutes to IP, sir."

He tapped his co-pilot's knee. "Time to take her down, Jack."

They continued to fight off the bandits until they leveled off at nine thousand feet and went off oxygen. As the first black puffs of anti-aircraft fire erupted around them, the German Fw 190s suddenly peeled off and disappeared, apparently unwilling to chance being shot down by their own ground-fire.

Chalk up a big one in favor of the target's being a decoy. If that factory was the real thing, the Jerries might sacrifice a few fighters to keep the bombs from falling.

Spears did a crew check. They all answered but Florey, the tail gunner.

Savage pressed his throat mike. "Rich, you okay back there?"

No answer.

He sent the flight engineer to check on Florey, stomach cramping. *Oh, Lord, don't let him be hit.*

The flak intensified and each close blast rocked the plane, sending pieces of shrapnel hurtling through the thin aluminum fuselage.

"Pilot to bombardier. Coming off the IP. Can you see our target?"

"Sure can, sir."

"Let me know when you've got your PDI centered."

In less than a minute, the bombardier radioed, "PDI centered, Colonel."

He made a small course correction until the needle on his own PDI was centered before lifting his hands from the yoke. "It's your airplane, Brian."

Seconds later the bombardier shouted, "Bombs away!" and the plane bucked higher into the air with the release of six thousand pounds of weight.

Savage took the yoke again and radioed the bombardier. "How'd it look?"

"Right down the smokestack, sir!"

Grinning, Savage let out a deep breath. "Good work." He turned to his co-pilot and pulled back on the yoke, adjusting his airspeed to compensate for the reduction in power. "Okay, let's get back upstairs and make a niner zero degree turn to the right, Jack.

Broken Wings

Let's go ho—"

A violent blast swallowed his words. Something slammed into his back and the breath left his lungs. Captain Spears fought the controls as Savage gulped in air. "Damage report," he gasped.

A moment later the flight engineer reported in. "Wings and fuselage took a lot of hits from those fighters. Got a six-inch hole in the right side next to the waist gunner's station and Florey's dead. Blasted Krauts got him."

Another burst of flak shook the plane, then another. The two left engines trailed flames.

Savage fought the yoke. "Set the fire extinguisher valve and stand by to pull charge." He'd been hit, but how badly? Strangely, he felt little pain in his back. The engines still trailed smoke. "Pull both charges, then feather." The pain he felt over losing his tail-gunner was another matter; Rich Florey had been like the younger brother he never had.

The co-pilot feathered both left engines. "Engines off. You all right, Colonel?"

"Just some cramps in my thighs. Handle the rudders for me while I work them out."

The flak gradually dissipated.

Savage looked at the falling altimeter. "Let's see if we can goose a little more out of those right engines."

The next two hours passed in a blur. Flying on only two engines, and both on the same side, made the flight extremely difficult. Both he and the co-pilot fought to keep the aircraft steady and on course.

The constant bone-rattling vibration took its toll. Savage's strength waned and it became harder and harder to keep his eyes open and focused on the instruments.

When they were over the English Channel, he pressed his throat mike. "Sparks, radio Ground Control we're coming in on two engines."

"Yes, sir."

Spears tapped his arm. "Better make that one engine," he said, indicating the oil pressure gauges. "Our outboard must have sprung an oil leak. Pressure's diving."

"Tell the crew to 'chute up," Savage ordered. He stared at the gauge. The image blurred and he blinked his eyes. If he had to order a bailout, he could never survive a jump when he couldn't move his legs. The engine sputtered five minutes after they cleared the top of the chalky Cliffs of Dover.

Though the co-pilot feathered the engine, they lost more altitude. They were getting too low—it was now or never.

He toggled the bailout button and the buzzer rang one long ring throughout the airplane. "Pilot to crew, bail out, bail out!" He looked at his co-pilot. "You, too, before we're too low."

"But the rudders ..."

"I'll take them now."

Spears unbuckled his harness. "Let me stay and help get her down."

"Get out now, Jack!" Savage thundered.

The captain left his seat as the airplane began to yaw.

Without the use of his feet on the rudders, Savage couldn't keep the B-17 stable with only one functioning engine. He thumbed on the autopilot and prayed the last engine would hold out for another few minutes without throwing the plane into a cartwheel.

He switched on his overhead mike. "Army one-six-eight to niner-four-seven Control, do you read me? Approximately two miles due east on the neck. Coming in on one engine. May be a little short."

"Roger, Army one-six-eight. We read you five by five. You are cleared for straight-in emergency landing on runway two-one-oh. Good luck, sir."

He stared at the altimeter. Down to one thousand feet and sinking fast. If he could only hold on long enough to reach the field. He shook his head again to clear his vision. The pain in his back was almost gone and a strange euphoria came over him. He peered through the pitted, milky windscreen.

There, straight ahead: Edenoaks.

He thumbed off the autopilot and gripped the yoke tightly.

Three hundred feet.

Too low.

Two hundred feet.

He had a fleeting image of the Scottish leftenant, her blue eyes raised shyly to his and he was sorry he had never had the opportunity to see her black hair spilling down her back.

One hundred feet.

Fifty.

Twenty.

He could see the runway ahead. If he could just make it over that security fence. He hit the switch to kill the engine.

He'd lost the elevation to clear it.

"Lord, help me!" He brought his arm across his face and braced himself.

Chapter Nine

Exhausted, Rob lay quietly for a long time, his breathing ragged. Reliving that last flight convinced him there was nothing he could have done to alter the ultimate outcome.

Had he ordered the bailout soon enough? He could have called it over the Channel, but that would have put his men in the drink, always a dangerous alternative. And as for himself, it was just his time. He could have been killed, like ... like Rich. In so many ways, that would have been easier. If what he had believed since childhood was true, it was Earth one second and Heaven the next.

The thought of spending the rest of his life in a wheelchair was unbearable. Did that make him a coward?

Probably.

⁂

Maggie served him his dinner of tattie brie.

He took only a few spoonfuls before pushing the tray away.

"Are you in pain?"

"No."

"Aren't you going to finish your coffee?"

"I'm full." He looked out the window, eyes narrowed.

She took the tray out into the hall.

He didn't look at her when she returned.

"What's the matter with you? You've been quiet and distracted all day."

He suddenly sat up straight in his wheelchair. "Put in a phone call to Operations at Edenoaks Airbase and ask to speak to Major Hank Hirsch. If they squawk about the long distance charges, tell them I'm good for it."

"A phone call, is it? And who is Major Hirsch?"

"My aide. Tell him Colonel Savage wants to talk to him.

Privately."

"But there are no private phones at the infirmary."

He exhaled noisily. "Wheel me down to one of those doctor's offices where we can close the door. It's imperative I talk to the major. I need some answers to a couple of questions."

His voice was so impersonal, so cold, she almost saluted. "Verra well," she said, her tone icy. "I'll take you down to Father's office. And don't worry about the charges. He's 'guid for' it, too."

After the connection was made, his hand trembled as she handed him the receiver. He dismissed her from the room with a curt nod. "Hank? This is Rob Savage."

She closed the door quietly and stood with her back to it.

The rumble of Rob's deep voice and long silences as he listened to the major came through the door. His brusque order had taken her completely by surprise. Yes, he had been withdrawn and quiet all morning, yet since that momentous afternoon when he moved his toes, his smile had come easily and he even teased her when she used more Scots than he could understand. Granted, he still had occasional dark moods, but now that shadow of grief was back in his eyes.

She worried her lower lip. Was he in pain and hiding it for fear of being put back on morphine?

He reminded her of an eagle with broken wings, straining, striving to heed the innate call to flight, yet unable to soar into the heavens. But it wasn't just Rob's paralysed legs that grounded him. Why couldn't he dare to hope that God would help him if he only asked?

The call lasted ten minutes.

When she heard nothing but silence, she tapped on the door.

"Come in."

Rob slumped in the wheelchair, hand over his mouth, forehead bathed in sweat.

She knelt in front of him. "Rob?"

He reached for her hands, smiling. "They made it, Maggie. All eight men are okay and already back to duty."

She knew immediately whom he was talking about. "Your

crew."

"Yes. Thank God, they all made it out okay. I've put in a verbal request for an Air Medal for my bombardier and a posthumous one for Rich Florey, my tail gunner. He was ... killed on the strike. Maybe it will help ease the pain for his sister, Ellie."

So this is why he'd been so worried. "I'm so happy for you. At least one of your questions resulted in guid news."

"Make that two. Reconnaissance photos showed the target we bombed was an empty warehouse. The Jerries were setting up a trap for the men in my group. We always flew that sector." He threw back his head. "Well, it didn't work. There was no reason for another strike."

She retrieved a towel from the sink in the corner and blotted his forehead. "So your mission was a success."

"It was. And Rich didn't sacrifice his life for nothing. That's what I'm going to say when I write his sister, Ellie. And I asked Hank about Den—Major Anderson," he said, rubbing his face. "He's fine, still acting as second-in-command to the new CO. I feel like a sack of bricks has been lifted from my back."

"And you're starving."

He smiled. "You're right. Think you can rustle up a little something from that magic pantry of yours?"

"Of course, Colonel."

"Uh oh, there's a burr under your saddle again."

She straightened and threw down the towel. "Och, you men and your secrets. Did it never occur to you that twa backs could have lightened that load you were carrying on just one?"

"What are you trying to say? That I should have burdened you with my worries?"

"It might have eased some of your fears."

He sighed. "Oh, Maggie, they tell you command is a lonely position and they're right. I made decisions every day that involved the lives of hundreds of men. If I'd shared my concerns, I'd have been second-guessing myself until I was worthless."

"This is the first time I've seen you wearing your 'Colonel's hat.' You must be very formidable when you argue with Wing."

"Can we have a truce, bonnie Maggie? I'll try not to order you around again. Old habits die hard."

What a complex man Rob Savage was. But one thing had just been proven to her; his loyalty to those under his command, which was legendary, was very true. "Truce."

As time for their departure to Innisbraw drew near, Maggie looked forward more and more to showing Rob her home. "Of course you'll be seeing it coming into its best," she said while they waited for her father's final instructions. "'Tis almost summer."

"Good."

Doctor McGrath entered the room. "If it's the weather you're talking about, I'll have to agree." He turned to Rob. "Already in your chair, I see, Colonel."

The two men stared at one another for a long moment.

"I'm ready for a change of scenery."

Her father turned to Maggie. "Have everything packed, lass?" He handed her an envelope. "I've written down all the exercises the colonel will need until I get to Innisbraw. Just remember to keep a detailed account of his progress."

She took the envelope and tucked it into her bag. She felt the same tension she always did between Rob and her father.

Not hostility, just wariness, like two male dogs circling and eyeing one another when meeting unexpectedly.

"The ambulance will be here any moment," she said brightly. "Then it's off to Oban for the night, and tomorrow morning the beginning of a long, long boat ride."

"I've contracted with Malcolm MacNeill to use his fishing trawler. He's the skipper I trust the most."

"'Twill be grand to see Malcolm again."

Rob wheeled his chair closer to the doctor and extended his hand. "I want to thank you again for all you've done for me."

Her father clasped Rob's hand tightly. "I'm delighted with the outcome so far. I'm especially happy your appetite has returned. You'll find the food more to your liking on Innisbraw. Almost everyone has a pig or chickens for eggs and meat and a vegetable garden. Our fishermen will keep the infirmary kitchen stocked with all kinds of fish and shellfish. There's even beef available occasionally if one of the crofters butchers a cow, and mutton is plentiful. That's one advantage of island living during rationing."

"You'll radio us with the time of your return?" Maggie threw her arms around her father.

"Of course." He hugged her close and kissed her cheek. "Remember, if you have any problems, you can reach me through my office, though with all the good folk on Innisbraw, you should get along fine."

"I'm sure we will. Guid-bye, Faither, and Godspeed."

"The same to you, lass, and to you, Colonel," he said, voice thick with emotion. He closed the door softly behind him.

Rob interrupted the silence. "What's this about a radio? Aren't there phones on Innisbraw?"

"We're only a wee spot of land far out in the Atlantic. There were plans for laying the cable to Innisbraw, but the war intervened before it could be installed. Also, the only places on the island with electricity are those on the south side by the harbour, the infirmary, the kirk properties, and primary school. A few of those with larger crofts have generators, but petrol is too dear to use them often."

His eyes narrowed, as if he wasn't pleased, but he didn't press her further. "I know I promised not to complain, so I'll phrase this as a question. 'Why an ambulance? Can't we travel by automobile?'"

"You can't mean it. The ride to Oban is so long you'd be in agony by the time we got there. No, 'tis a stretcher for you, even on the boat, though we will take the wheelchair so you can sit when you feel like it."

※

Maggie watched over Rob as he slept a great deal of the ride. He always seemed to sleep deeply when there was motion involved—first in the train and now the ambulance. It was she who paid the price once they reached Oban where they were spending the night in a small, two-bedroom, rented cottage.

He fidgeted in bed and talked in spurts as she tried to smile and carry on a conversation while fighting to keep her eyes open.

When she brought her hand to her mouth to cover another yawn, he frowned. "You're out on your feet, but before you go to bed, please take down that blackout curtain and open the window so I can look out at the garden and smell the fresh air."

She turned out the lamp, pushed back the heavy black curtain, and slid the window open.

Moonlight flooded the room.

"It is bonnie, isn't it?"

"It certainly is."

"I'll just take a wee nap."

"No nap. You'll take a nice hot bath, climb between the sheets, and sleep until morning."

"Och, you're giving orders again."

"Only because they're necessary. But don't go before I thank you for that stroll through the garden after supper. I don't think I've ever seen so many flowers all in one place at one time."

"Then you'll have to see my garden on Innisbraw. It might have suffered from neglect with me being gone so long, but my mither planted that garden and I'm hoping most of the flowers have survived."

"I'm looking forward to seeing it."

She sighed. "So am I."

"You've missed your home."

"Of course. 'Tis only a wee croft, but my faither built the cottage and infirmary when he and my mither were first married." She looked out the window for a moment. "Is there something I can get you before I go? There's water on the table, but I can bring you a scone if you're hungry."

"I'm fine. Good-night, bonnie Maggie."

"Guid-night, Rob."

He stared out the window for a long time after she had gone, mind leaping from one conflicting thought to another. What was he going to do about Maggie? She stirred something in his heart he hadn't even known was there. She gave him courage and the will to ignore the pain when he wanted to give up—and the hope that he might walk again.

The promises he had made the doctor were harder to keep than he had ever imagined. The scent of heather still hung in the air and he closed his eyes, trying to ignore a vision of her smiling face.

Though he knew it was a waste of energy and there couldn't be a worse time for it, he found himself fantasizing about what it would be like to fall in love with Maggie and spend the rest of his life with her. He had always dreamed about marrying and having children, but what if the doctor was wrong and he was never able to walk again? He could never burden her with a cripple, with someone who was less than a whole man.

And he couldn't imagine giving up his Air Forces career after the war and spending the rest of his life on some God-forsaken island far out in the Atlantic. The thought of civilian life itself was so foreign it made his stomach cramp. He didn't have the slightest idea how to go about doing what the average Joe on the street tackled every day. He'd never owned a single piece of furniture, never bought a house or an automobile or paid a utility bill, never planted a tree or mowed a lawn. The Army Air Forces fed him, clothed him, provided him with medical and dental care, and even cut his hair and did his laundry. When he made full-bird colonel, he had a driver, jeep, and staff car at his disposal.

All those obstacles paled when he thought about having to give up flying. He couldn't do it. It had been the focus of his life for over twenty years and the joy it brought was irreplaceable.

He wanted to pray as he had as a child—pour out all of his fears and longings and hopes—and still believe with youthful innocence his prayers would be heard and answered. But he was a man now. Life had taught him that though he could still pray for others and trust he would go to Heaven someday, God was much too busy to hear every personal petition, especially with the world torn apart by war.

Regardless of how much a part of him wanted to, he couldn't get too close to Maggie. He had meant what he told the doctor about his life being filled with losing those dear to him. He wouldn't survive going through it again.

By tomorrow evening, they would be on Innisbraw. Would it be the beginning of a new life or the beginning of the end?

Chapter Ten

The ambulance pulled up at the commercial dock in Oban at 0600. "I'll see our bags and your chair aboard, and then we'll come for you," Maggie told Rob as the two attendants unloaded the storage area behind the front seat.

One of the attendants threw open the two back doors as Maggie climbed out of the ambulance. She crossed the gangplank, looking smart in her RAF Nurse's grey-blue tunic and skirt with its matching short cape and dark stockings and cap. Oh, for the day she allowed him to see her with her shiny black hair released from its bun and spilling down her back.

He waited impatiently, looking out the open back doors. A dense mist hovered over the harbor, transforming masts and hulls into macabre shapes of ghostly white. The surface of the water was so still, it reflected those shapes as effectively as a piece of polished pewter. The muted clang of bells aboard British naval ships riding at anchor and the muffled shouts of fishermen readying their trawlers at the commercial dock competed with the shrill cries of a few gulls foolish enough to be looking for a handout this early in the morning.

Maggie suddenly appeared at the open door. "That didn't take long, did it?"

The attendants unloaded the stretcher and Rob finally had his first look at the trawler, the *Sea Rouk*.

"Where do you want him, Nurse?" asked one of the attendants as they carried him on board, "On deck or in the wheelhouse?"

"On deck," Rob said quickly.

She eyed the dense overcast. "You'll get wet out here and the diesel fumes are a wee bit smelly."

"Beats that hospital smell anytime. Besides, a little damp is better than being cooped up all day."

Broken Wings

They positioned his stretcher against the wheelhouse wall for stability before taking their leave.

A large, older man with a weathered face, vivid blue eyes, and wearing a heavy sweater, rugged tweeds tucked into rubber boots, and a well-worn seaman's cap came aboard, smile wide. "Maggie, lass!" He held out his arms.

"Malcolm!" She ran into his arms. "'Tis so guid to see you."

He hugged her before holding her at arm's length. "You're looking bonnie, but all grown up. It seems like only yesterday I was taking you to Oban to start your nurse's training."

"On you come." She laughed. "There's someone I want you to meet." She pulled him over to Rob's side. "Rob, I'd like you to meet a dear friend, and the owner and skipper of the *Sea Rouk*, Malcolm MacNeill. Malcolm, this is Colonel Robert Savage."

MacNeill leaned down and shook Rob's hand. "'Tis guid to make your acquaintance, Colonel."

"Same here. Appreciate you giving us a ride. And please call me Rob."

"Och, 'tis my pleasure, Rob, and I answer to 'Malcolm.'"

"Malcolm it is."

"Then we'll be under way as soon as my wayward hand gets here. As always, I've had to receive clearance from the Royal Navy to make our journey. They've taken over the harbour as a naval base so we'll have to dodge their ships and flying boats, but it shouldn't take long to clear the harbour and make our way into Mull Sound."

"What's the name of your boat mean in English? I don't speak Scots." Rob squirmed, the deck hard beneath his shoulders.

"Sea Mist."

"Name seems appropriate this morning."

"I take guid care of the auld lady. Took me weeks filling out all the government permits, but I had a diesel engine installed just last winter. She's provided me a living all these years, though since the war, nobody fishes the Atlantic because of the U-boats—only the Minch."

"Minch?"

"'Tis what we call the sea between the Outer Hebrides Islands and Scotland."

"How do you make a living, then?"

"I get by with delivering the mail from Oban to Innisbraw every other day and picking up supplies for our island folk. Also, the government has used me quite a few times for rescue work since even the Minch isn't all that safe now."

"They don't have a Coastal Rescue Service?"

Malcolm snorted. "Every boat and ship around these parts has been put into service. Those Germans and their U-Boats have caused many a muddle." He got to his feet. "Well, I've things to do. I've a nice low box you can sit on, lass." He wiped a crate off with a rag from his back pocket, pushed it over, and prodded the wheelchair with his foot. "When you want help getting Rob into this, just call out. Sim MacPhee should be here any minute. You remember Sim. He's young, but strong."

Maggie smiled at his retreating back. "The last time I saw Sim he was only a young lad," she said, sitting on the crate. "His family are crofters on Innisbraw."

"Crofters? Like in the Selkie story?"

"I thought you'd forgotten all about that. But yes, they raise sheep for the wool and mutton, and Angus adds to his income by breeding and selling fine herding dogs."

"Mutton. That's one meat I've never liked."

"Unless you're raised on it, it can be a wee bit strong."

A lanky young boy with fiery red hair and blue eyes hurried aboard. He tipped his flat cap to Maggie and Rob and mumbled a shy "guid-mornin" before pulling in the lines he had untied from the pilings. He stuck his head in the wheelhouse doorway. "Clear, Skipper."

When the diesel engine sputtered to life, the boards beneath Rob vibrated. "Whoa," he said, "looks like this trip comes with a massage."

They putted away from the pier and down a waterway between moored boats and ships, most belonging to the Royal Navy. As soon as they were clear of other vessels, Malcolm upped their speed and the rough vibration of the deck boards settled into a pleasant, tingling throb.

"Och, my stomach's all aflutter," Maggie said. "I haven't been home in almost four years." She looked up at the sky. "'Tis already starting to clear. Before long you can sit in your chair. We'll be passing through the sound and you'll get a guid view of Mull."

"Mull?"

"'Tis one of the Inner Hebrides Isles. Later, we'll catch a glimpse of Tiree, which has a large RAF airbase now, and see the shore of Coll off the starboard. After that 'tis open sea all the way to Innisbraw."

"I didn't know about the airbase on Tiree, but I have heard of the one at Benbecula. The Brits vector a lot of our planes there. Will we pass that?"

"Och, no, that's many islands north of Innisbraw which is at the verra southern-most tip of the Outer Hebrides."

He covered a yawn. "I have a feeling I'm going to desert you again."

"Don't fash—upset yourself. You look like you didn't sleep well last night. Close your eyes and drift off."

He awakened.

Maggie sat beside him, shielding his face from the sun with a towel.

"Good morning," he said. "Again."

"Guid-mornin again to you."

"Is it time to sit up yet? My back's as numb as my bottom."

"Och, of course it is."

Getting Rob from the stretcher lying on the deck up into the wheelchair proved difficult. Sim was not strong enough and Rob wouldn't allow Maggie to do any of the lifting, so the lad was finally ordered in to handle the helm, while Malcolm lifted Rob outright and placed him in the chair.

Rob was so embarrassed he could scarcely face the skipper. "Sorry about that," he said through clenched teeth. "I'm way too heavy."

"Don't think a thing of it," Malcolm said. "I've lifted heavier before."

"When?"

"When I've had a load of fish I didn't want to lose, dangling over the sea in a snarled net."

"Well, thanks."

"My pleasure. Now, I'd better get back to the helm, for the lad's green. Don't want him running us onto the rocks."

Rob gritted his teeth. He hadn't had to rely on so many people since he was an infant.

A large British warship blasted its horn at the *Sea Rouk* as it passed to their starboard, decks filled with busy seamen.

Here I am, flat on my back, while my men suck oxygen high over France. This is so blasted frustrating.

Maggie held his shoulder as the trawler rocked violently in the large ship's wake. "That's a common sight in the sound now, so don't let it fash you." She waited until the rocking steadied before placing a blanket over his shoulders and pushing the wheelchair toward the port side. "The view's the best from here." She locked the brakes and pointed. "That's Mull."

He glanced up. "Nice," he grunted.

She pulled the crate closer. "Don't take all this to heart. You're so impatient. Soon, you'll be doing for yourself again and all this will only be a memory."

"An unpleasant memory."

She took his hand. "Do you realize how far you've come in one month? Just three weeks ago you couldn't even move your toes."

"A lot of good a few inches—centimetres—does," he muttered. The internal battle he fought tore him apart. He *never* shared his innermost fears, and yet the urge to do so was overwhelming. He swallowed convulsively. He was about to go against his own tenet for survival. "I'm ... I'm not so sure things will turn out the way we want."

"Remember, it takes time for nerves to heal."

He could not stop himself now. "If they heal."

She grasped his hand. "Och, you cannot allow yourself to think that way, for if you do, you'll only be sabotaging your future. First, you have to pray, and then you have to believe and work, and work some more to make it happen. If you give up now, you'll only fulfill your worst fears."

"It's not the work."

"Is it the pain? I know how much those exercises hurt."

"Not the pain. I've always believed anything worth having comes at a price."

"Then what is it, if it's no' the work or the pain?"

He was silent for a long time, mind racing. This was the moment to either shut up or bare his soul. But if he couldn't trust Maggie to handle it, whom could he trust? He took a deep breath. "Sometimes I feel like a conceited jerk thinking I deserve to walk again. What makes me so special?"

"What have you ever done to condemn yourself to never walking again?"

"I'm no angel."

"None of us are."

"You're a saint compared to me."

"You don't know what's deep in my soul any more than I know what's in yours." She looked down at him with her eyes navy blue. "You once told me you don't like making idle conversation, that it makes you uncomfortable. I'm thinking you find it much harder to share your innermost thoughts."

Could she see through him?

She turned and walked away a few paces, then whirled about, wrapping her arms around her body as though the brisk wind had given her a sudden chill. "I never knew you were so afraid of the operation turning out badly because you never told me. I've been with you all day, every day for weeks since your operation and you never once said, 'I'm afraid,' or 'Hold me and tell me why you believe everything will work out well.' Who or what has hurt you so badly you cannot allow anyone a glimpse of the real you?"

He dropped his head and closed his eyes, unable to reply.

Her hands covered his. "Please don't go away from me again, for I can't stand it when you do that. It's as if you don't care enough, or trust me enough, to tell me what you're really thinking."

"It's not you, it's me. I have a problem with relating to others. I've told you that."

"You have that."

"There's no one I trust more."

"Then, unless you want to miss all of Mull, you'd better start paying attention." She pointed again. "We just passed the small buoy lighthouse marking the entrance to the harbor at Tobermory, the westernmost village on the island. There's also a large naval base there."

He took a deep breath and studied the island. "Lots of mountains and trees on Mull. Is Innisbraw like that?"

"Och, no," she said. "Mull's a verra large island with room for bens and great rushing burns and some fine fresh water lochs and many sea lochs. Innisbraw's so wee you cannot compare them."

"What's a ben?"

"'Tis a mountain."

"And a burn?"

"A stream, or even a wee river."

"So there are no mountains on Innisbraw?"

"There are a few braes and hillocks. One, Ben Innis, is verra tall—twelve hundred sixty metres—and there are several fells. High rocky cliffs."

"Any lochs?"

"We have one fine fresh water loch, Loch Domhnall—Donald. 'Tis where we get our drinking water. Innisbraw's three large fells take up much of the shore, so though there are inlets, there are only twa small sea lochs."

"No forests?"

"Och, no, but there are a few trees." She hesitated. "Innisbraw's no' like Mull at all."

He had to know. "Then what makes it so special?"

She was silent for a long time. When she spoke, he caught a sparkle of tears in her eyes before she turned to face the west. "'Tis home. 'Tis the long, bent, marram grasses waving in the wind, the splattering burns with their low-hanging greenwood, the heather sending its scent through the air and wildflowers everywhere you look. 'Tis the crofts with their thatched cottages and peat piles, and the sky as big as the world, and living in a place where you're surrounded by the sea sooking on the shore day and night." A tear trickled down her cheek. "'Tis the finest folk in the world calling a 'guid-mornin'' to you on their way and knowing that you belong there and that everyone else on that wee piece of land feels the same way. And perhaps most of all, 'tis our minister, Hugh MacEwan, teaching in the kirk what it means to love God first so you can love one another. That's only a bit of what Innisbraw is to me." She pierced him with her eyes.

His heart beat wildly.

"I'm sure you feel the same way about your own home in America."

His throat constricted. "Don't have a home."

"You don't have a home? What does that mean?"

"Grew up in New Hampshire." He could read the question in her eyes. "On the eastern coast of the States," he added, his voice sounding strangled, even to his own ears.

"And?"

"That's all. Went off to West Point when I was seventeen. Haven't been back."

"Rob!"

She looked so shocked, he felt ashamed. Another secret from his past he hadn't shared. He'd dug a hole this time and was already in it up to his neck. He drew a ragged breath. "Never had time. From the Point I went directly to Cadet Flight Training at Randolph Field in Texas."

"But they surely gave you leave at some time. What about your parents? Did they have to come find you for a visit?"

A chill crept over his body. "Don't ask about that."

"They must be verra painful memories."

Why couldn't she just let it go? This was something he had never shared with anyone. No one knew he was completely alone in the world, not even Den. For all of his adult life he pushed the painful memories to the back of his mind where they could not hurt so badly. His mouth tasted bitter. "I'm sorry, but this is something

I'm not ready to talk about. It has nothing to do with you."

She was quiet for a time. "That's all right. Perhaps I'm expecting more of you than I have a right to." Though she smiled and raised her chin, she was upset. "I can understand you no' wanting my pity," she said very softly. "After all, you're a proud man." She leaned over and cupped his chin in her hand, forcing him to look up at her. "But what about friendship? Will you finally accept that?"

After all he had put her through, how could she possibly make such an offer? He rubbed the side of his nose. "A man would be a fool to turn down an offer like that." He reached for her hand and laced his fingers through hers. "Will you really be my friend, Maggie McGrath?"

Her smile was radiant. "Aye, Rob Savage. I'll be your friend."

He returned her smile. His entire body grew light, like he could float right out of the chair. Forget Doctor McGrath and the promises he'd made. He had never felt so good in his entire life. Her mouth looked so sweet. He wanted to kiss her so badly, wanted to pull her into his arms and feel her body pressed against his, wanted to taste her, to inhale her very essence.

A sudden image of the doctor passed before his eyes and he couldn't have been more shocked if someone had thrown him into the sea. *Don't hurt my daughter. She's led a sheltered life.*

It was too much. His weakened body could no longer handle so many emotional extremes. First, he'd hurt Maggie and then he'd almost betrayed a trust. He groaned and shook his head. "Guess the sun's too much," he gasped. "I'm getting dizzy."

She leaped to her feet. "Malcolm, come out here. I need your help."

Rob fell into a troubled sleep peopled with amorphous beings who danced away on beams of pulsating light, chanting, "We belong, we belong." He reached out time and time again, but they were always just beyond his grasp. Finally, they flickered and died. He grieved to see them go.

The next image stunned him with its clarity. The Selkie and her crofter ran through the shallow surf, bare feet churning the dying waves into foam. The Selkie's long, black hair caught the sun, glistening like rain-slicked tarmac as she smiled up at her companion. He laughed and pulled her up the sand, leading her toward a dark opening in a small rise of stone. Rob raced after them, but every time he drew close, they receded farther away. As hard as he ran, they were always just out of reach.

※

Maggie watched him sleep, her mind teeming with conflicting thoughts. She had never met a man like Rob Savage. He was so complex she seldom knew what to expect. She poured a cup of tea from the thermos, sipping it slowly. Nothing in her twenty-two years had prepared her for a close friendship with a man older than herself. Rob was no callow lad like those young aviators who had taken her to the cinema in London and gripped her hand with sweaty fingers. And what if it turned into more than friendship?

He moaned and moved his head from side to side.

What filled his dreams—his last dreadful bombing mission, or some painful memory from his past?

She placed her hand over his, hoping to bring him comfort.

※

He awakened, bathed in sweat. Maggie's face swam into view. When he reached out to touch her, she clasped his hand.

"I'm here, Rob." She blotted his forehead. "You've slept for hours. How do you feel?"

He shook his head. "Weird dreams," he whispered.

"Are you hurting anywhere?"

"No more than usual."

"Can I get you anything?"

"Don't think so."

"How about a cup of tea? I'm sorry, but there was no way to make coffee at the cottage."

"Sounds good." He shook his head to clear the cobwebs.

"I thought you hated tea."

Her surprise tickled him and he couldn't help but smile. His

Selkie. Once he was settled on Innisbraw, he'd ask for the rest of the story. His skin tingled in anticipation,

She reached for a thermos. "I also have sandwiches I made this mornin, and scones I brought in this basket from the infirmary."

At that moment, Rob Savage did what he always did when faced with an uncomfortable situation. He pushed all of the previous unpleasantness into the back of his mind, placing it into a compartment labeled "Do Not Touch," and then relaxed. Things appeared to be back on an even keel between them and friendship was safe. He suddenly realized he was famished. "Bring it on. I could eat a horse."

She rummaged in the basket. "No horses. Only cheese and pickle sandwiches and sweet scones."

After he had eaten three of the sandwiches and finished off the scones, he looked up at the sky. "What time is it, anyway? Hope you packed my watch. I feel naked without it."

She checked her watch. "Almost 1600."

"I slept that long?"

"Aye. The sun must have been too much."

"We must be almost there."

"We are."

"Then, what are you doing here? Go on up to the bow. I want you to call out, 'land-ho,' or whatever it is they say, the minute you see land."

Her laugh was so girlish, he was sure he felt his heart turn over. "All right. Land-ho. Is that it?"

"Aye, lass, that's it." He winked at her. "As you always say, 'on you go then.'"

When she disappeared from view, he sighed and stared up at the sky. What was so special about Maggie that she took his breath away? Oh, she was definitely beautiful. The first truly beautiful woman he had ever seen who neither needed, nor wore, face-paint. Her cheeks and lips were naturally rosy, her brows expressive and her smile would fill an angel with envy. Yet, it went far beyond her physical beauty. Her voice with its soft burr was so comforting he could listen to her talk for hours. There was something so genuine about her, so unpretentious. She was kind, she was trusting, she had a bit of a temper when pushed too hard, and she was *real*. She had no need to put on airs.

He was the exact opposite. He carried enough emotional baggage to fill a proverbial freight car. He seldom faced unpleasantness. Instead, he played games with himself; *hide this, reveal that—no, not that, it might show how vulnerable you are.* Who was he truly? A hard worker, he tried to be as honest as possible and he felt a deep commitment to anybody under his command, but everything else lay shrouded in the ambiguity he had made of his life.

The hour of reckoning was near; he would soon get his first glimpse of Innisbraw. If he hated it on first sight, that would put a stop to his foolish fantasies. His hands clenched at an unbidden thought.

Maggie had only three months on Innisbraw. Even if he did eventually walk, once she reported back to duty, they would probably never see one another again. Could he ever find another woman like her, or was she unique? Would he become one of those lonely, acerbic old generals who were married to the Air Forces and went home every evening to an empty apartment—an empty life? He envied the love in Maggie's eyes when she spoke of her "wee" island. How would it feel to be so committed to a piece of real estate and those who peopled it? His apprehension made each breath a struggle.

Chapter Eleven

"Land ho! Innisbraw!"

Maggie's excited shout sent Rob's stomach plummeting. Eagerness at seeing the island disappeared beneath the thought of another humiliating transfer to the wheelchair. That piece of shrapnel had robbed him of more than the ability to walk. *Feels like I'm on a roller coaster with an incompetent idiot at the controls.*

Maggie skirted the wheelhouse. "Och, Rob, I have to get Malcolm so he can put you in your wheelchair. This is something you cannot miss—your first glimpse of Innisbraw."

"Makes no sense. Sim docking this boat would be as foolish as my radioman trying to land my B-17."

The sparkle left her eyes. She knelt beside him, taking his hand. "Then I'll have to tell you what you're missing so you can picture it in your mind."

"Paint me a picture with your words, Maggie."

"There's Ben Innis thrusting its broad shoulders above everything, already covered with light green shoots of heather, and the waves breaking on Innis Fell, blowing spindrift in billowing clouds high up onto the rocks." She squeezed his hand. "And though the tide's almost in, what you can see of the shore is glistening with a million points of light from the sun."

"Did you see your house?"

"Only a glimpse of one end of its thatched roof, for 'tis on the top of Innis Fell, just above the harbour." Her face glowed. "I could see the infirmary much better. It hides most of our wee cottage."

"No Selkie, basking on the rocks?"

"That's only an old tale."

Her fading smile reined-in his impetuous tongue. "Then get back to the bow and drink it all in. You've waited almost five long years for this."

"I have no need to see it. I've come into this harbour every hour of the day in all kinds of weather. I've seen it with the sky louring where the island looks dark and most mysterious, all in shadow. And on a misty day where 'tis like seeing a magical place with only bits and pieces revealed at a time because you couldn't bear to look on its beauty all at once." Her eyes soft with memories, face so filled with delight.

A tremor ran through his body.

"Most of the folk on Innisbraw are here and I saw Angus McPhee with his cairt and cuddy waiting on the path. Angus is Sim's faither. Malcolm must have radioed ahead so we'll have help getting you up to the infirmary."

He cleared his throat. "What's a cairt and cuddy?"

"Och, I forgot again you don't speak Scots. A cairt is a cart and a cuddy is a horse, especially one used to pull a cairt."

"Wouldn't an automobile or truck be faster?"

That delightful laugh again. "There are no roads on Innisbraw, only wide paths. There's never been any kind of car or truck here."

No roads? No automobiles? He'd not only be stranded for an indefinite time on a tiny piece of real estate surrounded by water and with no telephones, the only way to get around was on foot or in a cart. But he couldn't complain now and ruin her homecoming. "You mentioned people waiting. Anyone in particular?"

"Aye." She shielded her eyes from the sun. "Remember when we first met, I told you a friend made soap and sent it to me? 'Tis Elspeth NicAllister. She's ninety-eight and 'tis hard for her to make it down from the fell on foot. Angus must have brought her."

The boat bumped the dock.

She fell against him.

He could not stop himself. His arms encircled her, face buried in the hollow of her throat. She smelled so sweet, so warm. He longed to feel her lips against his again. She would taste as sweet as the fragrance of her skin and hair.

It took every ounce of resolve he could summon to transfer his hands to her arms so he could help her up.

Her cheeks flushed bright red.

He forced himself to break the uneasy silence. "Are you all right?"

She nodded. "Did I hurt you?"

"Not at all."

She smoothed wisps of hair from her face and brushed at wrinkles in her skirt.

"You're sure you're all right?" he asked again, struggling to stay focused.

"Of course." Her hands trembled as she fastened the top button on her cape.

He had to do something, say something.

"You're home, Maggie, lass." Malcolm's booming voice saved him. "Move that chair over here, lass, and I'll lift Rob. Sim's got us all tied up to the dock."

"Wait," Rob said. "I'd better stay on this stretcher. I'm no sailor, but I'm even a worse horseman."

Maggie rolled her eyes. "You aren't going to ride—och, you did it to me again." She smiled, her nose wrinkling in delight as it always did when he teased her. "But he's right, Malcolm. The cairt ride is rough. 'Tis easier on his back if he's lying down."

"Whatever you say, lass." He dropped a canvas bag stenciled *Royal Postal Service* to a woman waiting on the dock. "Put down the wide plank, Sim, lad. We don't want to drop Rob in the water."

Rob rolled his tense shoulders and neck. "Let's get it done. My bottom's killing me."

"You're sure it's no' your back?" Maggie asked.

"Definitely lower. And to think you prayed I'd really feel something."

"We all did. And our prayers were answered."

Her statement of faith sobered him. Another thing that set them apart. He'd been firmly grounded in Christianity as a small child, but her trust in God always to answer prayers went far beyond his experience as an adult. Sure, he prayed when he was in a tight jam, and sometimes he came out okay and sometimes he didn't.

He also prayed silently beside the bed of every man he visited in the base hospital. Not all of them made it. Had God said no? How could he know He heard?

Exhausted, the confusion overwhelmed him. He forced himself to look around as Sim and Malcolm lifted the stretcher, carried him across the deck, and down the gangplank to the dock.

Innisbraw stunned his senses with vivid colors: the brilliant sapphire sky, sparkling turquoise water in the shallows, glittering white sands. An enormous hill rose in the distance, its sides blanketed with soft green. And all around, the dazzling emerald of new spring growth, broken by patches of brilliant yellow, pink, white, and red wildflowers fighting for footholds among rocky outcroppings. The lack of trees and the profusion of rocks gave it a stark beauty, but this island offered far more than he expected.

Scores of people lined the sides of the pier and spilled over onto the narrow, sandy shore below. Their faces mirrored their delight at welcoming home one of their own.

Most of the women wore high-necked, calf-length, floral cotton dresses and knitted shawls. Some red-haired, a few brown and two or three blonde, but most black-haired and fair-skinned with rosy cheeks and lips and blue, blue eyes.

The men were clad in a variety of tweeds and tightly woven wools with flat, small brimmed caps on their heads. Some wore vests, others sweaters. There were a few white-haired old men wearing plus-fours tucked into fishing boots, or knitted stockings and heavy brogans. Wide, colorful braces held up their pants.

Children darted about. Boys in sweaters and shorts, feet bare, hair slicked back and still damp from water and comb. Girls wearing skirts and sweaters or dresses, hair in braids or flowing loosely down their backs. Apart from their fair skin and ruddy cheeks, they reminded him of kids from his childhood.

The crowd parted to make a path for the stretcher.

The people they passed smiled and nodded and he tried to return their smiles.

A middle-aged woman with her graying hair pulled into a tight bun at the top of her head looked grim, her expression making her stand out from the others. She greeted Maggie with a pat on the arm, but when she stared at him, her thin lips turned down in a sneer. Her look of contempt reminded him of an old-maid English teacher who didn't believe in giving any male student an *A* no matter how well he did.

Maggie stopped often and exchanged embraces and kisses, her laughter falling easily on his ears, happiness and delight so evident.

What would it be like to be loved by so many?

She stopped at the end of the pier and asked Sim and Malcolm to lower the stretcher.

A tiny, very old woman leaned on a cane, a smile of welcome lighting her lined face. The white braids wrapped around her head reflected the sun like a shining halo. Her worn, simple, floral dress and faded blue shawl spoke of humility. She held out her arms and Maggie stepped into her embrace.

They hugged one another, tears slipping down their faces.

The woman pressed Maggie away, touching her cheek. "They didn't feed you enough, lass," she said in heavily burred English, voice low and pleasant.

"Och, Elspeth, you always say that."

"The truth is always fitting." She pulled a handkerchief from her sleeve and dabbed at her eyes. She stepped forward, cane tapping on the boards, and stood over him, her keen gaze reaching into his soul.

This must be how his gunners felt when a German Fw 190 came straight at them, guns belching fire. His face burned.

The crowd quieted. Not a whisper or cough. He could be lying at the feet of royalty by their reaction.

Her smile was so bright it radiated warmth that settled into his bones.

He relaxed.

"So, you're our Maggie's Rob. John radioed you were coming." She knelt and rested her tiny, gnarled hand on his, her touch warm and soothing. "Welcome to Innisbraw, Rob Savage. May your stay here fulfill all your expectations and much, much more."

He hadn't been this tongue-tied since a teenager. "Thank you."

His voice sounded hoarse to his own ears.

Her faded blue eyes crinkled at the corners as she smiled again. She turned to Maggie. "Help me up, and then you'd best get this lad to the infirmary. It's been a long day at sea for the both of you."

"You're right," Maggie said, "we must get settled in. Will you be coming with us, Elspeth?"

"On you go. I'll catch you up on the mornin after you've both had a guid, long rest." She kissed Maggie's cheek. "Och, I almost disremembered to tell you, our Hugh wanted to be here, but he's meeting with one of our aulder folk with a spiritual problem."

"I wondered where he was."

"He did ring the kirk bell to tell everyone the *Sea Rouk* had been sighted on the Minch. He said you'd understand."

"Of course."

The ride up to the infirmary was amazingly short and the climb gradual, though the hard, wooden bottom of the cart sent a sharp pain through his back with each jarring bounce. They passed several stone buildings, one with a Scots flag snapping from a tall pole in the breeze.

The only home they passed, a quaint, thatch-roofed, stone cottage, stood high on the north side of the path, overlooking the harbor. Two rocking chairs and a table with a pot of bright pink flowers offered a warm welcome on the covered porch. Lace curtains lined the windows and a riot of colorful flowers filled the front yard behind a low stone wall.

"That's Elspeth's home," Maggie said. "She's lived there all her life."

So tired he could barely think, but curious about the old woman Maggie obviously loved, he asked, "She never married?"

"Och, no. She says the folk on Innisbraw are her family. They keep her on her knees so long every day, there's never been any time for a family of her own."

"On her knees?"

Her eyes softened. "Elspeth prays for each and every one of us at least once a day. By name."

"Everyone on Innisbraw?"

"Every man, woman, lass, lad, bairn and bairnie—baby—and of course, those away at war or jobs."

It was getting harder and harder to speak. "That's how many people? A hundred? More?"

"A wee bit over twa hundred right now. But the way things are going, with the U-Boats keeping our trawlers from fishing the Atlantic and the young folk either in the military or at war-related jobs—and the aulder men taking their families and moving away to find work—once this dreadful war ends, there'll only be the auld folk here."

The cart bounced off the path toward a large, imposing, single-story building, its stone walls pale gray and its many deeply recessed windows reflecting the light. Instead of thatch, dark clay tiles adorned the roof. A broad, flat-stoned porch, surrounded by a low railing, stood in front of the wide plank door. Once again, lace curtains graced each window and here and there pots of pink, white, and lavender flowers offered a bit of color. A stone chimney rose above the rooftop at each end of the building. This looked more like a very large home than any hospital he had ever seen.

"Here we are then." Maggie leaped from the back of the cart. "I'm sure everything's ready, but I'll just have a quick peek before we take you inside." She ran up the steps.

"I'll go see if the lass needs any help," Malcolm said, climbing down from the bench.

Maggie opened the door wide and Rob caught a glimpse of shining wood floors and white walls through the slatted sides of the cart before she disappeared, Malcolm at her heels.

Angus, his ruddy face wreathed in a smile, tied the reins over the brake handle and turned in his seat. "'Tis a fine day, what with the sun. 'Twill be guid to have the summer at last."

Rob nodded in agreement. Maggie had warned him that few of the islanders knew English, but Angus spoke enough to be understood.

It was obvious where Sim got his red hair and blue eyes. He estimated Angus's age to be around forty. His calloused hands and wiry frame evidenced toiling long and hard to make a living on his croft.

Angus took a small pipe from his shirt pocket and shook some tobacco into it. He glanced back at Rob. "Should I smoke my pipe, then, you being sick and all?"

"No problem. Like the smell of a pipe." So much effort for so few words.

Sim poked his father in the ribs and laughed. "You said the right thing, Colonel Rob. Faither does luve his clay pipe, but he canna smoke in the hoose. Mither winna abide it."

Maggie appeared in the doorway, Malcolm behind her. "Everything's ready," she said, as they hurried across the porch and down the steps. "There's even scotch broth and bannock in the kitchen. Flora picked the best room for you, Rob. It has a grand view of the harbour and fell."

Hang on, you're almost there ... hang on.

Angus took a hurried draw on his pipe, tapped it clean on the sole of his boot, and returned it to his pocket before he and Malcolm took care unloading the stretcher. Maggie walked beside Rob as they mounted the steps, and stood aside while they maneuvered the stretcher through the wide doorway.

He was so tired his mind couldn't register another impression. There'd be weeks, months even, to explore the interior of the infirmary. Right now, he wanted to lie in bed where he could close his eyes and lose himself to sleep.

She led the way down a wide hallway and indicated an open door at the end. "This is the largest patient's room in the infirmary with twa windows overlooking the harbour. Isn't that grand?"

He could no longer respond to her enthusiasm.

She leaned over him. "Are you hurting? What's the matter?"

He tried to speak.

Couldn't move his lips.

He attempted to shake his head, but his muscles no longer obeyed.

Sinking, sinking.

"Hurry," she said, voice hollow and muted. "Put the stretcher on the side of the bed. Malcolm, you take his legs, Angus, support his back and I'll take his head and shoulders."

She could hurt herself.

The sun hid behind a cloud.

Her face blurred.

No pain. Floating, floating free into the welcoming darkness.

Chapter Twelve

A dream startled Rob from sleep. He looked at the wall beside his bed. White, not gray. Where was he?

A flutter of movement caught his attention. A window just beyond the foot of his bed was open a few inches. Lace curtains billowed inward on an ocean-scented breeze.

Innisbraw.

Curious, he looked around.

His breath caught.

Maggie slept on a chair pulled up beside his bed, head resting on the sheet beside him. Her hair spread over the blanket and spilled down the side of the bed in lustrous ribbons of black.

Had to be another Selkie dream.

She stirred and looked up.

He knew it was no dream when she leaped up and leaned over him. "You're awake. How do you feel? Are you in pain?"

"Just thirsty." *Mouth's so dry, I sound like a bull-frog.*

A blue robe, belted loosely over a long white gown, matched the color of her eyes, but her hair left him speechless. It fell in black waves over her shoulders and down to below her waist. He picked up a lock, running its silky length through his fingers.

Her cheeks flushed. "Och, you've caught me. I'll give you some water, and get dressed. I didn't mean to fall asleep."

"Don't go."

Her throat convulsed, but he couldn't make his fingers release that curl.

"Last night, you had a bad dream and cried out. I'm across the hall, and with the doors open, I heard you."

He cleared his throat, stalling for enough time to paint a permanent picture of her in his mind. "I ... I didn't mean to go away from you again. I just couldn't stop myself."

"You didn't go away, Rob. You fainted." She squeezed his hand. "If you'll let go of my hair, I'll pour you some water before you dry up and blow out the window."

Still reluctant, he let her hair slip through his fingers.

She poured water from a pitcher on the bedside table. She didn't crank up the head of the bed, but sat next to him and lifted his shoulders, placing a large glass to his lips.

The scent of heather intoxicated him and he choked while draining the glass in hasty gulps.

She smoothed the wrinkles from his pillow before laying him down. "Better?"

"Best water I've ever tasted."

"'Tis the peat in it. But I'm thinking you could drink another."

One glass had quenched his thirst but the thought of her arms around him and the sweet scent of her hair brought an eager nod.

"I'll put the head of the bed up first so you can reach the water whenever you like."

Caught. This was no naïve girl, but a canny Scots nurse. She must have noticed how the proximity of his face to that tangle of black hair affected him. She'd never let him see her hair loose again.

She cranked up the head of the bed and poured him another glass before replacing a square of linen over the top of the pitcher. "Now, you can drink as much as you want. I'll get dressed and make you something to eat."

"I'm not hungry."

His words caught her halfway across the room and she whirled around. "No' hungry?" She hurried to his side. "Where are you hurting? And don't give me any of your blether this time. If you're no' hungry after so long without food, you're in pain."

He massaged his temples. "Only a headache. Slept too long."

"I'll get you some APCs. There's no reason to suffer in silence. Haven't you learned that by now?"

When she returned with the aspirin, she looked so beautiful, he fought the urge to bury his face in her fragrant hair.

"You lie there and rest while I get dressed. Mebbe by then

you'll have your appetite back." She left.

He'd fainted. How embarrassing. Grown men didn't faint. Passed out, maybe.

The crisp, saltiness of the sea filled the room as the curtains moved rhythmically in the breeze. He took a deep breath, stretched his arms over his head, and inched his legs apart. He drew his legs together before moving them even farther apart. A little progress there.

He wanted to leap out of bed and feel the cold floorboards beneath his bare feet. He wanted to walk completely around the island, exploring as he went. He wanted to walk anytime, anywhere—that's what he wanted.

He eyed the wheelchair sitting in the corner. Friend or foe? For now, it would have to be friend. At least it would get him out of this bed.

Maggie came in, carrying a steaming mug, hair pinned into her usual bun. She wore a gray tweed skirt and pale blue sweater. She looked so beautiful in mufti he stifled a groan.

The unexpected aroma of coffee made his mouth water. "Not tea?"

"You hate tea."

"Didn't think you'd have coffee here."

"Father sent it with us. It's no' rationed like tea, but it is hard to find. He had one of his staff search all over Edinburgh for a large enough supply."

He grabbed the mug. "Satan, get thee behind me."

"There you go again." She laughed, wrinkling her nose. "Drink your coffee. Angus will be here soon to help you into your chair. We'll get your wash-up and shave out of the way and by then, you'll be starving and we can have our breakfast outside on the front entry."

"Entry?"

"I believe 'tis what you call a porch."

⁂

When she washed his legs and feet, he could swear he felt more. "Feels guid," he said, using the Scots word. Since he'd be stuck here on Innisbraw for months, it would be a good opportunity to pick up the language.

"You feel more, then?"

"Must. Never felt the water trickling down my outer thigh before."

"That's wonderful." She dried him briskly. "Does this feel guid, also?"

"Verra, verra guid."

"Now, I'll shave you and find you some fresh nightclothes."

He was tired of feeling like an invalid. "What I'd really like is a shirt and pair of pants. That okay with you?"

"I don't see why no', as long as you don't mind having to change in the mornin and again at night."

"I don't. Are there pants and shirts in that duffle-bag the base hospital sent with me?"

"I've never opened it. But first, I'll get a clean basin of water and a razor."

She settled a fresh towel over his chest and hummed as she lathered his face. He savored her closeness and the scent of the heather soap she used to soften his whiskers. He closed his eyes as she drew a straight razor carefully over his neck, chin, jaw, and upper lip, opening them when she jumped back and picked up the basin.

"I'll empty this and fetch your bag."

The thought of getting into real clothes pleased him. He had no idea what they packed or who had done the packing—probably Hank Hirsch. He noticed his watch on the bedside table and strapped it on, grinning. A little past 0800, the hack-hand ticking off the seconds. Maggie must have wound and set it.

She dragged a large duffle bag through the doorway and up to the side of the bed, untied the bag, and began pulling out the clothing. "Here are your breeks." She held up a pair of uniform trousers.

"Breeks," he repeated, stiffening his resolve to learn the language. "They'll do, though I should wait to see if there's another pair. I doubt you have a dry-cleaner here and I'll need something clean to wear when I return to duty."

She smiled. "'When I return to duty.' I like the sound of your optimism."

"Keep it coming, lass. I had a pair of denims but I don't know if they packed them."

"Denim ... breeks?"

"Right—I mean, aye. They're dark blue."

She brought out another pair of uniform pants, his crush cap, two uniform shirts which she insisted were called "sarks," and a uniform blouse and tie, carefully folded between tissue. Several khaki skivvy shirts and boxer shorts followed, then a V-neck sweater he had bought in London, his dress boots and, at last, a pair of denims. "Is this what you want?"

"Perfect. Any socks in there?"

She tossed a pair on the bed. "That's all, except a heavy leather jacket."

"Yes!" He took it from her hands. "My A-2 jacket. This has been a lot of places and seen a lot of things."

"Really?"

"I've had it since I graduated from flight school."

"Tell me what you want to wear so I'll know what to repack until I can find time to put everything in the clothes press."

She stacked what he named on the bed and finished re-packing the bag. "They forgot your sleeping garments."

"Don't wear any."

"Och." She pulled the strings tight. "'Tis a guid thing I packed your pyjamas from the Royal Infirmary. The legs and sleeves are too short, but you'll have to wear them here."

"Don't try to move that. Wait, and I'll ask Angus to put it over in the corner behind the chair."

Didn't say much for a life when most of it would fit in a duffle bag. Of course, they hadn't packed everything: the rest of his uniforms, a few old clothes, his books, framed pictures of various flight crews, his one football trophy from high-school, old letters, and his raincoat. He hoped they were stored in a dry place. The new

CO would be using his quarters.

He put on his skivvy, then the sweater. It felt so good to be wearing clothes again. "I'm going to need your help getting these on," he said, waving the boxers and denims. "And my socks."

By the time she had him dressed, sweat gathered at his hairline. This was work.

She pulled up his khaki socks. "Those breeks are so tight they make you look taller, even lying in bed. Are you sure they're going to be warm enough?"

"Don't care. What's keeping Angus?"

She looked at her watch. "He is a bit late."

"I gathered that." A bite crept into his tone.

"You're in a bad mood."

"Not at all. It's just that I was taught punctuality is a mark of civility."

"Really!" She placed her hands on her hips. "Well, I suppose if you're fortunate enough to have work you can leave any time you wish, that might be true. But there are some who don't have that choice."

He must have insulted the crofter.

Angus arrived, full of apologies for being late.

"Had a ewe yean with twa wedder lambs, and so ahint the others. Took a while to get them suckling."

"He said one of his ewes gave premature birth to twins very late in the season, and it took time to get them nursing." Maggie shot him a haughty look.

"Are the lambs going to make it?" Rob asked, adding the proper amount of concern to his voice.

"Och, aye, they were going at it with great slaiger, they were."

"He said—"

Rob interrupted Maggie's translation. "I get the picture."

She lowered the bed, helped Rob to the side, and Angus took over from there. He was relieved to find the transfer almost pain-free.

She helped him into his A-2 jacket and pushed him out to the stone porch—entry—where Angus took his leave with a smile and a wave.

"Are you starving yet?" she asked.

"If you mean is my stomach touching my back-bone, the answer is yes ... aye, definitely."

"I'll heat up the broth and bannock and be right out."

"Is there another cup of coffee in there?"

"Another one? With all that caffeine, you'll be jumping out of your skin."

"I have to get to work on those exercises. It'll give me the energy."

"Any excuse for another cup of coffee. I'll catch you up in a minute. Are you warm enough?"

"Plenty."

He smiled at her retreating back and sat looking out at the harbor and sea.

A brisk breeze whipped the tops of the waves into frothy whitecaps. Far in the distance, a large convoy of British warships headed up the Minch, probably on its way to the North Sea.

He closed his eyes, demoralized by guilt. While he sat here doing nothing, his men were far into German-occupied airspace on their way to take out some rail yard or manufacturing plant.

But he couldn't allow himself to think about what he would be doing right now if that piece of shrapnel hadn't done its damage. He had enough on his plate without adding guilt.

He opened his eyes and studied the harbor below.

A deep expanse of white sand ringed the natural basin, the tide being out. Only one old fishing boat rocked beside the dock. Malcolm must have left for another mail-run and all the other boats tied up there the evening before were probably out at sea.

Seals barked stridently, wrestling and fighting for the best perch on several large, flat rocks at the base of the tall cliff on his right.

His binoculars—another thing missing from his duffle bag.

He rested his head on the back of the chair. Innisbraw wasn't at all what he'd expected. The little he'd seen of the island was very nice if he made allowances for the lack of trees. If only it wasn't so far from everything. It must be a real chore having to take an all-day trip on a smelly fishing trawler to reach the nearest town in Scotland or walk to get anywhere on the island. And no phones. And for many, no electricity.

Maggie came out the door, carrying a tray laden with bowls, cups, and a large iron pot. She set it on a broad bench and motioned him over. "'Tis a little low for a table, but it will have to do."

"Smells great."

"It will taste grand, too. Flora is a verra guid cook."

"Who's Flora?"

"She's Angus's wife. Father pays her to keep the infirmary clean and ready while he's away."

"Is it used as an infirmary now?"

"When Father's here. And Alice Ross, our postie—Post Mistress—is a midwife so she uses it for a difficult birthing. I'm certain I'll treat a few minor illnesses or wounds, but I'll have to send anyone in need of a doctor to the Cottage Hospital on Barra."

"Barra?"

"'Tis several islands north of us. Anyway, when the war is over, Father hopes to retire from the Royal Infirmary and University and be here full time, though he's been saying that for so many years I'm no' sure I believe him."

Eyes dark blue. So this was a sore spot. What he'd assumed a perfect relationship between father and daughter had at least one bone of contention. McGrath's insistence that Rob do nothing to hurt Maggie was not as ingenuous as he'd thought.

She handed him a bowl. "I know 'tis unusual to have Scotch broth for breakfast, but it was there and fast to heat."

As he balanced the bowl in his lap, she reached over and tucked a napkin into the vee of his sweater-neck.

"We don't want you slubbering all over your special jacket."

"Sure don't."

He ate a spoonful. "This is great. How about a piece of that bread? Is that what you call bannock?"

"Aye. 'Tis oat griddle bread. It might be a little plain for your taste, but it goes well with the spicy broth."

He ate half a piece in one bite, then dipped the other half into the broth and ate that. "This is verra, verra guid," he said, wiping his chin with his napkin. "Why didn't they have this at the Royal Infirmary?"

"You've forgotten about the rationing. We're fortunate here, for we grow most of our food on the island."

"I hope you have plenty. I really am starving."

She laughed and sipped her own broth. "Say the word and I'll hand you your coffee."

He ate three bowls of the rich broth and four pieces of bannock, then leaned back, coffee mug in hand, sipping contentedly. "Pass on my compliments to Flora. What was the meat in that broth?"

Her eyes twinkled. "Lamb."

"Lamb." He choked on his coffee. "I hope it wasn't one of those premature ones."

"Och, Rob."

He laughed, holding the mug out to one side so it wouldn't spill. "Gotcha."

"You can be a terrible tease."

"Can't help it. You wouldn't believe some of the pranks—uh, tricks—Den and I pulled at the Point."

"But surely you didn't do what you call 'pranks' there. Isn't that like University?"

"We had to do something to break up the tedium of study, study, study."

"Och, you men. You talk about women never being serious, but you have your own way of making fun."

"I guess we do. Is it about time for those exercises?"

She stacked the used bowls on the tray. "If you don't mind waiting a minute, I'd like to go over to the cottage. It's been empty so long I'm sure it's in need of a guid cleaning."

"Empty?" That surprised him.

"What did I say?" she asked, expression anxious.

"Oh, nothing. I just thought, I mean I assumed ... I just thought your mother must be there, that's all."

"My mither!"

Her shock drove the words from his mouth.

"I thought you knew my mither died when I was eight."

"I'm sorry, Maggie, I didn't know." He squirmed. Why had he made a thoughtless remark that caused her pain? "You never talked about her so I thought that maybe the two of you were not close ... or something."

"She died birthing my brother, Calum."

He leaped at the opportunity to change the subject. "You have a brother? You've never mentioned him."

"I must have done so when your thoughts were muddled with morphine, for he's in my prayers daily. He's fourteen and at the boarding academy on the Isle of Harris, where I went to school."

"Is he going to be a doctor like your father?"

"Though Father would like him to, no. Calum will either sit for his Highers—those are advanced A-level examinations—and go on to University after he finishes academy. Or, if Calum has his way, he'll apprentice on one of the fishing boats. All he's ever wanted is to be a fisherman."

"I'm sorry about your mother. I feel like a fool, bringing it up like that."

"You didn't know so you have nowt—nothing—to be sorry for." She placed their utensils and her teacup on the tray. "What about your mither? Is she still living?"

Her casual question caught him off-guard. He set his empty coffee mug down with a clack. "I'm all talked out."

She took the mug and put it on the tray. "Of course," she said before picking up the tray and walking off, shoulders stiff, head high. "I forgot. You ask about my past but don't want to talk about yours."

He'd done it again. She talked freely about losing her mother. Why couldn't he be as open with her?

But she grew up with a loving father and a younger brother. She had a *family*. He took a deep, ragged breath.

If he couldn't overcome his reticence, Maggie might ask her father to send another nurse to take her place.

He couldn't bear to think about enduring the following weeks of therapy without her encouragement. How much more would it take to make her dislike him, to drive a wedge between them that could never be removed, even by a thousand apologies?

Chapter Thirteen

On the far side of the island, Una Hunter bolted upright, eyes wide with confusion. As her gaze traveled over the familiar furnishings in her cottage, she took a deep breath and unclenched her hands. She had fallen asleep in her chair late the night before and had a nightmare.

Head pounding, she made her way unsteadily to the mirror she had hung so proudly in front of a makeshift dressing table when she was a lass. Streaks of black now tarnished the silver backing and dark green smudges from her fingers marred the once-bright gilt frame. But there was none like it on Innisbraw.

She studied the distorted image of her face. Even as a young lass, no one had called her "bonnie," but her long nose, dark, almost black eyes, pointed chin, and high cheekbones were once considered "braw." Her hair had been her crowning glory. Thick, dark brown, tending to wave over her shoulders and down her back.

Now, her nose turned down and looked much closer to her pointed chin, thanks to the thin lips that had almost disappeared in the past few years. Only her eyes were unchanged. Dark, intense, glittering in the light from the single oil lamp she had left burning. She plucked the pins from the tight bun at the top of her head and released the limp strands, scratching her scalp in relief, then rubbed her throbbing temples before picking up her hairbrush. Carved from exotic wood and set with boar bristles, it was made in Italy and given to Una by her mother's sister when Una was only a lass—another treasure from the past.

"One hundred strokes from root to ends," she said in the Gaelic, mimicking her mother's voice—Scots was for the lowbred and its use forbidden. "You've a nice enough body, but your hair is your one redeeming feature. Since you're unfortunate enough to favor the Hunters in looks and not the Munros, you'll never attract a suitor if you don't keep it shiny."

She dutifully drew the brush through her long, greying hair, her thoughts crowded with a litany of her mother's complaints about her father's family. "The Hunters are all good-for-nothings," she said aloud, making sure to interject the right amount of venom. "Allowing your grandfather to force me to marry one is the most dreadful mistake I ever made. Look at your father now, already in bed and snoring, and the sun not even set. Him and his sheep. Couldn't go into business with my father on Skye. Had to be a man and make it on his own. Rubbish! If my family didn't send a stipend every year, we would eat nothing but skirlie every meal."

The brush faltered in her hand as she pictured her father staggering into their thatched cottage every night, calloused hands filthy, clothes covered with grass stains and worse, and dark brown eyes dull with fatigue. Over the years, she grew to hate the man who sired her and stamped his unattractive features on her face. But she nursed him faithfully through his last lingering illness and saw that he had a proper funeral and burial. Pride would not allow her to do otherwise.

Her mother's sudden passing from a violent seizure a year later almost laid her low. Her auntie had been too ill to come for the funeral and take her back to her lovely home on the Isle of Skye as a live-in companion. Now she was alone in this desolate, dreadful cottage with only her own voice to break the silence.

She returned to the present with a start. "Why haven't you sent for me, Auntie?" she asked her image. "Surely you need help now you're so old." She sneered. "But until you do, I've other things to keep me busy. That Yank who came here is up to no good, and Maggie McGrath will rue the day she brought him here."

She placed the brush on the table and extinguished the lamp, berating herself for wasting precious paraffin. She walked to the tiny, deeply recessed front window, removed the black cardboard she used in lieu of a blackout drape, and pushed aside a corner of the lace curtain so she could see the cottage across the path. "That low-bred fisherman husband of Susan's is home today, but I don't see him out mending his nets, or her spinning. Most likely spending the day in their bed, doing unspeakable things beneath the covers."

Her flesh tingled sinfully.

Had that Yank already sweet-talked Maggie into more than friendship?

She had grown weak-kneed when he passed by on that stretcher. Same brown hair, same hazel-brown eyes as—

She clamped her eyes closed. No time to linger on her own bitter betrayal. "It won't do for that stranger to have his way with an Innisbraw lass, then leave her when he's ruined her life." The corners of her mouth turned down. "Stupid islanders. I'm the only one who knows what is going to happen. And with the help of those gullible widows who are always visiting, I'll make sure it doesn't."

Chapter Fourteen

Maggie walked slowly through her weed-infested garden, heart heavy. She stumbled over a clump of blackened foliage. A honeysuckle her mother planted as a newlywed, overpowered by native wild carrots and sow thistles with their invasive roots. Catching a glimpse of unexpected colour, she stopped and knelt beside a broad patch of purple vetch, pulling aside clumps of its tiny-leaved foliage. *"Och, thank Ye, Faither,"* she whispered as she uncovered a delicate purple orchid.

She studied its familiar broad lip, three lobes, and spotted leaves, a new resolve taking root in her mind. It would take time and labour, but before she had to leave in August she would have this garden well on its way to its former glory.

She stood and glanced toward the infirmary entry where Rob sat in his wheelchair. He looked dejected, jacket hanging loosely on his thin, lanky frame. Their lovely morning lay in ruins. It was so unfair. Coming home lifted her spirits to an all-time high, but how could she remain cheerful when he fell into another of his dark moods? *Och, Heavenly Faither, I need Your help. Please give me Your strength to see him through this painful time.*

Though he faced her, he appeared to be studying the cottage.

She turned and looked over the tiny stone building, trying to see it through the eyes of an incomer. Not a pleasing sight. The cracked, peeling paint on the deeply recessed door betrayed years of neglect. The two small, salt-encrusted windows at the front of the cottage, their lace curtains hanging limp, gave the cottage a sad, abandoned look. She eyed the stained thatched roof, crisscrossed with wires weighted down at the eaves with large, smooth stones. The soot-streaked stone chimney on the far side and front entry flags covered with soil and sand looked disgraceful. Och, what must he be thinking?

She had to push the sagging front door open with her shoulder. She eyed the interior, hand pressed to her lips in dismay. Thick dust covered the table, rockers, and every other flat surface and even the kitchen jaw box filthy with grit and dark stains where the faucet dripped over the years. No odour of mildew, but a musty, airless smell made her eyes burn. Och, she would have to scrub and air out the inside of the cottage before her father came.

She walked into her tiny bedroom and scooped up an armful of light summer clothes from their pegs along the walls. Too bad she hadn't taken them when she left the island, but there hadn't been room in her bags. Thank heaven Flora left several bars of handmade laundry soap in the largest infirmary bathroom. It would take several washings to rid the garments of their grimy shoulders and stale smell.

Intent upon depositing her dirty clothes in the large bathing tub, she only said, "Some summer things," as she passed Rob. He didn't even grunt an acknowledgement. She washed her face and hands and pinned some errant strands of hair into her bun before fetching him from the entry for his exercises.

He worked harder than usual, his face a mask of determination.

She gasped when he winced, his leg wobbling and dropping. "Och, you've done it now. Where does it hurt?" Without waiting for an answer, she levered the back of the chair until he was lying down and rolled him onto his side.

"I'm fine." His clenched lips and pale face belied the first words he had spoken since her return from the cottage.

She took a pillow from the bed and pushed it behind his back to keep him from rolling over. "What's the matter with you? You're so crabbit and quiet I'm thinking I must have done something to make you angry." When he didn't reply, a flare of resentment ignited. She placed her hands on her hips. "You're going to talk to me, or if this continues, Faither can send another nurse to take my place."

His look of panic almost made her recant but she had to break through his recalcitrant silence.

"I ... I ..."

A sentence from a nursing lecture flashed through her mind. *Touch is one of your most effective means of communication.* She knelt beside him and took one of his clenched hands, straightening his stiff fingers until she could lace them through hers. *Give me Your words, Faither.* "Tell me why you're in a fankle. And don't mumble."

He squirmed. "I ... I don't like questions about my past."

What was he talking about? "Och," she exclaimed, remembering their last conversation. "You mean me asking about your mither?"

He raised his eyes. "Yes."

Anger smothered to ashes of shame. "I shouldn't have asked that. You told me you didn't want to talk about it. Please forgive me."

She watched the expressions flitting across his face. He was fighting the impulse to retreat within himself again. Who had wounded him so badly he couldn't bear to talk about his own mither?

"I've hurt you again."

His sudden words startled her. "Hurt me?"

"You've been upset since we ate dinner."

Had she been that transparent? "Didn't it occur to you I could be in a fash without it involving you? That I have guid reason to be unhappy right now?"

"About what?"

Perhaps if she continued to be open with him .... She stood and looked out the window. "Like finding the garden I've worked on for years in a shambles with only the hardiest of plants surviving. And walking into the home I was born in to discover it dusty and so rundown after the years I've been away, it's only fit for beasties." She forced herself to meet his gaze. "Who appointed you responsible for my feelings?"

"Don't leave me, Maggie," he said, voice husky. "I'll never walk again if you go."

Humiliation burned her cheeks. "I should never have said that about leaving." She knelt beside him again. "I get so frustrated when you don't talk to me, but I never should have said that."

He groped for her hand. "I'm trying to talk more, Maggie. There are just some things I'm not ready to share with anyone."

At least he was talking again, even if only to remind her of something she had already heard. "Then you shouldn't. No' until you feel the time is right." She sighed. "Och, we're a fine pair. You hold everything inside and I can't help but show my feelings." She sat him up. "You did far too much this time."

"I always sweat when I'm exercising."

She left him for a moment, found what she needed in the pharmacy, and returned to his side with two APCs and a glass of water from his bedside table. "To help with the sweating."

"Why don't I sit here in the chair for a while and then we can run through those exercises again?"

So impatient. "Twice a day doesn't mean only an hour apart—and don't interrupt. Angus is due back any time and you'll take a nice rest in bed. This afternoon, he's sending his youngest lad, Edert, to help you back into the chair, but it's no' for exercises. We'll have our supper out on the entry and enjoy the sunset."

"That's a big imposition on the MacPhees. If I could just get into that chair and back into bed without needing so much help ..."

She decided to share part of a secret. "Malcolm made a run back into Oban last night. This een, he's bringing something that should be the answer to all of your transfer problems."

"A male orderly?"

"I said some*thing*, no' some*one*." She took his right hand and studied it for a moment. "You've calluses on your fingers. I didn't think pilots did manual labour." She pointed to a ring he wore, praying it wasn't a present from his mother. "And that's a verra fancy gold ring. Does it mean something special?"

"So you're not going to tell me what he's bringing, huh?"

"A little surprise spices the pot. First the ring, then the calluses."

"It says 'West Point' around the sides and top of the stone with the year I graduated, '1937,' at the bottom."

"It must be verra special for you to still wear it."

"The four years I spent there changed my life."

"Why are those words there?" She picked up his hand and pointed to the side of the ring. "Country, Honor, Duty."

"That's what we stand for, what we swear to live by. It's why we have to win this war and why I try my best to take care of my men."

"'Tis verra admirable. Now the calluses."

"Oh, all right, but this isn't as simple to explain." He looked out the window. "Look, a B-17 isn't the easiest bird to jockey around in the air, especially when it's loaded with a crew of ten, plus ten fifty-caliber guns and their ammo, enough fuel for a nine-hour flight, and a full load of bombs. We're talking about sixty-three thousand pounds of plane to maneuver through all the flak and bandits—that's enemy aircraft—and other Forts—Flying Fortresses—all going to the same place at the same time, stacked in the sky like cordwood."

She felt a stab of guilt. It had not occurred to her that the calluses had anything to do with flying. "I didn't mean to remind you—"

"You asked, so hear me out." He took a deep breath. "Anyway, the B-17 doesn't have power-assist or power-boost on the controls. It takes all your strength to keep that plane from bucking up and down if there's turbulence, so you set your autopilot to free up your hands because when you're flying at twenty-five angels—that's twenty-five thousand feet—the air's thin and the engines starved for fuel. So each one has to be individually adjusted to keep the correct pitch. Since there are four engines, even with your co-pilot helping, that takes a lot of pushing and pulling on knobs." He held up his hands, waving his fingers. "So—the calluses."

She had never seen him so animated. His face lit up, voice strengthened, and words flowed. No one-word grunts, no strangled voice as he searched to express himself. "I didn't know any of that," she said. "How do you remember to do so many things at once?"

"Training, training, and more training, like those exercises you have me doing, over and over again until you can do it in your sleep, because there are times when you're so sleep-deprived, you doze off at the controls for a few seconds. Hopefully when you're on autopilot."

"That's barbaric. How can they expect you to do your job if you haven't had enough sleep?" Nursing became harder the less sleep she had.

"There's a war on, remember?" He exhaled noisily. "And there are never enough airplanes or crews to fly them."

She had never given a thought to what the pilots faced on every mission. "And you do this day after day, month after month? How can you take all that pressure without going daft?"

"You take it one mission at a time." He leaned back and wiped his sweating forehead with his palm. "You learn never to borrow trouble by thinking about tomorrow because today will take all your energy and then some. And when you're in command, you have too many men you're responsible for."

"I know you take good care of your men. Everyone at Edenoaks said so."

"Like I said, I try. A language professor I had at the Point told us to give a lot of thought before asking anyone to do something we weren't willing to do ourselves. That's why I fly lead plane on the most dangerous missions."

"What a strange thing for a language professor to say."

"He was something of a philosopher too, and he was the only language teacher I ever had who could have you conjugating verbs in German or French and enjoying it."

"So you speak both German and French?"

"Enough to get by. I also have enough Italian to do more than order a mean plate of pasta."

"You're fluent in a few languages, so it appears our language differences can be solved."

"What language differences? What are you talking about?"

"Dinna ettle tae sook iz, Rob, aw wull skelt it ye."

"What?"

"Didn't understand the Scots?"

"Of course not."

Broken Wings

"I said, 'Don't try to fool me, Rob, or I'll swat at you.' Surely now, you must agree we have a language problem."

"It's all right when you speak enough English for me to understand. I hardly ever had any trouble at the infirmary, and when I did you always explained the Scots you were using."

Men. They could be so dense. "Is that fair?"

"What do you mean is that fair?"

"Just what I said. Why should I have to try to explain things just because you don't understand them?"

He sat up straighter in his chair. "I always have to explain the idioms I use."

"That's exactly what I mean. American idioms are no' the same as Scots or even English. If you're going to understand most of the folk on Innisbraw, you must learn to converse in our language."

"That's easier said than done."

"I'm thinking 'twill be verra easy. You're already fluent in four languages, counting American English. You'll learn Scots, of course."

He stared at her for a moment and then, for the first time since they met, he threw back his head and laughed aloud. "Maggie, lass, you got me."

His laugh was so infectious she couldn't help but join in.

A flurry of activity caught Rob's attention. Elspeth stood in the open doorway, Angus behind her. He dropped Maggie's hands and tried to compose himself, mortified to realize he had no shirt on and nothing to pull over his bare chest.

"Well, aren't you going to ask me in?" Elspeth asked with a smile. She winked at Rob. "Don't fash yourself. I've seen a few naked chests in my ninety-eight years."

Maggie raced to the bed and grabbed Rob's skivvy, slipping it over his head. "Of course we're happy to see you. We were having a bit of a laugh," she added, helping him into his sweater.

Elspeth hobbled in, extending her hand to Rob. "You look much better. Isn't it grand what a guid night's sleep can do?"

He took her hand. Was he hallucinating? It seemed to radiate warmth. "It's good to see you again," he said, surprising himself by how much he meant it.

"And 'tis guid to see you and our Maggie. She's been sorely missed." She motioned to a chair beside the bed. "If you would be so kind, lass, these auld legs don't appreciate standing for verra long anymore."

Maggie immediately brought the chair over and Elspeth sat, smoothing her dress over her knees. "Now, perhaps you would be so kind as to get Angus here something to eat. Having to pick me up cost him his dinner-time."

"There is a bit of Scotch broth and bannock left," Maggie said, eyeing Rob. "Is your backache better?"

Normally, he would have leaped at the chance to escape a conversation, but something about her made him look forward to talking to the old woman. "The backache's a lot better, so don't hurry on my account. I'll be in that bed far longer than I want."

Once Maggie and Angus had gone, Elspeth smiled warmly, her faded blue eyes sparkling. "You're a cannie lad, Rob Savage, and no' one to run from a challenge."

"I can't run from anything right now."

"Och, don't play word games with me. You know exactly what I mean." Another smile softened the stern words. She leaned closer. "I understand you're an aviator."

He nodded.

"And in the American Air Forces."

"Yes."

"And a colonel in charge of Edenoaks Airbase."

"You know a lot about me."

"There's nowt I've said that shames you, is there?"

"No."

"Then, perhaps you can help me know you better for I've a feeling we're going to be spending quite a bit of time together. How old are you?"

"Twenty-eight."

"Och, so young to have so much responsibility. But war often brings out the best in our young folk. Where were you educated?"

"West Point Military Academy."

"I've heard of it, though for the life of me, I cannot remember who from." She tapped his knee. "And you luve flying."

"Very much."

"You're a man of few words. That's an admirable trait."

"Used to be. I'm trying to talk more. Maggie doesn't share your opinion of my one-word answers."

She sat back in the chair with a chuckle. "For such a cannie lad, you've missed something verra important about our Maggie. It isn't how many words you speak to her, but what those words are. Her heart is tender. She can be hurt."

That struck an uncomfortable chord. He studied his hands. "I know."

"Well, since you're smitten with our Maggie and her with you, things should sort themselves out over time."

He raised his head in alarm. What was she talking about?

"Don't go getting all fashed." She chuckled again. "Nobody's told any tales on you. And there's the little matter of you walking. I'm certain you don't want to declare yourself until you're out of that chair."

He squirmed. This conversation was getting out of hand.

"Don't look so surprised. When you've lived as long as I have, you know what's important to a proud man."

She was beginning to sound like Doctor McGrath.

"You're getting way ahead of me," he said. "I like Maggie—a lot. She's become a close friend. Without her help and encouragement, I wouldn't have a prayer of ever walking again. But there are a lot of other things I'd have to clear up before I could ...." He let it drop, his thoughts about the future too tangled to share with a stranger.

Her deep, throaty laugh filled the room. "You're a cautious one then, but there's nowt wrong with that." She sobered and leaned close again. "Just be verra careful no' to break Maggie's heart in the meantime," she cautioned. "Tread lightly, Rob, lad."

"I'm not leading her on, if that's what you're afraid of."

"I'm sure you aren't. And, if you'll take some advice from an auld woman, don't let John McGrath intimidate you. His love for his only lass is understandable, but any faither can be overprotective." She reached for her cane and pulled herself to her feet. "I know I've said things that have made you uncomfortable, but that wasn't my intent. Perhaps 'tis my age that makes me so plain-spoken, but there are times when the truth needs to be sorted out quickly before the opportunity is lost." She patted his shoulder. "Don't get in a fash. I've had my say and I'll no' mention any of this again. Now, I hear Angus returning. 'Tis time to take my leave."

"Come back soon, as I can't come to visit you."

She leaned over and lightly touched her lips to his cheek. She smelled of heather, like Maggie. "Courage," she said. "God has great things planned for your future."

Maggie came in, followed by Angus.

"Are you ready to be put into bed?" the crofter asked with a good-natured smile.

"I'll be in the foyer," Elspeth told him. "Just catch me up when you're ready to leave."

Rob was surprised by how much he hated to see her go. Her directness made him squirm, but everything she'd said had been motivated by her love for Maggie. Though she was dead wrong about Maggie and him being anything more than good friends, she'd obviously spoken what she believed to be true. But what had she meant by "great things in your future?" "Thank you, Elspeth," he said. "I hope I'll see you again."

Her eyes sparkled. "Och, 'tis sure you will, lad."

By the time Angus took his leave, Rob's face was pale and he looked exhausted.

"I know you're tired, but getting back into bed is difficult," Maggie said. "Are you in pain?"

"I could use twa of those APCs."

She brought the aspirin and cranked up the head of the bed before handing him a glass of water. "Drink it all. You need to keep hydrated."

He swallowed the pills and emptied the glass.

"Guid. As soon as that aspirin works, I want to ask you a question."

"Don't have to wait. It helps to talk. So what's your question?"

She hated to bother him but he always asked her to talk or sing when he hurt. "What do you think of Elspeth?"

"How could anyone not like her? She's special."

She sighed with relief. She had been so afraid Rob would find her dearest friend too opinionated. She sat on the side of the bed. "Elspeth taught me so much when Mither died. How to care for a wee bairnie, and over the years how to dye, spin, and knit, or weave the wool from Innisbraw's sheep into clothing. She also showed me how to clean and cook, plunge butter and clot cream, and cultivate a kailyard garden filled with herbs and vegetables to fill the stomach and flowers to nourish the soul."

"No wonder you're so fond of her."

"Aye, but I didn't know how an incomer would react. She has strong opinions."

"Is that what you think I am? An incomer?"

"No. I didn't mean it that way. I just meant ... well, you're new to Innisbraw. I didn't mean to sound like you don't belong. You do." When he didn't reply, she said, "Now do you see how important it is to learn Scots? If I'd been speaking in Scots with you understanding, we wouldn't be in this muddle."

"I'll learn Scots."

"Because I want you to or because you want it for yourself?"

"For both reasons. Nothing's that simple."

"Elspeth will teach you."

"Elspeth? She can't be tied down to teaching me every day. Don't forget the transportation problem. She can't walk up here and there's no way I can get down to her cottage."

"We'll find a way. There's nothing she enjoys more than teaching Scots or the Gaelic." Despite Rob's protest, Maggie's spirits soared. *Och, thank Ye, Faither.* Rob would have a diversion from his painful exercises and she would be free to spend time in her garden.

Chapter Fifteen

Rob's Scots lessons began the following morning. Maggie talked several neighboring crofters with carts and cuddies into volunteering a shuttle service between Elspeth's cottage and the infirmary.

Elspeth brought a slate, chalk, paper, and pencils—and an ironic wit that soon won him over completely. She started their first lesson by explaining the origin of the Scots language and how it was now spoken, although differently in each region of the land, by most of those who were not Gaelic speakers and a few who were.

"Then, Scots isn't the same, say, on Innisbraw, as it is in the rest of the Hebrides?" Rob asked.

"Other Hebrideans don't have Scots at all. Their auld-timers all have the Gaelic and the young people speak English. 'Tis too bad you had to come to the only Scots-speaking island in all the Hebrides. It started on Innisbraw so many years ago the reason is obscured by a heavy mist—what we call a thickness—too dense for me to breach no matter how hard I try."

As a skilled teacher, she also gently questioned his relationship with God. Once she knew he was a Christian, she spent a few minutes at the end of each lesson explaining the importance of prayer and how much the Lord loved to have His children spend part of their days talking to Him.

"Maggie's been telling me the same thing, but how do you know He hears you?" Rob asked the first time she told him this. "I mean, with the war and all ..."

"Have you never heard that He is omniscient—all-knowing—and also omnipresent—anywhere and everywhere—at the same time? Don't fall for the de'il's trap of thinking our Heavenly Father is as limited as we humans. He has promised to listen to and answer our prayers." She held up a hand to keep him from interrupting. "I know you wonder why some of your prayers don't seem to be answered, but you have to realize that sometimes His answer is no because He has other plans for you or those you have prayed for—better plans than you could ever imagine."

His mind flashed back to the moment Rich Florey had not answered his interphone. "Even if it means someone you care for dies?" he asked in a voice hoarse with grief as he pictured the tall, bony young man with large gray eyes and infectious, lopsided grin.

"Aye, even then," Elspeth said. "Our days on earth are numbered, lad, and that number known, thankfully, only by God. Was this friend of yours a Christian?"

He nodded. "Rich Florey, my tail gunner. We talked about it sometimes, Rich and Gunny and I. I suppose that's why we three felt so close. But he was so young. They're always so young."

She bowed her head. "Leadership during war is too heavy a burden to be carried alone. I'm sure you prayed for your friend before he was killed, as you must have prayed for all of your young lads. Just remember this. Our precious Lord loves every one of those young lads even more than you do. Trust Him to work out His will in their lives."

After a few lessons, she startled him by saying, "You're a marvel, you are, Rob. You'll have the Scots mastered in no time and then we can begin on the Gaelic."

"I won't be here that long. I've got an air group to run."

"But you'll be back." She ignored his bemused look and reached for her cane. "Before I go, I want you to tell me about that machinery on your bed. I've been meaning to ask about it."

"Malcolm brought it over from Scotland. That's a trapeze, so I can pull myself up in bed. Those bars sticking out from under the mattress are to grab onto when I want to lower myself into my chair or pull myself into bed again. Pretty ingenious, isn't it?"

"It is that. It must have been invented by a Scotsman."

※

"I can't believe how quickly you're learning Scots," Maggie said several days later, "but you must stop exercising when you should be sleeping."

"I want to walk. I can catch up on my sleep once I'm on my feet."

Her blue eyes glittered with irritation. "I know you're eager to walk, but you're doing more harm than guid by no' allowing your muscles to rest. What you're tearing down by the exercises has to have time to rebuild."

She was right, but he couldn't stop himself, even when Elspeth changed the lessons to every other day and spent the entire morning.

Late one night, Maggie heard Rob's groans and found him writhing from cramps in both calf muscles. She pressed his toes upward but the cramps persisted so she untucked the bottom of the sheet and pressed his bare feet against the cold metal bed frame. Within minutes, the spasms eased and he fell back against the pillow, panting.

"You're soaking wet." She ran for a face flannel and a bowl of water and bathed his face and arms. "I've told you over and over no' to exercise when I'm no' here."

"What makes you think I was exercising?"

"Och, what else would cause such deep cramps?"

When he tried to reply, she pressed her palm over his mouth. "Don't tell me you were no' exercising when you're covered with sweat."

She would never understand. They had less than two months. He couldn't quit. A sudden vision of her sailing toward Scotland flashed before his eyes. He turned his head so she couldn't see his devastation.

"What is it? Have you hurt yourself that badly, then?"

He couldn't speak.

She sat beside him, cradling him. "Please talk to me, Rob. If you don't tell me I can't help you."

He pulled one arm free to rub the side of his nose. How could he tell her his fears without revealing how much she meant to him— how much he needed her? But he knew if he refused to answer her this time, he could drive her away forever. He took a deep breath to calm his raging emotions. "There's ... there's so little time left," he mumbled.

"Time for what?" she asked. "They'll surely take you back at Edenoaks no matter how long it takes you to recover."

"Not Edenoaks. You."

"Me? What do I have to do with this? I'm here for another ... och, Rob, you're surely no' expecting to walk before I leave?"

"I want to, more than anything."

She framed his face between her palms.

He couldn't meet her gaze.

"If only you could learn to tell me what it is you want, what it is you need, we could be working together."

"I can't. It isn't only the walking again before you leave. It's something I promised someone." Och, he'd done it now.

"I don't understand. What kind of a promise would require you no' to share your needs with me, and who would exact such a cruel promise?" Her hand covered her mouth. "Faither," she whispered.

Though he didn't allow himself to react, she would demand an explanation.

"What did you promise Faither?" she asked. "If best friends cannot be forthright, their friendship is nothing but a sham, or even worse, a lie, and you've told me you don't lie."

His throat convulsed as he fought for the right words, any words to put an end to this. He couldn't mention his promise not to take her away from Innisbraw or the lifetime commitment her father had demanded—not when he was still so torn by the thought of having to give up flying. "I ... I promised him I wouldn't hurt you and I've already broken that promise a hundred times."

"You've never taken advantage of me. The one time you kissed me, I liked it as much as you."

For one of the few times in his adult life, and the second time in the same conversation, he spoke without thinking. "You don't understand. You'll be going back to duty in August. What if I can't walk by then? I need to see your bonnie face smiling at me—hear your soft voice telling me I can do it, no matter how it hurts. Having you close gives me a reason to work as hard as I can. I want to walk again for you, Maggie—for you." He froze. He had blurted out his innermost secrets.

The bed shifted as she climbed up beside him. She put her arm around his shoulders and lay down, resting her cheek on his chest. "I'm no' a bairn, to be protected by half-truths and promises to my faither. I know you'll walk again but I don't know when. You've told me your fears and I appreciate it, for I didn't know they involved me. I thank you for the truth. Now we can have a new beginning based on trust."

"But I—"

"Don't talk anymore. We're both verra tired." She pulled a corner of the cover over herself. "Close your eyes and go to sleep. I'll be right here."

⁂

It was wrong to be lying on the bed next to Rob, even with the covers separating them, but he needed more comforting than a few words could bring. Maggie nestled against his chest. Did he feel more than friendship? He hadn't said so and he certainly didn't act like it, but why else would he want to walk for her? She felt a stab of fear. It was too soon. She wasn't ready for that.

Her thoughts drifted to her growing concern for his safety when he returned to duty. No. No negative thoughts now. She would allow herself the pleasure of relaxing against his warm body and stay with him until he was asleep.

Her eyelids grew heavy and she closed her eyes for just a moment.

⁂

Rob lay awake long after Maggie's breathing deepened. He had tried so hard not to allow it to happen, but he was beginning to wonder if Elspeth could be right. Did he love Maggie? He didn't think so, but he didn't know what love was supposed to feel like.

He'd met a few local girls who worked near the fighter base he'd been stationed at in England, but his inability to carry on a normal conversation ensured they never got beyond a first uncomfortable date. He'd given up on dating then, decided he'd have to wait until the war was over before trying to find someone he felt comfortable being around.

But Maggie was unlike any woman he had ever met. He breathed in the clean, warm-honey scent of heather that always surrounded her and finally admitted she could be what had been missing from his life.

Oh, God, I really need Your help. I have such a hard time revealing my past. If Maggie and Elspeth are right and You really can hear me and answer my prayers, please help me do the right thing now. I'm afraid I care for Maggie too much and I feel torn. I don't know for sure I'm going to walk again, and I know I can never take Maggie away from her home. But I can't bear the thought of not flying when the war's over. Please help me. Oh, Lord, please help me.

The rising sun tinted the white walls of his room soft orange when he awoke. Lace curtains shivered in the cool morning breeze and the seals barked their guttural greetings on the rocks below Innis Fell. Maggie's warm breath caressed his neck as lightly as a murmured sigh. She still lay with her arm across his shoulder and her body pressed against his. Even with the covers between them, he could really *feel* her.

Her black hair lay tangled across the blanket. He picked up a slight curl and brought it to his face, closing his eyes as he rubbed it across his cheek. It reminded him of a crow's feather he found in the grass when he was a lad—so soft and sleek. He saved that feather for years, trailing it across his face whenever overpowered by feelings of being trapped. It spoke of freedom, of soft winds and vivid blue skies, of flying.

A sudden thought brought a shiver of excitement. This must have been the sight that greeted the crofter when he looked at his sleeping Selkie. Did she stay on the island or submit to the siren calls of her Selkie-lover? He'd waited long enough. He had to know.

Maggie stirred. The curl pulled from his fingers as she scooted as far away as she could without falling off the bed. Her eyes widened, cheeks flushed. "Och, I didn't mean to spend the entire night."

He should have known she would be embarrassed. "I'm glad you did," he said, his voice hoarse with sleep—and much more. "It ... it helped."

He watched her face reflect her inner turmoil, certain the need to comfort him would soon overcome her embarrassment.

She smiled suddenly as she brushed tendrils of hair from her forehead. "How did you sleep?"

"Like a bairnie. I dreamed the verra beautiful Selkie crawled into bed beside me."

"Och, Rob, you didn't. How do your calves feel? Sore?"

"What calves?" He looked in wonder at this bonnie lass who gave so much of herself.

"Well, I don't know about you, but I'm thirsty." She slid off the bed and reached for her robe—och, dressing gown. "Water or coffee?"

"Water first, then coffee."

She poured him a glass of water and sat on the bed so she could lift him up. Their hands touched and he shivered when a frisson passed between them.

He drank the water slowly, savoring her closeness, inhaling the fragrance of heather wafting from her skin and hair.

When the glass was empty, she filled it again and took several sips.

Sharing a glass. So intimate. *Control yourself, Savage.*

"Why are you looking at me like that? Do you want more water?"

He shook his head, not trusting his voice.

She stood and stretched. "If you did dream about the Selkie, which I'm still doubting, 'tis most likely because you heard the seals."

"You never did finish the story. I need to know if she stayed with the crofter."

"Of course I'll finish the tale, but what makes you *need* to hear it?"

He had to say something to get himself back on the straight and narrow or he would lose control and do something rash. "Since the day is exercise day, you're going to see a changed man."

"Whatever do you mean?"

"This day, I start listening to you. No more sneaking around doing leg-lifts behind your back. You give the orders and I'll follow them."

"About time."

※

That night, Rob savored the feel of Maggie smoothing his covers.

She pulled a chair up close to his bed. "You need to hear the ending to the Selkie tale, so I'll tell it now."

Only if I can touch you. He reached for her hand, relieved when she laced her fingers through his.

"You remember how the crofter fell in love with the Selkie, and his gentleness won her trust? How she stopped wading into the sea and listening to the calls of her Selkie-lover?"

He nodded.

"Well, after several weeks of hiding from the fishermen, the Selkie knew she had to tell the crofter the truth about what she was—where she came from. She told him of her journey through the sea, something inside her breast urging her on and on until late one night, too exhausted to swim any longer, she reached an island and pulled herself up onto a large, flat rock and fell into a deep sleep.

"She awoke just before dawn, the need for food gnawing at her belly. But when she tried to slide from the rock, she discovered she had no flippers—only pale-looking hands and feet. The warnings of her mother were true. 'There is one island you must avoid,' she'd said, 'for if you beach yourself on a rock there, you will turn into a human. If that should happen, you'll find your fur beside you. Slip into it immediately and escape!'

"She'd seen a few humans before, on boats or other islands, their pale bodies clothed—not in fur—but strange coverings of many colors. Frightened, she scrambled to her knees and reached for the bundle of fur beside her.

"But, before she could slip it on, she heard angry shouts. Two humans ran through the sand toward her, waving their arms and long, pronged weapons. She grabbed the fur, scrambled from the rock, and raced across the shore, amazed by how fast her human legs could travel.

"'And that's how I came to your cottage,' she said to the crofter. 'And you covered my body and hid me in that first cave.'

"The crofter pulled her close, feeling her body tremble. 'I don't care what or who you are. I love you. Stay with me, please. Without you I'm nothing and I have nothing.'

"The Selkie gently pushed him away. 'There's something I must do before I give you my answer.' She picked up the seal fur and left the cave, wading out into the sea until the waves lapped at her knees. She tossed the fur into the water and watched it float, then disappear. When she turned, the crofter stood on the shore, his arm raised toward her. She began to sing.

"She sang of her love, that she would be his forever, that the love in her heart would never fade, but grow stronger each day.

"So the Selkie and her crofter married, had many children, and lived on their wee island in the sea, forever and ever and ever."

Rob's fingers tightened. "That's it? That's the end?"

"Aye, that's the end of the Selkie tale."

"But what about the fishermen who wanted to kill her?"

Maggie smiled. "'Tis a tale, Rob, no' something that really happened. It's been told over hundreds of years, and I'm sure some of it—like the angry fishermen—has been lost in the telling."

"Was the island Innisbraw?"

She pulled her hand away. "Of course no'. There are no caves here large enough to hide in." She stood and pushed the chair away. "Now, you've had your ending and 'tis time for sleep." She poured a fresh glass of water for his bedside, said a soft "Guid-night," and crossed the hall to her own room.

Sleep? How could he sleep? The Selkie had stayed. The last few words of the story echoed in his mind.

And they lived on their wee island in the sea forever and ever and ever.

In the days that followed, he found the exercises much less painful, but he suffered an entirely different kind of pain. Maggie's naturally affectionate nature drove him crazy. She didn't spend another night on his bed—he didn't expect her to—but he often caught her looking at him with such fondness, he had to bite his tongue to keep from blurting out that he might be falling in love with her.

He could imagine how she would react to such a ridiculously immature disclosure.

"Might be," she'd say, nose in the air. "You sound like some luve-sick lad with fuzz on his chin."

He kept such thoughts to himself and stuck to his word, only working his muscles when she asked. The transfer apparatus helped ease his frustration. He could now use the trapeze to sit up without any help. After much practice, he used the bars to lower himself into the wheelchair and pull his body back onto the bed. The transfer took a lot of time and arduous effort, but it was heartening not to have to rely on so many others for mobility.

Every day, he regained more feeling in his hips and legs. He could even feel the difference between the harshness of his denims and the smooth texture of ironed sheets. If only he could make more progress toward controlling his emotions—a problem he hadn't experienced since a small lad.

Maggie constantly encouraged him to talk more, but somehow he had to learn to keep from revealing how he *felt* about everything. He'd have to ask Doctor McGrath if there were a physical reason. The commander of an air group could never wear his emotions on his sleeve.

Chapter Sixteen

Hugh MacEwan, the minister of the Kirk on Innisbraw, trudged back toward the manse from a visit with several of the older widows at their cottages on the western side of the island. Why did he feel so tired? Granted, he had been up over half the night preparing his lesson for the Sabbath, but he often spent the quiet, uninterrupted hours studying Hebrew, Aramaic, and Greek texts to get a more precise translation of the original languages of the Bible than the early church scholars had provided.

At almost fifty-three and at least a stone too heavy, he might not be in the best physical condition but he walked this far almost every day without feeling so spent. His fatigue must be a symptom of emotional turmoil.

"Och, Heavenly Faither, I don't like what those auld ones had to say about Maggie and that Yank patient of hers one bit," he muttered aloud. He paused, took off his eyeglasses, polished them on his handkerchief, and looked toward the freshwater loch.

A pair of mute swans hugged the far shore, protecting a clutch of tiny cygnets.

He veered onto a narrow footpath leading to the banks of the loch, choosing a route as far away as possible from the shy, wild birds. He took off his heavy tweed jacket, folded it carefully, and sank onto a large, flat rock with a sigh.

Common butterwort, one of the earlier wildflowers, bloomed among the rocks that cluttered the peaty soil. In a few weeks, the bell heather would be in its full glory, along with bog myrtle and large patches of white cotton grass in the less stony places. This was exactly what he needed—time to revel in God's handiwork while attempting to deal with the unsettling thoughts those old women evoked.

They were in a fash about something, but he could not understand what. Yes, Maggie spent her days and nights alone at the infirmary with a young man, which could be considered improper in any other situation. But how could it compromise the lass's reputation when the lad's legs were paralysed? After all, John McGrath sent his daughter and her patient here because she was trained to administer the therapy the young man needed.

He had led several prayer meetings since the colonel arrived on the island, beseeching God to heal the aviator's broken body, and to give Maggie the strength and wisdom she needed. The entire congregation prayed for them every Sabbath.

But he did miss Maggie and looked forward to the time her patient had healed enough for a long, blethering visit.

He unbuttoned his top shirt collar and rolled up his sleeves, turning his face to the brisk sea breeze rippling the dark, peaty loch water. Those widows needed more to keep their minds busy. They should no' be spreading their gossip about Maggie and her patient. That could stir up a bee skep of problems island-wide.

He stood, threw his jacket over his shoulder, and picked his way through the rocks back to the main path. He needed to spend the rest of the day on his knees. Only God could solve this fankle.

Chapter Seventeen

Rob awakened with a start.

An agonized scream from across the hall sent a rush of adrenaline through his body.

Maggie!

He struggled to sit up and bolt from his bed, mind galvanized into action. His legs refused to cooperate.

"Maggie?" he shouted. "Maggie, what's wrong?" He pulled on the mattress, rolling over onto his side.

Her heart-rending sobs tore through him.

He reached for the bars connected to his bed. "Maggie!" he shouted again. "Och, Lord help me. I can't get to my Maggie." He grasped one of the bars and slid his left leg off the bed.

Grabbed the other bar.

He stopped, gasping for breath. Thank God the moonlight streaming in through both windows illuminated the wheelchair in the corner.

But even if he could move his right leg off the mattress, he would be hanging in space with nothing to break his fall when he let go. "Help me, Lord," he panted, "please help me."

Maggie staggered into his room, doubled over, violent sobs wracking her body.

"Maggie! Come to me. I can't get up. Please come to me."

She stared at him, brushing her tangled hair from her face. "Rob? Rob, is it really you?" She stumbled across the room and collapsed against him. "I thought I lost you," she cried. "I thought you were dead."

"Help me back into bed. I'm about to fall."

She raised her head and gasped. She lifted his left leg onto the bed and pried his hands from the bars before rolling him onto his back. "You could hurt yourself even more. What have I done to you?"

He grabbed her shoulders. "Crawl up here beside me. I need to hold you close. Och, please, Maggie, I need to hold you close."

She climbed up beside him, throwing her arms around his shoulders.

He hugged her, heart filled with anguish. "You screamed. What happened?"

She held onto him, shoulders shaking. "I thought I lost you," she repeated.

"You didn't lose me. You must have had a bad dream."

"It was dreadful." She moaned. "The most dreadful dream I've ever had." She looked into his face. "I wouldn't want to live if that happened to you. And it will ... if you go back to duty."

"It was only a dream, Maggie. Dreams don't come true."

"This one will. With all the missions you've flown, this one will."

"You dreamed I was killed on a bombing strike?"

She buried her face against his chest. "'Twas after a mission, when you came in for a landing. And I watched it happen. Your landing gear wasn't down and your plane skidded off the runway on its belly until one wing hit the ground, and then it ... it just exploded and tore into ... into pieces with black smoke rising high into the air. I tried to run closer but I couldn't move." She wept, clutching him while her body shook.

"Och, you've heard too many stories." He smoothed wet tendrils back from her forehead. "Aye, planes can crash land when they're damaged, but they never have enough fuel after a mission to explode." He continued to hold her, pressing his cheek to her hair.

So she feared for his life when he returned to duty. She must have been thinking about it a long time to suffer such a terrible, graphic dream.

Jerking and whimpering, she fell asleep in his arms.

He pulled a blanket off himself and covered her with it. His back ached. Probably pulled muscles, but that didn't matter. He had to convince her he would survive another round of duty. *Och, Lord,*

I know her faith is far stronger than mine, but for some reason, she's afraid for me. Help me show her that You'll take care of me, no matter how thick the flak. Give her back her faith, Heavenly Faither, for that sets her above so many others—especially me.

~*~

False dawn lightened the bruised sky to pale grey-blue when she raised her head. "I've made you hurt yourself." She slid from the bed and pulled the covers over him. "And you're cold." She sat on the bed and smoothed the forelock back from his forehead. "Where do you hurt? And don't you dare say nowhere. I see it in your eyes."

"'Tis the pain I feel for you." He brushed her cheek with his fingers. "I didn't know my returning to duty frightened you so much."

"Neither did I, until last night."

"We have to talk about it. We can't have something like this torturing you."

"It doesn't have to. You can resign your commission and stay here on Innisbraw. You don't have to report back to duty when you can walk again."

This was no time to tell her he could never give up flying. "It doesn't work that way. A member of the American Army Air Forces can't suddenly decide he wants out, especially a career officer like me."

"Why no'?" Her chin rose. "You told me you've flown over eighty missions if you include the time you spent in fighters. Surely that's enough for any man, officer or no'."

He needed time to think about how to handle this. "Make me some coffee, will you please?" He knuckled his burning eyes. "I'm going to have to educate you about how the American military works and I'm a wee bit groggy."

"I doubt you slept at all after what happened. And I'll make some tea. I need a clear mind, too."

"I could use some APCs."

"So you did hurt yourself."

"My back just aches a wee bit."

"Then you get the APCs first. I'll be back in a tick." She brought him aspirin and straightened his bedding, pulling up another blanket before leaving for the kitchen.

Eyes closed, he lay thinking. He couldn't bring up his own indecision about the future. She had presented him with a problem and there could be only one answer. The truth.

He'd have to talk as forcefully as he had when facing a room full of generals. Could he make her understand, truly understand, what he was about to tell her? He prayed for the right words. Face pale and eyes swollen, she had dressed and put her hair into a bun by the time she brought their coffee and tea.

He pulled himself up with the trapeze and patted the side of the bed. "Up you come. I want you close while we talk."

She settled beside him.

He swallowed some coffee and set the mug on the bedside table. "Before I interrupted, you said I could resign my commission and remain on Innisbraw, and I was trying to explain it isn't that simple."

She nodded, sipping her tea.

"Now, I'm going to tell you what would happen if I did that." He glanced out the window at the orange-flushed sky. "First, an officer on active duty can't just resign his commission. Even in peacetime, it isn't easy. When there's a war on, it can't be done." He shook his head when it looked as if she might interrupt. "Let me say it all, and then you can ask your questions, all right?"

She nodded again.

"Second, if I don't show up for duty after I've been declared physically fit, I'll be considered AWOL. Do you know what that means?"

"Is that like French Leave?" Her voice trembled.

"Aye, but Americans call it 'Absent Without Leave.' The American Army Air Forces will send their military police here to Innisbraw and return me to London in handcuffs to face a court martial. I'll be appointed council for my defense—a member of the Army Air Forces who specializes in law—and he'll present my case with the Judge Advocate prosecuting before a military judge and a panel of five officers who've been appointed to try me.

"Witnesses will be called, including your faither who will already have stated in a sworn affidavit I was fit for duty." He took another swig of coffee. "And John won't do that 'til I can no' only walk, but run, do sit-ups, and anything else the flight surgeon at Edenoaks might throw at me before allowing me to re-take command of the 396th.

"Anyway, after your faither testifies, my defense will probably call witnesses to attest to my diligence to duty before this happened, to my service record and combat decorations, even all the way back to my graduation, with honours, from West Point."

Maggie opened and closed her mouth.

He reached for his coffee and drained the mug, gathering his scattered thoughts. "Then I'll be called to testify. What can I tell them? That I don't want to return to duty because I'm afraid I'll be killed?" He shook his head. "That would be a lie because I'm no' afraid of dying. Or that I've found a life for myself on an island in Scotland and I can't give it up to help defeat Hitler? Another lie. There's nowt I wouldn't do to help win this war."

The whirr of a vacuum broke the uneasy silence. Flora was Hoovering the foyer.

He again looked out the window, searching for the words to make her understand, but unable to meet those pleading, navy-blue eyes. "So, after all the evidence is given and sworn to, the panel would meet together to make their decision." He took the teacup from her, put it on the table, and gripped both of her hands. "They'll have to come back with a guilty verdict, Maggie, and desertion during war has severe penalties. The worst is death by firing squad."

She jerked her hands from his and covered her face. "No, that's no' possible."

"But it is. Another penalty would be life in prison, and I'll tell you right now I prefer death."

"They're all barbarians. Don't they have hearts? Don't they care about the men who die and all those they leave behind, broken-hearted, their lives ruined?"

"No, they don't—they can't, because if they did, they'd soon have no Air Forces to bomb German fuel depots or take out their airieplane factories, rail yards, and manufacturing plants." He framed her face with his palms. "When I joined the American Army Air Corps, I swore to uphold my duties to my country. And since America entered the war, those duties include helping everyone who's fighting the Germans. I didn't take that oath lightly, Maggie.

"I'm no' a liar, as I've told you often enough, but I'm also no' a quitter. When your faither finally signs that paper stating I'm fit to return to duty, that's exactly what I'll do because 'tis who and what I am."

She closed her eyes, a tremor shaking her body. "Then ... then 'tis up to me to be as brave as all the others who have someone they ... they care about in danger." She laid her head on his shoulder. "Please pray for me, Rob. Somehow, I've lost the faith that God will bring you home safely and I don't know how to get it back."

"I have been praying. And I'll keep on praying. Your faith is the one thing that will keep me safe." That, and God's plan.

She was quiet the rest of the day and he didn't push her to talk. She fought a spiritual battle. Only the Lord could help her regain her faith.

Maggie paced her room, wringing her hands, fighting tears. What should she do? How could she sleep, especially after hearing Rob's determination to return to duty the moment he could? Sleep would surely bring another horrible dream.

If only she could spend the night close to him, hear his steady breathing, feel the beat of his heart beneath her cheek.

Her face burned. Och, what kind of lass allowed such thoughts?

She dropped to her knees beside her bed. "I'm in a terrible, terrible fash, Heavenly Faither. I can't stand having another nightmare, I just can't!" She clasped her hands beneath her chin, body quivering. "I know I shouldn't even think about spending the night with Rob. 'Tis wrong because I'm his nurse—and I could be tempting him to sin."

I AM YOUR FORTRESS.

In brilliant yellow letters.

Written behind her closed eyes.

Words from a Salm she memorized as a bairn echoed in her thoughts: 'For You are my rock and fortress; therefore, for Your name's sake, lead me and guide me.'

"Aye, lead me, Lord. Guide me. I want only Your perfect will."

Her mind flooded with memories of that first night she spent on Rob's bed—when she awakened to find him holding a lock of her hair.

Just her hair.

And last night, he only held her while she cried, somehow sensing she needed proof it was only a horrible dream, that he hadn't been killed. She didn't mean to fall asleep, but when she opened her eyes, he held her hand.

Just her hand.

"I don't want to act like a wanton lass. Give me an answer, Lord, please! I don't know what to do." She remained on her knees, listening for the quiet, small voice of the Holy Spirit.

She awakened hours later, slumped on the floor beside her bed, shivering, muscles cramped. The first flush of dawn tinted the walls with a warm, yellow glow.

No bad dream.

The Lord heard her prayer.

And answered.

Chapter Eighteen

Over the next few days, she seemed more like the old Maggie who smiled and teased, but this wasn't a problem that could be solved quickly. A dark shadow deep within her eyes saddened Rob. He could do nothing to help her but pray, and he had failed God too often to be certain He would answer, even if his pleas weren't for himself.

On Saturday evening, he suggested Maggie take time off the next morning to attend services at kirk. "You haven't been once. I'm afraid your minister thinks I'm too selfish to allow you the time away."

"Och, Hugh knows better than that. He understands I don't want to leave you alone while I go to kirk."

"What's twa or so hours? Please, Maggie, go on the morra's mornin. You've told me how important your minister's lessons are to everybody on the island, and it's been a long time since you've heard him."

"I can't leave you alone for over twa hours. I can't."

He laid his head back. "Och, I can't believe this."

She walked over to the window and looked out at the sea. "I suppose I could ask Morag MacDonald to stay with you, for she's been begging me to give her some wee task."

"Well?"

"But she has her own reasons for never missing kirk. Her only lad, Graham, is in the British Army and she's verra concerned about him."

"I already feel like I work you near to death. I hate you giving up the spiritual food you need."

"Don't talk daft. Doing things for you brings me joy and 'tis guid to feel needed."

"Mebbe Morag would like to feel needed, too."

She worried her lower lip, fingers tapping on thighs. "I'll raise her on the radio and ask."

She returned in minutes. "Morag said she'd be verra glad to help. She's been wanting to meet you and this gives her a guid excuse."

He may have opened a can of worms but he would just have to bear all the personal questions. At least Maggie was going to kirk.

Morag arrived at the infirmary fifteen minutes early so her husband could meet Rob before driving Maggie to kirk in their cart. Alec, a tall, sturdy, open-faced man with strong, masculine features, wore a tweed suit, the jacket stretched taut over his broad shoulders, a white shirt, and tie. He held what Maggie called a "bunnet"—a flat cap with a small brim in front—clasped beneath his arm.

Morag had the same black hair and blue eyes as her husband but she was slim with a heart-shaped face. The hint of a dimple decorated her pointed chin. Even though she was not going to kirk, her dress looked too fancy for every-day wear.

They greeted Maggie with hugs and kisses. "We've missed you, we have that," Alec said, face beaming.

"She's been verra busy," Morag said, holding out her hand to Rob. "And you're our Maggie's Rob. I have to say, 'tis guid to see you in a wheelchair and no' in bed. If you're as bad a patient as my Alec here, you're already giving our Maggie fits to be up and about."

Rob shook her hand, grateful for her warm smile and the effort she put into speaking English. "I can't thank you enough for taking Maggie's place this morning. It's been too long since she went to kirk."

"Och, 'tis my pleasure. And 'tis grand you realize how much a bit of time spent at our Lord's house will mean to her."

"I do that."

"We'd best be on our way, then," Alec said. "'Tis a bonnie day oot there. If you're allowed on the entry, Morag can wheel you oot so you can enjoy the sunshine and the sound of the sea sooking on the shore."

Maggie ran her fingers over his shoulder. "Do have Morag take you ootside. We'll no' be gone long."

As soon as they left, Morag released the brakes on the wheelchair. "Maggie told me you're a coffee drinker, and since our son Graham is too, I'm thinking I'll brew a pottle to take out on the entry."

"Now that sounds guid," Rob said with a wide grin.

"I don't know how much you know about coos, but they can be contrary though loving beasties," she said, pouring his second mug of coffee. "We raise the Hieland cattle, bred for generations in Scotland, mainly because they are so gentle and hardy. But if you treat them too well, they soon forget they're coos and think they can come into the cottage any time it pleases them."

"You mean they just show up in your house?"

"They do that." She laughed. "We had one heifer that wouldn't stay out of the cottage. She found a way to nudge the latch on the gate open. If the door to the cottage was ajar, we'd find her in the bedroom or the bathroom Alec put in when we got a generator, smelling everything with her broad, wet nose, her long, curved horns covered with towels and anything else she happened to get them tangled in."

Rob chuckled. "I can just see that. What did you do with her?"

"Och, we put up with it 'til winter and then kept her in the byre. By spring we'd bred her and her thoughts turned elsewhere."

They talked briefly about her son, Graham. "I admire you trusting the Lord to bring him home," Rob said, thinking about Maggie's fears.

"My faith isn't always so strong, but then I get on my knees and turn him over to the Lord again. After all, our Faither luves Graham even more than Alec and I do."

By the time Alec and Maggie returned, Rob considered Morag a friend. She hugged him and said she hoped they would meet again soon. "I don't think I've ever seen our Maggie so happy," she whispered.

The moment they drove off, Maggie sat on the stone bench beside his wheelchair. "I can't express how grand it was to see Hugh again." She smiled at the memory. "And you must have been a mind reader. His entire lesson this mornin was on intercessory prayer and having the faith to believe it would be answered. My Bible is filled with passages I've underlined, so every time my faith falters, I have our Lord's words to help me back to the right path, especially Philippians 4:6-7."

"And what does that say?"

She reached for her Gaelic Bible and thumbed through it quickly. "Here it is." She took her time translating from the Gaelic into English. "'In nothing be anxious; but in everything by prayer and supplication with thanksgiving let your requests be made known unto God. And the peace of God, which passeth all understanding, shall guard your hearts and your thoughts in Christ Jesus.'"

"Sounds familiar. The wording's a bit different."

Her breath froze. "What do you mean—different?"

"I grew up with the King James version of the Bible. A lot of thee's and thou's."

Her apprehension evaporated. "Och, is that all?"

"That's a guid passage. About sums it up, doesn't it?"

"It does that. I'm certain I'll have that one memorized by day's end."

"I hope to meet your Hugh someday. He sounds like a man who takes his orders directly from the Lord."

"So many times his lessons seem directed right at me, like this mornin, and I've heard other folk say the same. I'm sorry Morag had to miss it, but I did see Alec taking notes as fast as I was."

"Then you're feeling a wee bit better?"

"I am, but don't stop praying for me. I've a ways to go before you report back to duty."

He was alone in the back cockpit of a Stearman PT-17 bi-plane trainer, five thousand feet over Randolph Field in Texas. He tromped on the rudder and put the bi-plane into a deep bank, reveling in the keening song the wind played through the wing-wires and the early morning chill on his face. He caught a glimpse of the sun just peeking over the horizon between the two yellow wings and grinned like an idiot. There was no feeling like this anywhere on earth.

He tromped hard on the right rudder and put the plane into another steep bank. The moment he recovered, he checked his altitude and pulled the P-17 into a climb. His head pressed back as he gazed through his goggles at the vast, cloudless sky above him.

A sudden harsh noise drove the dream from his mind as the raucous barking of seals brought him awake. Not now! He closed his eyes and concentrated on recapturing the dream. But it was gone, and with it the peace, the sensation of being a whole man again and at one with the heavens.

He wiped his stinging eyes. Oh Lord, he could never give up flying. He couldn't!

Chapter Nineteen

Elspeth came every other morning. As the weather warmed, they moved out to the flagged-stone entry for Rob's lessons. His vocabulary grew at an amazing speed. Scots was easy compared to the German, French, and Italian he'd spent years learning.

An expert on island folklore, the old woman delighted him with tales of the early inhabitants of Innisbraw.

"Do you know the Selkie tale?"

"Everybody on Innisbraw knows it, young and auld. Why? Has Maggie shared it with you?"

"So many times I've lost count. I'm just wondering if you know why the fishermen stopped chasing and allowed her to marry the crofter."

She laughed into her sleeve. "I told that tale to Maggie many times when she was a young lass. If a reason ever existed, it's been lost over the years."

No help there.

His imagination was caught by her description of the skerries—large, sharp rocks far from shore, hidden by high seas, and visible only because of the conflicting waves they generated.

"You are certain to hear our skerries mentioned by the fishermen here on Innisbraw," she said, "for the nearest lifeboat is on Barra, over twenty-five kilometres north of us. Over the years, many of our trawlers have been lost to the rocks lurking out there in the Atlantic to our southwest. Of course, the German U-Boats keep our trawlers from fishing the Atlantic now, but once the war is over the danger will still be there."

That night Rob tossed and turned as he sought sleep. Once the war ended, how could the fisherman of Innisbraw be expected to brave the Minch and the vast Atlantic without a rescue boat of their own, especially with the added danger of hidden rocks? There had to be some way to get the island its own rescue service.

On an afternoon toward the end of his third week on Innisbraw, Maggie tiptoed into his room. Calf and thigh cramps had plagued him from midnight to dawn and by noon he was so exhausted, she insisted he take a nap.

She stood over him, studying his braw face, so peaceful in sleep. Though she cooked large dinners and suppers from the poultry, fish, and vegetables the folk brought almost daily, he insisted on only scones and coffee for breakfast and he still looked much too thin.

His dark moods were less frequent as his physical progress accelerated, but he remained a complex, secretive man. Remembering his tenderness the night she suffered the nightmare brought a flush of warmth and unbidden thoughts flooded her mind. What would it be like to be married to him, to be living together in a wee cottage, perhaps planning a family? Och, how could she even think such a ridiculous thought?

He woke, staring straight up into her face as though he could read her thoughts.

"You've been asleep for almost three hours." Her words tumbled out fast as a rain-swollen burn. "Any longer and you'll no' sleep the night."

He stretched and grinned. "Right. So what's on the agenda? I'm no' up to exercises 'til after supper."

Calm down. He's too perceptive by half. "There will be no exercises the day. And you have a visitor."

"A visitor? Who?"

"'Tis Hugh. He told me on the Sabbath he's wanted to come ever so long but he hasn't wanted to bother you."

His look of dismay surprised her. Hadn't he said he wanted to meet Hugh?

"If you don't feel up to seeing him, I know he'll understand. I told him you had a bad night." Was he afraid to meet Hugh? Had she given him the impression Hugh was an unapproachable spiritual giant? "Hugh's always been an anchor in my life. All the time I was growing up, he was never too busy to offer encouragement. And he has a fine sense of humour. His face always crinkles like a smiling wee elf when he's especially pleased."

Rob rubbed the side of his nose, a habit she recognized. He was uncomfortable.

She hated to keep Hugh waiting, but sat on the side of the bed. "I remember one time when I was only a lass he told me about my mither and faither's courtship—how Faither was like a golden eagle, already a physician and exploring the vast, unlimited reaches of his profession. He compared Mither to a rock dove, young, tender, wanting nothing more than her warm cottage nest filled with healthy bairns."

"Why don't I meet him out on the entry? I could use some fresh air to clear the cobwebs—och, moosewabs."

Relief replaced anxiety.

He reached for the trapeze while she retrieved the wheelchair and set the brake. By the time she guided his legs into the chair and he sat, sweat beaded his forehead.

"Do I still look fit for company?" he panted.

"Och, you look grand." She laughed, releasing the brakes. "On you go then. I'm going to start coffee for the both of you."

"Coffee?"

"Some Americans drink tea and some Scots prefer coffee. Our Hugh's one of them."

He propelled his chair down the hall. Though the few people he'd talked to on Innisbraw said only good about Hugh, the preachers he'd encountered growing up tended to be a bit smug or sanctimonious. He hoped he wouldn't have to sit through a lengthy lecture on redemption, or even worse, sinning. He gritted his teeth, wheeling his chair through the foyer. This was one encounter he wasn't ready for.

Come on, Savage. Stop acting like a sacrificial lamb going to the slaughter.

The front door stood open. A short, rather stocky man stood at the railing, looking out at the harbour. He had thinning brown hair with greying sideburns and wore dark brown tweed slacks, jacket, and a white shirt, open at the collar. He turned as Rob approached. "Colonel Savage." He extended his hand. "I'm Hugh MacEwan. I've been looking forward to meeting you."

"Rob, if you don't mind." He gave a good shake.

"And I'm Hugh. We don't stand on formality here on Innisbraw." He gestured with a wave. "I'm always astounded by the view from up here on the fell. The kirk and manse are hidden by so many trees, I seldom have an opportunity to drink in so much of God's bonnie handiwork." Voice pleasant, manner relaxed.

"Sit down, Hugh." Rob wheeled his chair closer. "Maggie says the bench is comfortable."

Hugh sat with a sigh. "'Tis grand to finally put a face to the man we've all been holding up in prayer."

"That's verra kind of you."

When the minister smiled his round face transformed from a man in his fifties into a mischievous imp of indeterminate age. If he were heavier—with a white beard and eyebrows—his round cheeks, cherubic nose, and twinkling eyes would make him the perfect model for Faither Christmas on a Yule card. "Och, 'tis our obligation, and indeed our privilege, to ask God's help in your recovery."

"Appreciate that. Never was a man to turn down prayers."

Hugh studied the lad. He was a bit older than expected, pale and thin, but a verra, verra tall man, broad-shouldered and braw. Perhaps this was what set the auld widows' tongues flapping. "We'll have to get you over to the kirk. 'Tis one of the few places on Innisbraw with tall trees."

"Is the rest of the island too rocky?"

"Och, Innisbraw was once heavily forested. Most of the trees were cut down for boat building by the Norlanders who conquered our Western Islands long ago. Also, in the spring of nineteen and twenty-one, a fierce gale uprooted more. With the harsh winds stripping the soil away every winter, much of the island is now too rocky to support strong, healthy tree roots."

"How do the crofters get by then? If the soil's so bad is there enough girse for their sheep? And I'm told there are quite a few coos on the island as well."

"Indeed there are. Coos are no' a problem. They don't eat the girse down to the soil but sheep crop it too close and the soil erodes. The crofters are having a rough time, though I must say, they are a hard-working, optimistic lot."

Rob eyed the minister. He sounded kind and seemed sincere. "So, how long have you been here on Innisbraw?"

"Almost twenty-five years. This was my first kirk, and if our Lord is gracious enough to grant my fondest desire, 'twill be my last. The guid folk of Innisbraw are unique. Have you met many of them?"

"Only some of the MacPhee family, and Alec and Morag MacDonald, and Elspeth, of course."

"The other folk are most likely wanting to protect your privacy. I know everyone's been most curious about our newest resident." Again, the impish smile. "So you met Alec and Morag. 'Tis folk like them that are the backbone of this island. Did they tell you they are both members of the Innisbraw Island Council?"

"Nobody's said anything about that."

"I only mentioned it because it shows how dedicated they are in trying to save our dying island, which is the focus of the Council right now. But tell me, what do you think of our Elspeth who chairs the Council?"

"I'm becoming verra fond of her. She's one of the most comfortable—yet stimulating—folk I've ever been around."

"She's also the prayer warrior who has held the folk of Innisbraw up before the Lord most of her life."

Maggie appeared, carrying a laden tray.

"Och, Maggie, lass, is that coffee I smell?" Hugh patted his belly. "And scones. How could you know I missed my dinner?"

"I didn't." She placed the tray on the bench next to him. "But Rob is always starving about now. He never makes it from dinner to supper without a bite of something he calls a 'snack.'"

"A man after my own heart."

She handed Rob his mug and a scone. "Don't eat too much. Sim brought us some partans. I'm making partan bree for supper."

Thank God for the Scots lessons. Partan was what the Scots called crab. Crab soup. Sounded delicious. He bit into his buttered scone and took a swig of coffee. "Maggie's a grand cook. If I'm no' careful, I'll outgrow my verra limited wardrobe."

"Och, you look like you could stand to gain at least twa stone."

"A stone is fourteen pounds," Maggie said.

"I know. That was one of those obscure facts I learned in school."

They ate in companionable silence. Hugh MacEwan was unlike any minister Rob had ever met. Not once had he approached, either obliquely or head-on, the state of Rob's immortal soul. "So, how large is your congregation?"

"Everyone on Innisbraw is a member, though we've lost most of our young folk either to the war itself or war-related turns. We only kept our young fishermen because they're considered a part of the Merchant Service, sworn to use their trawlers and creelers for rescue work, and their catches provide much needed meat. The lack of guid turns has caused a large problem we're going to have to solve before this war ends, or we're going to go the way of the other Western Isles."

"From your tone of voice, I take that as a negative. What do you mean?"

The minister fidgeted, brushing crumbs from his knees and tapping his fingertips on his empty mug.

Rob prepared to plead fatigue to give Hugh an out.

"Och, the folk of the Outer Hebrides, I'm ashamed to say, have been slowly losing their moral fibre. The war has helped halt it to a degree, taking the young lads from the street corners where they used to congregate every evening, swilling whisky before moving out into their villages, causing damage and mayhem with never a thought to anything but their own dark pleasures."

Rob glanced at Maggie.

Her teacup shook as she raised it to her lips.

"Maggie's never mentioned a problem with drunkenness and law-breaking here."

"No' on Innisbraw as much as the other islands, though it was quickly heading in that direction when I first came here."

Maggie refilled his mug.

The minister took several sips before continuing. "When the government set up the dole, the crofters began turning more and more of their labour over to their womenfolk while they drowned themselves in whisky they bought with the silver they were given for doing nowt."

"How could one man stop all the men from doing the same thing?"

"It was the Lord, no' me," Hugh said. "The Lord, with the help of all of the women on this island who were hearing the truth from the pulpit every Sabbath. They refused to do all the work and the men faced three choices." He ticked off his raised fingers. "They could beat their wives into submission, which would have dire repercussions, do the work themselves, or lose their crofts because they weren't being productive."

Rob sat back with a frown. "I'm confused. Maggie told me that the Laird of Innisbraw, Donald somebody, gave the crofts to the folk a long time ago, doing away with the need to pay rent. Who could take their crofts away?"

"The Donald also set up an Island Council to govern the island," Maggie said, "and when the folk on the Council saw things going awry, they got verra strict. If a crofter was unwilling to try to make a living, his land and cottage were taken away from him and given to another"

"And this actually worked?"

"Over time," Hugh said. "Remember, Innisbraw was never in such dire straits as the other islands. Over the past years, the men of Innisbraw have regained their sense of duty, refusing the dole, working hard, and no' abusing their womenfolk." He dabbed at his forehead with his napkin. "But I suppose we'll always have the problem of no' enough work for those lads about to graduate from school."

It never occurred to Rob such conditions existed far from the large cities in Scotland. "So you're afraid that when the war ends your young lads will either no' come back or those who do will begin drinking and carousing because they have no work to do?"

"Aye. 'Tis most unfortunate there isn't any industry to keep our young folk here and occupied with skills they can be proud of."

"Has anybody looked into starting something?"

Maggie set her empty teacup on the tray. "I don't know what it could be. The soil is too poor and rocky to support more than coos and sheep and a few goats or cuddies, and the fishing is too difficult to bring in much silver."

"How about boatbuilding?" Rob turned his chair. "What's that large shed down by the pier used for?" he asked, pointing to a structure at the east of the pier.

"Nowt now," Hugh said. "It's stood empty for as long as I've been here. Maggie, lass, did John ever tell you why it was built?"

"I remember him mentioning it was a herring-processing plant before they built so many on Barra."

Rob continued to study the shed, his mind churning with ideas. "With some fixing-up, it looks big enough to house a boatbuilding business—and the first boat built would have to be a rescue boat for Innisbraw."

"But who would we find to run such a business?" Hugh asked. "There isn't a boat-builder amongst us. Or, are you planning such an enterprise once the war is over?"

"What I know about boats, you could put in a thimble, but surely there are some old-timers around here with a wee bit of experience."

"Perhaps there are, but there is no silver for such a venture."

What right did he have to interfere in other's lives? "Leave it to an incomer to appear on their shores and tell the folk how to improve their lot."

"Och, 'tis never presumptive to offer ideas," Hugh countered. "We will have to give it some thought." He grasped Rob's hand. "I hope I haven't given you the wrong impression of our island. The vast majority of our islanders are guid, God-fearing folk." He didn't wait for a reply but got to his feet. "I'd best be off for I've a lesson to work on, but before I go I would like to offer a prayer." He continued to hold Rob's hand as they bowed their heads.

"Our gracious Heavenly Faither, we thank You for this bonnie weather and I thank You for guiding my steps this way the day, for it has been a joy and a pleasure to meet our Maggie's Rob." His fingers tightened. "Give this lad Your strength as he works to regain the use of his legs, for we are reminded by Your Word that where twa or more are gathered together, You will be in their midst, to listen, to council and to give help in time of need. We also ask that You give Maggie guidance as she ministers to Rob. We pray this in the name of Your Son, who gave His life for us on the cross. Amen."

Rob shook Hugh's hand again. "I'm happy to have finally met you."

"And I'm most happy to have met you. I must say, for an American who's only been here a few weeks, your Scots is remarkable."

"Thanks to Elspeth's lessons."

"Then, knowing our Elspeth, I expect you'll be learning the Gaelic next."

"She's mentioned it but I don't think I'll have time before I report back to duty."

"Och, you'll be back here once this terrible war is over."

Again, that simple statement, first Elspeth and now Hugh. Perhaps their prayers didn't concern only his recovery.

***

"So what do you think of our Hugh?" Maggie asked as the minister made his way out to the path.

"I like him. He's no' like any minister I've ever met."

"Since he's the only one I've ever had, there's nobody I can compare him to, but I am glad you like him. He's the glue that holds us together. Hugh just teaches the Word of God. He's no' consumed by kirk rules."

"He didn't mention religion much."

"He won't, unless you bring it up. And, as far as religion is concerned, I know what you mean, but our Hugh always says Christianity is no' a religion, but a relationship between folk and their Lord. His teaching from the Word every Sabbath is his greatest gift."

Rob mulled the afternoon over while trying to get to sleep. The problems plaguing the other islands had been news to him.

His thoughts returned to the business solution he had presented. A boatbuilding enterprise intrigued him. It would surely help with the problem of unemployed lads after the war. He knew nothing about boats, but he could learn. He was certain the shed would be ideal, and as he had said, the first boat built would have to be a rescue vessel for Innisbraw.

But what about this talk about him coming back to the island after the war? Even if things worked out between him and Maggie, how could he return if it meant giving up flying? And despite what he'd told Maggie, there was a good chance once he reported back to duty, he would be killed. With all the sorties and missions he'd flown since the beginning of the war, the odds were stacked against him. Only the Lord having a plan for him to fulfill here on Innisbraw would change those odds. Could that be possible?

Chapter Twenty

Una Hunter swept the last of the sandy soil from her stone flags and eyed Susan and Mark Ferguson's cottage across the path, hoping to see Susan bring her spinning wheel out into her yard. Her thin lips curled in a semblance of a smile when she recalled her luck at cornering Flora MacPhee after kirk last week. Thank the gods Flora liked to talk.

Flora had mentioned one succulent morsel Una had been passing on for days. This was the information she had been waiting for since that Yank appeared on Innisbraw and the folk greeted him with open arms. But she needed to tell some of the younger lasses closer in age to Maggie McGrath if she hoped to stop that lass from making the biggest mistake of her life.

"Fools," she muttered aloud. "Don't they know Americans are liars who spin such a beguiling tale of love and commitment even the 'wee folk' in Scots lore would hide in shame in their small, dark caves at being so outdone?"

She sat on a stool, plucking aimlessly at a small hole near the hem of her apron, thoughts reeling with mind-pictures of betrayal and heartbreak. She had been about Maggie's age when she met him. "Edmond," she whispered. Oh, no. She had promised herself years ago never to think his name again, let alone speak it.

Repressed spectral shadows coalesced into burning images.

Young, tall, handsome.

Brown hair and hazel eyes beneath heavy eyebrows.

Wealthy enough to afford a holiday on the Isle of Skye.

He swept her off her feet at a ceilidh in the village of Portree where she and her mother were visiting her mother's family. She lied to her mother, pretending to be out with cousins and their friends when she met him every day on a hidden grassy hillock behind the village. They walked and talked for hours, holding hands, the spark of attraction so palpable she could scarcely breathe. Their first kiss chaste, barely the meeting of lips. But to a lass who had never been kissed, it filled her soul with ecstasy. She returned his next kiss with abandon, tears flooding her eyes.

They met every day for over a week. His promises of undying love soon broke her weak protestations. They found a secluded glen where they lay on the soft grass, expressing their love.

He would start his last year of university in New York. Next summer, he would return and take her to America, where they would be wed. He described his family's huge, palatial home where they could have an entire wing all to themselves.

He left her in the glen, alone, heart afire with love.

Three months later, she knew she carried his child. Emotions vacillated from ecstatic happiness to dread that her mother would banish her from the cottage before Edmond returned. Somehow, she would have to hide her condition.

That fear never became a reality.

She awakened one night, clutching her abdomen in agony. She pleaded to God repeatedly for help as she crept from of the cottage and made her way through the darkness and cold, biting wind to the sheepfold where she collapsed, thighs sticky with blood.

She was so weak, it took hours to clean up the mess, both in the fold and on her body. Just before dawn, she sneaked back to her pallet, shivering from pain and the icy water she used from the burn. She curled into a tight ball beneath her thin bed-cover, grieving.

She had lost Edmond's child.

No one would ever know, not even him.

"And I swore then I would never again pray to the Christian God who turned a deaf ear to my pleas," she muttered aloud. Her favorite aunt spoke the truth. The Christian God was a myth. Only the ancient goddesses of the Celts would help her from now on, especially Scathach, the Dark Goddess, a warrior woman and prophetess who once lived on the Isle of Skye.

She clenched her fists. Day after day, hours at a time, she waited on the dock the following spring and summer, eagerly meeting each trawler that unloaded its fish in Oban, hoping Edmond had booked passage to Innisbraw on one of them.

"You never came, you liar," she spat.

His vow of undying love, of marriage into a prestigious family—the flame that flared inside her so high for well over a year—was quenched to an ember by the first rains of autumn.

Every year it became more brittle until it hardened into a tiny kernel of black hatred, sharp and unforgiving.

※

Susan Ferguson spent a delightful hour at the shore, wading through the surf, the hem of her dress held high above her knees, face turned to the warm sun and brisk, salty breeze.

Several gannets took off from a nearby rock, their nearly two-metre wingspans still amazing after all the years she had watched them. Her attention turned to the dark bed of kelp bobbing in the surf far offshore, and the white-crested breakers marching slowly over the shallow seabed toward the sandy strand. She breathed a prayer of gratitude she lived on such a bonnie island.

She held a bouquet of daisies, buttercups, and eyebrights picked from among the myriad of wildflowers to decorate the middle of the supper table when Mark came home from his three-day fishing trip this een.

She tingled at the thought of his braw, broad face breaking into that heart-stopping grin when he spied her waiting on the dock. He would toss back his unruly mop of red hair and run toward her, strong arms outstretched.

They did not have many worldly goods and their cottage, which had belonged to his long-buried parents, was small and auld, but they had each other and that was enough—aye, that was more than enough.

She crossed the main path and turned her bare feet toward home, glancing over her shoulder at the sun. There was still plenty of time to make a hearty skillet of skirlie and a batch of bannock to go with whatever fish he brought. Mark was always ravenous when he got home and it wasn't only for food. Her cheeks flushed at the thought of the very thorough luving they would share this night.

Her happy thoughts were dashed when she spied Una Hunter crossing the small path. No' now, when she was in such a guid mood. It was so difficult having a nosey neighbor always spying on them from between the lace curtains over her front window. The bent, greying spinster with her sunken cheeks and almost lipless mouth was the last person she wanted to see the day.

"Susan!" Una called out in the Gaelic with her high, irritating voice. "Why didn't you ask me to join you on your walk?"

She brushed past the older woman and opened the door. "I'm in a hurry, Una. Mark will be home this evening and I have supper to start."

"Isn't that just like a man, staying away for days at a time, expecting you to drop everything when he decides to show up again?"

Susan's irritation grew. "That's not true. Mark works hard to fill his fish hold."

Jealousy churned in Una's belly as she eyed the comely young woman with eyes the colour of the sea and a thick black braid thrown carelessly over her shoulder. Stupid, lovesick girl. How did she know her husband spent all his time in Oban unloading and selling fish? After all, he was a man.

She followed Susan into the small cottage. "Of course Mark works hard," she said, forcing a calmness she didn't feel. "But I must talk to you about Maggie, you being a friend of hers."

"Maggie?" Susan reached into her aumrie, removing a canning jar turned blue with age. "What could you possibly know about Maggie?" She filled the jar from a bucket of burn water and arranged the flowers on the table. "She spends all of her time at the infirmary tending her patient."

"That's just it," Una said. "Rumor has it he won't even allow her out of his sight."

"Rumor, is it," Susan grumbled, reaching for her griddle. "You'd do best to keep such thoughts to yourself. You know what our Hugh says about sins of the tongue, and I saw Maggie at kirk last Sabbath. Alec brought her while Morag stayed at the infirmary."

Una opened her mouth. "She—"

Susan said, "I'm certain Maggie doesn't want to leave him with others for long. Remember, his legs are paralysed."

Una edged closer. "Flora told me he's in a wheelchair now and getting around fine. You were at the dock when they landed, so you know he is a handsome man, though much too old for our Maggie. Not only that, but Flora hinted that the two of them are ... you know ... carrying on improperly." All the older women she shared this with were aghast, and promised to pass the word on.

Susan laughed. "Good for them!" she exclaimed, pulling a tin of flour from the aumrie.

Una sneered. "You young girls are all alike, your heads turned by a handsome face and sweet words." Una wagged her finger. "You can consider yourself warned right now, young lady. Yanks cannot be trusted. They'll lie for no reason, except to get what they want, and then walk away from the mess they've made of other's lives without a backward glance."

Susan measured the coarse oat flour into a large bowl. "I'll not listen to any more of your gossip, Una. It's hurtful and wrong—as wrong as Flora was for 'hinting.'"

Una wanted to strike the impertinent lass. She strode out, slamming the door.

Susan would see. All of the young girls would soon see what came from trusting a man—especially a Yank.

Chapter Twenty-one

Sunday morning, Rob once again urged Maggie to attend Sabbath services. "And I don't need a nursemaid," he said, deflecting her protest. "I'll stay on the entry with the brakes locked on my chair. I can't get into any trouble doing that."

Maggie glanced at the wheelchair. But what if something happened? What if he fell or—

"Please, Maggie. Do this for me."

"For you?"

"For me. I mean it, Maggie. I need you to go to kirk."

She looked into his pleading, green-flecked hazel eyes. "You really won't move? No' at all?"

"No' even a centimetre."

※

She savored the walk down the fell. A light onshore breeze teased tendrils of her hair, tickling her forehead, while the sun flickered across the waves of the Minch, and transformed delicate wildflowers into fluttering butterfly wings. Overhead, the vast, cloudless sky offered a glimpse of heaven.

How could her father bear spending most of the year in Edinburgh with its dreich grey buildings, wee twisted streets, and soot-blackened seventeenth-century tenements collapsing against one another like decaying teeth crowded into a narrow jaw?

Only the MacPhees, Elspeth, Alice Ross, and five fishermen and their families lived on this side of the island. She hoped they had already left for kirk. She needed time to be alone to thank God for the bonnie day and for Rob's progress, and to prepare herself for hearing the Word of God.

Once she passed the pier, Maggie's eyes darted eagerly over the landscape. So many details had escaped her when she rode in

Broken Wings

Alec's cart. She eyed the large fish-packing shed Rob had pointed out from the infirmary entry, a part of the scenery so long she had forgotten all about it.

Her steps slowed as she passed the five small fishermen's cottages tucked into a wee cove on the shore. Crab, lobster, and crayfish baskets, buoys, and an old upturned rowboat cluttered the sandy girse between the thatched dwellings. The keening cry of a gull interrupted her reverie. She glanced at her watch and hastened her pace.

The tall trees surrounding the manse and kirk brought a smile to her face. Horse chestnuts shot forth their tall, white blooms and broad rowans crowded out small firs trying for a foothold. When the kirk came into view, her heart swelled with love. Over one hundred years old, it stood proudly, stones darkened by the harsh winter weather, stained-glass windows rising majestically to the eaves. It had been a haven of peace and strength all her life.

Hugh still stood on the broad entry, his arms open wide in welcome.

Not late, after all.

"So how's our lad?" he asked, hugging her.

The familiar texture of his tweed jacket, rough against her cheek, brought tears to her eyes. "Getting stronger with each passing day."

"That's guid to hear. 'Tis an answer to all our prayers."

He released her to greet another latecomer and Maggie walked to her usual pew. Usually several of the older women stopped her for a short blether, but this day they didn't even return her smiles. Only a few women smiled warm greetings, Morag, Susan Ferguson, Elspeth, and Flora among them.

She dropped to the kneeler, confessing her confusion and unease. Rob had sacrificed a lot to give her this opportunity. Unwilling to allow her foolish mind to conjure up anything to interrupt her joy at being in kirk to hear Hugh's lesson, she raised her gaze to the large stained-glass picture of the Risen Christ behind the altar. As always, peace washed over her. "Thank Ye, Faither," she breathed.

When she got to her feet, Una Hunter turned in the pew in front of her and gave her a glance that chilled to the bone. How she disliked the woman. Una had a wicked tongue and often stirred up unrest out of bits and pieces of nothing. Och, Maggie needed to pray to love her enemy.

She lost herself in the first hymn and then in Hugh's message. His lesson that day concerned seeing that one's relationship with the Lord was strong and healthy before attempting to help others. She took copious notes and marked several passages in her Gaelic Bible. How had he known exactly what she needed to hear?

After the Benediction, she made her way out to the entry and hugged Hugh, thanking him for the lesson. "You always feed my soul."

His brown eyes danced. "That's because we are all so much alike," he said with his elfin smile, "and our needs so similar."

Morag and Alec and then Elspeth, Flora, and Angus stopped her at the bottom of the steps. They talked for several minutes before she turned her steps toward home. As she approached the main path, a large group of older widows, Una Hunter in the lead, stepped in front of her.

"We need to hear how you are faring," Una said in the Gaelic. "I do hope you aren't working your fingers to the bone over that stranger."

"Stranger? What do you mean? What stranger?"

"Why, that Yank airman you have to take care of," Catriona Douglas said with a shake of her head. "Your father must not have a brain in his head, asking his own daughter to do such difficult, thankless work."

Maggie's temper flared. So that was it. Una had latched onto Rob as a sacrificial goat for her viper's tongue. "I would hardly call my patient a stranger," she said, voice cold, "since he was the commander of the air base I served on. As for the work, you seem to forget I'm a nurse well trained in rehabilitative therapy. 'Stranger,' indeed."

She stepped aside but the women pressed forward, stopping her again.

"We're only here because we care about you, Maggie," Una said. "We don't want that Yank to turn your head with sweet words and then leave you alone and broken-hearted."

Maggie placed her hands on her hips glaring at the faces around her. What had Una stirred up this time? "I won't listen to another word of such nonsense. I'm in a hurry," she said, pushing through the group. "The colonel has been alone far too long as it is."

"Watch what you two do in private," Dolly MacSween called. "After all, we've always thought you a good girl."

Maggie had heard enough. She shot them a scathing look and walked quickly up the path, all thoughts of savoring the walk back to the infirmary pushed from her mind. *What they did in private.* What did that mean? Who had been spying on them, and why? And what did they think they had seen?

Tears welled in her eyes. How dare those old women lay in wait for her, pretending to care, when they only wanted to stoke their small-minded, gossipy minds?

Angus stopped his cart and offered her a ride but she refused, saying she needed to stretch her legs. Elspeth and Flora both smiled and wished her a "guid-day." Had she imagined it, or were Flora's cheeks redder than usual? Flora. Och, dear Lord, had she somehow started all of this? It seemed hard to believe. Like most of the women on the island Flora did love to gossip and often eagerly took part in spreading news across the island, but never in a mean, hurtful way.

Maggie walked quickly, climbing the hill as fast as she could. Her heart fluttered when she saw Rob, sitting in his wheelchair on the entry, close to the railing, where she had left him. He smiled broadly and she waved, choosing to wipe the past unpleasantness from her mind. She couldn't wait to share Hugh's lesson with him.

Chapter Twenty-two

John McGrath radioed Maggie Monday morning to inform her he would be arriving on Innisbraw the following Friday and apologizing for the delay. She acted giddy with excitement as Rob lowered himself from the bed into his wheelchair.

"Faither'll be amazed at your progress." She hugged him the moment he was seated. "Then, if he thinks you're ready, he'll let you start raising your hips, and I've told you what the next step is—walking!"

Her exuberance contagious, Rob's heart pounded. "That's what I've been working for." Not long now and he'd be free of this chair and the frustration of being dependent on others for things he'd always done for himself. "Believe me, I'm ready."

"I know you're ready. Do you realize how far you've come in the few weeks we've been here? Though you have some numb spots on your lower back, the feeling in your legs and feet has returned." She gave him a saucy smile. "And your appetite, too."

She looked like a delighted lassie who had just bested him in a game. "My appetite's back because you're feeding me real food." He grinned. "Only somebody on their deathbed could eat what they put on those trays in Edinburgh."

"What do you expect with rationing so tight? Be careful what you say or I'll skite your lug—och, box your ear."

That afternoon, Maggie left Rob sitting in his wheelchair on the entry with firm instructions not to move while she walked down to the harbour to get the mail. He thought about the doctor's visit, how he'd hoped to find an answer about how to alter McGrath's opinion of him in the Selkie tale. But nobody knew what had changed the fishermen's minds.

He fidgeted, hoping Maggie would return with copies of the

Broken Wings

Edinburgh *Scotsman* newspaper her father posted to them every few days. Being out of touch with world news frustrated him so much he read the papers from cover to cover—with the exception of the section devoted to the Gaelic readers.

The moment he caught sight of Maggie walking slowly up the hill, he realized something was wrong. She held her handkerchief pressed to her mouth and her steps were hesitant. Twice, she pulled something from her sweater pocket, stopping to read it.

She must have received bad news.

She would be fashed, but he unlocked the wheelchair brakes and moved closer to the steps. "What's the matter?" he called when she turned off the main path.

※

Maggie couldn't trust herself to reply without breaking down. There had to be a mistake. When they were at the Royal Infirmary, her commanding officer had given her until late August before she had to report to duty in London. She pulled her new orders out of her pocket again, but her eyes were so filled with tears she couldn't read them.

Rob called her name.

Och, he was far too close to the steps! She dashed forward, tossed a roll of newspapers into his lap, and grabbed the back of the wheelchair, pushing him away from danger. "I told you no' to move," she cried. "What were you thinking? You could have fallen."

"Why are you crying? What's happened? Maggie, talk to me."

She closed her eyes for a moment before wheeling him over to the bench where she handed him the letter from her pocket and sat, tears trickling down her cheeks.

He read it quickly, then let it drop to the stones. "They can't do this. They can't just order you to report to London in a week."

She swiped angrily at her tears. "Of course they can. They can do anything they want."

He pulled her onto his lap.

"I'll hurt you."

"You're light as a newly hatched pewlie gull. We can't let

them do this, Maggie," he whispered as she buried her face against his chest. "We haven't had enough time."

⁂

Rob felt like his heart would beat out of his chest. He couldn't lose her so soon. He pressed his cheek against the top of her head. He'd been a fool, tiptoeing around the thought of returning to Innisbraw after the war, concentrating on what he would lose if he did, agonizing over the thought of having to someday give up flying, refusing to admit even to himself how much she meant to him. If what he felt for Maggie wasn't love, he couldn't imagine what love could be.

Faither, please help us. I've been blind, thinking I had so much time left to make up my mind. And now ... it might be too late. How could he bear the following months without Maggie's smile, her soft voice, even the short but well-deserved tongue lashings she gave him?

But worst yet, what if he lost touch in the confusion of war and had to live the rest of his life without her?

⁂

Maggie's thoughts tossed like a burn in winter, water dodging and boiling over rocks. It had been hard enough knowing she would have to leave before Rob was walking completely unaided, but how could she leave him now, just before his first steps between the parallel bars? How could she give competent care to other injured aviators when she'd only be thinking about how he was doing, fretting about his progress, and how they could manage to meet again? He was right. They hadn't had enough time.

He raised his head and held her at arm's length. "Radio your faither. He's the one who got your orders taken care of last time. He can surely do it again."

"I ... I don't know." She wiped her face with her soggy handkerchief. "He did warn me my orders could be changed."

"We have to try, Maggie. We can't give up without a fight." He pulled her close again. "Please, Maggie. Please say you'll try."

She nodded.

⁂

Doctor McGrath reacted to her news with disgust. "What are they thinking? We haven't the room to bring the colonel back here. Every bed is taken and we're even turning away patients who want to schedule elective surgery. I may have to send somebody from my staff to Innisbraw to take over his therapy, though I don't know how I can do what I must with one less qualified nurse."

"So you will call Leftenant Colonel Smythe and try to get my orders changed back to the original date in late August?"

"Of course. But it will take time to reach her. And don't count on me being able to convince her to rescind your latest orders. I've been afraid this might happen, with the war in the sky escalating and never enough RAF nurses. I'll call you the minute I have some sort of resolution to this muddle, but it could take days."

※

Neither Rob nor Maggie ate supper that evening. Both slept poorly and were exhausted when dawn broke. Maggie fixed his coffee but he asked her not to bake any scones. "I couldn't swallow a bite of food around the lump in my throat."

Too upset to argue, she acquiesced.

※

Elspeth sat in her rocker before her peat fire, rubbing her throbbing knees. After all the years she'd spent kneeling in prayer, her body should be accustomed to the abuse. She couldn't get Maggie and Rob out of her mind and her aging joints added to her frustration. Though she had prayed for them for over an hour—for Rob's continuing progress, for Maggie's strength to care for him properly—her distress had not eased.

She picked up her walking stick and pulled herself to her feet, hobbling to the window overlooking the entry where she pushed aside the lace curtain. Usually, the first glimpse of the riot of colorful flowers and vegetables in her garden brought a burst of joy, but this morning they appeared only an inconsequential blur. Something was happening in those precious lives and she had to find out what, so she could pray effectively.

Angus's cart pulled up in front of her cottage and she smiled, pulling her shawl over her shoulders.

Right on time.

※

Though Rob and Maggie were reluctant to burden Elspeth, it didn't take the cannie old woman long to wheedle out of them the reason for their long faces.

"Then there's no time to waste. Our Heavenly Faither needs to perform one of His miracles. I trust you've prayed about this?"

"Of course," they said in unison.

"Most of the night," Maggie added.

"I'm going into the foyer where I can petition our Lord without any distractions," Elspeth said. She paused in the doorway. "Have faith. Our Lord will no' abandon you in your hour of need."

Elspeth waved Angus off when he came to pick her up an hour later, telling him Maggie would radio when it was time for him to return. She prepared tea and coffee and took it into John's office. "Drink this," she ordered. "What guid will it do if you become ill?"

Their drawn, exhausted faces brought tears to her eyes. Och, the de'il worked hard to keep these twa from fulfilling what the Lord had planned for their lives.

By suppertime, they still hadn't heard from John. Maggie insisted that Elspeth go home. "It's too late to hear anything," she said, voice breaking. "Please say you'll continue to pray."

"You know I will. And I'm going to have Angus radio Hugh. If ever there was a need for the folk to gather for prayer, 'tis now."

※

Una Hunter heard the kirk bell pealing and removed her apron. She always heeded a call to kirk, not to pray, but to find out why the bell had rung. She joined the flock of folk heading for the kirk, hurrying to join the group of widows walking together. "Perhaps that Yank has taken a turn for the worse," she told them, keeping her voice low. "Wouldn't that be a convenient way to get him off the island?"

"I'm not certain that would be a good thing," Dolly MacSween said. "After all, he was injured fighting those wicked Germans."

Una bit back a sharp retort, careful not to antagonize Dolly who had lost her husband and only son in that first, terrible war.

"I don't think our talk with Maggie has done any good," Catriona Douglas said after looking around to make sure she couldn't be overheard. "That patient of hers is still on Innisbraw."

"Leave it to me," Una said. "I'm far from finished with the likes of him."

Once she heard the reason for the call to prayer, Una was furious. That meddling Hugh. Without Maggie's nursing, that Yank would have to leave. She dropped to the kneeler and bowed her head with the rest of the congregation, plotting another way of get rid of that aviator in case Maggie found a way to stay.

The plan she'd hatched several nights ago was meant for later, but she might have to implement the idea. It could be dangerous, involving one of the men-folk, but the old sot she'd thought of had no scruples and constantly sought ways to make easy pieces of silver. She had no silver to spare but she did have a case of whisky she uncovered only days before when she'd been digging a hole in back of the cottage to make a wintering-over place for the potatoes someone was sure to give her. Probably spirits from the shipwrecked *Polly,* buried years ago in a hasty flight from the revenuers and forgotten. She'd have to make sure the old fool kept his mouth shut.

The folk took turns praying aloud, Elspeth offering the longest, most heart-felt prayer. While many of the younger men and women also offered prayers, Una clenched her hands into fists and locked her knees to keep from leaping to her feet and walking out.

Though her queasy stomach rebelled, Maggie fixed a pot of chicken bree and browned bannock on the griddle for supper. When she took the tray of food into Rob's room, she found him lying in bed, staring out the window, eyes bleak. He looked so pale she would have to force him to eat.

"I've made us some bree and bannock." She set the tray on the clothes-press. "I know you're no' hungry, but we both need to put something in our stomachs besides the tea and coffee we've had the day."

He didn't answer.

She bent over him and cupped his chin in her palm, forcing him to look at her. "You've worked too hard and too long to allow owt to keep you from walking. Please eat, Rob."

He grasped her wrist with a trembling hand. "I can't do it without you, Maggie. I'll never walk if you're no' here."

His desolate words penetrated her numbness. "Don't say that. You are going to walk again. You told me you're no' a quitter, Rob, but I'm no longer certain that's true."

His grip on her wrist tightened. "I also told you I'm no' a liar. Are you thinking that's also no' true?"

She tried to pull away.

He wouldn't release his grip.

Good. He was angry. She didn't like doing it, but it was a price well paid if it kept him from giving up. She stared down at him, willing herself to meet his steady gaze. "You may be right. If you can mislead me concerning your tenacity, how can I trust you to tell the truth about owt?"

His eyes darkened. "I've been called a lot of things, but nobody has ever called me a liar."

She didn't trust herself to answer. She couldn't back down now. He had to realize he couldn't quit even if he lost her encouragement. She swallowed and tried to still her trembling legs.

He continued to stare at her, as though delving into her soul.

She couldn't bear it. She pulled away, fled his room, and ran outside where she collapsed onto the bench, gasping for breath.

What had she done? She knew how important he considered truthfulness. No matter how good her intentions, she had just accused him of being a liar. *Heavenly Faither, help me. I've said such a cruel thing, and I didn't mean it. Help me, Faither, please*

Broken Wings

help me.

⁂

Rob pulled himself up with the trapeze and twisted and turned, ignoring the pain, fighting his reluctant muscles until his legs were off the bed. The wheelchair was not far away. He'd crawl to it on his stomach if he had to. Maggie thought he was a liar. He had lashed out in anger but only to cover his anguish. How could she even think such a thing?

He had to get to her.

He gripped the bars and lowered himself until he was hanging several inches above the floor.

His hands slipped.

He grabbed for the blanket at his side.

It slid from the bed.

He tumbled to the floor, hitting his nose on the bedside table leg, and upsetting the water pitcher, before landing on his left hip.

He lay stunned, panting as blood ran from his nose. He couldn't take a deep breath. His hip burned. He turned to face the wheelchair, gripping the floor with his fingertips to pull himself around. The boards were too slippery with water from the upset pitcher. He ground his knuckles into his smarting eyes and laid his cheek on the cold floor. What had he done?

But it didn't matter anymore—not walking, not flying—nothing mattered. Maggie had run away from him. He would never have an opportunity to tell her he loved her.

If she thought he was a liar, it didn't make any difference.

He would have to add her to that long list of those he had loved and lost.

⁂

A crash of breaking glass.

Maggie leaped from the bench, looking toward Rob's window. What happened? She swiped her sleeve across her wet face and tore into the infirmary, running hard.

When she reached his room and saw him on the floor, she dashed forward, bending over him. "Rob!" she cried. "Och, Rob, what have you done?" She leaped up and turned on the lamp, almost collapsing when she saw the blood on his face and the floor. She pulled a blanket from the bed and covered him, gasping with relief when he turned his head and looked at her. "Don't move," she said. "You're bleeding. I'm going to radio Angus for help."

He blinked as she reached the door.

"Talk to me, Rob," she said when she returned to his side. She brushed aside shards of broken glass and knelt beside him. "Please tell me where you're hurting."

He mumbled something.

She leaned closer. "Your nose is bleeding, but I'm more concerned about your back. How did you fall out of bed?" Her fingers shook as she took his pulse.

Racing.

She wanted to untangle his legs from the bedding on the floor but couldn't move him until she had help.

"Just ... just go, Maggie," he groaned. "It doesn't matter anymore."

"I don't understand. What doesn't matter?"

"Nowt."

Chapter Twenty-three

Maggie leaned over him, dabbing at the blood on his face with her handkerchief. "Och, what have I done to you? I didn't mean a word I said. I only wanted you to get angry so you wouldn't quit trying to walk. I'm sorry, Rob, I didn't mean to hurt you like that. 'Twas me lying, no' you."

He fumbled for her hand.

Angus and Edert pushed through the doorway. "We rode auld Jack up the hill. Didn't want to take time to hitch up the cairt," Angus panted. "What's happened?"

"Rob's fallen out of bed. Move that table aside and use one of those blankets to brush that glass and water away so we can straighten his legs."

It took several minutes of struggling before the three had Rob back on the bed, lying on his belly. "Should I raise John on the radio, lass?" Angus asked.

"No' yet." Maggie probed the healing scars on Rob's lower back with her fingertips. "You have to tell me if this hurts," she said to Rob.

"Left side," he mumbled. "Hip."

"No' your back?"

He shook his head.

She studied a red mark on his left hip carefully. "Angus, Edert, I'm going to untuck the bottom sheet and you can help me roll him over on his back."

The moment they had him turned, he groped for her hand. "Did you mean it? About making me angry?"

"Every word."

Rob wanted to believe her. It made a kind of perverted sense that a young lass who had never known the weight of loss and loneliness would blurt out such hurtful words thinking it would help. He had to believe her or their future together was over. "Och, lass, you didn't have to scare me to death to get me to eat," he whispered, trying to smile.

"I want you to move your legs as far apart as you can."

"Now?"

"Right now."

She watched him slide his legs apart. "Any pain?"

"No."

"Then lift your right leg, slowly, slowly. Aye, like that. Does it hurt any more than usual?"

"The same."

"Then your left, verra slowly." He had landed on his left hip when he fell. Her breath froze as he raised and lowered the leg.

Was his face paler? She pressed her trembling knees against the bed. "How much did that hurt? And don't make light of it. The absolute truth."

"Same deep ache as always."

Breathing deeply, she hugged Angus and Edert. "I can't thank ye enough for coming so quickly and all your help. He can't have injured himself badly if he can do leg-lifts."

"Och, then the guid Lord answered our prayers, isn't that right, lad?" Angus said with a broad grin.

Edert mumbled something unintelligible, his shy smile answer enough.

"Thank ye," Rob said as the two left the room.

Maggie washed the blood from Rob's face, relieved at the colour returning to his cheeks.

"You bumped your nose on something when you fell," she said, helping him into clean pyjamas.

"Sorry I made such a muddle of the bed covers."

"Och, 'tis easily remedied." She pulled the top sheet from the bed, tucked in a fresh one, and finished with two clean blankets.

He took her hand as she raised the last blanket to his chest.

Broken Wings

"And I broke your pitcher. Hope it wasn't a family heirloom."

She sat beside him, smiling. "Well, if it was, we had a far larger family than I ever imagined. There's one exactly like it in all the patient's rooms."

"I'm ready for a bowl of that bree."

His hand no longer trembled and her stomach felt hollow. "So am I. Be back in a tick." While it heated, she sat beside him on the bed. "I only wanted you no' to give up." She rested a hand on his forearm. "I'm afraid it got out of hand and I didn't know what to say to undo my hurtful words."

"Och, you know what a clumsy oaf I am. 'Tisn't your fault I act before I think."

"But everybody at Edenoaks said you never do anything without planning every move."

"Something personal is different. I told you once I always put my foot in my mouth, only this time I forgot how high this bed is and ended up shoving my whole body in."

His attempt at levity could never erase his words as he lay on the floor, body twisted, face bloody. *"Nowt matters anymore."*

"The bree is surely hot by now," she choked, escaping to the kitchen for another cry, praying for forgiveness the entire time.

They each ate a bowl of bree and a piece of bannock before she swept up the broken glass, stacked the bowls, and took them into the kitchen. She didn't wash them. That could wait for morning.

※

Rob's hip had a light bruise the next morning, and a small red mark rode the bridge of his nose. "I'm fine, only a little stiff."

Maggie watched him do his exercises before rubbing his back and legs with lotion, kneading each muscle carefully.

※

They spent two more fruitless days staring at the radio, willing John to call. Their only messages were words of encouragement from Hugh and a few of the other islanders.

Next morning, Rob slumped in his chair in John's office. Would this waiting never end? Losing Maggie now could mean the end to everything that made life worth living. He felt like a waist-gunner about to take off for his twenty-fifth and final bombing strike. Would he survive to step out the fuselage door at the hardstands, or be carried out with a blanket over his face—

"I know we've each prayed about this," Maggie said, breaking into his dark thoughts, "but we've never prayed together." She scooted her chair closer and reached for his hand.

He clutched her fingers like a drowning man grabbing a lifeline.

"Our precious Heavenly Faither, we come to You with fearful hearts. Please forgive our lack of faith to trust in Your plan for our lives." Her words flowed with ease, as if she were having a conversation with a dear friend. "Give us Your peace, Lord. And above all, we pray for Your perfect will." She squeezed Rob's hand.

His turn. He had not prayed aloud since childhood and hesitated, stumbling over his words, overly conscious of Maggie's presence. By the time he offered a hoarse "Amen," he was ashamed. Such a long way to go and so much to learn before he could consider himself worthy of God's attention.

Their call sign came over the radio. John McGrath's voice.

Maggie snatched up the mike.

"Maggie, lass, I'm sorry it took so long to get back to you, but Leftenant Colonel Smythe refused to give me an answer until this mornin. I threatened to go over her head to Brigadier Jones-Hilton with a complaint that I could no' be expected to do my best for our own lads if I had to work so short-handed. I'm afraid I may have made an enemy of Smythe ..." His voice faded for a moment before coming back strongly. "So I hope you haven't packed yet. You're to follow your original orders and remain on Innisbraw until late August. Over."

She fumbled with the Broadcast switch, hand trembling. "Och, Faither, I can't believe it. And I can never find the words to thank you enough. Over."

"I'll take a warm hug when I arrive, lass, but I'm thinking your gratitude should be to our Lord. I would have had to wait until next week, but Smythe had to postpone a meeting in London. Something about suffering a sudden bout of hives."

"Hives!" Maggie's bubble of elation threatened to lift her from her chair. "Och, at least it wasn't a plague of frogs."

McGrath's deep laugh echoed over the airwaves. "I'll see you Friday een, luve. Give my best to the colonel. Out."

"I can't wait. Thank ye again, Faither, and guid-bye. Out."

She threw her arms around Rob's neck, laughing and weeping, relief so palpable she wanted to shout her joy. "Hives, can you believe? Who says the Holy Spirit doesn't have a sense of humour."

Rob's laugh bubbled up from his belly. Had God really done this? Of course He could—but had He?

No matter how the Lord arranged it, his Maggie was staying. He inhaled deeply, feeling the knot of tension in his chest dissolve. He stroked her hair with trembling hands, eyes smarting with unshed tears.

Though he'd been in England for over a year, Rob had a difficult time adjusting to what they called "Double Summertime" in the UK. Clocks were set two hours ahead of Greenwich Time during the summer and one hour in winter, unlike the one hour President Roosevelt had established as "War Time" during the summer only in the States.

Because it was summer, and the island so far north, it never became completely dark at night and the sun rose a little after four in the morning. Knowing how he loved fresh air, Maggie never put up the blackout curtains in his room.

As Friday approached, it was not only the half-light coming in the window that kept him awake, but John McGrath's impending arrival. Once the doctor spent a few minutes with them, he would realize how much their relationship had changed since they left the Royal Infirmary.

They teased one another constantly and Maggie was very open with her affection. She occasionally kissed his cheek or rested her hand on his arm or shoulder, and they held hands while sitting outside on cloudless evenings, watching the vivid sunsets bathing the island in a brilliant scarlet, purple, and magenta glow.

Now that Rob could admit to himself that he loved Maggie, he wanted to tell her. It became harder and harder to keep his hands to himself. He longed to unpin her hair and bury his face in its soft, fragrant, ebony glory. He wanted to kiss her hands, neck, lips—oh, how he wanted to kiss her soft, full lips.

A small niggle of worry that his progress might hit a brick wall and leave him tied to a wheelchair lay at the back of his mind. But because feeling had returned to his legs and feet, he began experiencing a newfound confidence that in time, he would not only walk again, he would fly.

Fly.

If he resigned his commission and returned to Innisbraw after the war, he would never fly again. Even his dreams haunted him now. The dream he'd had about piloting the PT-17 had opened a floodgate of memories and he often dreamed of flying. He was always alone at the controls, feet working the rudders perfectly, while he lost himself to the feeling of peace that being at one with the sky always brought.

But he could not go much longer without telling Maggie he loved her, and his indecision about returning to Innisbraw could very well break her heart—or even drive them apart.

Though he prayed repeatedly, no solution presented itself. If only he had someone to talk to. Like Colonel Hal Fielding, his flight instructor at Randolph and again in the P-47 fighter. When they first met, Hal had seemingly ignored Rob's obvious fear of close relationships, never pushing, but always being a consistent sounding board. Over the years, they had developed a strong friendship. But that had been put on hold indefinitely when America entered the war and Rob was deployed overseas, caught up in almost daily sorties and missions. He had no idea where Hal was now. What could he do?

By Thursday afternoon, he needed guidance and he needed it quickly.

"Maggie, could you radio Hugh and ask him to drop by?"

"Hugh?"

"I need to talk to him about something—personal." Her understanding smile dissolved the knot in his stomach.

"Of course. Does it matter when?"

"The sooner the better."

Hugh walked up the infirmary steps an hour before suppertime. Maggie was in the kitchen, preparing their meal.

"I understand you want to talk," the minister said, taking a seat on the entry bench.

Rob locked his wheelchair nearby. Though no longer intimidated by the minister, he would still have a hard time voicing his fears. He cleared his throat and opened his clenched fists. "I have a problem I can't work out. I've prayed about it endlessly, but it's still there, as tangled as ever."

"Have you asked that God's perfect will be done?"

The minister's quiet question confused Rob. "Perfect will? I don't understand ... though now I think on it, I heard Maggie say that at the end of a prayer."

Hugh leaned closer. "God has a perfect plan for each of our lives, but there are times we pray for something that is no' included in that plan. Even though it might seem a logical, legitimate prayer to us, His answer may no' be what we expect or want."

"But how can we know His perfect will?"

"We can't. That's why every time we petition our Lord, we add, 'if it be Your perfect will.' That way, no matter how the prayer is answered, we're assured it complies with the plan He has for our lives."

Rob laid his head back and looked at the clouds playing chase across the sky. "I actually have twa problems, though they're all mixed together. The hardest is making up my mind to resign my commission in the Air Forces after the war so I can return here to Innisbraw with Maggie."

"So you luve her, then?"

"I do. But the second problem is, I can't tell her I luve her when I don't know where I'll be living when the war's over."

"Have you thought to make a list of the pros and cons of each choice?"

"I don't have to. Och, I know I'd miss being an officer in the Air Forces, but ..." His heart throbbed painfully. "I can't give up flying. I've wanted to be a pilot since I was a bairn and getting my wings was the happiest, proudest moment of my life."

Hugh nodded, steepling his hands. "And what and where will you be flying after the war, if you stay in the American Air Forces?"

"I don't know. I have no idea what the Air Forces will even look like after the war ends. There's only one thing I know for sure. I'll never fly a desk. I've known that since I took my first flight."

"Fly a desk? Do you mean having some sort of office turn instead of flying an airieplane?"

"Aye."

"So you have no particular aversion to living on Innisbraw?"

"I don't think there's owt I can't learn to live with, though I haven't really seen the island. It'll take time getting accustomed to the isolation, and I know there will be a lot of things I'm no' used to, like the lack of telephones and having to burn peat instead of wood. If it weren't for no' flying again, I'm sure I'd come to like it ... even all the walking."

"So you're confident you'll walk again?"

"I'm determined to make it happen. I just don't know how long it will take."

Hugh leapt to his feet. "Have you thought about getting one of those airieplanes that land on water? Though I've never seen one, I understand they make them."

"A floatplane?"

"Och, I don't know what they're called. I only know Malcolm's told me about the large ones the RAF uses. He's always having to avoid them in the harbour at Oban. Calls them flying boats."

"I never thought about that." Rob grinned. "And they make smaller ones than the Catalinas and Sunderlands the RAF uses. They don't have the speed or versatility of other small planes, but at least I'd be in the air." He turned and studied the short pier leading from the packing shed to the harbour. "I could build a hangar for her right down there, and though I wouldn't get in any flying during the winter gales Maggie's been warning me about, at least I'd have something to look forward to when the weather clears." He rubbed his stinging eyes. "Och, you've given me my answer, Hugh. I should have known the Lord would answer my prayers through you."

Rob couldn't share this conversation with Maggie yet. He had more praying to do. His thoughts kept returning to his talk with Hugh the first time they met. Yes, Rob had always had a love of planes, but could he build a rescue boat for Innisbraw after the war ended, too? He knew nothing about boats, but he could learn, couldn't he?

Hugh had suggested making a list of pros and cons. Rob used a sheet of paper Elspeth had left behind.

On the con side: he knew nothing about boats. Though he wracked his brain, he couldn't come up with another.

On the pro side: he could follow written directions, knew how to draft a plan and build something using that plan. He'd taken wood shop in high school and even helped build a house and several pieces of furniture when he was a senior. *And there are plenty of fishermen who will give me ideas if it means having their own rescue boat.*

But even after he built the rescue boat, he'd have to find a way to make a living. Could he gain enough experience building a rescue boat to start a boat-building enterprise on Innisbraw? He'd saved most of his pay for years, so silver shouldn't be a problem, and equally important was what a viable business could do for the island's dying economy. Boat building took a crew and that crew could come from some of those lads who were in the Army or Navy or had been forced to relocate to Harris, Lewis, or Scotland to find war-related, paying jobs. Perhaps he could even help in seeing that the young lads growing up on Innisbraw didn't take to whisky to fill their empty, aimless lives.

He slept poorly. So little time to make up his mind. John would be here the following evening, and if Rob wanted to let Maggie know how he felt about her, he had to face her father first. He prayed over and over for the assurance he was headed in the right direction, always adding, "if it be Your perfect will."

The moment Friday morning dawned, Maggie raced from task to task. She and Flora cleaned the infirmary while several crofter's wives solicited by Maggie cleaned the McGrath cottage.

It was a good thing she kept busy. Mind occupied with the pending conversation with her father, Rob would have upset her with grunts or one-word replies. He prayed constantly for the words to say to McGrath, unwilling to alienate the man who had done so much for him.

※

Elspeth voiced her concern when their morning lesson was over. "You're verra quiet this morning. Are you feeling poorly?"

"I'm fine. Just a lot on my mind."

"You look like a lad who's done an ill-tricket prank and is about to face an angry faither. Don't try to fool me. 'Tis John's return has you fashed, isn't it?"

She was too cannie to fool. He nodded.

Her faded blue eyes held his gaze. "Remember what I told you when you first came to Innisbraw? John is a verra protective faither, but that does no' give him license to run Maggie's life. 'Tis time you told him how you feel about the lass."

"So you know I luve her."

"Och, I knew that even before you did. Are you going to tell John?"

"Aye, but he's no' going to be pleased. I'm sure he has someone verra different in mind for Maggie. At least a Scotsman if no' an Innisbraw lad, and certainly no' a Yank tied to a wheelchair."

"John's an adult. He knows how time, especially during war, can alter our expectations. And surely you don't think you'll be in that chair much longer."

"Maggie thinks I'll be on my feet soon."

"And what do you think?"

"That I'll walk if it has to be on my hands." He shook his head and lowered his eyes. "I've been praying for God's perfect will but so much depends on what I say to John McGrath."

"Asking His perfect will can frighten you, can't it?"

"It can do. I don't want to make an enemy of the doctor."

"Your superior officers weren't your enemies, yet Maggie's told me how you argued with them to protect your men." She picked up her walking stick and waved it at the sky. "Just think of this as another problem when you're flying over perilous land, and your target is no' an object but John's implacability. How would you argue your position?"

He looked up at the sky, searching for the answer. "There would be so much flak and so many enemy aircraft over the target, the objective should be changed to an alternate. Too big a chance of casualties."

"I don't believe that for a second. Since when does Colonel Robert Savage back down from a fight?"

"It's been a long time since I've worn my colonel's cover."

"John's always seen you in bed or in a wheelchair—as a patient. Wear your uniform this een. 'Tis time to show him the real Rob Savage."

"You think that's the real me?"

"Of course. You were born to lead, Rob. Surely you know that."

He dressed carefully. He even asked Maggie to help him into his dress boots. Perhaps his crush cap would be a bit much, but he would have it handy. It amazed him how different he felt when he buttoned his blouse. Resolve replaced dread.

He had met two of his promises to the doctor, that he would love Maggie forever and not take her away from Innisbraw. The final one—not hurting Maggie—he would work on as hard as he could. He straightened his tie. Bless Elspeth. This was what he'd needed.

Maggie stood back and looked at him, face pale.

"Why the long face?" he asked.

She attempted a smile. "Och, 'tis just the sight of the uniform, I suppose. It brings the war into this room."

"And your nightmares with it?"

"I hope no'." Words so soft he could barely hear them. "It's just that there's so much more work ahead and it will take time, and I—"

"We have eight weeks left before you have to report for duty. And after this een, things are going to be different."

"Different? How?"

"You'll see." He tapped the end of her nose. "Have a little faith in Colonel Savage. I can still give a good argument for what I believe in."

"You'll ... you'll ask Faither to release you from your promises?"

"I will, but 'ask' may be too mild a word."

Her lips trembled. "Then, I'll pray Faither realizes what a good man you are, Robert Savage."

Rob waited on the infirmary entry while Maggie went down to the dock to meet her father. Elspeth had it right. John McGrath was no enemy. More like a commanding officer with an agenda of his own. Well, arguments about objectives were his specialty. He reached for his cap—might as well make the picture complete. He adjusted the crush and put it on, wheeling himself over to the railing.

Malcolm's boat was at the dock. Not long now.

Chapter Twenty-four

Maggie and John McGrath walked up the hill. The doctor talked with animation, his arm draped around her shoulder, but Maggie kept her face turned toward the infirmary entry and seldom replied. As they drew closer, the apprehension on her face brought a stab of guilt to Rob's heart. A fragile lass about to be caught between two strong wills.

When they reached the entry, Maggie pulled away from her father and ran up the steps. She dashed to Rob and kissed his cheek.

He squeezed her trembling hand. "Welcome home, Doctor," he said in English, tone calm but resolute. "I trust your tour was successful." Den called it his kick-butt-and-take-no-prisoners voice.

McGrath pinned him with a steely gaze. "It's good to see you again, Colonel, and in uniform. Very impressive." Stern, confident.

"Seemed only right to dress for your return."

"Maggie's told me how far you've come. It appears you have made amazing progress."

"I have, and I'm ready for more."

"You realize it will take time."

"Of course. But the sooner we begin, the sooner I walk."

"Back to war."

Maggie's trembling increased.

Rob cleared his throat. "I'm certain your father could use some tea and I'd luve a cup of coffee. Take your time."

Smile fleeting, she rushed into the infirmary.

He wheeled himself next to the bench and removed his cap, running his fingers through his hair. Hoping he hadn't misread the man's character, he said, "Won't you sit down, Doctor? You must be tired after your long boat ride."

McGrath hesitated.

Surely, he wouldn't take the advantage by looming over his adversary.

The doctor sat on the bench. "I take it you wish to speak to me in private."

"I do."

"About what?"

"Aboot Maggie, and the promises I made," Rob said, slipping easily into the Scots. "I wint ye to release me from them."

Doctor McGrath, visibly shaken by Rob's command of the language, stared at Rob. "You've been busy, I see," he said in Scots. "But why should I release you from your promises? Nowt's changed."

"Och, but it has, Doctor. A great deal has changed."

"I still don't want Maggie hurt."

"Neither do I." Rob's deep voice brushed the silence like a steel blade over a well-oiled whetstone. "The last thing I want to do is hurt Maggie. I luve her too much."

John McGrath blinked rapidly. "Luve her! How can you say that now when only a few weeks ago, you said luve was too strong a word. Or were you no' being truthful?"

"I've luved her from the first moment I met her. It's just taken me a while to realize it."

"But you're certain now?"

"I've never been so certain of anything in my life."

"And what happens after the war, when you return to America?"

"I'm no' going back to America. I'm returning here to make a life with the lass I luve."

"On Innisbraw?"

"On Innisbraw."

McGrath leapt to his feet and began pacing. "I cannot believe this. How will you support her? Take up fishing? Or crofting?"

"I plan to start a Coastal Rescue Service on the island. The folk need it."

The doctor halted in mid-stride. "A Coastal Rescue Service? As admirable as that sounds, if you intend to crew a certified lifeboat, 'tis all volunteer work. There's no' a drop of silver in it."

"Somebody has to build the boat and that's only the beginning. With what I've saved from my pay, I have enough reserves to open a boat-building business."

"Och, you're daft. What does an American aviator know about building lifeboats or Scots fishing vessels?"

"I'm a fast learner. I've always luved working with my hands and I know my way around a wood shop."

Doctor McGrath sat again, face haggard. "So you no longer have any doubts about a complete recovery?"

"I have feeling now in every part of my body from the top of my head to the bottoms of my feet and no matter what it takes, or how long it takes, I will walk again." Rob met the doctor's steady gaze without blinking.

"And if you're killed when you return to duty? What happens to Maggie then?"

Rob felt the blood drain from his face. "Then she'll get over me in time, find another, and settle down on Innisbraw with the lad of her choice."

"You'll no' marry 'til you both return to Innisbraw?"

"Another promise?"

"Aye, another promise."

"No more promises, Doctor. Neither of us knows what the future holds."

"You'd risk Maggie's future on the whims of war?"

"There's a lot more than her future riding on this war we're fighting. Everyone's future hangs in the balance."

The doctor ran his hand over his face, his shoulders slumped. "I'll no' ask for your promise concerning marriage, then," he said, voice weary. "But I'll hold you to part of your previous promise. I don't want you to do owt that will hurt my daughter."

"I'll never intentionally do anything to hurt the woman I luve with all my heart. And I'll go even further. Unless something unforeseen happens, I'll no' marry her 'til I can walk her back down the aisle at kirk."

McGrath sat back, stroking his beard, internal battle obvious.

He must have been certain that sending an American to such a remote, primitive island would ensure his daughter's future on Innisbraw, would send the "incomer" back to the comfortable, easy life he'd always enjoyed. And how he must regret fighting to get Maggie's orders changed.

Two pewlie gulls swooped low over the entry and out to the path in a never-ending search for scraps of food. One suddenly dived, scooping something up in its beak. Wings flapped in ragged beats as it sought to escape its attacking companion. The frantic struggle of white wings, black heads, and rapacious beaks ended when one pewlie broke free, victorious.

No way to tell which won.

Rob's attention returned to the doctor.

John McGrath remained silent, competent surgeon's hands clenched together in his lap. It must be hard to realize that a child he'd nurtured and treasured since birth had grown up, that their relationship would never be the same. At least the doctor had one promise to hang onto—his precious Maggie would someday return to Innisbraw.

McGrath heaved a deep sigh and met Rob's gaze. "I can see why they put you in command of the 396th. I'm thinking 'tis time you stopped calling me 'Doctor.'" He extended his hand. "I prefer 'John.'"

Maggie appeared with a tray. The cups rattled as she set it on the end of the bench.

"I'll take my tea and retire for the evening," John said. "It's been a long day."

"Are you certain, Faither?" Maggie asked, voice quivering. "I can put together a late supper."

"Thank ye, lass, but Malcolm shared his tea and buteries with me and I'm verra tired." He kissed her cheek and turned to Rob. "Get a guid night's sleep, lad. On the morra's mornin, the real work begins."

"Guid-night, John. I'll be up bright and early."

Rob watched the doctor walk slowly toward his cottage. When the door closed, he reached for Maggie's hand. "On you come," he said, pulling her into his lap. I've something to show and tell you."

"Show and tell again?" Her eyes revealed her apprehension.

His heart raced when he took her face between his palms.

What if Maggie didn't luve him? He had often either hurt her or made her angry, which she had every right to be.

Perhaps she decided long ago she preferred a man without so many emotional hang-ups.

He took a deep breath and moved her face closer. "I want to kiss you, Maggie." He tipped her chin.

Their lips met.

She tasted every bit as sweet as he remembered—even sweeter—and her lips were soft and pliant as they moved beneath his.

He pulled her closer and kissed her lips for a long time, then the sides of her mouth, her cheeks, her forehead, her pulsing throat. He groaned. Och, he was drowning in the warm-honey fragrance of heather. He tasted the salt from her tears and he held her away. "Guid tears, or bad?"

"Guid, definitely guid."

He kissed her again—couldn't get enough of her—wanted to lose himself in her sweetness, her softness.

But she had to hear how much he loved her.

He held her away again. "That was the show. Now the tell." He took her hand, kissing each finger. "I luve you, Maggie McGrath. I luve you with all my heart and soul, and I always will."

Her face glowed. "And I luve you, Rob Savage, with all my heart and soul, and I always will."

Her tears wet his face as their lips met again.

Their kisses were gentle and sweet and so filled with mutual luve, he could barely contain his joy.

After weeks of longing, of a yearning so bittersweet, Maggie was in his arms where she belonged.

He chuckled.

"What's so funny?" she asked, smiling.

"There's something I've been dying to do since that first night we met." He rested a hand on her hair. "May I?"

She nodded.

His fingers sought the pins holding her hair.

They fell to the stones, one by one.

She shook her head and a mantle of soft, black, heather-scented glory surrounded him. He ran his hands through it, raised it up and let it slip through his fingers. He could scarcely contain his joy. He knew how the Selkie's crofter felt when she sang of her undying love. She was his. Maggie loved him.

Much later, she helped him into his pyjamas, two bright spots of colour staining her cheeks. "I'll help you with the transfer, and then I'll—"

"Come here, luve."

She stood before him, her chest rapidly rising and falling.

He took her hands and looked into her eyes. "I need to tell you something," he said, fighting for control. "As you already know … Och, I want to show you how much I luve you—but no' now. We'll wait. Someday, I'm going to pick you up and carry you to our marriage bed. Do you understand?"

She nodded hesitantly. "I understand," she said, her voice soft in his ears. "'Twill be hard to wait, but 'tis the right thing and a small price to pay for knowing you luve me."

"You doubted that?"

"Aye, though I wasn't even certain I luved you until I had that terrible dream. And even after, I feared to trust my feelings. I … I've never been in love before. It was only when you were so upset about having my orders changed that I began to hope you wanted to be more than my friend." She lowered her eyes.

He pulled her into his lap again and tilted her head up so he could kiss her soft lips. "Och, my Maggie," he breathed when their lips parted. "I've never been in love either. And you getting those new orders made me realize I couldn't live without you." He picked up a lock and brushed the side of his cheek. "I've thought of kissing you a thousand times, but I wanted to be certain I could walk again. And I had to talk to your faither, assure him I would never take you away from Innisbraw."

"The talk appears to have gone well."

He rested his forehead against hers. "As for being your friend, I want us always to be best friends, for that's the foundation for a lasting luve."

"It is that."

He grinned. "Then help me with the transfer before I lose control and ruin a guid friendship."

She leapt up and wheeled him into position. "Are you certain you can make it? 'Tis much later than usual and I know you're verra tired."

"I'll make it." He grabbed the bars and pulled himself up as she guided his legs.

Not a single bead of sweat. He could have flown into bed.

She pulled the sheet and blanket over him, and sat on the side of the bed. She leaned over, soft breath caressing his cheek, and kissed his forehead and cheeks, lowered her lips to his, their kiss gentle, and filled with mutual longing.

"Guid-night, my Maggie, my luve."

"Guid-night, my dearest Rob."

Chapter Twenty-five

Rob couldn't sleep.

Overcome with joy and gratitude, he couldn't even close his eyes. At last, he knew how it felt to love and be loved. *Thank Ye, Faither, thank Ye for my Maggie.*

A strange, new sensation tingled on his face. He touched his cheek with a fingertip.

Wetness?

Tears?

He brought his arm over his eyes and sobbed for the parents he couldn't remember, for all the days and nights he spent surrounded by others and yet so alone, for the countless young airmen who made the ultimate sacrifice. He wept until his breath came in broken gasps.

Maggie crawled onto the bed beside him. "'Tis all right." She nestled close, cheek on his chest. "Tears are guid for the soul," she whispered. "They water the seeds of joy."

It was time to tell her everything.

His fingers sought her hair. "I know I've hurt you by holding things from you, but I want to tell you now."

"What things?"

"My parents." He took a ragged breath. "My mither and faither."

"Only if you're certain you're ready."

"As ready as I'll ever be. I've never told this to anyone, no' even Den."

"You've never shared your grief?"

"I've wanted to so many times, but I couldn't. Not since I was a bairn. I couldn't cry when I watched my crewmen, bright young lads I considered family, being carried off on stretchers with blankets pulled over their heads, or saw planes go down piloted by men I've known for years." He fingered a lock of her hair. "I couldn't even cry when I thought I might be losing you. I've spent hours with my eyes burning and the tears so ready I felt like I was being torn in twa, but they wouldn't come."

"Och, luve, no wonder you've always had a sadness deep within your eyes. Everyone needs to cry. 'Tis a release our Lord built inside to help us bear our grief."

"You can't imagine what your luve means to me. I've never truly belonged to anyone until now."

She sat up, eyes swimming with tears. "Then tell me now and we'll cry together."

He almost lost himself again. His chest heaved with the effort to breathe. "My ... my mither and faither were killed in an automobile accident when I was a wee bairnie. I survived the crash somehow. Neither of my parents had family. I grew up in an ... an orphanage." He reached for her.

She closed her eyes and returned her cheek to his chest.

He could remember the orphanage so vividly, could still smell the pungent odor of caustic cleansers, the fishy odor of tinned tuna—one of the staples in a monotonous diet, prepared in oily casseroles or spread sparingly on thin slices of dark bread—and the scent of urine lingering in the hall outside the nursery.

And the noise. Thundering feet on old wooden floors and stairs, the constant babble of voices, babies crying, the squeak of un-oiled hinges every time someone opened or closed a door.

The constant confusion became harder and harder to bear as he grew older. The feeling of not belonging there, of not belonging *anywhere*, grew worse, especially after he spent almost a year in a real home with a man and woman who called him Son.

He cleared his clogged throat. "When I was five, a couple took me home with them. Said they wanted to adopt me." He took several deep breaths. "It was wonderful. They had a bedroom fixed up, filled with toys and books. Even a shiny new bicycle on the back porch they wanted to teach me to ride. They showed me how to play games I'd never heard of, took me for walks and to Sunday School, and taught me a special bedtime prayer. Gave me a red wagon and even a pup. I named him Shep. He slept with me."

"But something happened," Maggie said, voice soft.

His chest heaved again. "Aye," he gasped. "I don't know what. The day before I was to start first grade they called me in from the front yard. I'll never forget their faces. They were so serious and I could tell they'd both been crying. They told me they couldn't keep me, that they were taking me back to the orphanage." His voice dropped to a whisper. "And they did take me back. All the way there in the car, I felt numb, like something inside me died. I couldn't even find the words to tell them guid-bye. I wish I'd been aulder, braver. I never did ask them why. But I didn't need to. I wasn't the lad they wanted after all. They were always trying to make me laugh, but it was hard and I knew I hadn't laughed enough."

"That couldn't have been the reason."

"Mebbe no'. But to a lad almost six it seemed logical."

"They never came back? Even to explain?"

"No' even once. After that, I don't think I laughed, really laughed, for years. And I never could cry."

"Did anyone else choose you?"

"No, I ..." Memories shuffled through his mind like the pages of a photograph album turned too quickly: blurred images of disappointed faces and heads shaken as couples looked sadly at one another before turning their backs and leaving him alone again.

When he was young, he took each rejection hard, but as he matured, if he felt anything, it was relief. Never again would he love and lose. By the time he became a teenager, the interviews stopped and he found that secret, safe spot within himself where he felt nothing.

"Rob, please don't go away from me."

Maggie's tearful plea broke into his thoughts.

"Quite a few were interested but after spending time with me, they all decided I was too serious, too quiet. The aulder I got, the fewer times I was called to meet with visitors. By the time I was eleven or twelve, the interviews stopped."

"Och, how could you survive such rejection?" She buried her face against his chest, tears wetting his pyjama top.

"Please don't cry, lass. The staff didn't mistreat me. They tried their best, but there were just too many bairns and never enough silver. One young lass, Beth was her name, made certain I said my prayers at bedtime and even brought me books from the local lending-library." The memory softened his sorrow. "I devoured them. Couldn't read enough, for those books took me to places I never imagined existed—places far, far away."

An image of Beth's plump, dimpled face swam before his eyes. Always smiling, always happy. And it was Beth who arranged the outing that changed his life.

"And one day when I was seven, twa flying barnstormers came to a nearby farm. All us aulder lads were crowded into cars to see them perform." He paused, caught up in the wonder and joy of that special day. "I watched those twa auld Jennies take off and land with their paying passengers, the tall grass shivering from the spinning propellers, the smell of castor oil they burned making my nose tickle. I had no silver in my pockets, but in my imagination I made every flight they took."

She raised her head, smile filled with understanding. "And you wanted to fly from that day on."

"Och, and I did! I flew my bed, my desk. I even flew an old Sycamore tree out in the yard until I broke my arm in an unexpectedly rough landing. But that didn't stop me. I had it bad." He scrubbed his face on his sleeve.

"When did you actually get to fly?"

"No' till years later. But the most amazing thing happened when I was twelve. A United States senator stopped at the orphanage on one of his campaign tours. I'm sure he only stopped for the pictures and publicity, but his visit changed my life forever."

"How could that be?"

"For some reason, he took an interest in me. I was the tallest lad there by far, so mebbe I was hard to miss. He was easy to talk to, didn't ask personal questions, only wanted to know my favorite subjects in school. I had a hard time answering because I luved them all—Languages, Science, Math, English, History, Wood Shop. Before I could stop myself I even blurted out my secret desire to become a pilot. I must have piqued his curiosity, because he started writing me several times a year. By the time I was seventeen and graduated from high school, I had a stack of letters from him. I still have them, plus others. We corresponded for years."

"Then what happened?"

"Something I still find hard to believe. Senator Keyes sponsored me for admittance to West Point Military Academy."

"You were finally chosen."

He kissed her forehead. "I was finally chosen. And had the grades to make it."

"And your chance to fly."

"That's right. Four years later I was a commissioned second lieutenant in the Army Air Corps with a train ticket to Flight Training School at Randolph Field in Texas. And the rest is history."

Maggie lay silent for a long time, heart aching with mind pictures of that lonely, love-starved lad. She understood now why he couldn't talk about his past. He had hidden from the pain so long a deep scar covered the still-raw wound.

She sat up, looking down at him. "No wonder you've always felt socially awkward. You never had the normal experience of verbal give and take, of expressing yourself with confidence to your family, to those who would love you no matter what you did or said."

"I suppose you're right."

She gazed into his eyes. "Someday Rob Savage, you'll have that family of your own. I want a whole croft-full of bairns. I want eight."

"Eight?"

"Aye, eight."

"But Maggie, you'll be pregnant for years."

"With your bairns. You have your dreams. That's *my* dream."

He pulled her into his arms, head buried in the hollow of her throat. His husky whisper tickled. "I've died and gone to heaven."

Maggie stayed until Rob's breathing deepened. She slid from the bed and groped her way through the half-light to her room. She knew she wouldn't sleep.

She knelt beside her bed, remembering her grief when her mother died. But she had her faither and Calum. How could Rob bear losing both faither and mither?

And unlike her, he had been so wee, he had no memories to sustain him. She buried her face in the quilt, allowing the tears to fall, beseeching the Lord to ensure Rob never felt alone again.

John gave Rob a thorough physical and watched him do his leg lifts. "I'd say you're almost ready for the last steps before I put you on the parallel bars," he said when they sat on the entry that evening. "Your incisions have healed verra nicely and you feel the pin prick all the way from your hips to your toes. You've made an astonishing recovery."

"I had a lot of encouragement." Rob squeezed Maggie's hand. "I wonder if you could do me a wee favor."

"A favor, is it?" John snapped his fingers. "Och, I forgot to tell you about the wireless radio I promised to bring. There isn't a single one to be had in Edinburgh. Several of those working at the Royal Infirmary live across the Firth of Forth in Dunfermline or Kircaldy, so I have them asking about. I'll let you know when I have any news." He studied Rob, his gaze penetrating. "Now, what's this favor?"

Rob couldn't fault him for being suspicious. "I want you to talk this lass into going to kirk with you on the mornin. She's only been twice and, besides hearing Hugh's teaching, she needs to get outside more."

John grinned. "That sounds like an excellent idea. Maggie, we're going to kirk on the morra."

John assured Maggie it was perfectly safe to leave Rob alone and he could see no reason why he had to stay on the entry. "Let him either wait in his room or outside, whatever he wishes."

Though still concerned, Maggie acquiesced and at 0930 she and her father left Rob on the entry while they walked down the path. A few wispy clouds parted for the brisk wind. Invigorated by the salty breeze, she listened as her father spoke about some of his work at the Royal Infirmary and the rumor they were thinking about adding on yet again to the frequently altered establishment.

"For a place of healing that was begun in the seventeen hundreds, that institution has outgrown its surroundings and moved more than most tinkers," he lamented. "I just hope they're no' thinking about another move before I'm ready to retire."

Maggie knew better than to ask when that might be.

When they reached the kirk, men and women greeted John, relating how sorely he had been missed.

Susan Ferguson ran to Maggie's side. "'Tis so guid to see you at kirk again." She kissed her cheek. "With Janet, Siobhan, and many others off to war jobs, 'tis so different from when we were young lasses. I was just telling Mark this mornin how much I miss blethering with you."

"I'm afraid you'll have to come up to the infirmary for that blether." Maggie returned her childhood friend's hug.

"That's what Mark told me, but you must be run ragged with a patient to look after and I never know when would be a guid time."

"I hang the wash every Monday mornin around 1100 hours while Rob's having a rest in bed. Come around to the back of the infirmary and keep me company."

"I will. Och, Mark's waiting. See you later."

Maggie's smile faded when she saw the pitying glances many of the old women cast her way. Her heart plummeted when Una Hunter, surrounded by a group of widows, hurried toward her father.

Not again.

⚜

"It's so good to see you home, John," Una said in the Gaelic, her cold, piercing gaze belying her words. "It's about time you came back to Innisbraw to rescue your daughter from the clutches of that Yank."

"What are you talking about?" His voice often grew gruff when talking with the only woman on the island he could not bear to be around. Her wicked tongue caused many a muddle over the years.

"Why, it's all over the island how he's working that poor lass to the bone, keeping her captive in that infirmary and turning her head with sweet-talk before he leaves her here alone and heartbroken as soon as he can walk."

"Have you lost your mind?" He took a step back. "What nonsense have you been spreading?"

Una pressed forward. "You're her father, John, and as her father it is your responsibility to protect that poor, innocent lass."

As he opened his mouth to rebut her tirade, Hugh came down the kirk steps, arms outstretched in greeting. John took Maggie's elbow and pulled her toward their minister.

"John," Hugh exclaimed. "'Tis so guid to see you attending kirk with Maggie. Welcome."

The two men hugged shoulders and shook hands before Hugh greeted Maggie. "You're looking a bit pale, lass. You need more time in the sunshine." He pulled out his pocket watch, face creasing into an elfin smile. "Och, 'tis time to begin the service. Walk in with me."

Una stood in the kirkyard after the service, watching John and Maggie ride off in Angus's cart. The corners of her mouth pulled down. So much for thinking John would rescue his daughter. Men were all alike—blind to each other's faults and untrustworthy.

It was her duty to rescue the lass before that handsome Yank with the silver tongue broke her heart.

And she had devised a perfect way to make it happen.

Chapter Twenty-six

The joy of newly declared love brought the same euphoria as taking off into a heaven ceiled with cloudless blue skies. Rob floated through the hours. The only thing bringing him back to earth was the grueling, painful therapy.

"You have to build up your abdominal muscles before you can raise your hips," John told him. "The abdominals act as a girdle that supports your back when you stand and walk."

"All right, how do I get started?"

"Modified sit-ups. Let me show you what I mean."

John's demonstration didn't impress. "Is that all? At one time, I could do several hundred sit-ups on an incline board."

"Then isn't now. Some of the nerves sending impulses to your back muscles were badly damaged and you haven't used your abdominal muscles for some time. 'Tis amazing how quickly they lose their tone."

"Do you know how the crew stationed forward of the wings enter B-17s? We grab the top of a small hatch in the fuselage, which is above our heads. Then, we lift our legs up through the opening and pull our bodies in. It might sound simple, but it isn't."

"Then you should progress quickly."

Rob laced his fingers beneath the back of his head and spread his elbows, took a deep breath, raised his head. Shoulders off the bed. Another deep breath. Pain shot through his back. *Use your abs.* He sat, sucked two deep breaths, and slowly lowered himself. *Forget the pain.* Down, slowly. Success. One sit-up.

The second one came easier, finding a rhythm. *Forget the pain. Control your landing.* Two sit-ups.

The rhythm faltered and the hurt grew. *Abs—use your abs, eejit! Exhale—louder! Falling too fast. Crash landing.*

John handed Rob a towel. "You meant what you said. I never imagined you could do almost three before you tired."

Rob scrubbed his dripping face, sucking in air. "Can't count the last one. Should have used full flaps on my descent."

"Och, you pilots." John's beard tilted with the breadth of his smile. "When you can do twenty of them in one session without severe pain, it will be time to start the hip-raises."

"Twenty?"

"Aye, twenty."

Rob worked every other day for the rest of that week, starting very early in the morning. John's return to Edinburgh loomed and he wanted to accomplish as much as he could before the doctor left. By the end of the week, he was up to fifteen controlled sit-ups and the pain in his back, though severe at first, gradually lessened.

The doctor congratulated Rob and gave Maggie his parting instructions. "I won't be able to come back for at least a month, so you'll have to proceed without me. Remember, lass, don't put him on the parallel bars at the beginning without Sim or Edert or some other lad at hand to catch him should he fall. If you try it alone, you could hurt your back badly."

"I'll remember, Faither."

Maggie walked her father down to the dock and saw him off. When she returned, she flew into Rob's arms. "Och, he's so impressed with your progress," she exclaimed, "and your determination." She kissed him with exuberance. "And, he says he's absolutely certain you'll walk again, and soon."

"I know I will."

By the end of the week, Rob completed twenty controlled sit-ups.

Maggie clapped her hands, laughing. "I'll give you five days of hip-lifts, and then we start the bars."

The hip lifts were very painful as more muscles were put to use, involving nerves still regenerating, but they became easier every day. At the end of the five days, he could do them smoothly and almost pain-free. Why had he dreaded them so?

Maggie sat on his lap on the entry after supper. "On the morra's mornin, we start the parallel bars. That's when the real work begins."

"I think I'll need a little extra luving the night. Need to build up my strength."

"How's this for a start?" She pulled his face to hers and gave him a very thorough, very long kiss.

That night, he had a hard time falling asleep. "Lord, I know I shouldn't be, but I'm so afraid. I could never have gotten this far without Your help, so I thank Ye. And please, please give me the faith I'll walk come mornin."

Angus showed up after breakfast. "I'm here to help," he said to Rob, "and 'tis a fine mornin indeed to take your first steps."

"But you've sheep to tend. Isn't it still shearing season?"

"I didn't bring my shears, but if Maggie has some scissors, I can give you a guid, close haircut." Angus laughed, slapping his knee. "Och, if you could see your face."

Rob attempted a smile.

Angus patted his shoulder. "Sorry, I'm a wee bit kittled up. Maggie asked me to send Edert but I wouldn't miss this for owt."

Maggie led the way as Rob wheeled his chair down the hall past John's office to the therapy room. Weights, benches, an incline board, and a set of long parallel bars filled the narrow room.

"Wheel your chair between the bars and wait." Maggie nodded to Angus. "Once Rob's on his feet, I'll remove the chair. Stand behind him and grasp him as high on the chest as you're able. Lock your elbows, but don't support his weight unless he falters."

Rob moved into position.

Maggie leaned over and kissed him.

Angus's mouth gaped.

"Och, Maggie lass." Rob groaned. "You turned my knees to jelly."

"On with you. Are you ready?"

"I'm ready." He set his mouth in a grim line of determination. For months, he had feared this day might never come. *Please,*

please Lord, I'm verra afraid. If it be Your will, help me walk.

"Reach up and grasp the bars," Maggie instructed. "Keep your weight evenly distributed and pull yourself to your feet as slowly as you can. When you feel in control, give a nod. I'll remove the chair, and Angus will be right behind you."

"On we go then." He grasped the bars and pulled himself to his feet, grateful for all the exercises to strengthen his arms and shoulders. He reeled as the room spun around him. "Och, I'm wobbly." He nodded.

"Take your time." Maggie removed the chair.

He took several deep breaths, toes tingling. How strange but exhilarating to feel the floor beneath his feet.

Angus's arms circled his waist, the man being too short to reach his chest.

"Is standing painful?" Maggie asked.

"Just the usual deep ache."

She moved in front of him. "Concentrate on sliding your right foot forward. No' far, only fourteen or so centimetres. Imagine you're doing leg-lifts." She beckoned him forward with her hands.

This was it. Only a few centimetres determined his future. If he failed he would have to give up Maggie, and without her ... He looked deeply into her eyes and concentrated with all his might.

Chapter Twenty-seven

Rob slid his right foot forward. Sweat stung his eyes.

Maggie blotted his forehead. "Perfect. Now, your left. Be careful, you're off balance."

Again, Rob concentrated. His legs trembled, but only a dull ache throbbed in his lower back. "Come on, Savage," he muttered beneath his breath. "Move."

His left foot moved several centimetres.

Maggie's eyes sparkled. "Now, slide your hands forward so you're balanced. That's right. Can you do it again? Both legs? Don't start until you're certain."

Angus's arms tightened.

Rob gulped in air and nodded. His right leg responded, then his left. Both legs trembled so hard, he feared collapsing into a heap on the floor.

"Angus, you need to move and support his weight from the front," Maggie said.

Angus slipped around to Rob's front as Maggie got behind him.

The wheelchair seat bumped against the back of his legs.

"Do you have the strength to lower yourself slowly? Just nod or shake your head. And be honest."

"Don't know," he groaned between clenched teeth. "Hurry."

The chair pressed his legs and they gave way. His sweaty palms lost their grip on the bars.

Angus grasped his denim waistband tightly, easing him down.

At last, he sat, chest heaving, leg muscles quivering.

Maggie wiped his face with the towel. "Och, Rob, you're the only patient I've ever had who's taken four steps on his first try."

He didn't care if his smile felt lopsided. It was only a few centimetres, but he had done it.

He had walked.

///

They spent most of the evening on the entry while Maggie explained the next phase of his rehabilitation, interrupted often by exuberant hugs and kisses.

"I can't wait to run again," he said as she walked beside his chair into his room. "I've always done a lot of running."

"Now, why doesn't that surprise me?"

When he lay in bed that night, he thanked God for allowing him to walk again—and for giving him Maggie. He turned onto his side, grateful he no longer had to spend all night flat on his back. He tucked his arm beneath his pillow, felt something on the sheet below his elbow, and pulled out a piece of paper, grinning. It was so like Maggie to leave him a note after such a momentous day.

He couldn't turn on the lamp because the blackout curtains weren't in place so he squinted in the half-light coming in the windows.

Yank.

This wasn't from Maggie, but it was written in English.

Be warned. You are being watched.

He held the paper closer to his face, stomach cramping. The tiny, old-fashioned handwriting was almost unintelligible and the pen had been pressed into the paper so hard the ink blurred in places. He narrowed his eyes and continued reading.

You may have fooled a few of the folk, but not all. Maggie is too sweet for her own good. Bad things can happen to good lasses. You are not welcome on Innisbraw, not now or ever! You must leave now before it is too late.

There was no signature, only a strange symbol, like an eye with an enlarged pupil, drawn at the bottom of the page.

He read it again and then again. How could this be? Sometime today someone had sneaked into the infirmary—into his room!—and left this paper for him to find. What was this all about? And who was it from? Few of the islanders even spoke English, let alone wrote it.

He started to wad up the note, then changed his mind and placed it in the drawer of the bedside table and lay down on his back, staring at the ceiling.

He was being watched. When? Why? But most importantly, by whom? He pictured all of the folk he had met on Innisbraw. They were so friendly. *Fooled a few of the folk, but not all.* Fooled them how?

They had mentioned Maggie. *Bad things can happen to good lasses.* Were they threatening her?

The meaning of the last two sentences was crystal clear. Someone on the island wanted him gone—forever. Those last words were definitely a threat.

He took a deep breath. It caught and splintered in his throat. His plan of making a life on Innisbraw no longer seemed as easy as he hoped. And right now, he was so vulnerable. Taking a few faltering steps on the parallel bars was a long way from being able to defend himself, let alone Maggie.

The pinched, old-fashioned penmanship probably meant the note had been written by a woman. But who? And what did that strange symbol mean?

He couldn't share this with Maggie. She worried enough about him. He could show it to John, but it would be almost three weeks before the doctor returned to the island. He punched the mattress in frustration. Why did this have to happen now, after he decided there was a way for him to return to Innisbraw after the war and still fly? He thought about the note most of the night, only falling into an exhausted sleep early in the morning.

When Maggie brought him breakfast he was dismayed by the amount of food on the tray. "What did I do, sleep through breakfast? That looks like enough for dinner."

She slid the tray onto his bedside table and placed her hands on hips. "You're on your feet now, so 'tis a real breakfast with sliced sausage, eggs, tinned beans, and fried bread. If you're still starving after you eat it all, you can have your scone."

He choked down every bite.

Broken Wings

The next three weeks dragged so slowly Rob was sure he was caught in a nightmare where time moved backward. Normally, that would have pleased him. He dreaded Maggie's impending return to duty. Now, he feared for her life. That note had mentioned her name so she could be in danger. He kept a close eye on her, spending as much time as possible with her and keeping such a tight rein she finally balked when he told her she didn't have to hang the washing yet again.

Though obviously puzzled, Maggie said, "If you're thinking I'm lonely oot there alone, I'll send word to Susan Ferguson, a friend. She spent last Monday helping me with the washing and I know she won't mind coming again."

He was wary every time they were on the entry or when she worked in her garden next door, keeping a sharp eye out for anyone on the path, fearing for her safety when not at her side.

Did he really want to return to Innisbraw after the war? He'd spent his childhood in a small village where taunts of "orphan brat" were a daily occurrence. Could he spend the rest of his life on an isolated island where he wasn't wanted?

Though he tried to press such negative thoughts from his mind, they returned night after night, interrupting his sleep. This must have been how the crofter felt when he hid the Selkie from the fishermen.

Only his work on the parallel bars took his thoughts off the note. Though exhausting, he kept at it, and after a week, could walk over two metres without having Angus or Edert nearby to catch him if he faltered.

Not good enough. He had to work harder so he could protect Maggie.

Chapter Twenty-eight

John McGrath watched Rob walk the entire length of the parallel bars and lower himself into the wheelchair with no help. "Grand. Maggie tells me you've been unusually quiet, but I can see you've been working hard. How's the pain?"

"Much better." Rob wheeled over and closed the rehab room door. "There's something I need to show you."

"Is there a problem with your legs, then? Or your back?"

"Och, no." Rob reached into the back pocket of his denims and pulled out the threatening note, handing it to the doctor. "I found this the night after I took my first steps."

John unfolded the paper and adjusted his glasses on his nose. He read it quickly, glanced at Rob, and read it again. "Where did you find this? And why didn't Maggie tell me about it?"

"I haven't told her. I found it 'neath my pillow before I went to sleep."

John read the note again. "Have you shown it to anyone else?"

"No one. But I'll be honest, John, I haven't slept well since and I've had the de'il's own time trying to keep Maggie in sight as much as I could. I don't like whoever sent that saying what they did about her."

"Nor do I." John leaned against the top of a parallel bar. "Now I can see why Maggie's worried. You look like you've lost some of the weight you put on."

"That symbol at the bottom of the page? Do you recognize it?"

John stroked his beard as he studied the paper. "I do, though I haven't seen anything like it in years. 'Tis called 'drosh shuil' in the Gaelic—an ancient Celtic symbol for the evil eye."

"Evil eye?"

"Och, just a bit of nonsense about a curse to bring you bad

fortune."

"Then, forget it. But I can't plan on coming back to Innisbraw after the war if Maggie's in danger or if I'm no' wanted here. I wo—"

John snapped his fingers. "Of course. 'Tis only one of our folk who don't want you here, no' many. I'm almost certain I know who wrote this."

"Who? I've wracked my brains, but I can't imagine anyone I've met doing something like this."

"I doubt you've ever met her."

"So it *is* a woman. I thought it might be by the writing."

John stuffed the note into his jacket pocket and thumped Rob on the shoulder. "The morra is the Sabbath. How would you feel about attending kirk and bearding the lion?"

"You mean face her down?"

"Exactly."

"As long as it doesn't endanger Maggie, consider it done."

The following morning, Angus, accompanied by Flora and their two younger bairns, pulled his cart up in front of the infirmary. Edert, black-haired and blue-eyed like his mother, had often helped Rob. The lad greeted the McGraths and Rob with a shy "hoy," before ducking his head. Rinait, their thirteen-year-old red-haired lass, gave Rob a saucy smile, blushed, and hid her face, coyly peeking at him from between her fingers.

After Rob and his chair were lifted into the cart, the two bairns jumped onto the back, dangling their legs. John climbed in to stand beside Rob, grabbing a slat on the side for stability.

They stopped for Elspeth, who smiled at Rob, eyes twinkling. "Och, what a joyful day this is going to be," she said as Angus helped her onto the bench beside Maggie and Flora.

Under other circumstances, he might have enjoyed the ride. Finally, a chance to get away from the infirmary. Instead of drinking in all the sights, he dreaded reaching the kirk. A direct confrontation with another man would be guid, if only for the mental stimulation, but a woman? He had no idea what to expect. His stomach clenched.

He made himself look at the scenery. The ever-present gulls lazily circled the inner harbour and old trawlers and creelers crowded the dock, rocking softly from side to side on an incoming tide. At the bottom of the hill, opposite the main pier, stood several stone buildings with slate roofs.

The only thing that held his attention was the large fish-packing shed. He turned in his chair to look at it until it was out of sight. His plans might go up in smoke this morning. So tense he couldn't swallow, he undid the top button of his uniform shirt and loosened his tie.

The kirk spire rose from tall trees ahead.

Lord, I'm verra nervous about this. I don't know what's going to happen, so I'll just have to ask You to handle it according to Your perfect will.

The cart pulled into the kirkyard. A larger than expected crowd gathered. Numerous carts stood behind a long driftwood pole, cuddies flicking tails and twitching ears at swarms of hovering midges. Bairns of all ages raced about, laughing and shouting as adults gathered in clusters, gesturing and talking.

The men all wore shabby woolen suits, white shirts, ties, and bunnets, and the older women, print dresses with knitted shawls. The younger women were clad in woven skirts and dressy sweaters.

The kirk caught his interest. Stone, like all of the buildings on Innisbraw, with a long covered entry, stained glass windows soaring to the top of a large nave, and an imposing square bell tower. The spire pierced the cloudless sky with a cry of victory.

Angus pulled the cart close to the entry. Edert and Rinait leaped to the ground before John alighted and hailed Alec MacDonald and several men Rob did not know to lift the wheelchair. Angus helped the women to the ground and drove off to park the cart.

Maggie rushed to Rob's side. "Well, what do you think?"

"'Tis magnificent. I'd no idea it was so large. It must seat everyone living on Innisbraw."

"Och, it does, and with room to spare now with so many leaving the island."

Broken Wings

John took Maggie's elbow. "I want to introduce Rob to some of the men. Why don't you and Elspeth go on in and take a seat in our pew?"

"Already? But Hugh isn't even out on the entry to greet everyone yet."

"Take Flora, Edert, and Rinait, too," Rob said, casting a meaningful glance at John.

"Aye, 'tis a guid idea," the doctor agreed.

"I need help checking on the flowers I sent down yesterday." Elspeth said. "On you come, everybody. Let the men-folk get acquainted."

Had John told her about the note or did she sense the tension?

Rob forced a smile. "On you go. I'll catch you up in a tick."

They walked up the entry stairs, Edert and Rinait hanging back, gazing with longing at the other lads and lasses racing about the yard.

Though John had said he wanted to introduce Rob to some of the men, the moment Maggie disappeared inside, he leaned down and whispered in Rob's ear, "The person we're interested in is approaching as I speak. I'm going to leave you to it, lad, but I won't go far."

Rob watched John herd the men a short distance away. A flurry of activity off his left shoulder caught his attention and he turned the wheelchair. A large group of older women hurried toward him, led by a small, bent-shouldered woman with greying hair pulled into a tight bun at the top of her head and a deep frown on her face. Why did she look so familiar?

She stopped inches from his knees. "How dare you!" she screeched in English. "How dare you desecrate this holy place with your vile presence?"

He stared at her, startled by her vehemence.

"You have been warned," she said, in a high, irritating voice. Her dark eyes glittered with malice as she glared at him.

"Your penmanship is a wee bit slutterie," he said in Scots. "It would help if you didn't press so hard on the pen."

Her mouth flew open.

He pressed the advantage. "Of course, at your age, you should be grateful you've been schooled to write."

"Did you hear that?" she asked the old women gathered around her. "Did you hear him insult me?" She repeated his words in the Gaelic.

Several of the women tsked and shook their heads, but the evil on the face in front of him gripped his attention. "Nowt I say could insult you," he said in Scots, meeting her malevolent gaze. "I'm too much of a gentleman to tell you what I really think of you and your kind."

She recoiled as though slapped. Nothing broke the silence, not a word or a bairn's laugh. Even the ever-present breeze held its breath.

She leaned so close he gagged at the sour odor of unwashed hair and body.

"Listen carefully," she hissed into his ear. "Leave Innisbraw, or Maggie is going to suffer a very unexpected and fatal accident. There is no way she can be protected every minute of every day." She pinched his arm as though emphasizing her words. "If you don't believe me, look in Maggie's room when you get back to the infirmary. A very able helpmate has left you my last warning."

Irritation flamed to rage. He grabbed the tops of her arms, pressing his fingers into her bony flesh. "If you so much as touch my Maggie, I'll break your scrawny neck." He shoved her away, chest heaving with the effort not to lash out with his fist. He reached to release the brake.

Something wet struck his cheek.

His hand came away with a glob of spittle and a red mist curtained his eyes. He wheeled after Una, catching her before she could reach the safety of the crowd. He grabbed her shawl and wiped the spittle on it, then turned the wheelchair toward the main path. He had only gone a metre when something hard and sharp struck his shoulder, then the back of his head, stinging enough to bring a grunt of surprise.

Shouts followed him but he couldn't stop. He fought the urge to return and strike the woman, an act he would ultimately regret.

He pushed the wheels as fast as he could.

Hands reached out to stop him.

He shoved them away, stopped his chair, and whirled around, fists raised.

John leaned over him.

"Let me go," Rob snarled, "or so help me, I'm going to lose it and knock that witch flat on her back."

"Where do you think you're going?"

"Someplace to cool off."

Maggie rushed toward them.

"Then I'm going to get Maggie back to the infirmary, use your shortwave to call the polis in Oban, and arrange for somebody to get me off this island."

"Polis! I doubt they'll arrest Una for what she's done. You can't let her win, lad. I didn't think she'd go so far, but you can't let her chase you off now."

Maggie's warm breath drifted over his face as she took out her handkerchief and wiped his cheek, then turned it over and pressed it to the back of his head. "You've a cut there, luve."

"Forget it," he said, voice gruff. "Please get away from me, Maggie. I don't want you hurt."

"I'm in no danger." She hugged his shoulders. "Morag told me what Una did to you. It was terrible, but Faither's right, you cannot let her run you off. No' when so many of our folk want to be your friends."

"Friends, is it?" He snorted. "I'm thinking the Jerries are friendlier than some I'll find here."

Maggie's lips brushed his cheek.

He flinched. "Don't kiss me there. No' there."

"But I must." She kissed his cheek again. "Una has been a bitter, vile woman for as long as I can remember. But the other women are just lonely auld widows with nothing to liven their tedisome lives. You can't throw away everything for one woman. Please, luve, listen to me."

"You don't understand. You didn't hear what she told me. As soon as I know you're safe, I have to leave Innisbraw, Maggie. As much as I wanted to belong here, I never will."

She stared at him, eyes wide. "Then ... then we'll leave Innisbraw together."

"You can't leave. This is your home. These are your folk. You belong here."

"Without you?"

Her anguished cry pierced his heart. That evil woman would do exactly what she threatened, and he had to see what she meant by looking at Maggie's room. But how could he tell Maggie her life was in danger? How could he bear watching her fear each day?

He pulled Maggie close and buried his face in her hair. He couldn't stay on Innisbraw if it put her in danger. He was about to break Maggie's heart.

A hand gripped his shoulder. Hugh leaned over him, face pale and drawn. "Please listen to me, Rob. I think Angus should take you and Maggie back to the infirmary now, but I wouldn't be in a hurry looking for a way off the island. In a few days all the terrible things that happened this mornin will seem like a bad dream."

"It isn't what she did to me, Hugh. They could hurt my Maggie." Rob wanted to take the words back. He had revealed too much in front of her.

"John came to the manse last night and showed me the note. No one will hurt the lass," Hugh said. "I guarantee you that."

"What note? What are you talking about?" Maggie asked. "Who wants to hurt me?"

"Somebody left a threatening note beneath Rob's pillow a few weeks ago. He's concerned about your safety."

"That's why you've barely let me out of your sight and didn't want me to hang the washing alone? You don't understand. Nobody on Innisbraw would harm me."

He reached for John's arm. "I need to talk to you alone. Now."

John nodded. "Lass, go tell Angus to get his cairt and bring it around. We need to get Rob back to the infirmary so I can have a look at the cut on his head. Hugh, why don't you get the folk settled down inside the kirk?"

The moment they were alone, he bent over Rob. "I saw her

whispering to you. What did she say?"

"That unless I leave Innisbraw Maggie is going to die. Now do you see why I want to call the polis?"

"But that's just nattering. What can an auld woman do to a young lass like Maggie?"

"She said she has a man helping her."

"But who? I can't think of a single man on Innisbraw who would harm my lass."

"You don't know what's in every man's heart."

⁂

While John rounded up some men to lift Rob into the back of the cart, Maggie looked for Una in the crowd. Alec and Mark Ferguson held her arms at her sides. Maggie marched forward, chin high, chest heaving. She stopped and stared at the one who had hurt her Rob.

The woman's smirk was more than she could bear.

She slapped Una's face.

Una staggered for a moment, then tore her arm loose from Alec's grip. She raised her hand with thumb, pinkie, and forefinger clasped together, only ring and middle fingers standing straight up. She waved the hand at Maggie, eyes glittering. Some of the older folk in the crowd gasped at the ancient hand sign for the evil eye.

Maggie raised her two forefingers and made them into a cross, staring into Una's eyes for a long time, before whirling around, and making her way to Angus's cart.

Chapter Twenty-nine

The Sabbath service was brief. No music, just prayers, and a short lesson. When silent prayer ended, Hugh quoted scriptures in the Gaelic concerning the sins of the tongue, most from the book of Proverbs, the last from James 3:6. "And the tongue is a fire, a world of iniquity. The tongue is so set among our members that it defiles the whole body, and sets on fire the course of nature, and it is set on fire."

His gaze lingered on the pew filled with guilty women. The widows sat in stricken silence. Only Una's cold eyes glittered with defiance.

Grief clouded his thoughts. He paused and prayed silently for guidance from the Holy Spirit.

"I must tell you," he continued, "that I am ashamed. I believed the sort of behavior we witnessed this morning had long disappeared from our fair island. I have often taught you about the sins of the tongue, but it is obvious either some of you were not listening, or I was not emphatic enough. The constant gossip continues. Though usually without malice—not motivated by evil like this morning—it is still a sin." He took a deep breath and let it out slowly. "But there is no excuse for what took place a few minutes ago."

He left the lectern and walked to the center of the dais. "It would have been bad enough had this happened anywhere else on the island, but this evil took place in our own kirkyard."

Dolly MacSween, the old woman sitting next to Una, slipped to her knees and wailed.

Morag made her way to Dolly and helped her to her feet, leading her outside.

Hugh returned to the lectern. "As believers in our Lord Jesus

Broken Wings

Christ, how can we hope to undo the terrible hurt suffered by one of our most vulnerable? I know a few of you have offered your support and friendship since the colonel arrived on Innisbraw, and Maggie told me how much he appreciates your kindness and looks forward to meeting everyone."

His eyes traveled over the troubled faces before him. "At this point, I have no instant, easy answer. I urge you to do what I am going to do. Pray. Pray about this, and then pray some more. Ask the Lord for guidance and He will give it. Just remember these words from our Savior in Matthew 7:12. 'Therefore, whatever you want men to do to you, do also to them.'"

He nodded at Elspeth. "Those of you involved in the fracas this morning will remain in your seats where our Elspeth will join you in prayer. I apologize for the short service this morning, but Elspeth and I are needed at the infirmary as soon as she can leave. The rest of you, go with God, and rely upon Him to guide you."

He remained on the platform as Una stood and made her way out of the Sanctuary, head held high. How foolish to hope she would stay. *Och, Faither, I must leave her soul in Your hands. Only You can deal with the darkness overcoming her.*

⁂

After John examined the cut on the back of Rob's head, Maggie washed his face and hands, cleaned the cut, sprinkled sulfa powder over it, and taped a piece of gauze in place. She handed him two APCs and held out a glass of water. "I'm going to fetch an ice-pack to put under your head while you climb up in bed and we talk about what happened this mornin."

"Don't need to lie down."

His first words since leaving kirk.

"Please get up on the bed. You don't have to undress, just take off your blouse and tie, and I'll help you with your boots." She leaned over him. "If you won't do this for yourself, do it for me, luve." She regretted her trembling voice, but no matter how hard she held onto her emotions, the breaking point loomed near.

He unbuttoned his blouse and she pulled it off, draping it on a hanger before placing it on its peg on the wall. She brushed her palm over the rows of theater, combat, and decoration ribbons below his silver pilot's wings. How could any of the folk she had known all of her life make him feel so unwelcome? She took his tie from his hand, removed his dress boots, and wheeled his chair closer to the bed. "Do you need Faither's help?"

He shook his head.

She set the brake, cranked the bed down, and he climbed on top of the blanket. "I'll catch you right up."

※

Rob called John over. "I forgot to tell you that Una said to have a look in Maggie's room. I have a feeling that man she has helping her left something really bad in there, so you'd best do it while Maggie's no' here to see it. Be careful. It could be a trap."

John ran a hand over his face and walked quickly across the hall. He wasn't gone long. He closed the door to Maggie's room before he returned and pounded his fist against the doorjamb. "Somebody has been here while we were at kirk and 'tis a rare muddle. Her clothes have been slashed to pieces and strewn about. But the most frightening thing ... "

"What? What is it?"

"A knife is stuck in the mids of her pillow."

"Knife?" Rob grabbed the trapeze and pulled himself up. "Radio the polis right now! No, first find Maggie. I don't want her alone for a minute."

John rushed from the room.

A knife! He'd have to tell Maggie everything, even if it did frighten her. Una gave the impression Maggie would be safe if he left the island but he couldn't leave her now. Even if he wasn't in good enough shape to defend her physically, he could ask John to find him a pistol. Surely someone on Innisbraw had one.

※

John found Maggie washing her face and hands in the small bathroom.

"What's the matter?" she asked. "You look like you've seen a ghost."

He walked her silently back to Rob's room.

Unhappy to see Rob sitting up, she said, "Lie back down so I can put this beneath your head."

He took the icepack and tossed it on the table. "We have to talk." He scooted over. "Up you come. Sit beside me."

She looked from Rob to her father. Their faces were grim. "All right, talk," she said, sitting beside Rob.

As the men who loved her most described the threats against her life and the violence perpetrated against her home, she couldn't even speak. Finally, she looked at them in horror. "I don't believe it. Why would Una, or anybody else, want you off Innisbraw enough to threaten to kill me?"

"We don't know, lass," John said. "I'm going to leave you twa here and radio Oban. When Rob mentioned it earlier, I thought he wanted Una taken to task for throwing stones at him, but after finding your room in such a muddle, I agree. We need the polis."

Rob pulled Maggie close. "I won't let anything happen to you. Until your faither found that knife stuck in your pillow, I thought I should leave the island so you'd be safe. But now, there's no way I'll leave 'til that man is caught and jiled."

※

The policeman John talked to, a Sergeant Grant, told him to expect at least three officers who would arrive on the island later that night. "We've a good, fast 18-knot motor-launch, but it will take us that long to gather what we need and cover the distance from Oban."

"Then you think you can help?"

"I don't know what we can do about the woman who made the written and verbal threats, but we can certainly seek out and arrest the man who did the damage and left the knife. Just make sure your doors are locked and that the lass isn't left alone."

"This is an infirmary. There is no lock on the door."

"Then I suggest you set up a guard or barricade the door," Grant said curtly before signing off.

※

Maggie insisted on seeing her room. Rob agreed only after

John helped him into his wheelchair so he could be with her.

As her father opened the door, she grabbed the door frame to keep from falling.

"Don't touch owt," John warned. "The polis will want to see everything as it is."

She walked around the room, hands clenched at her sides. "That leaves me only one uniform." She looked at the tattered, gray-blue skirt and tunic fragments strewn across bed and floor. Tears blurred her vision. "That was my favorite skirt. And Elspeth knitted that sweater for me."

She eyed the knife buried in the pillow, then whirled around. "Why, Faither? What have I ever done to deserve this?"

"You've done nowt, lass," John said, taking her into his arms. "Whoever did this evil wants to frighten Rob into leaving the island."

She swiped angrily at the tears in her eyes. "Then he and that dreadful Una are in for a disappointment." She stood behind Rob, throwing her arms around his neck. "They don't know Rob if they think he'll leave Innisbraw before he has to report back to duty, and by then I'll be gone, too."

*

Rob and John stayed in the kitchen with Maggie while she made coffee and tea. "I'll take this outside to the entry," she said, placing everything they needed on a tray.

"That's no' safe," Rob said. "You shouldn't be ootside until the polis arrive and arrest that man."

"But what could he possibly do with the both of you beside me?"

"Please take the tray, John," Rob said. He reached for her hands and gripped them tightly. "There are hiding places behind rocks and bushes along the path. I don't want you oot in the open where somebody could take a shot at you."

"A ... a shot at me? Och, Rob, your imagination has run away with you. Nobody shoots guns on Innisbraw. There's no game here."

John led the way up the hall. "You've forgotten the fowl, lass, and there are a few long-guns on the island. Alistaire MacIver has one and I've heard several of the crofters who came here from Mull and Skye hunt corncraik, so they surely brought their shotguns with them. Since we have no idea who else has a gun, let's go out to the foyer where I can safely open the door. The cliff across the path from the front of the infirmary is too steep to allow cover." He set the tray on the foyer table.

Maggie asked Rob to lie down on the sofa with his head in her lap, but he insisted on having some coffee first. He took several thirsty swigs. "Do you know of a handgun available?" he asked John.

"A handgun!" Maggie exclaimed.

"For your protection. I'll settle for a long-gun but it won't be nearly as handy."

"Och, I doubt anyone has one here," John said, stroking his beard. "I don't know if Maggie's told you, but many of our crofters keep watch on the western shore every night in case a U-boat surfaces and tries to send a landing boat ashore. A few are armed, though I don't know what with."

Rob's stomach twisted. "You've a shore-patrol on Innisbraw and nobody's ever mentioned it? Is the island in danger of being invaded?"

"I'm sure it's no', for Innisbraw is so small we have no airfield or British military stationed here like on Tiree, South Uist, and Benbecula—and of course Lewis, far to the north, with its large naval base at Stornoway. But who knows? Several of the Outer Hebrides have been shelled by U-boats using the Atlantic to reach their western shores. I'll radio Angus and Alec and see what I can find. I agree with you, a handgun would be more practical. Do you know how to use one?"

"The Army Air Forces made a Smith and Wesson .38 Special available to each pilot when we got to England, and they gave us plenty of time for target practice. I wore it 'neath my flight suit on every sortie and mission."

"I remember seeing it," Maggie said. "Doctor Larson took it out of a leather holder when you came into the hospital."

Hugh and Elspeth appeared in the doorway, interrupting their conversation.

"That tea looks good," Hugh said.

Maggie jumped up to get two more cups from the kitchen while Elspeth examined the bandage on the back of Rob's head. "I'm so sorry, lad. Though I doubt Una has any regrets from the way she disappeared after Hugh dismissed everyone, all the auld widows feel most terrible for how they acted."

"I hope you know those women who fell for Una's lies were the only ones who had anything to do with what went on this morning." Hugh clasped Rob's shoulder. "Unlike many of the smaller villages of Scotland, who never accept those they call 'incomers,' the folk on this island welcome everyone who wishes to make Innisbraw their home."

"I'm thinking you and Elspeth should have a look at Maggie's room before you decide that," Rob said. "John, why don't you show them?"

Obviously puzzled, they followed John down the hallway

While the three were gone, Maggie returned to the foyer with the cups. "Here. Finish your coffee first," she said. "Then you're going to lie down and I won't take no for an answer."

Exhausted, but keyed-up, he wanted to pace the floor. "I can't stay that still," he said, after draining his mug. "Come sit in my lap so we can be close." He clasped her to his chest, inhaling her sweet, innocent fragrance. "This is worse than fighting the Jerries. At least with them, I knew who the enemy was."

"The polis will find him, if it really was a man who did this. Una may have lied."

"There's something I have to tell you. I swore to myself—and your faither—I'd never take you away from Innisbraw after the war, but what's happened may change all that."

She placed a finger over his lips. "If there's a reason we can't come back here, we'll have to look for a home somewhere ... somewhere else. Perhaps in America."

He traced the arch of her eyebrow with a trembling finger. "But if we don't come back to Innisbraw, there's no need for me to resign my Air Forces commission, and you have no idea what it means to be married to someone in the military. They don't station you in one place for long. I could be deployed a great deal of the time, leaving you alone with only other wives for company and no one to hold you in the night."

"Rob—"

"You grew up surrounded by folk who luve you. Some of the bases are out in the middle of nowhere without villages nearby. And those eight bairns of ours would have to change schools every time they put down roots. I can't do that to them ... or you."

Tears escaped her eyes. "But surely we don't have to look that far ahead."

"Och, I'm sorry, luve, I know we don't. But after thinking it over, I don't see how I can stay here any longer than it takes the polis to arrest that man. Una can always find another to take his place. You'll be in no danger if all she wants is me leaving the island."

"All? Isn't that enough? If you leave before the end of August, even if you can somehow get into an American military hospital in England, you won't have Faither's rehabilitation program to make certain you walk unaided again and ... and I can't go with you. I'll have to return to duty."

"Don't say that. Don't even think it."

"But 'tis true." She collapsed into sobs.

Chapter Thirty

Rob held Maggie while she wept. *Get control, Savage. Think. Think!* Only logic could solve this problem. No emotion. Just thought. His ability to focus on logistical problems had always been his primary problem-solving device when planning bombing strikes, especially those with two or more approaches. His actions depended on weighing choices, but those choices were so limited. Leaving now was not an option.

The most obvious choice was remaining on the island until the polis arrested the man responsible for the knife, and then leaving so Maggie would be safe in case Una found another to carry out her dirty work.

Where could he go?

Maggie couldn't leave with him.

Finding the man and enough proof to arrest him could take a long time and the end of August was only a few weeks away.

So only one choice remained. Stay on Innisbraw and protect Maggie. *Just like the Selkie's crofter.*

"I'll be here 'til you have to return to duty." He rubbed his cheek against hers. "Though I'm worried sick over what Una might do to you if I don't get off the island."

"And ... and after I have to leave? What about your therapy?" She pulled back and looked at him, face filled with despair.

What would he do when Maggie returned to duty? Another choice, but not as difficult. His Maggie would be off the island and he was determined to walk without a limp once this was all over. "I'll stay here until my therapy is finished. I'd be daft to quit before John thinks I'm ready for duty."

Their lips met, an uncertain future drawing them together.

Elspeth, Hugh, and John interrupted the kiss, John saying, "I'm sorry we took so long. We prayed for guidance before having a lengthy discussion about what steps to take."

"Hugh has Alec's cairt and cuddy outside," Elspeth said. "He's going to take me to my cottage so we can spend time together on our knees where we belong." She trailed her fingers over Rob's shoulder and kissed Maggie's cheek. "After seeing what was done to your room, lass, your faither is going to contact some of the menfolk and try to find a gun. I know it sounds dreadful, but we're all convinced it's needed for your protection."

Hugh grasped Maggie and Rob's hands and said a brief prayer for God's perfect will before they took their leave.

John spent over an hour on the radio before searching for Maggie and Rob. He found them in the kitchen. "Alistaire MacIver, a cannie auld-timer with a keen memory, is certain there are no handguns on the island. He also said his shotgun is so auld and in such poor condition, he doubted it would be safe to fire."

"So we're back where we started," Rob said.

"No' quite. Alec, who heads up the men patrolling our shores every een, told me about one of the sheep crofters who came here from Mull in the mid-thirt—"

"He has a gun?"

"Och, calm down, lad. 'Tis Colin Stewart, and Alec paid him a call. He has twa shotguns—a newer one he carries every time 'tis his turn to guard the western shore—and a verra auld one in guid shape. I don't know anything about guns so I wrote down what Alec said it was." He pulled a paper from his shirt pocket. "'Tis a J. D. Dougall 12-gauge single-shot. Collin will bring it over the day with some shells and show you how to use it."

"I don't like taking it away from one of the shore patrol."

"Och, Alec said the men who know how to shoot all have their own shotguns and nobody else has the skill or desire to use a gun of any sort."

"I've never fired a shotgun, but from what I understand, you don't have to aim as closely as you do with a handgun. The shot in the shell scatters enough to stop a man, often without killing him."

Maggie shivered.

"I'm sure I'll never have to use it," Rob said, expression grim, "but if anybody tries to hurt you, they'll have to climb over me first."

"Why don't you start some supper, lass?" John asked. "I know none of us is verra hungry but Rob, in particular, cannot go without food."

"Only if you agree to get into bed," she said to Rob. "You've missed your nap the day and if you lose any more weight, you'll soon be as thin as when we arrived."

John retired to his office so the two could have some privacy. He stared out the window at Ben Innis, her sides a blush of soft purple as heather blossoms opened in the burgeoning warmth. How could something like this happen on Innisbraw? Och, the folk were far from perfect, but if Una hadn't lied to Rob, what man on the island would threaten his Maggie with bodily harm?

He prayed for divine intervention before making his way to the kitchen. Maggie would surely be there by now and he didn't want her left alone.

He found the MacDonalds in the kitchen with Maggie. "There you are," she said. "Alec and Morag decided to walk up from their croft to see how Rob is feeling before they drive Hugh home in their cairt. I'm starting supper."

"We had a peek at Maggie's room," Alec said. "'Twas most awful."

"I can't imagine who would have the nerve to do such a thing," Morag said. "Surely they knew they would be missed at kirk."

"A few of the men-folk seldom go," Alec reminded her.

"That narrows the suspects down right there."

Maggie swept the potatoes and an onion into a large kettle and added water. "Faither, will you go make sure Rob is asleep? 'Tis still difficult for him to get out of bed by himself, but he's in such a fankle, I don't trust him to stay put."

Rob sat on the side of his bed, doing leg-lifts.

"You should be resting," John said.

"I can't stay still. Jump at the slightest sound."

John nodded and went to the window, pulling aside the lace curtain. "At least there aren't many who use this path. Only a few fishermen and those crofters who live on the southwest end of the island getting their post."

Rob grunted in agreement. "I want to ask you something." He rubbed the side of his nose. "And I want you to level with me."

John dropped the curtain. "I'll do my best."

"Then, speaking as my doctor, I want to know if there's a physical reason why I can't get a handle on my emotions. I've never been as angry in my life as I was this mornin—'twas like looking through a red fog. And for weeks, I've gotten so caught up in how I'm feeling, I can't make decisions, even after praying and thinking about problems for hours."

"Of course there's a physical reason." John pulled a chair up next to the bed. "Anybody who's come so close to death and suffered excruciating pain for a long period of time will be emotionally affected, especially if the injury involves damaged nerves."

"Please tell me it will get better. I hate this."

"Over time."

Rob hung his head.

"Our bodies are marvelous creations of God, but they're no' machines. If an engine breaks down, you can replace the defective part, but the human body is far too complex for that, especially the nervous system. And you can't leave the brain out of the mix." He patted Rob's knee. "The injury you suffered dealt you a double blow—both physical and emotional. The possibility of spending the rest of your life paralysed from the hips down has left you reeling."

"But I'm walking now. No' well, but I know I will in time. I can't expect to take command of an Eighth Heavy Bomber Group again if I can't make instant decisions without deciding how I *feel* about it."

"You haven't given it enough time. The more physical progress you make and the better you walk, the more control you'll have over your emotions. 'Tis as simple as that."

Though John's words made sense, they were not what Rob wanted to hear. "When can I start using crutches?"

"Och, I've never seen anyone in such a hurry. Crutches are dangerous. First, you must learn to turn and walk much farther than you are now. One hard fall and that wheelchair could be your constant companion for the rest of your life."

Anger flared. No matter how much he accomplished, something always slowed him down. He remembered his first landing in a Stearman PT-17 trainer. A three-bounce landing was embarrassing enough, but if he didn't lighten up on the stick and rudders, he would be washed out of flight school, or even the Air Corps.

Luckily, his instructor, Colonel Hal Fielding, a World War I ace, explained his rough landing. "You can't wrestle a plane to the ground. Try to sense the landing before the wheels hit. Feel it in your gut and you'll learn to let her land herself."

Is that what he was doing now—trying to wrestle this problem to the ground?

"Then why waste time? It's going to be hours before the polis get here, so let's start now. Tell me what I need to practice and I'll do it, no matter how long it takes."

"Maggie'll have my skin if you don't get some sleep. Lie down and try to at least rest for an hour."

"Och, you're as bad as Maggie," Rob grumbled, lowering himself to his back.

Colin Stewart arrived with his shotgun tucked under one arm and a handful of shells in his pocket.

John greeted him with a warm handshake. "Maggie has a fish and tattie bree simmering on the stove, so this is a guid time to show Rob your long-gun."

Rob put down the copy of the Edinburgh *Scotsman* he'd been trying to read. Once introductions were made and Rob sat in his wheelchair, they made their way out to the foyer.

"I want Maggie to stand back inside the doorway," Rob said.

Broken Wings

Maggie propped her hands on her hips. "But I can't spend days or even weeks inside. I'll go daft. There's the peat to bring in, the butter and milk to fetch from the cooling shed, the washing to hang, my garden to tend and—"

"Let's wait to hear what the polis advise," John said. "Until then, you've no business outside where you could come to harm. I'll keep you company."

※

Stewart was a husky, sandy-haired man with keen blue eyes and square, calloused but very dexterous hands. He showed Rob how to use the Dougall, demonstrating the loading of the gun several times. "Remember to keep some of these shells in your pocket all the time. And practice using the break-open lever at the top of the tang 'til you can do it in your sleep." He showed Rob again, breaking the barrel. "There's no shell in there, so you just load it, lock the break, cock the hammer the way I showed you afore, and pull the trigger."

"What about the kick you talked about?" Rob asked. "I don't want it knocking me oot of this chair."

"Och, you're too big for that. But you don't need to bring it up to your shoulder to aim. Just keep it on the chair's seat against your hip. When you need to use it, load, raise it to your waist, tuck it in firmly, and shoot. Keep a guid firm hold on the grip and don't aim for the head. A body shot, even from a single shell, should knock a man over before he can hurt Maggie."

This would be a good time to assuage his curiosity about the men patrolling the shoreline every night. "Tell me about this shore watch you're a part of."

Stewart lowered his eyes and studied the floor. "I'm no' certain 'tis doing much guid, but all us able-bodied crofters take four-hour shifts, walking the shore or hunkered down behind a rock, studying the sea for a bit of light blinking where it shouldn't. In nineteen and forty-one, a U-boat surfaced off Benbecula and tried to land several small boats. If the Home-Guard hadn't been watching, those Krauts could have done some rare damage to the airfield there."

"And you're armed with shotguns?"

A broad grin creased the crofter's face. "Most have only knives and digging forks, but we're no' expecting a fight. Those Krauts can't see us with a guid smear of peaty soil on our faces and hands and wearing dark clothes. All it takes is one of us whistling like a pewlie—no' a sound you'd expect to hear at night—and the man with the radio calls Tyree and Benbecula and has them radio their closest coastal search airieplane while we keep watch. One of those RAF lads spent time here showing us how to use their radio."

"Have you ever had to send a signal?"

"No' yet, but we'd like nowt better than to see one o' their large airieplanes dumping a load of bombs on some U-boat and watching it blow oot of the sea."

After Stewart left, Rob mused over what the crofter told him as he practiced grabbing up, phantom-loading, and dry-firing the gun while Maggie watched from inside the doorway, wincing every time he pulled the trigger. When satisfied he knew how to hold and use the gun effectively, Rob pocketed the shells and tucked the shotgun on the seat against his right side so he could wheel his chair through the doorway. "Where's your faither?"

"On the radio seeing if either Alec or Angus would be willing to wait at the dock later to meet the polis." She stepped several feet away, eyeing the gun warily.

"It isn't loaded, lass," he said. "On you come and I'll show you."

"I believe you."

"Then why are you shaking?"

"It ... it's ugly," she whispered.

His right eyebrow rose. "Ugly? 'Tis actually a fine looking weapon, especially considering its age. On you come," he repeated, holding out his hand. "Touch it."

She drew back another step. "I can't. It's fearsome."

"It's just wood and metal. The only thing fearsome is what it can do in the wrong hands." Again he offered his hand, leaving it extended. "It'll be beside me in this chair or on my bed 'til they catch that man. Are you going to refuse to come near me 'til then?"

She gnawed her lower lip before placing her hand in his.

Broken Wings

"Sit on my lap."

She sat, legs trembling.

He hugged her to his chest, nuzzling her neck. "You know I'd never ask you to do something dangerous, but 'tis important you lose your fear. Understand?"

"I suppose."

He picked up the shotgun and balanced it on the arm of the chair. "I don't want to raise it any higher with you in my lap, so you'll have to turn to the right a wee bit."

She turned slowly, looking down at the gun, eyes wide.

"That's perfect. Just don't touch any of the metal." He pointed. "See that large wooden grip at the back of the barrel? Cup your hand around it."

She hesitated. "Why don't you want me to touch the metal?"

"Because salt from your skin will penetrate the bluing and pit the metal over time. Stop stalling, lass. It won't bite."

She touched the grip with one trembling finger. Slowly, she worked up the courage to do more, slipping fingers beneath the grip and closing them, glancing back at him, a tiny smile on her face. "'Tis so smooth."

"It's been handled a lot."

She reached her hand back, trailing her fingers over the checker-carved wood. "What's this for?"

"'Tis called a stock. When you put the butt of the stock against your shoulder, it gives the gun enough length so you can put your finger on the trigger.

Her smile grew wider. She wrinkled her nose. "If I stand up, can I hold it?"

Talk about a one-eighty. "It's no' heavy. Give it a try."

She slid to her feet and he demonstrated what she needed to do. She picked up the shotgun and brought it to her waist as Rob had done. She was tiny but strong, and held it steady several seconds.

Rob took it from her. "Do you think you can get used to having this around for a while?" He stifled a grin when her shoulders straightened and her nose went up.

"And why no'? 'Tis only metal and wood."

Maggie accompanied John and Rob to the rehab room. Rob propped the shotgun in the corner nearest the parallel bars and pulled himself to his feet, grabbing the bars as he looked at John. "You said you'd tell me what I need to accomplish before I can use crutches."

"You start by learning how to pivot and turn at the end of the bars and go back again. Everybody has his own way of doing the pivot, so I'll leave that up to you. As your legs strengthen, use the bars mainly for balance. Do that over and over, adding a lap as often as you can without hurting yourself. Understand?"

Rob exhaled and straightened his shoulders. "Yes, sir," he said in English. "It's very clear."

"Then why don't you work at it until suppertime? I've some things to see to in my office. I'll wedge a chair beneath the knob on the front door."

Rob waited until he was gone. "Maggie, stand where I start so I'll be walking toward you after the pivot and turn." He concentrated on each step, keeping his grip on the bars as light as possible. As he walked, he tried to figure out how to accomplish that pivot and turn.

At the end, he hesitated, then took several small sliding steps toward the left bar. Off-balance, he grabbed that bar with both hands, stepped back with his right foot, and turned on the ball of his foot. Awkward, but it got him facing in the right direction. He stepped sideways with his left foot and transferred his left hand to what was now the left bar. He looked at Maggie.

She smiled and blew him a kiss.

Now the long walk back.

His heart ached for her, so innocent, so trusting. It agonized him, having her fear someone she must have known all of her life.

A sudden, terrifying thought leaped into his mind. Would she still love him if he decided they couldn't return to her island home after the war? And if they had the bairns she wanted, would she come to resent him because they were growing up so far from her family and friends—from the island she loved so much?

His legs tired. He had not yet walked so far but determined not to stop until they could no longer bear his weight.

She continued to smile.

Another stab of panic jolted him. No matter what the constables accomplished, in only a few weeks she would be gone from Innisbraw. It was unlikely he'd be walking unaided before she reported back to duty. How could he bear to see her leave? She was his sunshine and joy, and their minds worked almost as one.

A few lines from one of John Milton's poems came to his mind. *For what thou art is mine; our state cannot be sever'd; we are one, one flesh; to lose thee were to lose myself.*

How could he stay here without her?

When he reached the end of the bars, she pushed the wheelchair behind his knees. He collapsed into it with a grunt.

"You did it." She hugged his shoulders. "You walked twice as far as before, and I couldn't believe how well you pivoted and turned."

"I felt like a dog with one front paw caught in his collar and the other in his water bowl." He wiped his forehead on his sleeve.

Her girlish laughter brought the ghost of a smile. "I've never seen a dog in such a fankle. But you did exactly what you should have for your first attempt." She surprised him by picking up the shotgun and handing it to him. "On you come, brave warrior. I need to warm the bannock for supper."

Chapter Thirty-one

The three policemen arrived at the infirmary just before 1900. The senior officer, Sergeant Grant, was a stocky veteran with closely cropped grey hair, a slightly crooked nose, and soft grey eyes beneath jutting brows. His two companions, both constables in their mid-to-late forties, slender, erect, black-haired and brown-eyed, looked so much alike, Rob wondered if they were kin. He grinned when Grant introduced them as Ian and David Thompson.

"As I told you on the radio, Doctor McGrath, we don't normally take action so quickly unless there is an attempted homicide," the sergeant said. "But your daughter being a nurse working in an infirmary, and an injured American pilot involved, I feel it is our duty to find this man before he attempts to carry out the threats that were made."

The policemen all eyed the shotgun tucked into the wheelchair beside Rob, but none of them commented as they followed Maggie to the kitchen for a cup of hot tea.

"This is much appreciated." Sergeant Grant warmed his hands over the stove. "It might be July, but that wind on the Minch is as cold as a worn-out prost—" He stopped, cheeks flushing as he eyed Maggie. "As if it were already winter," he finished in a rush.

Ian Thompson choked on his tea.

Rob stifled a laugh.

"I have often found that true," Maggie said, a hint of laughter in her eyes.

"I apologize, Miss McGrath," Grant said, his voice sounding strangled. "I've been in the company of men entirely too long."

"Our minister, Hugh MacEwan, has offered the manse as a kind of headquarters while you are here," John said.

"Mr. MacDonald already informed us of the hospitality offered and has taken our personal bags to the manse, thank you." Grant's stiff stance relaxed. "I realize it's rare late, but we would like a look at the lass's bedroom and take your statements before we drop in at your pub."

"The howff?" Maggie's eyebrows rose.

"Och, on the ride up here from the harbor, Mr. MacDonald told us about the old-timers who congregate in the evening if the owner has whisky. Apparently, he heard a rumor that tonight could be such a time. I thought it a good place to start." He pointed at the shotgun. "I hope that isn't loaded."

"Of course not," Rob said. "But being in a wheelchair, it gives me a bit of confidence."

"I understand you're a colonel in the American Air Forces," Grant said, grey eyes no longer soft, but piercing. "How long have you been here on Innisbraw?"

"He's been here almost twa months," Maggie said. "He was transferred here from the Royal Infirmary in Edinburgh so he could have extensive therapy. I'm his nurse."

"And my daughter," John added.

Grant stared at Rob. "Don't do anything foolish with that shotgun. It would be a tragedy to have to arrest you."

"Arrest him?" Maggie's eyes darkened with anger. "If that's what you're thinking, you can get on your boat right now and go back to Oban."

"Aw can spek—speak for myself, Maggie," Rob said, wanting to kick himself for the lapse into Scots. "I suggest you stop dancing at shadows and start investigating, Sergeant. I'm career military and, while I understand your concern, you have my promise that using this gun will be my very last choice."

"If you'll follow me, I'll show you Maggie's room," John said.

*

They watched from the doorway as the three policemen gathered evidence. Their meticulous actions fascinated Maggie. They took photographs of her room from several angles and each piece of evidence where it lay. Handling everything with care, they never touched anything with their bare hands before putting it into its own bag.

Sergeant Grant drew a clean handkerchief from his pocket, draped it over the haft, and worked the knife free from the pillow, using only his thumb and index finger placed firmly on the guard above the blade. He laid it flat in his covered palm and held it out. "Do any of you recognize this?"

She and Rob studied it. "Never seen it before," Rob said.

"It looks like a kitchen knife." Maggie shuddered.

John stroked his beard. "I agree with Maggie. I'm thinking there's one like it in our own kitchen."

"Would you please see if it's there?" Grant asked Maggie.

"I don't have to. Morag MacDonald used ours the day to dice the tatties for our bree."

Grant lowered the knife into an evidence bag. "We'll take this back to Oban and see if we can lift some fingerprints from it." He turned to John. "Now, Doctor, if you will be so kind as to tell us where it will be the most comfortable, we'll take each of your statements before we leave for the pub."

It was 2200 before all their statements were heard, written, and signed. "We'll be on our way, then," the sergeant said. "But we'll be back in the morning to ask your help in locating those we should question, especially Miss Hunter."

"You're not planning on going to the howff without an interpreter, are you?" John asked with the tiniest of smiles.

"Interpreter? I thought everyone in the Outer Hebrides speaks English."

"You've obviously been misinformed," Rob said, not bothering to hide his amusement. "Only a handful of folk on Innisbraw speak any English. The rest use Scots or the Gaelic, but the old-timers have only the Gaelic."

Grant whirled around and eyed his cohorts. "I don't suppose either of you have the Gaelic?"

They shook their heads.

"I'll go with you," John said. "Besides the language problem, you won't get any answers to your questions unless somebody they know and trust does the asking."

Broken Wings

After they left, Maggie insisted Rob go to bed immediately. "Your face is pale and your hands are shaking," she said when he protested. "And I'm so tired I can hardly hold my head up. Faither has given me another room for the night and he's going to stay here, also."

"But he'll be gone for a long time. I don't want you alone in another room."

"I'll be alone even after Faither returns. And with the polis on the island, nobody will dare try anything."

He pondered her words, fingers tapping. "Then up you come. Sit in my lap for a few minutes. I'll even put the shotgun on the back of the couch."

"No, I will," she said with a mischievous smile.

※

Much later that night, John tiptoed down the dark hallway, directed the hooded torch he was carrying into Maggie's room, saw her sleeping, and continued to Rob's room.

As he expected, Rob sat in front of the window in his wheelchair in the grey half-light, staring out at the moonlit waves dancing across the harbor.

He turned his chair at John's approach. "I hoped you'd come in here when I saw you walking up the path. Did they find owt?"

John pulled over a chair and sat with a tired grunt. "Och, a few things that could be relevant."

"Like what?"

"Well, for one thing, there were far more men there than usual. And for another, the whisky was flowing."

Rob's eyebrow rose. "So Alec was right. But I thought whisky was scarce because of the war."

"It is, and though auld man MacGinnis hid the bottles when the police walked in, every man there had some in a glass, and I don't mean just a wee dram."

"But what does that have to do with the knife left in Maggie's room?"

"Would you like a cup of coffee? My throat's so dry from talking, I need some hot tea."

"It must be bad if you can't tell me straight out."

"No' bad, just long."

"I don't like leaving Maggie alone. That's why I haven't gone to bed."

"I wedged a chair beneath the door handle. On you come, we don't want to chance waking Maggie with our blethering."

※

John closed the kitchen door and turned on the light. He added some peats to the stove and put the coffee pot and teakettle on. "I need to give you a bit of history if you're to understand what I'm about to say." He sat down, propped his feet on another chair, and leaned back, linking his fingers across his belly. "In the winter of '41, a large steamer, the *Politician*, went aground off the shores of Eriskay—that's a wee island north of Barra. It didn't take long for the word to get around that the ship had in its hold thousands of cases of the finest single-malt Scotch whisky. In no time at all, men from every island around were rowing to the wreck of the *Polly*—what they took to calling her—in the dark of night and carrying off as many cases as their small boats could hold." He got up, emptied the whistling kettle into the teapot, and moved the coffee pot to a cooler spot to perk.

"Were the men of Innisbraw involved?" And how was this story relevant?

"Word didn't filter down here until quite a while after the steamer wrecked. When our Island Council heard what was going on, they held an island-wide meeting and warned all the folk that anybody found with whisky would be turned over to the authorities in Oban. I'm certain there are still a few bottles hidden on the island that haven't been found yet, but there's been no evidence of out-and-out drunkenness."

"Sounds like Innisbraw got off lightly."

John massaged his stiff neck. "We did. You cannot imagine the harm all that drinking did to the folk on the islands from Sanderay all the way up to North Uist. 'Tis said whisky was so plentiful folk were using it to make their peat fires burn more vigorously and as fuel instead of paraffin in their Tilly lamps."

"Tilly lamps?"

"What you Americans call 'lanterns.'" He poured himself a cup of tea and filled Rob's mug before returning to his chair. "In time, the Ministry of Shipping and Customs got word and sent watchmen to stand guard on the *Polly*. Revenuers and constables made the rounds of the islands, arresting those they caught with whisky." He shrugged his shoulders. "Of course they didn't find even a portion of what had been taken. Bottles of whisky were hidden inside peat piles, tucked beneath bairnies asleep in their cradles, stuck into the thatch of cottages, byres, and faulds, and buried by the case in the soil of the machair—what didn't make its way down the throats of the islanders, that is."

"The whisky at the howff is somehow involved in this story you're telling?"

"It is that. Sergeant Grant pulled a bottle from beneath the bar and read the label aloud. It was Hieland Nectar, the finest whisky aboard the doomed *Polly*, and much too dear for a struggling howff owner on Innisbraw to afford."

"What did MacGinnis have to say?"

"No' a word. If he admitted he'd bought it from somebody, he was breaking the law as much as if he admitted taking it from the *Polly* himself. That would make no sense since he's been turning away folk off and on for months, saying he couldn't get any whisky—though we all know he manages to find an occasional bottle of cheap John Barleycorn so the auld men can have their wee drams."

"What did Grant do?"

"He and his twa constables searched the pub but couldn't find the wooden case. Grant sent those Thompson brothers to the shed at the back of the howff where MacGinnis lives and sure enough, they found it beneath his box-bed, well over half-full."

"Is MacGinnis under arrest?"

"I offered the use of the cooling shed behind my cottage and he's in there right now, door tied with a rope so he can't escape."

"But what guid does this do us? We have no way of knowing MacGinnis is our man."

"Grant thinks he is. He says Una Hunter could have given MacGinnis that whisky in exchange for threatening Maggie. None of the men questioned the night admitted knowing owt, which wasn't surprising, drunk as they were. But several did say that Fergus MacCrae and Alistaire MacIver were there earlier and left, after their usual one dram, in a rare fankle over something MacGinnis whispered to them. Both of those men are on the Island Council. If they know owt, they'll tell Sergeant Grant."

"Could Una have been hiding the whisky all this time?"

"'Tis doubtful unless she found a case somebody secreted away. But the police have a lot of questions for her after they talk to Alistaire and Fergus."

"Och, I'd hoped we could settle this the night."

"Don't forget, if there are fingerprints on that knife that match MacGinnis's, we'll have our proof, but that will have to wait till Grant takes everything back to Oban to be analysed."

"So we wait till the morra to find if we discover owt." Rob drained his mug and knuckled his eyes, yawning.

"Aye, the morra." John rinsed their cups and set them in the jaw box to dry. "You'd best get to sleep, lad. 'Tis well past the turn o' the night."

⁂

Sergenat Grant made the doctor join the group of policemen the next morning when they left the infirmary to interview Fergus MacCrae and Alistaire MacIver. Doctor McGrath had told Grant both old men were noted for being testy when confronted with situations they couldn't control. According to the doc, though Alistaire had some English and understood Scots, Fergus spoke nothing but the Gaelic and was proud of it.

Grant looked around at the scenery from his seat beside John, who drove Alec's cart. How could anyone live on such a primitive island? The lack of motorized transportation most likely kept Innisbraw from attracting a larger population—that, and the dearth of any industry apart from crofting and fishing. The islands north of Innisbraw all the way to Barra were also in the Inverness Constabulary and he had spent many a day on Barra. But in the ten years he'd been with Oban Polis Headquarters, he'd never received a call to investigate a crime on Innisbraw.

John turned the cart up a path meandering between thatched cottages. "Alistaire and Fergus both live on this path, but I'm thinking you'd best interview them separately. When they get together, they're worse than twa ravens fighting over a place to shelter for the night."

"Whatever you deem best."

John pulled the cuddy to a halt. "This is Fergus's cottage. We'll have to talk to him outside. He has a badly crippled aulder sister and Christina would be verra upset by the sight of your uniforms."

The Thompson brothers stepped gingerly down from the back of the cart to join the sergeant, dour faces revealing how miserable they'd found the bumpy ride.

"Keep your gabs shut and your ears open," Grant warned in a low voice as John came out of the cottage followed by two old men, both with erect postures and grey hair.

The similarities ended there.

The one John introduced as Alistaire MacIver was clad in clean, mended tweed pants, a tweed jacket over a yellowing white shirt, and heavy, worn brogans, hair neatly trimmed, cleanly-shaven cheeks and chin, blue eyes keen with interest.

Fergus MacCrae looked like MacIver's poverty-stricken kin. His grey hair and stubbled chin were in drastic need of a barber and wild, untrimmed eyebrows jutted out over etiolated blue eyes. Faded red braces held up rumpled tweed pants, at least two sizes too large. Tattered rubber boots, newspaper peeking from holes in the toes, swallowed his feet and calves.

John asked Alistaire a question in the Gaelic and listened to the terse reply.

"Alistaire came visiting to bring Christina some heather honey," he said in English, "so I suppose we'll have to talk to them together after all."

Fergus spouted something in the Gaelic, hands gesturing wildly.

John spoke to the old man for a moment before turning to the sergeant. "Fergus wanted to know what the police are doing here. I assured him you only want to ask them some questions about their visit to the howff last night."

Another spate of Gaelic from Fergus ignited Alistaire. Both men were incensed at being questioned about having a "wee dram" the night before—their first in weeks. Alistaire was so upset, he refused to speak any English and constantly interrupted Fergus's tirades in the Gaelic with his own.

After a short time, Grant pointed a finger in Fergus's face, then Alistaire's, and roared, "You tell them to shut their gabs! I'm going to ask some questions and I want truthful answers, or I'm going to arrest them both for obstruction of justice."

Both old men jumped back.

John translated.

Alistaire blinked rapidly. "Why didna he just say so?" He turned to Fergus and the two exchanged a few words in the Gaelic. Nodding, he faced them. "We're biding on ye."

They answered Grant's questions quickly and, he was quite certain, truthfully.

Aye, MacGinnis bragged that the whisky came from the *Polly*. Aye, he traded it for a "wee bit of a turn."

"No, he did not offer a name, but he hinted he had dealt with a 'cailleach' or 'old witch.'"

※

A cart rumbled to a stop outside Una's cottage. She hurried to the window and lifted a corner of the lace.

The polis!

And that meddling John.

She dropped the curtain. Fierce, hot anger exploded through her body. How dare they invade her privacy.

She ignored the rapping on the door. She was a Monroe, not a sniveling, cowardly Hunter. Monroes had money and prestige. Monroes bowed their knees to no man—not even the King.

No longer polite knocking. Pounding on the door like ill-bred, uneducated crofters.

Her anger cooled to smoldering resolve.

Even if that old sot had betrayed her, it was his word against hers. Keep them outside. Let them ask their questions. Deny everything. They couldn't make her answer.

Chin high, shoulders straight, she opened the door.

⁂

Grant seethed. Who did this old bag of bones think she was, refusing to allow them to enter her decaying cottage? He turned and eyed the group of neighbors gathering on the path. "Are you sure you want us to question you out here, in front of your neighbors?"

She opened the door wider, eyes cold, mouth turned down in a sneer.

Don't smirk at her. It isn't befitting an officer of the law.

He let John step inside before beckoning to the constables, voice a gravely whisper. "Examine the grounds for a spot of recently forked-up ground." He joined John.

"There will be no snooping inside my home," Miss Hunter said, voice dripping with venom.

High, irritating voice, like a wheel starving for a wee drop of oil.

"If I feel the need, I'll look anywhere I please, but for now, I want you to look at this." He held out the note Rob had found, jerking it back when she tried to take it from his hand. "Read it. I've been assured you know how to read and write."

No outward reaction, but if looks could kill …

Her eyes moved down the page. "What does this have to do with me?"

"You deny writing this?"

"I have never seen it before."

⁂

Because Una spoke English, there was no need for John to translate. His gaze wandered over the small, cluttered room while he listened to her hostile denial. He strode to a table, picked up a piece of paper, read it, then handed it to Grant. "If I remember correctly, 'tis the same writing."

Una tried to snatch the paper from Grant's hand, but John

restrained her.

"That's my letter," she screeched. "You have no right to take what's mine."

"A perfect match," Grant said, "right down to the ink smudges."

The two constables ducked through the doorway, stomping dirt from their feet. "We found a patch of broken earth," David Thompson said. "It looked like it had the imprint of a case at the bottom, but there was nowt in it. We took a photograph, anyway."

※

Once the policemen arrived back at the infirmary the sergeant told Rob and Maggie all they had discovered.

"Does that mean she gets off with what she did?" Rob's eyes narrowed. "Just because you couldn't find proof the whisky came from her croft?"

"Och, this is a complicated case," Grant said. "We'll transport MacGinnis back to Oban to stand for receiving stolen whisky, and if his fingerprints match any found on the knife handle, to be charged with destruction of property and malicious mischief with the intent to do harm. But you must realize we cannot prosecute Una Hunter for writing that note since it wasn't an overt threat and that imprint in her yard wasn't clear enough to be admissible proof." He held up his hand when Rob tried to interrupt. "However, if MacGinnis implicates her in his deeds, she will face the same charges."

"And if he doesn't?"

"Then all the law allows us is to ask for a Writ from the Court to forbid her talking to or even getting near either of you."

"So we're still in the same fankle." Rob pulled Maggie into his lap and rested his cheek against hers. "I'm sorry, luve. I thought this would be settled by now."

"You have to be patient a few more days," Grant said. "We'll be taking our leave as soon as we pick up our personal effects, secure our evidence bags, and take possession of our prisoner. We have a sworn, signed statement from Mr. MacIver. Because Mr. MacCrae has no schooling, he made his mark on his."

Rob huffed. "But there is more evidence."

Grant nodded. "We have well over half a case of Highland Nectar whisky from the *Polly* and matching samples of Miss Hunter's handwriting." He started for the door before hesitating. "The moment the fingerprints are analysed, we'll contact you. If they implicate Mr. MacGinnis, your worries should be over."

John ushered the three policemen out and thanked them for coming so quickly.

Sergeant Grant held his back ramrod straight as they walked down the path. "Take note," he said to the constables. "It is not always possible to satisfy those hoping for a quick resolution from the law, but I believe we have one more duty to perform before we leave this island. I know you lads are tired of walking, as am I, but Miss Hunter needs a very strong reminder that if anything happens to Maggie McGrath, she will be prosecuted to the full extent of the law. After all, good polis work dictates that we go the extra mile—even on foot."

His professionalism would not be questioned by an officer in the military, especially an American.

Chapter Thirty-two

John returned to his duties in Edinburgh and without the distraction his visit provided, waiting for word from Grant wore on Maggie and Rob's nerves.

She returned to her room across the hall from Rob. Though Angus installed a sturdy bar across the inside of the front door, which could be lowered to keep anyone from walking into the infirmary at night, Rob yawned often, as if he did not sleep well.

Maggie, an avid fresh air enthusiast, became more and more upset that she couldn't spend time outside, working in her cottage garden next door, or hanging the washing out to dry.

Her gloomy mood worsened when Rob wheeled his chair into the large bathroom and discovered her using a washboard in the tub.

He grabbed one of her hands and wiped the soapsuds away, examining her red knuckles. "There's electricity here so why haven't you a washing machine?" he asked, words clipped and harsh. "You've told me often enough, the island's behind the times, but that's no reason no' to have a betterment that's been available for years."

"I've been doing the washing this way since I was a lass." She jerked her hand away. "At least I have a bathing tub and don't have to go down to a burn and scrub the linens and clothes on a rock like most of the women on Innisbraw."

He caught her shoulder. "I don't care what the others do. Most of the washing's mine and you do enough for me without having to bend over a tub, rubbing your hands raw. You didn't have a fit when your faither told you to find a lass to hang the wash to dry."

She ignored his raised eyebrow and pulled away, bending over the tub. "Only because the polis told me I shouldn't expose myself to danger."

"When the lass you hired comes later the mornin you're going to tell her you want her to do the washing, too. I'll write the Bank of England in London to send me some silver from my savings to pay her."

"Och, you're giving me orders again."

"Please, Maggie. I have enough to worry about without thinking of you bending over the tub by the hour." His voice dropped to a whisper. "Please do this for me."

Her irritation vanished as quickly as it had come. She still wanted to defend her freedom to do what she wished, but the pleading in his eyes was too hard to ignore.

And he had said "please."

When Anna showed up for work, Maggie called Rob into the foyer. "This is Anna MacLeod. I've explained why you have the shotgun by your side, and she'll be verra happy to do the washing as well as hang it out for me."

Rob clasped Anna's chapped hand. "I'm verra pleased to meet you, and I want to thank you for doing this turn for Maggie."

The lass, caught in those awkward years between bairn and woman, with a nose slightly too large that would be perfect when grown into, a thin, pointed chin only needing a bit more flesh, and wearing a sweater and skirt several sizes too large—probably to cover her maturing body—blushed and lowered her eyes. "Och, 'tis my pleasure, especially after our Maggie helped with doctoring wee Beasag's belly-thraw."

He glanced at Maggie, eyebrow raised.

"Beasag's the Gaelic for 'Bessie.' The bairnie had colic and I told Katag, that's Anna and Beasag's mither, to stop eating so much cabbage and neeps. That often relieves breast-fed bairnies suffering from gas."

Rob wrote to the Bank of England in London, requesting two hundred pounds from his savings account.

"The lass doesn't expect to be paid that much." Maggie protested.

"'Tisn't all for her. It should last a long time. I never did like being without silver, and there were only a few pound notes in my uniform pocket in that duffle bag."

⁂

The days crawled by but the only calls they received were from Flora or Morag asking if they had heard anything from the police. They both looked forward to Elspeth's visits as a break from their anxiety. Maggie, who had always used the time to do something she delighted in like working in her garden, was surprised to find herself enjoying Rob's language lessons.

Amazed at how quickly he learned new phrases, she forgot her anxiety and teased him when he looked perplexed at a Scots idiom. "'Aff at the knot' doesn't sound any stranger than some of those American idioms you used at the Infirmary."

"Wouldn't it be easier just to say 'daft'?"

"Mebbe, but I remember you saying one of the new orderlies was 'off his rocker' when he said creamed calves-heads were tasty."

⁂

Maggie was washing the breakfast dishes when Rob wheeled through the kitchen door and said, "It's been a week. Don't you think we should call Oban?"

As anxious for news as Rob, Maggie made the call, asking to speak to Sergeant Grant.

"The sergeant's not at his desk," the dispatcher said, her bored tone irritating. "May I direct your call to one of our constables?"

"No, thank you. The Procurator Fiscal's office will call another time." Maggie smirked as she disconnected. "That should wake her up."

Rob, fuming, picked up a glass paperweight from John's desk and aimed it at the wall.

Only Maggie's horrified gasp kept him from hurling it, smashing it into a thousand pieces.

"What's the matter with that Grant? It can't take this long to compare some fingerprints. I'm about to crawl out of my skin."

"You're not the only one anxious to hear."

He slumped deeper into his wheelchair, head in hands.

Och, what right did she have to complain when he had been

either lying in bed or sitting in that wheelchair for so many weeks?"

"I'm sorry, luve." She took the paperweight from his hand and returned it to her father's desk. "I'm just weary of staying inside, and you've been confined far longer than I."

"I'm the one who's sorry." He rubbed his forehead. "I'm so tired of having my stomach tied in knots, fearing somebody's going to hurt you." He squirmed beneath her steady gaze. "What's the matter? Still upset, or did I miss a place shaving?"

"Let's go into the foyer and I'll give you a haircut." She pushed the forelock off his forehead. "If it grows much longer, you'll need a bit of string to tie it back."

"Can you cut hair? A barber did it at the Royal Infirmary."

"There isn't a woman on Innisbraw who can't give her menfolk a proper haircut." Though she had no clippers, she used a pair of sharp surgical scissors like a professional, and even lathered and shaved the back of his neck. When she finished, she wheeled him into his room and brought her hand mirror. "Well?"

"'Tis perfect. I've never had a better haircut."

※

Hugh, who had been dropping in for a visit every few days, noticed how the waiting upset them, made them sober and anxious. The lighthearted bantering between them no longer animated their conversation.

On his latest visit, he made a joke about Rob's short military haircut, saluting him briskly when he walked into the foyer. When neither reacted with a smile, he said, "Och, I've had enough of this. You are going to listen to me."

They stared at him as if surprised.

Granted, he was a spokesman for the Savior, but hadn't the Lord exhibited righteous anger at least once? He stood in front of Rob's wheelchair, rocking back and forth on his heels, hands clasped behind his back. "This fear and unhappiness has gone on long enough." He pinned them with a stern gaze. "I know you've been praying about the polis investigation, but 'tis obvious you're no' depending on the Lord to provide the outcome He deems fitting."

Maggie stood stiffly at Rob's side.

"Lass, I expected better from you. You spent years under my teaching and, though your schooling and war duties have kept you from hearing the Truth for a long time, you should have enough residual doctrine in your soul to see you through this."

Maggie blinked away tears. "I know."

"Then perhaps you could share your reason with me."

She lowered her head. "I've been afraid to ask for God's perfect will. I can't bear the thought of somehow losing Rob."

"This isn't about the threat on your life?"

"Och, no. I know I won't be called home to Heaven 'til our Lord deems it time." She knelt next to Rob's wheelchair.

Rob rested his cheek against the top of her head. "Maggie's just voiced my own fears about asking the Lord's perfect will," he said, words hesitant. "I haven't been able to end my prayers that way, because I'm afraid I'll lose my Maggie, either to a killer or because ..."

"Because you're no longer convinced you want to return to Innisbraw at the end of the war?" Hugh did not wait for an answer. He put his arms around their shoulders, praying silently for the Holy Spirit to guide his words. "For many weeks you've been beset by emotional and physical trials, Rob, yet you've told me you're reaching out to our Lord in prayer more and more. Why?"

"Because Elspeth and Maggie have just about convinced me God hears my prayers, no matter how inadequate I feel."

"They're telling you that every child of God is infinitely precious to Him and He is capable, through His omniscience and omnipresence, motivated by His perfect luve, and aided by the power of His Holy Spirit, to answer every prayer of each believer?"

"Aye."

"So, you once trusted Him to forgive your sins and accept you into His presence when your journey on earth is over, yet you can't trust Him enough to take care of this latest stumbling block to your future happiness?"

"I know He'll take care of it," Rob said. "I'm just no' sure I'll want to live with His answer." His arms tightened around Maggie.

"I prayed for His perfect will before I confronted Una. Yet, instead of changing her mind about hating me, she threatened Maggie's life. How could He want that?"

"Haven't either of you realized there are many, many more affected by Una's evil doings than only just you twa? There are all the folk on this island, John and his staff, the polis and their families and co-workers, the patients who could be waiting for your future care, Maggie. And the men you could someday command again, Rob. Even the results one load of bombs dropped from your B-17 on enemy soil could have on a war that affects so much of the world. Och, the list is endless.

"Our lives are never lived in a vacuum, but are interwoven with countless others, yet God's perfect plan is just that—a perfect plan for each and every life, worked out to His satisfaction, in the fullness of His time."

"I ... I've never considered that," Rob said. "You must think me selfish."

"No' selfish, just human with only finite knowledge and a limited exposure to the Truth." Hugh squeezed his shoulder, then looked at Maggie. "And you, lass?"

"I have no excuse for disremembering all you've just said. I've heard you teach the Truth all my life. I've allowed my emotions to overwhelm what I know."

Hugh couldn't help a wee smile. "I'm told first luve can be a bit overwhelming." He stood over them, the sorrow he felt for their fear of the future tightening his throat. "'Tis easy to trust the Lord when everything is going right, but when all is darkness, can you still see the bright beacon of His Word? He hasn't changed. He's the same yesterday, the day, and forever. He's waiting for us to trust Him so He can bless our lives. David said it so simply in Psalms 40: 1. 'I waited *patiently* for the Lord and He listened to me and heard my cry.'"

"Patiently." Rob shook his head.

Hugh placed a hand on each of their heads. "Take that step right now. Ask silently for His perfect will with this problem and you won't be disappointed."

They closed their eyes and prayed.

※

Their radio call sign came faintly from John's office only moments after Hugh's departure.

Maggie raced through the hall, pushing Rob's wheelchair. She answered the call while Rob leaned close.

"This is DS Grant." The formal, clipped tone of the sergeant's voice brought such a relief, she exhaled a deep sigh. "Is this Miss McGrath?"

"It is that."

"Is that shotgun-armed colonel at your side?" Grant asked, voice dripping with sarcasm.

"Of course." Maggie crossed her fingers, giving Rob a wicked smile. "And since it's taken so long to hear from you, he's threatening to keep the gun loaded."

"Och, tell him there's no need for that."

She and Rob exchanged smiles.

"It's taken longer than I expected to get back to you because we've been trying to convince MacGinnis to implicate the person who gave him the whisky. But he's a stubborn man and won't budge, even when threatened with extra jail time for being uncooperative. The man has been drunk so long his mind has gone soft. Every time it looks like he's about to give us a name, he mutters something about bringing a curse on his head and refuses to say owt."

"What about the fingerprints?" Rob shouted.

"There's no need to raise your voice, Colonel. I was about to tell you that indeed, there were prints on the handle of the knife, and though some were smudged, we did find a match to those we took from MacGinnis. He's definitely the man who damaged Miss McGrath's clothing and pillow."

Rob closed his eyes. "Thank Ye, Lord," he breathed.

Maggie shivered. "Is he going to jile?"

"The Procurator Fiscal has assured me he'll spend at least six months in prison, perhaps longer since his crime was committed in an infirmary with a patient in residence, and he'll also be charged with receiving stolen goods which will add at least another six months."

"And Una Hunter?" Maggie's voice trembled. How or when would God solve the woman's determination that Rob leave the island?

"As I already explained, without MacGinnis naming her as an accomplice, we have no legal recourse but to serve her with a Restraining Order, which will be delivered to her in person by two of my staff by the end of the week. I do want you to know, however, that before I left Innisbraw, I visited Miss Hunter and assured her that should an unfortunate accident befall you, Miss McGrath, she will spend the remaining days of her life in jail."

Maggie thanked the Sergeant before bursting into tears.

Rob fought raging emotions. She was safe. His Maggie was safe.

He took the shotgun from his side, put it on John's desk, and gathered her close, kissing her cheeks, her forehead, and fragrant hair, as he sent up a silent *Thank Ye*, to a very forgiving and faithful Savior.

Maggie radioed her father, Hugh, and Morag and Angus, and the word of the policeman's information quickly spread around the island.

Engrossed in sweeping her front stone flags, Una jumped when Mark Ferguson surprised her by coming home early from a fishing trip. He hollered the news from the path to Susan, busy at her spinning wheel in their croft yard. "Tormad radioed every trawler, lass," he shouted. "Auld man MacGinnis is guilty. His fingerprints were on the knife. He's going to jile!"

As he embraced his joyous wife, Mark looked over the path at Una who stood frozen in place, her heather-twig broom clutched tightly in her fingers. "You're next, you auld witch!" he yelled.

Una barely heard his taunt. *Did he betray me?* her mind screamed. *Did that old drunkard tell them about me?*

Rob and Maggie spent the evening on the entry, savoring the crisp ocean-scented breeze, gazing up at the startlingly vivid reds and purples undulating across the sky.

"I just pray your faither and Hugh are right, and Una won't be able to talk another man into doing her evil deeds," Rob said.

"I know they're right." She laughed as she grabbed his ears and brought his mouth down to hers.

Chapter Thirty-three

Angus's cart pulled up in front of the infirmary, Elspeth on the front bench while old women crowded the back.

Rob, who had been waiting for his Scots lesson, released the brakes on his chair and started to retreat until Elspeth called out to him. He turned his chair and watched through narrowed eyes as she slowly climbed the steps.

She leaned over and kissed his cheek. The familiar scent of heather brought an ache to his chest.

"I once said you weren't one to run away from a challenge." She hugged his shoulders. "Was I wrong, lad?"

"I have nowt to say to them."

She brushed aside his gruff words with a wave of her hand. "They haven't come to hear anything from you, but to ask forgiveness. You've told me a wee bit about your lonely days in the orphanage, but you aren't the only one in this world who has felt the pangs of loneliness."

He sighed with a reluctant nod.

The women hobbled up the steps, so frail they looked as if a brisk breeze could lift them from their feet and send them sailing off the fell like desiccated leaves. Clad in threadbare cotton housedresses with tattered shawls over their white hair or stooped shoulders, faces sunken-cheeked and wizened, gnarled fingers clasped tightly together, they huddled in silence behind Elspeth.

Maggie had told him about these women who spent their lives labouring in cottage and croft for eighteen or more hours a day, birthing their bairnies on straw-filled pallets and only hours later cradling them in crude cloth slings so the wee ones could suckle without interrupting their mother's unending tasks.

He could see no trace of the young lasses they had once been—

clear-eyed and dreaming away nights with visions of a bright future once they won the heart of a lad. The hard knot of resentment filling his chest began to loosen.

Maggie stepped from the doorway, smiling a greeting.

"Remember, none of our aulder women speak Scots," Elspeth said, "so I believe your Maggie should translate what they have to say."

"I'll be as true to their words as I can, luve." Maggie squeezed his hand.

He cleared his throat. "All right."

The first old woman to speak had been at that Hunter woman's side in the kirkyard. She began in a halting voice, her words so soft they were almost carried away on the brisk breeze. By the time she finished speaking, she held a frayed handkerchief clutched to her mouth, sobs shaking her body.

"This is Dolly MacSween," Maggie said. "She wants you to know she will never forgive herself for no' grabbing the stones from Una's hand when she saw her scoop them up from the ground. She begs your forgiveness, though she knows she doesn't deserve it. She also said she will have nowt to do with Una again and will never, ever allow herself to open her heart to the darkness that overcame her that dreadful day."

Dolly knelt before Rob and groped for his hands, sobs shaking her thin shoulders as she spoke again.

Maggie pressed his shoulder. "She said you remind her of her son who served and died in that terrible First World War, and she thanks you for caring enough to come all the way from America to help fight this war and prays you will return safely to Innisbraw when it is over."

Rob prayed for the Lord's help before laying a hand on Dolly's trembling arm. "Please tell her I'm trying to understand. And I hope we can be friends someday."

After Maggie translated his words into the Gaelic, Dolly kissed his hand, struggled to her feet, and collapsed into Elspeth's waiting arms.

An emotional hour followed. After the last woman apologized,

Rob slowly rubbed the side of his nose. "Tell them I understand how hard this was to do. I'm as sorry as they are about what happened, but it showed me something I never could have known otherwise—some of Innisbraw's folk might get wrong-footed at times, but they have the courage to admit their mistakes."

The encounter exhausted him, and Maggie insisted he take a nap. "I know you didn't sleep well last night after our guid news so don't look at me with that stubborn set to your jaw," she scolded when he started to protest. "Besides, I'm tired myself. I'll curl up in the chair while you sleep."

He soon lay in the bed.

Maggie wanted to ask if he felt better about making a life on Innisbraw someday, but he fell asleep so quickly, she didn't get the opportunity.

When he awakened an hour later, he broached the subject while she helped him into his boots. "I noticed one woman missing from that group this mornin."

"Och, if you mean Una, don't hold your breath for that one to ever show up here, though I'm thinking she's going to find herself verra lonely with all the auld widows shunning her."

"She'll just find others to take their place."

Maggie stood and brushed off her palms. "Never. After what Flora told me Hugh said at kirk, there isn't a woman, or man for that matter, who will listen to a word she says."

"What makes her so hateful?"

"I don't think anybody knows. All I've ever heard is that she suffered when no' a lad on the island showed any interest in her. It happened long before I was born."

He sat on the bed, looking out the window at the cloud-streaked sky. Was there a chance he could find himself accepted here on Innisbraw? He would have to meet more of the folk, see how they reacted to him. He'd read or heard someplace that the Scots were notorious for carrying grudges. Surely, the old men who enjoyed their wee drams would resent losing their only supply of whisky.

Many of the island's folk dropped by the infirmary. Sheila MacNab, the kirk organist, and her crofter-husband, Arthur, overcame their initial shyness and chatted amicably.

"We are most sorry about that awful Sabbath," Arthur said as they were preparing to leave. "Please know our folk will be most pleased if you choose Innisbraw for your home."

All the other crofters and fishermen and wives who came by voiced the same sentiments. Rob and Maggie had such a grand time visiting with Mark and Susan Ferguson, Maggie asked them to stay for supper.

Every time visitors left, Rob waited for Maggie to ask if he finally felt welcome and was relieved when she never did. He had no answer yet. Some of the folk in Newton, New Hampshire, resented having such a large orphanage in their small village and he had often been the target of their kids' taunts about his patched, second-hand clothing and rusty bicycle. Despite Maggie and Hugh's reassuring words about incomers being welcome, how could he live the rest of his life on such an isolated island where he wasn't wanted?

The visits slowed to a trickle. Rob worked on the parallel bars and spent the rest of the day in his wheelchair, accompanying Maggie as she went about her daily turns. If John didn't allow him crutches soon, he'd go daft.

Rob tapped his fingers on the arms of the chair during his new studies in the Gaelic.

"Are you feeling a wee bit pent-up, lad?" Elspeth asked. "The way you always have your fingers tapping, tapping. Or perhaps 'tis the swarms of midges making you so jumpy. Those meanbh-chuileags—wee flies—can be most irritating. I've an idea you'd be pacing the stones of this entry if you could."

"In a minute, and it isn't the midges." He slapped the arm of his chair. "You don't know how tired I am of sitting in this chair. I feel like I'm in prison."

She rapped his arm with her pencil. "How do you fill your time when you're no' exercising or studying with this auld woman?"

"I follow Maggie around from room to room, no better than a dog too lazy to chase his own tail. I've been looking forward to later this mornin when I'm going with Maggie to hang the washing. Hugh finally talked me into letting her do it again since 'tis one of her favorite chores."

"You mean you still fear for her safety?"

"I guess I'm acting like Maggie. I call her a 'mither hen' for the way she's always keeping an eye on me, but I'm just as bad."

"Why don't we go out to the back yard right now? You can wheel your wheelchair down to that stone walk over there and follow it to the back girse where she hangs the washing to dry."

He eyed the walk she pointed to. "She's told me no' to use that ramp without her beside me."

"Och, she is a mither hen." She struggled to her feet. "I'll be with you, so on you go. Let's go do some exploring."

His stomach fluttered with excitement as he studied the ramp. It must be used for access to the back of the infirmary, or even to the front path, without having to use the stone stairs. Taking care not to move too quickly, he maneuvered the chair down the ramp from the entry to the walk. "How are you doing?" he asked Elspeth, who walked behind him, gripping the wheelchair handles.

"I never did like a blethering traveling companion." She knuckled the top of his head. "Hold your tongue and let's see if this chair can go faster than a wee bairnie learning to crawl."

He wheeled faster, taking care not to outpace her steps.

"Maggie's been hard at work. Her garden is a wonder," she mused.

He looked over the stone dyke at the flowers in front of the McGrath cottage.

"I wish I was taller or that dyke shorter so I could see it all," Elspeth said.

"Once I'm on crutches, I'll take you over there. I've been wanting a closer look, too."

When they rounded the back corner, Rob stopped so abruptly, Elspeth scolded him and told him to move forward a few more feet so she could see what caught his attention.

He rolled the chair forward, gazing in wonder at the wide expanse of grass that led up to the stone dyke at the back of the croft, a profusion of tiny wildflowers covering the area with a carpet of yellow, blue, white, lavender, and pink. "Look at all the wee flowers," he breathed.

She stepped onto the grass and stood beside him. "Raise your eyes, lad, for that's where the real beauty lies. That is Ben Innis with her four stone sentinels standing guard at the top."

He shaded his eyes from the glare of the sun and looked up. "It's so big," he said, filled with awe. At the very top of the mountain peak, four tall, erect stones stood dark against the cloudless sky, reminding him of pictures he had seen of Stonehenge. Narrow paths meandered across and up the ben, skirting large yellow bushes, but most of its flanks were blanketed by heather bushes covered with flowers in varying shades of purple. The fragrance of heather brought an instant vision of Maggie's face.

"Aren't you happy you came now?"

"I am that." His gaze was drawn to a huge pile of peat at one side of the yard. He started to ask Elspeth about the intricate way it was stacked when Maggie called his name from the entry. Her voice rose in urgency every time she called.

"Och, I'm in trouble now," he said. "I shouldn't have gone off without telling her."

"Then call to her. There's no reason to frighten the lass."

He placed two fingers in his mouth and let out a shrill whistle. When footsteps raced over the stone flags toward him, he turned his chair. "I'm back here, Maggie. With Elspeth."

She careened around the corner, eyes wild, hair in disarray. "Och, Rob, what are you doing out here?" she cried, hand clasped to her heart. "And Elspeth, you could have fallen on that uneven walk."

Elspeth drew herself up to her full height of just under five feet. "I don't like that tone of voice from a wee sliver of a lass. Rob was fidgety this morning so I saw no reason to wait for you."

Rob held out his arms and Maggie fell into his lap, pressing her face against his shoulder. "I'm sorry, luve. I got so busy I disremembered all about you coming out here with me after your lesson." He raised her chin so he could look into her eyes. "I've never really seen Ben Innis." He brushed stray tendrils of hair from her forehead. "And there's a whole island out there to explore. When I'm finally walking, I'm going to cover every inlet, every path, every burn, and especially that fresh water loch you told me about." He took a deep, uneven breath. "A man has the right to see the place he ... he might want to call home the rest of his life."

Maggie nodded. "Then see it you shall but you won't have to wait that long. We'll put your chair in Angus's or Alec's cairt and allow you to explore even before you can walk on your own."

The idea excited him. What better way to gauge the reactions of the folk than getting out among them? "Can we really do that, Maggie? See the island? Someday, when I return to duty, I want to call up images of Innisbraw from my mind when I think it."

"And you shall, but I hear Angus with his cairt come to take Elspeth home. Can you stay here while I walk her out to the main path and fetch my laundry basket?"

"I won't move a muscle."

He helped Maggie fold the sheets so she could hang them on one of the four lines strung across the center of the grass, smiling when she stretched onto her tiptoes to reach the higher ends of the line where she hung the sheets. She had discarded the woolen tights she wore in cold weather and this first glimpse of her shapely knees flooded him with warmth.

She was quiet for a time, probably thinking about his reluctance to return to Innisbraw.

Before long, she sang as she worked—some ballad in the Gaelic—and the soft language and her clear soprano voice rising and falling to the lilting cadence brought tears to his eyes.

When she hung the last item, she ducked the sheets flapping wildly in the wind and danced from item to item, touching each once with her forefinger, then her pinkie, before moving on to the next.

He grinned when she returned to him, breathless, cheeks and lips rosy, and blue eyes sparkling. "You looked like a fairy casting a spell on everything so it would dry quickly and smell of heather and honey, the twa scents I'll always associate with Innisbraw—and you."

"A fairy, is it?" She grabbed the empty basket from his lap. "'Tis a dance Elspeth taught me when I was a verra young lass and it makes me feel so guid, I still do it."

"You all finished?"

"Unless you want to stay out here, though you do have an appointment with those parallel bars."

"Let's get it over with. At least it puts me on my feet for a while. Don't worry, I'll be back out here, and soon."

Chapter Thirty-four

Una Hunter paced from one side of her small cottage to the other, hands clenched into tight fists. Each day brought more irritation. She had tried to visit some of the widows but they slammed their doors in her face. "Good riddance. Stupid, weak, gullible old fools!"

Even those who lived on her path, like Susan Ferguson, turned up their noses and ignored any attempts at conversation. She would never go to kirk again, which meant no more catching up on island gossip. Hugh's public scolding angered rather than shamed her, but she could no longer tolerate anything that milksop said.

Pray for help and the Lord will answer.

Utter nonsense. Her ancestors, the Celts, knew the gods and goddesses to worship—the ancient ones with powers to shame the Christian God.

Her temples throbbed. Why did she have so many headaches? Surely, they were that Yank's fault, the way he talked down to her. She came from quality, from folk with money and prestige who paid for her education.

And the nerve of that policeman, first threatening to put her into jail if anything happened to Maggie, then sending a restraining order signed by a magistrate, forbidding her to get anywhere near Maggie or that Yank.

Threatening to put a curse on that old drunken fool sealed his mouth. The police hadn't taken her off to a jail cell. But she still lived in this miserable cottage on Innisbraw. "I've always hated this island and its ignorant crofters and fishermen." She spat. "It's even worse now, and it's all that Yank's fault."

She passed the hutch and her gaze caught on a sepia picture of her only relative still living in Scotland. All the other aunts, uncles, and cousins in the Munro family sailed off to America before the war. At least they sent her a little silver each month, enough to live on if she was careful.

Such a faded, old picture. She carried it to the front window to study each detail. Her mother's only sister, clad in a fancy silk gown, sitting in the parlor of her well-appointed two-storey home situated high on a hill above Portree on the Isle of Skye. She wrote her aunt every week, but her letters always came back, "Addressee Unknown" stamped in black ink across the envelope. She had checked the address several times. Fools staffed even the General Post office.

For years, she had waited for word that her very elderly aunt was ill and needed her. She would make herself indispensable and once the old woman passed, that stately home with its gardens and fountains and lovely furniture would be hers.

She looked around at the cramped, ugly cottage she had lived in all of her life and closed her eyes, picturing life in a grand home with roomy bedrooms on the first floor, up that broad staircase sweeping elegantly from the ground hall.

Her own bedroom, with a large bed, dressing table, and wide armoire for her clothes.

Not the narrow cot that had been hers for as long as she could remember. No privacy growing up, only an uncomfortable box-bed in the family part of the two-room cottage. She tried sleeping in her parent's bedroom the night after she buried her mother, but didn't last an hour. Too many voices were trapped in there—voices that tittered and whispered obscene words.

If Auntie didn't write for her to come soon, she would take the initiative and think of a way to go to Skye without an invitation. "But in the meantime, it's up to me to get rid of that Yank once and for all."

Rubbing her pounding temples, she made her way into the kitchen and checked that she had all the ingredients needed for one large scone. No sugar, but flour, and a few spices to mask the foul taste of her secret ingredient.

She took a small leather bag from the back of her writing desk and opened it, taking care not to get any of the oil from the toxic seeds on her fingers. Henbane, the deadly herb the Celtic goddess Scathach reminded her about in a dream just the past night. Everyone on the island knew the Yank had a taste for scones. At the right time, when no one expected it, she would find a way to leave the scone next to his bed.

No reason to hurry. She would be very clever not to be caught inside the infirmary. Safely back in her cottage, what evidence could link her to anything? It would be in his stomach.

"A healthy dose of Henbane to cure what ails you, Yank," she mused, "and you cannot be too angry with me. After all, it is said to be a most pleasant though lingering death."

Chapter Thirty-five

"Hope Angus isn't late," Rob said, fingers tapping.

"You're fidgeting like a hen on a hot griddle," Maggie replied. "We're out here a wee bit early. I didn't know how long it would take you to maneuver your chair down the ramp and to the path."

"You can't know how I've been looking forward to this."

"Your waiting is over." She squeezed his shoulders. "Here he comes."

Angus pulled his cart to a halt in front of the infirmary stairs. "Hear you'd do for a keek at Innisbraw," he said, grinning at Rob. He pulled two long pieces of wide, heavy lumber from the back of the cart. "I brought a sort of ramp I gathered together this mornin. With you wheeling, and me pushing, you'll be up there in a tick."

The ramp proved easy to use with minimal effort.

Angus angled Rob's chair. "You'll see more if you're riding backarts." He pulled Maggie into the cart. "Flora sent a stool so you can sit at Rob's side." The crofter climbed onto the driver's bench. "Where first?"

"Doesn't matter," Rob said. "I haven't seen much."

Maggie's smile evaporated.

He regretted his hasty words. "I remember Elspeth's flowers when you brought me here."

Angus took his cue from Rob and pulled the cuddy to a stop in front of Elspeth's cottage.

She wandered about her garden, deadheading blossoms, a light shawl pulled over her hair. "So, you're out broadening your horizons at last, lad? 'Tis only fitting."

"I owe it all to you. Without your prodding, I'd never have dreamed this possible."

"Och, on you go then. Explore. Find out all you can about the island you'll be calling home forever."

The certainty of her tone tied his tongue in knots.

Angus slapped the reins over Jack's broad, bony back and he and Maggie lifted their hands in farewell.

Half way down the hill, Maggie pointed out the path leading inland to Angus and Flora's croft.

Soon, Angus pulled the cuddy to a stop in front of a stone building with a large Scottish flag whipping in the breeze.

Several women standing by the building smiled and called out greetings.

He took deep breaths of the fresh, briny scent of the sea.

"That's Alice Ross's Post Office," Maggie said. "She lives in the back."

"And that run-down place next to it? That must be the howff."

"It is, but 'tis closed now since Donald MacGinnis will never be welcome back on Innisbraw."

Two older women came out of what Maggie told him was the weaving shop. They smiled and waved before hurrying up the path.

The knot in Rob's stomach eased.

His gaze took in the large abandoned shed on the harbour side. It looked in good condition, though the slate roof could use some work. From what he could see, it appeared perfect for a boat-building business. Too bad.

The path turned west. No more businesses. Only a post office, shuttered howff and weaving shop?

"Is the grocery store on the other side of the island?"

"Och, there isn't one on Innisbraw. We give Malcolm our ration coupons, a list of our needs, and silver. He brings our order from Oban."

No wonder everybody had a garden and at least a goat, pig, or chickens if they had a large enough croft.

They passed a large copse of tall trees, and he spotted the kirk spire and steeled himself when Angus pulled the cart to a stop.

Maggie pointed to a two-storey stone building. Several rocking chairs graced a broad, railed entry, offering a place to rest after a long walk. "That's Hugh's manse. The minister before him had ten bairns, so 'tis huge. Hugh doesn't even use a fraction of the rooms." She waved her hand at a dense stand of tall trees and hedge of bushes behind the manse. "The primary school is back there, but the leaves hide it from view in summer. There's a large hall around the side of the kirk where Hugh hopes to hold ceilidhs when the war's over."

"What's a 'kay-lee'?"

"A ceilidh 'tis a party with music, dancing, and story-telling. A guid time for a blether between friends."

Rob averted his gaze from the kirk. Too many bad memories.

Angus slapped the reins and they continued west, passing two large crofts with neat cottages, peat piles, and herds of cows. A few sheep, goats, and cuddies grazed on the lush grass.

Angus halted the cart and leaned back. "Up that path is Heuch Fell." He pointed to Rob's left.

"The stone quarry and broch are up there," Maggie said, "but that's a climb that'll have to wait 'til you're walking well."

A steep, deeply rutted path zigzagged across the face of the high fell. Sparse grass and a few wildflowers clutched the thin soil surrounding scattered piles of grey stones. A few huge rocks, lichen-covered and somehow menacing, crouched on the hillside, like giant behemoths protecting their young.

Now, Rob understood why all the cottages on the island were made of the same grey stone. From what he could see, the entire fell was nothing but rock. "I know what a quarry is, but what's a broch?"

"'Tis the ruins of an auld, round, stone tower that once served as a home and fortress to some of Innisbraw's earliest inhabitants. 'Tis said it goes back to the Iron Age."

He whistled. "Now, that's what I call auld."

Maggie pointed to the last and largest croft where a herd of broad-horned cows lay in their pasture, placidly chewing their cuds. "That's Alec and Morag's croft. Alec must have his bulls tethered out on the machair. Those are all coos and heifers."

"I thought only bulls had horns."

"They raise Hieland cattle only. The coos also have horns."

They rode in silence until the path took another abrupt turn and Rob spied the mighty Atlantic, waves combing far out over a shallow seabed. Between the shore and path was what Maggie called the "machair," heavy with wildflowers. Here and there bulls staked to long ropes grazed, their long, rough tongues pulling up the tallest grass. A few low stone dykes separated parts of the machair, where stretches of grain crops and turnip fields rippled in the breeze, a colourful patchwork of gold and dark green.

"So this is the western side of the island," Rob said. "Is there any way to get down to the water from this main path?"

"We don't have time to explore all the paths now. Angus, why don't you take Rob to that cove just past Scaur Fell? It has a bonnie strand with white sand and shallow water." She leaned close to Rob. "'Tis also where twa men patrol at night since it offers such a broad, shallow landing place for the Germans."

Angus turned Jack down a narrow path heading directly west.

Rob scanned the coast. Maggie was right—no rock outcroppings were high enough to form a cave. Och, why did memories of the Selkie's tale keep popping into his mind? Perhaps because he'd heard it so many times, clutching at the diversion from pain. He seldom thought of Maggie as the Selkie anymore—she was his lass, his Maggie.

Nearing the shore, the wind intensified. Maggie pulled her shawl over her hair. Angus turned the cart around and brought it to a halt in front of a shallow cliff above the sandy shore and Rob's breath caught at one of the most breathtaking panoramas he had ever seen.

Sand so white it almost blistered the back of his eyes, waves curling up to the shore in gentle undulations. Large, flat rocks to the north and south covered with basking seals. Several unfamiliar species of birds swooped overhead and clownish puffins rode the swells. Other smaller rocks, draped with clumps of seaweed, resembled misshapen heads with clumsy haircuts.

Och, how he wanted to take off his boots, climb down from the cart, and run on that sand barefooted. He turned to Maggie. "'Tis so grand it takes my breath away."

"It is that." She massaged his shoulders. "But we'd best be getting along. There's still a lot to see."

Angus clucked to Jack.

Rob burned the image of the cove into his mind.

They continued south, the cart's wheels juddering on a wide stone bridge over a rocky burn tumbling toward the sea. Just past the bridge, Rob's eager gaze took in a large body of dark water on his right, lined with large, uneven rocks, shores covered with masses of colorful wildflowers. "That must be the fresh-water loch. And on yonder brae's where they dig—och, cast peat. Please slow down, Angus, I want a guid look."

"Aye, that's Loch Donald," Maggie said. "'Tis the source of our drinking water and you can see how peaty it is by its dark colour. 'Tis fine water, which leaves our clothes without wrinkles and feeling soft, and you know how guid it tastes."

A breeze rippled the dark surface as flocks of birds dove and swooped over the water, feasting on swarms of midges. The cart moved again.

Rob tore his gaze away from the loch. Many small paths meandered off the main path toward the base of Ben Innis. "Where do those paths go?"

"Each is filled with cottages," Maggie explained. "'Tis where most of our folk live."

He looked at his watch. "Do we have time to go down one? I know 'tis getting late."

Angus tamped his clay pipe full of fresh tobacco and scratched a wooden match against the sole of his boot. "One I can do," he mumbled, sucking to keep the flame from dying. He inhaled deeply, smiling as the aromatic smoke drifted from between his lips. "I promised Flora I'd be home with time to do my turns before supper."

The voices of bairns laughing and shouting to one another in the Gaelic and Scots rode the breeze as Angus turned the cuddy into a narrow, twisted path. The cart rumbled between cottage crofts, some so small only a tiny, rocky yard, filled to overflowing with a struggling vegetable garden, that fronted the path. Pigs dozed in dusty wallows and chickens pecked about in sparse grass. Most of the cottages looked in poor condition, a few with newspapers and bits of cloth stuck into places where window glass belonged.

They passed an old woman using a butter plunger on her front door flags, and three cottages down, another, spinning wool. Both shouted greetings in the Gaelic, their smiles welcoming.

"You'll find only widows and auld folk on this path," Maggie said.

Rob studied the cottages. The deep-seated poverty sickened him. Something had to be done before Innisbraw slowly died away with its old folk.

He heard the bairns voices again and his heart fell. They were on the next path. He'd wanted to see them at play. When they reached the last cottage, Angus turned the cart and they returned to the main path.

The cart rumbled past a bent-shouldered old woman leading a shaggy cuddy with a large woven basket strapped to each side of its sturdy back. Both baskets bulged with slabs of peat.

Angus and Maggie called out a greeting, which the woman acknowledged with a shy smile and a wave.

"Shouldn't we stop and offer to help?" Rob asked.

"Sorcha's almost home," Maggie said. "She lives on the next path and would be embarrassed if we stopped. 'Tis guid to see somebody's cast her some peat and let her use their cuddy and creels. Her Murdo passed so long ago, our men-folk sometimes forget her needs."

Maggie had told him dried peat was light, but it still bothered Rob that a woman so old would have to walk to the bog and fill those baskets—creels—by herself.

They crossed several small stone bridges and passed numerous paths, exchanging greetings with the young women they met, all struggling to carry heavy buckets, bairns tugging at their skirts. "They've been to the nearest burn for water," Maggie said. "As I said before, most of our folk live on those paths, but after a bit you'll see our largest sheep crofts, stretching almost to the sea."

When the roar of heavy surf made conversation impossible,

Angus pulled the cuddy to a halt.

Vast areas of uneven, rock-strewn grass stretched behind on the right, countless sheep grazing or lying in groups, chewing their cuds with lazy contentment, black and white dogs keeping watch. Only a few thatched cottages with sheepfolds, peat piles, and low stone dykes separating crofts, kitchen gardens, and small turnip or oat fields broke up the vivid green landscape.

Angus clucked again and the cart made a turn to the east. Looking at the southern shore of the island, Rob understood why the crofters didn't bother patrolling it. What wasn't taken up by the steep cliff of Innis Fell on the far eastern side was given over to large jagged rocks marching in ragged, broken ranks out into the heaving waters of the Atlantic.

They made the long, slow climb to the top and across Innis Fell, pulling up in front of the infirmary.

Angus refused the pound note Rob offered him for his services. "'Twas my pleasure." The crofter ducked his head. Rob and chair unloaded, Angus left with a wave of his bunnet.

Maggie pushed the chair over the sandy path to the walk.

Rob wheeled up the ramp and stopped. "Come you on, luve." He pulled Maggie into his lap, hugging her. "I want to thank you for the day. Now, when I'm back to duty I'll have all those mind-pictures to take with me."

Her gaze, dark with anxiety, met his. "Do you feel better now, Rob? I mean about our folk?"

He thought for a moment. "I do that. I hope you understand I don't really know deep in my heart I can come back, but 'tis a guid start. I've a lot of praying to do."

"We both do. We can't let one bitter auld woman keep us from coming home."

"If that's the way it turns out, you're absolutely right." He removed her shawl and tangled his fingers in her wind-blown hair. "First in my memories of the day will be the picture of your smiling face with its rosy cheeks and those wee wisps of hair dancing around your forehead." He pulled her closer, whispering, "Thank ye, my Maggie," before lowering his lips to hers.

Chapter Thirty-six

The rapid pealing of the kirk bell woke Rob.

Maggie rushed into his room.

"What's wrong?"

"I don't know, but it's something bad. Hugh only rings the bell that fast to warn folk of an emergency and call them to prayer. I'm going to get dressed and run over to Angus's croft."

"What about U-boats? Could that be the problem?"

"Och, I don't know. Kirk bells have been banned in Great Britain since the war started, but because we have no siren, the War Department allows Hugh to ring ours. But U-boats never attack the islands during daylight."

He pushed back the covers and sat up. "Is there owt I can do?"

"Stay in bed and promise you won't try to get up."

"I'll stay right here. 'Tis a promise."

The long wait drove him crazy. Had the Germans landed on Innisbraw's western shore without being seen, and overpowered the poorly armed crofters? Gunfire couldn't be heard from the open window, though, and the sun had been up for almost an hour

Maybe it was a fire. Or someone had been injured. But wait, it was only—he looked at his watch—0500. Who would be up and about so early?

The fishermen.

A pain ripped across his belly. Was a trawler or creeler in trouble? He closed his eyes, beseeching the Lord to help whoever needed it and for whatever reason. He prayed the same prayer over and over, so frustrated he felt like shouting. If only he could be with Maggie.

The front door slammed and Maggie's running footsteps came from the hall.

He pulled himself up again.

She leaped onto the bed and threw herself into his arms, sobbing.

※

"What's happened? Is it the Germans?"

She shook her head, struggling hard to catch her breath. Her mind spun with more loss. "'Tis ... 'tis Gregor Boyd's ... trawler." She panted. "She must have lost her rudder and was swept onto the rocks on the southern shore of Innisbraw."

"Has Barra rescue been notified?"

"Aye. But they can't get here in time to help. There are six souls aboard that boat, including Gregor and his own twa lads. Six souls, and all such guid lads."

"What was it doing near the south shore? I thought they only fished the Minch."

"He must have been heading for the Atlantic. Fishing the Minch is so poor right now."

"Is there any way they can make it to shore by climbing the rocks if they have to abandon ship?"

"No' with the incoming tide washing higher and higher over the rocks. They'll be battered to death. They're already abandoning ship. She's being driven to pieces by the surf beating against the sharp rocks. I'm going with Angus to help, but you have to promise to stay in bed while I'm gone."

He held her away. "I want to go with you. I don't need my wheelchair. I'll sit in the back of the cairt and hold on."

She shook her head, unwilling to waste time on senseless blether. "Och, you can't go, and what could you do even if you did?"

"I know first aid and I've been trained to help in plane crashes. Mebbe I can't help physically, but my mind isn't paralysed. I use logic to save lives. Please, Maggie. I have to go."

"Angus has already gone to catch and harness Feona, his fastest cuddy."

"Then go stand on the path and wait for him. First, bring my chair over and set the brakes so I can get into it. And toss me my clothes. Hurry, lass, please."

She rushed for the chair. She'd have to see he stayed in the cart. In less than a minute, Rob was seated and pulling his clothing on over his pyjamas while she ran for the entry.

Rob couldn't manage his socks and boots but pulled his A-2 jacket down from its peg on the wall and shrugged into it.

Angus's cart rattled up the hill. He and Maggie rushed in a moment later.

"Angus can help you into the cairt and lift your chair in and while he's helping you, I'll gather up some saline, blankets, and my medical bag." Maggie unlocked the brakes. "On you go. I'll catch you up in a tick."

Angus looked at Rob's bare feet and pulled two pairs of socks over them. "'Tis cold out there," he said, pushing the chair down the hall.

When they reached the cart, Rob heaved himself into the back and scooted forward while Angus struggled to lift his chair. The crofter helped Rob position his hands on the side slats and pull himself to his feet, then pushed the chair up behind him so he could drop into it. Rob had just set the chair's brakes when Maggie came out the door, hidden behind a pile of blankets and the large medical bag she carried.

She tossed everything into the cart and Angus pulled her in. Burying her head against his chest, she leaned against him and he joined her in prayer as the cart tore along the path over Innis Fell. When they reached the turn at the bottom of the fell, Angus slowed Feona slightly but kept her on a straight western course, wheels juddering over the rough machair.

It didn't take long to see the trawler, or what was left of her. She lay on her side, the agonized screams of her timbers being torn apart by the rocks one of the most horrifying sounds Rob had ever heard. They sounded human, like the shrieks of women in excruciating pain.

The shore was lined with men, some clad in woolen trousers and sweaters, a few wearing heavy tweeds and fishing boots.

Angus pulled the cart to a stop and turned it around so Rob and Maggie could see. "I'm going to help." He jumped down.

Several men removed their boots and tied long ropes around their waists before handing the other ends to men to hold. As Rob watched the rescuers struggling towards the rocks, he had a sudden idea. He put two fingers in his mouth, let out several shrill whistles, and cupped his hands around his mouth. "Bring me your ropes so we can tie them to the axle of the cairt!" he shouted. "'Tis stronger than any man! Hurry!" He whistled again and repeated his instructions.

Some of the men holding the loose ends rushed to tie their ropes to the axle while others had to be coaxed. Soon, five lines were tied to the cart's axle.

The rescuers scrambled over the rocks, their clothing drenched by the pounding surf.

Off to the right, one of the men with a rope around his waist climbed onto a rock and shouted, pointing. He slid off the rock and disappeared. He must have found one of the victims. If only he would have the strength to pull his burden back to shore.

"Maggie, get that group of men to gather over here. If one of those ropes tightens, tell them to leave it tied to the axle, but to line up and start pulling that rope in. On you go, lass."

She jumped down from the cart.

Soon, the men, including Angus, squatted on the ground, watching the ropes tied to the axle. They all reacted at once when one of the ropes began to twitch.

Maggie's teeth chattered when she rejoined Rob. He took off his jacket, helping her into it and zipping it before rolling up the sleeves.

"You'll freeze," she protested.

"I'm the warm-blooded one, remember?"

When that rope tightened, several men formed a line and began pulling. Within moments, four of the five ropes were being pulled in. "I hope somebody found twa fishermen," Rob said beneath his breath, "or we're one rope short."

They pulled the first rope to shore.

Broken Wings

Maggie leaped from the cart, grabbed her medical bag and several blankets, and ran to the man who dragged a limp body behind him. "'Tis Ivor. Found him behind a rock out there," he shouted.

Rob suppressed a groan.

She leaned over the victim, placing her fingers against his carotid artery.

Rob shouted, "Would Artificial Respiration help? In that cold water, it can bring him around if he hasn't stopped breathing too long."

"It will do no good. His head is crushed." Maggie closed Ivor's staring eyes and pulled a blanket over him.

Every fisherman pulled in had been either pummeled to death by the surf on the rocks or was dead from drowning far too long to revive. When only one rope remained, four bodies lay beneath blankets on the shore.

Frantic voices.

Women ran across the machair. When they neared the blanket-shrouded bodies, some doubled over, keening in grief. Others stumbled forward, fell to their knees, and tore blankets away from faces, wailing with heartbreaking agony. One, a lass about Maggie's age, held her husband's lifeless body in her arms, rocking back and forth, kissing his dark blue, bloated face again and again.

Rob tore his gaze from the harrowing scene. "Any action on that last rope?" he shouted to Angus.

"It's been moving a wee bit, but ... wait! Here she goes."

Rob closed his eyes and prayed for the men at the end of this last rope. They'd been lucky so far, none of the rescuers lost, but he feared for the life of this last brave man. He'd been in the water, battling rocks and the roaring surf, a long time.

Miraculously, the last rope held three men. Rob leaned forward, stomach cramping. Men waded into the surf to pull the victims up onto the shore. The rescuer who had risked his life dropped to his knees and retched, spewing seawater onto the sand.

Maggie grabbed some blankets and rushed to the rescuer's side. "Get it up, Michael, all of it." She told one of the men to strip Michael and wrap him in blankets before she hurried to the side of the closest victim. Dead—a gaping wound in the side of his head. She stepped to the side of the last victim and dropped to her knees.

Her breath caught.

Dougal MacLeod.

Only thirteen years old.

Chapter Thirty-seven

Maggie searched for wounds. Not finding any, she placed her fingers on Dougal's carotid. "I've got a pulse! Some of you men strip off his clothes so I can cover him with a blanket, and hand me that black bag. Quickly!"

"Maggie!" Rob yelled. "I'll have somebody get me down so I can help. You start AR, or show one of the heavier men how."

"Aye!" After the lad's clothes were removed, she laid a blanket on the sand and told the men to place him on his belly. She covered him with another blanket, pulled his lower jaw forward, placed his arm beneath his face to raise it off the blanket, and drew his legs apart. She motioned to the burly man standing nearby. "Neil, I'm going to show you what to do. Watch me carefully."

She placed her legs between the lad's and put a hand on either side of his back, at the base of his ribs. She pushed with all of her might, and then fell back on her knees before leaning forward to push again. "I'm no' heavy enough, but that's how you do it."

Neil followed her example.

After two pushes, water gushed from the lad's mouth.

Maggie stayed at his head, her fingers hovering on his carotid artery.

Two men lifted Rob from his chair and carried him over to the victim. "Set me down here beside Maggie. I'll monitor his pulse and breathing while she starts an IV."

She palpated the lad's arm, sterilized a spot, tied a piece of tubing, and inserted the needle. It took two attempts before blood rushed into the syringe. She capped it with the plunger and attached the end of the tubing into the hole, screwing it in tightly, then connected the other end to the Saline bottle, holding it high. "Tape the needle to his arm while I open the drip wide," she said to Rob.

He reached for the bag.

"How's his pulse?" she asked a few moments later.

"Verra thready and weak, and he's only taken a few breaths. Doesn't look guid."

Neil performed AR on Dougal for what seemed forever. The lifeboat from Barra arrived, was waved off, and departed. The lad's pulse gradually faded and stopped.

Rob shook his head.

Maggie motioned Neil to stop. "I'm so sorry." Grief drained colour from her cheeks. "He was in the water too long."

A woman kneeling beside Rob thrust a baby wrapped in a thin blanket into his arms. She wailed and sobbed.

One of the men who had risked his life in the boiling surf knelt next to her, shivering convulsively as he clasped her to his chest, tears streaming down his wind-burned cheeks.

"Och, my laddie, my poor, poor laddie," the woman keened, rocking back and forth. "I begged you no' to go to sea. Och, my poor laddie."

Rob pulled the blanket over the infant's head and held it close, sheltering it from the cold wind.

A woman nearby removed her shawl and placed it over the baby. "'Tis Beasag, poor Katag's last bairnie. Dougal was their only lad."

The bairnie with the colic. He lifted the infant higher in his arms and laid his cheek against the shawl. What a terrible, heart-breaking waste. Something had to be done to stop this needless loss of precious lives.

Innisbraw would someday have her own rescue boat and, with the Lord's help, he was going to design it.

Other carts appeared on the path from the north and bounced over the machair toward those gathered on the shore. Alec, Morag, and Hugh, the first to arrive, went from mourner to mourner, offering prayers, words of comfort, blankets, and hot sweetened tea from one of the many thermoses they brought.

Hugh was shocked to see Rob, clad only in a thin shirt and a pair of denims, sitting in the sand beside Katag and Gordon MacLeod who were weeping over a blanket-shrouded body. It must be their lad, Dougal. He staggered beneath the pain tearing at his heart.

Rob clutched a bairnie to his chest.

Hugh retrieved a blanket from Alec's cart and placed it over Rob's shoulders before kneeling beside him. "You shouldn't be out here, lad," he said into Rob's ear. "You could get sick."

Anguish filled Rob's face. While at war, this lad had seen enough death and heartache to last a thousand lifetimes.

Hugh leaned close to hear what Rob whispered.

"He was their only lad. Och, Hugh, I'm so tired of death and dying. When is it all going to end?"

"Only our Faither in Heaven knows." Hugh got to his feet and looked for Morag. "We've got to get Rob into his chair and back to the infirmary," he said when he found her. "He's seen too much death already and he's still weak."

She followed Hugh back to Rob. "I'll take that wee lass from you now. Her auntie is in that crowd of women. She'll see to the bairnie."

Rob uncovered the infant's face. Wee Beasag still slept, impervious to the havoc and sorrow going on around her. He brushed his fingertips lightly over her tiny cheek and handed her up to Morag, tears shining in his eyes.

Hugh took Maggie's arm just as she finished adjusting the drip on Michael's saline. "I need to get back to Katag and Gordon. Twa of the men carried Rob to Angus's cairt. You should get him up to the infirmary as soon as possible."

She leaped to her feet. "What happened? He was sitting there on the sand the last time I looked."

"He's going to be all right." Hugh led her to the cart. "This has been too much for him. You have to remember, these aren't the first deaths he's seen, nor will they be the last."

⚜

She pulled herself into the cart and rushed to Rob, who sat

huddled beneath a blanket, head in hands. "Och, luve, I should never have let you come." She put her arms around him. "Have you hurt yourself?"

He raised his head. "I'm fine," he said, voice hoarse. Tremors shook his body.

Tears of relief filled her eyes when Angus climbed up onto the driver's bench. "We have to get Rob back to bed. This has been too much."

"I wondered about that when he came," Angus said, "but he did a fine turn. His idea for using the cairt's axle was grand."

Alec leaned over the back of the cart. "We'll put Michael into our cairt along with several of the others who have cuts and scrapes and take them up to the infirmary. You get this lad back to bed where he belongs."

Maggie asked Morag and Flora to get Michael settled into a room at the infirmary while Angus wheeled Rob into his room and helped him onto the bed.

She stripped off his sandy outer clothing but left him in his pyjamas, then covered him with his regular sheet and blanket and added two more blankets.

He still trembled. "I'm no' cold, lass," he said as she tucked in the added blankets. "Just tired."

She knew better. His eyes looked haunted—the look she'd hoped never to see again.

She brought him some APCs and a large glass of water, waiting until he emptied the glass. "Off to sleep." She smoothed the forelock back from his forehead.

"Don't know if I can," he whispered.

He fell asleep within five minutes. Maggie located Morag and asked her to sit in a chair by his bed and come find her if he awoke.

She spent the next two hours working on the men who had risked their lives, stitching cuts, administering penicillin and tetanus shots, and sprinkling Sulfa powder over every wound.

When all of the patients but Michael were on their way home, she poured a cup of tea, and returned to Rob's room.

"He's slept like a bairnie," Morag whispered. "Hugh was right. He's seen too much death. He didn't need what he saw the day."

"He wanted to help but I shouldn't have let him."

"Och, he's a grown man." Morag hugged Maggie. "And grown men will do what they must. I'm thinking he'll be fine once he's had a guid sleep."

After she sent Michael home later that evening, Maggie brought her comforter and climbed onto the bed with Rob. Though exhausted, she couldn't even close her eyes. She prayed for each of those suffering unspeakable grief that night. And for Rob—that he wouldn't fall ill or have a relapse.

Rob awakened just as the sun crept over the horizon. He lay quietly for a long time, praying for those who had lost someone they loved, grieving they had been unable to save even that last lad. He didn't dwell on what it would be like to lose one's only lad. The briefest thought was torture enough.

Maggie appeared in the doorway.

He waved her over to the bed. "Guid-mornin." He kissed her.

"Och, you're awake. How do you feel? Are you in pain?"

"My stomach feels like my throat's been cut."

She hugged him. "Then you're really no' hurting?"

"I'm really no' hurting," he said. "How about you?"

"Only my heart. I never should have allowed you to go with—"

He covered her mouth with his hand. "I'm no' your bairnie, lass. I know what I did ultimately meant nowt, but at least I was trying. It made me feel like a whole man again."

"Hugh was afraid you'd seen too much already to go through what happened."

He laid his head back on the pillow. "It did bring some bad memories but that was war, Maggie, no' the senseless loss of life because Innisbraw doesn't have its own rescue boat. I think that's what gets to me the most, how unnecessary ...." He reached for the trapeze and pulled himself up. "I'll tell you, luve, I'm thinking the Lord had a hand in me being there yesterday. It made me all the more resolved to find a way for Innisbraw to have its own rescue boat."

Maggie threw her arms around him, smiling for the first time since the ringing of the kirk bell the morning before.

Chapter Thirty-eight

When Hugh visited later that morning he found Rob on the stone-flagged entry, a pot of coffee on the bench and his lap filled with sheets of paper covered with notes. "I was afraid you hurt yourself yesterday, but you look guid."

"Och, I'm fine, but I appreciate your concern. If only we'd been able to save that last lad."

"You've endeared yourself to the folk for all you did yesterday mornin. Nobody can believe a man who can't even walk would put himself out so much for folk he doesn't know, especially after all the trouble Una caused you."

"Don't make me out to be somebody special. Nowt I did helped a single victim."

"They were beyond help when they were pulled to shore, which is the way it always is—though they're usually lost far out to sea. I'm going inside for another mug so we can share that coffee while we talk." The minister left a folder on the bench with the name "Dougal Peadar MacLeod" printed on it.

The young lad he and Maggie tried to save—Anna and Beasag's brother.

Hugh returned with a mug, poured it full, and refreshed Rob's.

"Is this something you wanted me to see?" Rob held up the folder.

"It is that." Hugh sat on the bench. "The first time we met, you mentioned starting a boat-building business on Innisbraw. I admit I wasn't verra encouraging, for such a thought never entered my mind. But the more I think and pray about it, the more it lingers in my thoughts." He opened the folder and handed Rob a sheaf of primary school reports. "Here, mebbe this will clarify my concerns about our wee island."

Rob scanned the material.

Hugh took a swig of coffee and smacked his lips. "The Island Council and I tried verra hard to get Katag and Gordon to accept our help in sending Dougal to the academy on Harris, but they were too proud to accept any silver."

"He certainly was bright. With grades like these, he could have gone far."

"Dougal wanted to be a teacher, and he'd have made a fine one," Hugh said, setting his mug down. "This is what brought me to see you this mornin. We must start some sort of industry here on Innisbraw so those lads who don't want to be fishermen or crofters have another choice. It isn't only bringing back the lads who have already left, but hope for the future."

Sheets of paper littered Rob's lap. "These are some design ideas for a rescue boat I'm planning to work on when Maggie has to go ... go back to duty. I'm no' certain I'll be around to build it after the war, so I'll leave the plans here. That could provide work for a few lads."

"I see."

First Maggie, now Hugh. Disappointment followed in his wake like a spent wave collapsing on shore. "I'll leave a list of all the materials needed. And I'll make the plans as complete as possible." Smile grim, he asked, "Who knows? Mebbe by the time we defeat Hitler and the Japs I *will* come back and do it myself."

※

Rob didn't attend the funeral service the following afternoon, though Maggie begged him to. "I don't want to call attention to myself. No' at a time like this. You all knew and luved every one of those men and lads. Everyone should be allowed to grieve for them surrounded by their own island folk."

"You're certain 'tis no' because of what Una did?"

"That has nowt to do with it. If it makes you feel better, I promise no' to leave my room while you're gone."

She shook her head, eyes sad. "I still think you're wrong, but I'll no' argue about it."

※

Broken Wings

Early the following morning, Maggie contacted John by radio and left Rob to talk to him while she fixed breakfast.

"I've a big favor to ask," Rob said. "You're too busy yourself, but I need you to have someone find all the books for sale about boat-building, from the smallest to trawler size, from laying the keel to shakedown cruises. I'll pay them for their time."

"You're really going to do it?" John paused a beat. "I thought 'twas only a foolish dream, but after watching your determination to walk, you've convinced me you're stubborn enough to design that rescue boat."

Rob laughed. "That's me, sorted then. And I'm also going to write an auld acquaintance in New Hampshire who owns a lumber mill. He might be able to fill in with a book about the American Coast Guard. I'll pay you when you tell me how much they cost."

"Och, don't worry about it. I'll bring everything we can find."

Rob threw himself into his work on the parallel bars, adding a lap every few days, refusing to be defeated by the passing of each day bringing Maggie's departure closer.

Hugh visited Rob often. Maggie took advantage of the time she had to herself, working in her garden before climbing the low dyke at the back of the croft and making her way down the brae to the wide burn spilling through a shaded glen. She swallowed tears when she brushed her fingers over the curly bracken fronds and pointed willow leaves bending low over the rocky burn or gazed up at the sky, so vast and blue. It tore at her heart to think she might never bring her bairns to wade and play in the cool water or smell the acrid, earthy scent of willow and sweetness of the heather on the slopes of Ben Innis.

Help me remember this, Faither, so I can tell my lads and lasses about the pebbles shining beneath the sparkling water and the feel of the wet, peaty soil pushing up between their wee, bare toes.

Rob, pressured to make up his mind once and for all, often ate more than he wanted, only to satisfy Maggie. Why couldn't he take a firm stand one way or the other? Every time he thought about coming back to Innisbraw he broke out in a sweat and his heart raced. He couldn't allow Maggie to leave for duty without knowing if she would ever come back to her home.

He mustered the courage to bring up the subject when Elspeth was giving him his first lesson in the Gaelic.

"You mean you still think there are those besides Una who don't want you here?" Her voice registered surprise. "I thought you had put that all behind you."

"But Maggie's told me there are over twa hundred folk on Innisbraw. Surely even you don't know how each one feels about a Yank moving to their island."

"Och, I'm ninety-eight years auld and I've lived on this wee island all of my life. I know every man and woman here and I don't have to question them to know what they think about you returning. As I've told you before, they're no' like some of the folk in Scotland who continue to ignore you like an incomer even after you've lived in their village for years." When he didn't respond, she leaned closer. "Have you prayed about this, lad?"

"So much I'm thinking the Lord is tired of hearing it. You must wonder how such a coward could ever serve in the military."

"Coward? As if I could ever think that of you." She sat back. "Where did you get the idea that everybody will like you no matter where you choose to live?"

"What do you mean?"

"'Tis time you faced reality. I know you didn't feel a part of the village when you were growing up, but that doesn't mean everybody who lived there was liked and wanted. You're still living a bairn's dream of what it means to settle down and make a home for you and yours, and you've never let it change as you became a man."

"I don't know about that." He exhaled loudly. "I got so tired of feeling trapped and alone I just crawled inside myself and stayed there most of the time."

"And shut others out so you couldn't be hurt."

He nodded.

"What you may no' have considered is that folk sensed your discomfort when they were having a conversation so they stopped trying. Perhaps that added to your feelings of loneliness."

"So you're thinking I'm having a hard time making up my mind about coming back here because of what happened when I was a lad?"

"Childhood hurts run the deepest, especially when there's nobody to share them with. Ponder what I've said, lad, and continue to pray for the Lord's perfect will."

⁂

Rob prayed. During his postings at various airbases in the States and the two in England, it was clear his fellow pilots considered him a loner. Yet, if the conversations in the officer's clubs concerned flying, they not only welcomed, but solicited his comments. Did that mean they liked him? How could he know? He'd seen respect in their eyes, but they seldom laughed or told jokes when he was around.

At the orphanage, every time he made a friend, the lad disappeared to become someone's son—and he was alone again. It took years of pain before he learned not to allow anyone close. Losing them wasn't worth the silly jokes, games, and shared secrets. Was protecting himself from the pain of loss worth such a lonely life?

But he had changed since coming to Innisbraw. He enjoyed talking to others now. Was it because the friends he made here weren't involved in the war, weren't facing death every day, so it was safe to allow them close to his heart? He doubted it. He'd been reluctant to make friends long before the war. Or was it because loving Maggie opened a door he'd slammed shut as a lad?

Och, it would be so much easier if that Hunter woman didn't dislike him so much.

⁂

Angus brought them a large box John had sent on the *Sea Rouk*. "'Tis right heavy, it is, so you'd better tell me where you want it now before I drop it."

"Put it on the admitting counter," Maggie said. "And you'd best stay 'til we find what's in it before you leave. It may have to be moved again." Maggie read John's note and squealed with delight. "Och, Rob, Faither has sent us a radiogram."

"What's a radiogram?"

She laughed, handing Angus the scissors so he could slit the sides of the box. "It plays records. He's only sent one record but he'll post more as soon as he can find them."

"A phonograph," Rob said in English.

She wrinkled her nose and lifted out a record sleeve. "I don't believe it." She sat in Rob's lap and showed him. "See? 'Tis a recording of songs from Vera Lynn's radio program, 'Sincerely Yours.' Och, it has 'Till We Meet Again,' 'The White Cliffs of Dover,' 'When the Lights Go On Again,' 'Shine on Victory Moon,' and even 'Wishing.'"

"I remember hearing her music on the wireless at Edenoaks." He grinned. "She's a grand singer. See if you can get that radiogram out, Angus. Let's hear some music."

When the record player was unboxed and plugged in, Maggie placed the record over the spindle and turned it on before carefully lowering the stylus into the groove.

"On you come, lass," Rob beckoned. "We can't dance, but at least I can hold you close."

Angus sat on the sofa, fiddling with his bunnet, embarrassed to be intruding on such a personal moment, but fascinated by the sound of the first orchestra he'd ever heard. When Vera Lynn's clear, sweet voice began singing, he closed his eyes and laid his head back. What a grand sound.

Rob buried his face in Maggie's hair, the poignant words washing over him. Aye, he and Maggie would meet again, and like the song, he didn't know where it would be, or when, but somehow they would make it happen.

She looked up at him, tears slipping down her cheeks, the love in the depths of her violet-blue eyes so pure that his own eyes teared.

He raised her chin, kissing her tenderly.

※

Angus got up quietly and tiptoed out, the lyrics of the second song bringing a strange welling in his heart as he crossed the stone-flagged entry. He'd never seen a blue bird or the white cliffs of Dover, but that was a never-mind. Innisbraw's own laverlock and plunging fells would do. The thought of a world without war—of never-ending peace—brought a longing to his soul. He climbed onto the cart bench, wiped his eyes on his kerchief, and blew his nose vigorously before releasing the brake.

※

They listened to the record several times that evening, Maggie nestled in Rob's arms on the couch. His warm embrace, his tender kisses, his words of love, brought to life each song's heartfelt words, strengthening her hope that the war would soon be over and they would spend all of their tomorrows together.

※

The next morning, Rob awakened early to find a napkin wrapped around a plump scone lying on his bedside table. He looked at his watch. Only 0550. Why was Maggie up and baking so early?

Maggie meant for him to wait until he finished his breakfast of sausage and eggs, but he was starving so he ate half of it in one bite.

What a strange taste and unpleasant smell.

He drained the water in his glass and lay down, waiting for her to appear in the doorway. He wrapped the remainder in the napkin.

Mebbe later with a cup of coffee …

Chapter Thirty-nine

Face burning. Pressure inside skull. Brains growing? Blood pounding. Feel it. Hear it. Instant fear.

He sat up, throwing back the covers. Brilliant flashes of light pierced the edges of his vision.

Instant peace. Well-being. He lay down, fascinated by the flashing lights.

"Guid mornin," Maggie called from the doorway. "You're already awake."

Voice hollow. Echoing.

So close.

Her eyes. Delicate petals of violet blooming in depths of azure-blue.

Her hair. Each individual strand of raven curls tumbling, tumbling over shoulders.

"Why ... you ... staring ... like. . . that. . ."

Her voice. Echoing, echoing.

Tongue thick. Mouth dry. Can't talk.

※

Maggie reached for Rob's hand. Something was wrong. His cheeks flushed deep red, the pupils of his eyes dilated. "Rob, speak to me. Rob!"

No answer.

Her fingers went to the base of his thumb.

His pulse pounded.

She grabbed the stethoscope from a drawer in his bedside table and pulled up his pyjama top. Listening intently, she moved the diaphragm over his chest.

His heart galloped. Lungs sounded clear. Though his chest rose and fell rapidly, no gasping or fighting for breath.

She tossed the stethoscope onto his bedside table, knocking aside a napkin lying there. Something fell to the floor.

She started to kick it aside but stopped, looking closely. Why was a scone on his table? She bent over and studied it. He'd eaten half but she could see the rest and it was the wrong shape. This scone had been dropped from a large spoon before baking. She always rolled hers out and cut them into wedges. She grasped his shoulders and shook him. "Rob, where did you get the scone?"

He opened his eyes. Pupils so large his eyes looked black.

She shook him again. "I have to know where you got the scone. Answer me, Rob!"

"No' ... verra ... sweet," he mumbled, "but ..." His eyes closed again.

A sudden thought made her legs weak. Och, they no longer put the bar across the door. Had someone left a poisoned scone on his table that night?

Una! It had to be.

She raced down the hall to the pharmacy and rummaged through shelves until she found the syrup of ipecac and a dosing spoon.

Rob lay so still.

She poured a glass of water before cranking up the head of the bed. "Rob, open your mouth," she cried, patting his cheeks. "Open your mouth."

When his lips parted, she emptied the spoon on the back of his tongue and watched him swallow.

"Mouth ... dry." He gulped down the water she offered.

Her mind raced. Flushed cheeks, rapid heartbeat, enlarged pupils, dry mouth. Something niggled at the back of her mind, but she couldn't grasp it. She had to know more.

"What do you feel? Is your stomach hurting? Do you have a headache?"

"Lights ... bright ... lights."

Bright lights with his eyes closed. She wrapped a pressure cuff around his arm and took his blood pressure. So high!

But what if it wasn't poison? She pressed her fingertips to her temples.

Think.

It had to be Una. What did she put in that scone?

She picked up the scone with the napkin and broke a piece off, spreading the crumbs across the table. Small flecks of something dark brown. She smelled the crumbled dough. Unpleasant, almost fetid odor.

Think.

Herbs. It had to be herbs of some sort. But what dangerous herbs grew on Innisbraw?

Jacob's Ladder? She hadn't seen any on the island in years and it wouldn't have the same symptoms.

Think.

"Och, Faither in Heaven, help me," she groaned. Flushed cheeks, raised pulse, flashing lights, dry mouth, dilated pupils.

Henbane!

Of course. That explained the odor. "Heavenly Faither, is there an antidote for henbane? Help me, please help me."

Rob retched.

She placed a blanket over his lap and lifted his shoulders. "That's right, get it all up."

When he finished vomiting, she wiped his lips and took his pulse again. Still so high. She wadded up the soiled blanket and tossed it on the floor. "Are you still seeing bright lights?"

※

Lost in an unearthly world, he whirled and undulated through brilliant colors in his weightless, unfettered body, a breath-taking landscape unfolding below him. He floated over a tumbling burn, water so clear, the iridescent scales on the small fish darting about glistened and winked in the sunlight. He soared over a copse of rowans and firs. Each leaf and needle dancing, quivering, every color of green he had ever seen or imagined standing out in brilliant relief. So beautiful. Such detail. He hoped this enchantment lasted forever.

※

Maggie dashed to the bathroom to wash her hands and jumped,

letting out a startled shriek when she turned and bumped into Flora in the doorway.

"Och, you skeered me," Flora said. "What's the matter, lass, you're pale as a ghost."

Maggie grasped her shoulders. "Thank God you're here early. It's Rob. He's eaten henbane. Do you know the antidote?"

"Henbane? Why would he eat that foul plant? I thought it had all been dug up and burned long ago—'tis deadly."

"I don't have time to explain. Think, Flora. How can I get it out of his system?"

"I don't know. Mither wouldn't let us near it."

"Run down to Elspeth's and ask her. She'll surely know. I have to get back to Rob. I can't wake him."

Flora whirled. "I'm on my way. You see to that lad," she called over her shoulder.

Rob still slept when Maggie returned. Not a good sign. First sleep, then coma, then . . .

She poured some water onto a towel and wiped his face.

He didn't stir.

She took his blood pressure again. Still terribly high. She clasped his limp hand. "Please, Lord, please help me. I'm so frightened and don't know what to do." She pulled up a chair and sat beside him, laying her cheek on his chest, listening to the rapid thrumming of his heart. Loud, it was, like storm-driven waves ravaging the shore.

It seemed like an eternity before voices neared. Angus ran into the room. "Milk! Elspeth says as much milk as you can force down his throat. Flora's in the kitchen getting it now."

"Milk? You'll have to help me wake him."

It took them over ten minutes to get Rob awake enough to swallow, and another ten before the milk dribbled from the corners of his lips. "That's all he can take," Angus said, "but we got most of a litre down him."

Flora patted Maggie's shoulder. "'Tis a guid thing I had a Women's Aid meeting the afternoon and came early."

Angus leaned over the scone. "Och, 'tis henbane, for certain.

Rare reekie, it is."

"Where did he get the scone?" Flora asked. "And why would he eat such a foul thing?"

"I'm thinking Una put it there sometime during the night," Maggie replied. "He probably thought I left it for him. He only ate half of it, thank the Lord."

"If Una did something like that, she should be in jile. Are you sure it was her?"

"Who else would want to hurt Rob? Spitting on him and cutting his head wasn't enough. She's wanted him off the island since he arrived."

"Then I'm thinking the Island Council should arrest her and hold her for the constables from Oban," Angus said. "I'll use your radio and see if I can raise Alec before she tries owt—"

Both MacDonalds, Hugh, and Elspeth crowded through the doorway. Elspeth dropped her walking stick and gathered Maggie into her arms. "I see from the empty jug you got some milk down him. If he didn't eat much of the henbane, it should save him but we have to pray now, and pray hard."

"I made him vomit, too," Maggie said. "I hope some of it came up before he absorbed the poison." She spent several minutes explaining what had happened.

Though reluctant to leave, Alec and Morag agreed that the sooner they contacted the other members of the Island Council, the quicker they could take Una into custody.

"If she has any henbane," Alec said, "we'll find it."

"I'm going to radio Arthur and Lachlan and have them ring the kirk bell for prayer," Hugh said. "I'll be back in a tick."

By early afternoon, only Elspeth and Maggie sat at Rob's side. Flora and Angus had taken Hugh to the kirk to lead the folk in prayer and Alec and Morag were meeting with the Island Council. Maggie checked his vitals often.

Unchanged. He lay so still, only the rapid rise and fall of his chest brought hope.

Shame burned her cheeks. For weeks, she had been consumed

Broken Wings

with the thought of having to leave Innisbraw forever and now ... she couldn't allow her thoughts to go there. Without Rob she would have nothing—no joy, no hope, no future. He had to live. He had to!

Alec and Morag tiptoed into Rob's room as the sun settled behind Ben Innis. "How is he?" Alec asked.

"No better," Maggie said. "I've pinched the inside of his thigh where the flesh is tender over and over, but I can't wake him."

"Och, what a muddle," Alec said, tossing his bunnet on the clothes press. "You'll no' believe what's happened the day." He pressed Maggie into her chair. "First, when we got to Una's cottage, we found a note on her door saying she had gone off to Portree on the Isle of Skye to live with her auntie and wouldn't be back."

"So she got away?"

"Hear me oot, lass." He paced the room, running his hands through his hair. "You can't imagine the midden we found in that cottage. She broke and carved up the furniture, tore all the linens, and smashed everything else. Though we searched through everything, we found no henbane."

"But how could she get to Skye?"

"That had us in a rare fankle. Mark Ferguson, who was taking a day to mend his nets, got the idea to radio all the trawlers that were out. I took him to my cottage so he could use the radio, and sure enough, she was on Tormad's boat. He said she paid him a wee bit of silver to take her to Skye and he thought 'twas a guid idea to get her off Innisbraw after how she treated Rob."

"Then she's going to get away with it?"

Alec grunted. "I told Tormad to contact the constable at Portree before he docked and have him check her bags for henbane. She was in the wheelhouse and heard what Tormad was saying. We could hear her screaming about finally killing Edmond for abandoning her and their bairnie."

"Edmond? There's never been anyone on the island with that name," Elspeth said.

"Did he contact the constable?" Maggie asked.

"He did that. Tormad radioed just before we came up here. One constable and twa home-guardsmen were waiting for his boat. They found a wee sack of henbane tucked into one of her bags. 'Tis going to take some straightening oot, but right now Una Hunter's in the Portree jile. Where she belongs."

Maggie looked down at Rob. "Och, luve, I wish you could know this." She brushed her lips across his forehead.

"The constable did say to save that piece of scone," Alec added, "and the napkin."

⁂

Morag spent the nights with Maggie, Elspeth the days. Though Rob's vitals gradually improved, he remained in a deep sleep forty-eight hours later.

Angus had just taken Elspeth home when Rob looked up at Maggie. He smiled, tried to take her into his arms, and frowned at the IV in his forearm. "What's this for?" he croaked.

"You're awake!" She leaned over and hugged him, tears burning her sleep-deprived eyes. "How do you feel?"

"I need water."

She filled the glass and held it while he gulped the water down. He motioned for another and emptied that glass, too, then lay back with a satisfied sigh and cleared his throat. "I feel grand. I don't know what happened, but I've some fantastic dreams to tell you about. I've been flying, Maggie, and without an airieplane."

She pressed her cheek to his. "I thought I was going to lose you. You came so close to dying." Tears long spent, dry sobs shook her body.

"Don't cry, lass." He rubbed her shoulders and back. "What happened? What do you mean, dying? Haven't I just been asleep? And why the IV?"

She pulled a chair as close as possible to the bed. "'Tis a long story, and a troubling one, but I want you to hear it all and then you can tell me about your dreams."

Rob didn't interrupt until she told him how long he had been unconscious. "You mean I've been asleep over three days?"

"Aye. You talked a wee bit at first, but your words were slurred and then they ... they just stopped."

He kissed her cheek. "I'm awake now, luve, and I feel fine, but

I still have some questions."

"Of course you do."

"That henbane? That's why my vision was so clear? Och, I've always had guid eyesight but the detail I saw from a distance was unbelievable. One time, I hovered over a flock of sheep and I could see each curly hair on their backs, and each blade of girse they were eating."

"I don't know anything about henbane improving your eyesight, only that it promotes visions and enhances colors—if it doesn't kill you."

"So when I thought I was flying over the countryside I was hallucinating?"

"Aye. That's one of the reasons the ancient Celts used to drink a potion made with a few seeds of henbane. It had something to do with their pagan worship. Some scholars think that is what started all the blether about witches being able to fly."

"But why do I feel so guid, so relaxed? I don't think I've ever felt this guid no matter how much sleep I had."

"Elspeth told me you'd feel that way ... when you woke up."

"You mean, *if* I woke up." Rob shook his head.

"Just think, that awful Una's gone forever—and all the hate and bitterness always trailing after her like reekie smoke from a smoldering midden."

"Without her around, I don't have any excuse for not making up my mind about returning to Innisbraw."

Maggie's breath froze in her throat. She only wanted to know what lay in store—a life in America or returning to the island of her birth? *Och, Faither, help me be patient. I don't want him deciding before he's ready.*

⁂

Time to make a decision. Had the Lord finally answered his prayers? Or perhaps they were answered long ago and he was too thickheaded to realize it. Una was gone and even if she didn't receive any time in jile for trying to kill him, she'd never be welcome back on Innisbraw.

He'd met only a fraction of the island's folk, but he was no longer that lonely orphan trying to fit in. No matter where they settled after the war, whether here or someplace in the States, there were bound to be folks who didn't take to him for some reason or other.

Why had it taken him so long to realize that? After what Maggie had been through, it was time to stop acting like a selfish lad.

He cupped her chin in his palm and looked into her eyes, anxious to banish the anxiety turning them dark blue. "I'm glad I got all that silver from the bank," he said, voice husky with emotion. "We'll need some of it to pay Malcolm for our trip back to Innisbraw when the war's over."

She melted into his arms with a sob.

Chapter Forty

The only after-effects Rob suffered from his narrow escape were a raging thirst and an appetite to match.

He and Maggie sat on the entry, sharing a handful of shortbreads. "I thought I'd get tired of the wind blowing most of the time, but it keeps away the midges." Rob swigged his third mug of coffee.

"It won't be long 'til they're gone for another year." Maggie brushed crumbs from her fingers and reached for his hand. "What will you do for a living when the war's over? And where will we live? I was so kittled up, I could hardly sleep."

He mentally kicked himself for being so close-mouthed. Surely, he must have mentioned something about his plans.

"Well?" she prodded. "Knowing how you always plan everything, I can't imagine you coming back to Innisbraw without knowing what you'll do once we get here."

"In other words, I haven't talked when I should have?" He wound a piece of her hair around his finger.

"If there's owt to say."

"You're certain I haven't told you? No' a single word?"

She shook her head.

He placed his empty mug on the bench. "Sorry about that. I've been on my own so many years I forget I have someone to share things with." He rubbed his cheek against hers and took a deep breath. "This is all up in the air right now because there are so many unknowns, but when we come back, I'd like to build Innisbraw a rescue boat and start a rescue service, then open a boat-building business."

She gazed at him, eyes wide. "You've been planning all of this and you've never shared it with me?"

Och, he was in trouble now. "That's why I radioed your faither. Asked him to bring me books, lots of books on boatbuilding. I do remember telling you I like to build things."

"You mentioned it once."

"Only once?"

"Once."

Deep trouble. He'd better start explaining or he'd soon be in it over his head. "I helped build the orphanage director's house the year I graduated from high school. His lad had a lumber mill and taught me a lot. Learned how to raise walls, frame and sash windows, install plumbing, and shingle a roof. Even made some furniture."

"My Air Forces group commander made furniture?"

"Nothing fancy, only tables and such." His stomach cramped at her intense stare. "It'll be a lot of work, doing things I've never done before, and you're going to have to help me plan our home someday."

She chewed on her lower lip. "I should be angry," she said, voice so low he strained to hear. "But I've known for months how hard it is for you to share your thoughts."

Her smile made him giddy with relief.

"Your idea sounds wonderful. Think of all the souls that could be saved, no' to mention the lads you could bring back to Innisbraw to help build the boats." She grabbed him, her kiss so exuberant his blood raced fast as a P-47 fighter coming out of a loop.

※

The days passed too quickly. Rob tried using a pair of crutches from the infirmary storeroom but his first attempt proved disappointing. Even with the crutches extended as far as they would go, they were a poor fit.

"I'll contact Faither and ask him to send longer ones."

"If they make them. This is ridiculous. I'm only a bit over six-five, no' seven feet tall."

"You have to remember to use each leg like you would in walking. Don't swing both legs together." Maggie stared into the distance. "Mebbe twa walking sticks would be better."

"If they make them long enough."

She burst into tears.

He'd expected a wee smile, not tears.

"What did I say, Maggie? I wasn't making light of your suggestion. Sounds guid to me."

She wiped her eyes with the back of her hand. "I just hate to see owt hold you back."

He hobbled over to a chair, dropped the crutches on the floor, and pulled her into his lap. "'Tis you going away from me these past days. Can you tell me what has you in a fash?"

"I ... I can't say it."

He buried his face in her hair. No time to be at a loss for words. "It's almost time for you to report and I'm no' fit for duty."

She nodded.

He kissed her cheeks and forehead. "Och, lass, you break my heart with your tears. Do you think I'm looking forward to ..." His voice faltered. "To seeing you sail off without me?"

Give me the words, Faither. I'm at a loss to say what I feel.

The knot of anxiety strangling his throat dissolved as quickly as a snowflake on a bairn's tongue. "It won't be long. If I keep working hard—and you know I will—it'll only be a few weeks at most before I catch you up in London."

She rested her cheek against his chest. "It hurts so badly to see how hard you've worked, how far you've come, and know I won't be here to see you take your first steps on your own."

"You may no' be here to see it, but you'll know when I do." He propped a finger beneath her chin and raised her face, his kiss gentle. "'Twill be your luve inside me holding me up."

"Och, Rob, I'm going to miss you so much sometimes I can't breathe just thinking about it."

"I feel the same way. But we're twa of the lucky ones. We're no' facing months or even years of separation like so many."

"But every day away from you will seem like a month."

"It will that, but we'll get through this as long as you don't close me out now." He parted her hair and kissed her neck. "You're mine, Maggie, and nowt will ever change that. You're part of my soul."

He slept poorly that night. He'd been selfish, thinking only of how he would feel when she left. It was time to pray for the Lord to ease her pain.

※

John sent extensions to bolt onto the crutches, enabling Rob to walk around the inside of the infirmary, exploring places he'd never seen: X-ray, pharmacy, operating and examining rooms. "I had no idea this place was so complete. John has a verra nice infirmary set up here."

"That's why I've been able to treat minor wounds and illnesses, though I've been verra careful no' to bring in anybody with an infectious disease."

"Always watching out for me, my Maggie." Rob's gaze swept the operating room. "Do you really think John will give up all he has and come back here to open the infirmary?"

"Perhaps, but he's put it off so long, I'm no longer certain he'll ever retire."

"Someday, I'm hoping there will be enough folk here to bring in a grocery store."

"That would be wonderful. Our folk get so tired of having to send to Oban for everything they can't grow or make themselves."

He led the way into the large foyer. "Why don't we have a fire in the fireplace the night and sit together on the couch?"

"That would be grand if you can get up when the time comes."

Maggie put the record on the radiogram and they sat close together, as the nostalgic words to Vera Lynn's songs renewed their hopes for the future.

※

Maggie was excited about something, but refused to tell Rob. Only that Angus would be bringing him something after breakfast.

The crofter arrived as they were having tea and coffee on the entry. He waved at Maggie and made a circle with his index finger and thumb.

"Guid, he's got it," she said to Rob. "Sit here and close your eyes. Promise no' to peek."

He closed his eyes, heard the cart drive off. A few moments later, hot air tingled his hand and a whimper sounded.

"You can open your eyes now."

A plump, furry pup, long tail wagging wildly, stared up into his face, pale blue eyes begging for attention.

"This is Shep. He's your new friend to keep you company on your walks when I'm gone."

He picked up the wiggling pup and buried his face in the soft fur, tears filling his eyes when the soft tongue slavered his chin. "Shep." He ran his fingers through the pup's soft coat. "Och, lass, how did you know my first Shep was an Australian shepherd?"

"I didn't, but I'm delighted to hear it."

"I've no' seen a sheep dog like him on Innisbraw. They've all been black and white."

"Those are border collies. Angus used to breed them, but he bought two Australian shepherds from a man in Oban several years ago and breeds them exclusively now. He had a new litter and this wee lad needed a home. Unlike his littermates who all had bobbed tails, he was whelped with a long tail and in order to get a decent price, Angus would have to dock it. Shep's too fine a dog for that."

"My first Shep had a long tail, too." Rob held the pup close, chuckling when its tongue covered his face with wet licks, leaving behind the warm scent of milky innocence. "'Tis the nicest thing anyone has ever done for me."

"I'm glad you like him. He certainly likes you."

Rob worked the crutches hard, practicing going up and down the steps of the entry, Maggie next to him in case he faltered. By Thursday, he could go almost anywhere without falling.

That afternoon, he waited, Shep at his side, while Angus drove Maggie around the island so she could say good-bye to all her friends. When she returned, face streaked with dried tears, he held her in his arms, whispering words of comfort.

Chapter Forty-one

John arrived at 1700 on Friday evening. Maggie went down to the dock to meet him while Rob waited on the entry.

In thirteen hours, Maggie would sail away on the *Sea Rouk*. He stared, unseeing, out at the sea, unable to imagine surviving without her innate sweetness, her warmth, and her gentle encouragement when pains shot down the sides of his legs from all the walking. His heart felt leaden, bones hollow. Without Maggie, there could be no joy, no laughter, no true meaning to life.

Shep leaned against his leg and whined.

He reached for the pup and buried his face in the soft blue-merle coat. "Och, Faither, help me make this easier for her."

John and Maggie were both subdued when they arrived, though the doctor praised Rob as he watched him maneuver on the crutches. The books he had requested were on Malcolm's boat and would be delivered to the infirmary later that night.

When John patted Shep and congratulated Maggie on her choice, she didn't reply. Her blue eyes were dark as the sea at gloaming.

They ate a somber supper. Rob picked at his food, but Maggie didn't chide. She ate little. John retired to the cottage immediately after Maggie finished washing the dishes.

Rob pulled her outside to the bench and took her into his lap. "We have the night," he whispered. "Let's make the most of it."

Maggie looked into his eyes, her heart echoing the grief in his hazel eyes. How could she leave him? How could she live without his strong arms around her, his deep voice speaking to her soul? This was the man God prepared for her. Her thoughts tumbled as joy battled sorrow. She traced the dimples beside his lips with her fingertip, tears blurring her sight.

He laced his fingers through hers. "We have memories to make," he said, voice thick. "Memories to carry us through the lonely nights. Help me make them, please."

She closed her eyes and raised her lips.

Their kiss tender, then urgent as they sought to savor every second, every minute of their last night together. They clung so closely together, their heartbeats blended into one.

"I luve you, my Maggie. I luve you as I'll always luve you, completely and forever."

"Och, Rob." She choked up. "You're my reason for living, for breathing. If I luved you any more, I'd surely die from the joy of it."

"Let's sit on the sofa the night. I want to hold you and feel your body against mine. I want to kiss your lips and your throat. I want to taste you 'til there is no other taste in my mouth but your sweetness."

"But 'twill hurt your back, sitting so long."

"I've spent the past three months sitting." He tapped the tip of her nose. "But I'm afraid you'll have to help me to my feet. My knees are so weak, I'll never make it on my own."

She tried to smile. Couldn't. "Then, who's to help me? My knees are no stronger than yours."

They struggled to their feet. He caught her hand and rested it on his before taking up the other crutch. "There's no reason to change into our night-clothes, but unpin your hair, please."

She brushed her lips across his. "I'll hurry."

He ordered Shep to lie down on the rug, added peat to the fireplace, pulled back the black-out curtains, and opened the window, before sitting on the sofa, staring into the glowing fire.

The ambient light from the evening sky poured into the room, softening corners, casting delicate shadows across the walls as she glided into the room. Her long black hair cascaded over her shoulders and down her back, tendrils flittering in the breeze from the open window. She sat beside him, cuddling close.

He pulled the knitted blanket over her, burying his face in the hollow of her throat. "Tell me the Selkie tale again, please. I need to hear all they went through, but especially the guid ending."

She laced her fingers through his. "There once was a verra beautiful seal, who lived in the deep sea." Her tears dripped onto his face when she reached the last sentence. "So, the Selkie and her crofter were merrit, had many bairns, and lived on their wee island in the sea, forever and ever and ever."

"Forever and ever and ever," he whispered. "That's what I needed to hear."

They didn't sleep. They kissed, embraced, and talked about all they would do together once the war was over. There were long silences when they expressed their love only with their eyes.

When dawn swept the shadows into corners, he said, "I'm going down to the dock to see you off. I've already asked Flora to have Angus pick us up."

"The pier and dock are rough with spaces between the boards. Are you certain you should?"

"I have to be there." He nuzzled her chin. "To remind you this is where we'll make our home together."

"I'll get ready and start your coffee while you shave and dress."

His hands shook as he buttoned his uniform shirt and fastened his tie. He propped his feet on a chair and pulled on his khaki socks and dress boots before straightening the lapels of his blouse. "Come, Shep."

When he entered the kitchen, Maggie set the coffee pot on the stove, uniform in perfect order, hair in a proper bun. She looked at him, eyes widening in surprise. "Why are you wearing your uniform?"

"To remind you what I'll look like when we meet again. Either here or London, look for the American colonel with the biggest grin you've ever seen."

Her smile lasted only until tears flooded her eyes. "As if I could ever forget." She put Shep's breakfast bowl on the floor before slipping into Rob's embrace.

Steps sounded from the hall. John appeared in the doorway,

face bleak. "I was going to make tea."

"The water's on," Maggie said.

"Angus will take us down to the dock," Rob said. "He'll be here at 0540."

"I've things to do in my office. Call me out when the tea's steeped, will you, lass?"

The coffee perked. She moved it to a cooler spot on the stove.

They ignored the teakettle's whistle until the water boiled over and sizzled on the hot stovetop.

Her smile looked strained as she poured the boiling water into the teapot. "It will have to steep a while." She raised her lips to his.

The coffee was strong and tea even stronger when they remembered it. She poured a cup of tea and a mug of coffee. He didn't want the coffee, but sipped it while she went to the office to fetch her father.

John entered the kitchen, head ducked in apology. "I heard Angus arrive as I was coming through the hall."

Time passed too quickly. Rob closed his eyes took a deep breath. "Bags all packed?"

"I did it yesterday while you were having your wash-up."

John took several sips before putting his cup in the jaw box. "We don't want to keep Angus waiting."

Rob fought to control his trembling voice. "If you'll fetch Maggie's bags from her room, we'll go oot to the cairt. We'll take Shep. He hasn't been oot yet."

⁂

John sat on the front bench with Angus. Rob and Maggie rode in the back, their hands laced together, Shep curled into a ball at Rob's side.

"Write to me," Maggie said, "every day. Your letters needn't be long. Just tell me what you're doing, of your progress, please."

"I will, every day. And you, also. I want to know every thought that passes through your bonnie head."

"I'll write. Every day."

They neared Elspeth's cottage. She stood on her entry, hand raised. "Godspeed," she called.

Maggie blew her a kiss and waved.

Time flew.

When they reached the pier, Angus unloaded Maggie's bags. She buttoned her cape against the early morning chill and climbed down. Rob lowered his crutches and slid from the cart.

"I'll take your bags, lass," John said. He lifted Shep to the ground before grabbing both bags and striding off.

Rob clasped her hand. "Only our bodies will be apart. Nowt can ever separate our hearts."

Her eyes brimmed with tears. "Only our bodies," she whispered.

They made their way up the pier to the dock where Malcolm and John waited.

Malcolm clapped Rob on the shoulder. "Coming along well, I see."

"Aye. Just no' well enough."

"Find a way to let us know when you arrive in London." John hugged Maggie. "Telephone my office if you have to, and they'll radio us you're there."

She kissed his cheek. "I will, Faither."

"I'll be on the path with Angus, lad."

Rob stroked Maggie's cheek. "Take care. Always go to the nearest bomb shelter the minute the siren sounds."

Tears cascaded down her cheeks as she threw herself into his arms. He clasped her against his chest, fighting for breath. His kiss was fierce, body shaking. When she stepped away, he almost fell over. He had to pull himself together for her sake. He squeezed her hand. "Only a few weeks, Maggie, we can do it."

"We can do it." A sob escaped her. She walked up the boarding plank, stepped aboard the *Sea Rouk*, and turned, tears streaming.

He stepped forward, swallowing his tears, and raised his hand. "Remember, only a ... a few weeks."

She nodded.

Sim cast off the lines. Malcolm pulled in the plank. A moment later, the engine coughed and throbbed to life.

The boat pulled away.

Maggie stood like a statue, arm high.

Rob raised his hand until he knew she could no longer see it.

The small boat plowed through the waves until it was only a small speck far out on the Minch.

This must be how the crofter felt when his Selkie waded into the water—heartbroken, afraid he was seeing her for the last time. He continued to stand on the dock, Shep whining and circling his feet.

Rob Savage, who thought he had known the true depths of loneliness growing up, had never felt so bereft in his life.

Chapter Forty-two

Three days after Maggie's departure, a young constable and two older members of the Home Guard from the Isle of Skye, arrived on Innisbraw. "Most of our lads have been seconded to the War Department, so we've resorted to using members of the Home Guard," the constable explained. He voiced his regret at missing Maggie, but questioned Rob and John, making copious notes, before interviewing Hugh, the MacDonalds, Elspeth, and the MacPhees. He also placed the napkin and remains of the scone into a secure container.

"Miss Hunter will definitely be charged with attempted murder, but because she's deteriorated both mentally and physically while in jail, there's every possibility she'll be found insane and confined to a secure mental institution, most likely Stoneyetts in Lanarkshire."

Neither Rob nor John felt like talking after the trio left the island. Una Hunter had been an evil influence on Innisbraw, but no one suspected she was insane.

"I pray she receives help," John said. "It must be terrible to be consumed with such evil thoughts." Shoulders slumped, he walked to the patient room he had slept in since Maggie's departure.

Rob prayed a long time, asking the Lord to help him forgive Una. Already saddened by Maggie's departure, his heart felt even heavier and he spent the night sitting on the couch in the foyer, stroking Shep's soft fur, staring into the glowing peat fire.

By the end of the first week of September, clear, windy days gave way to louring skies and frequent gusty rain showers—what the men on the island called "pishing-doons." Clouds often obscured the top of Ben Innis. Even on the days when the sun shone, it cast a weak, tenuous light upon Innisbraw, its rays carrying little of the remembered warmth of summer. The crofters took shelter in folds and byres, praying for enough dry weather in October to harvest their oats and barley when the grains would be plump and ripe.

The dreich weather matched Rob's spirits. He felt hollow, drained of all joy. On the mornings he didn't meet with Elspeth for his Gaelic lessons, he spent hours on the entry, looking southeast toward London. If he did have a Gaelic lesson, he went out to the entry after dinner.

Even rain didn't stop his daily vigil. He huddled on the bench in his leather A-2 jacket, hands in pockets, shoulders hunched as he gazed off at the horizon, Shep at his side. The pup pressed his body against Rob's legs, shivering occasionally as he looked up at his master's face.

Elspeth climbed from Angus's cart on a morning not scheduled for a lesson. "Rob, 'tis time to take advantage of our first clear day for that trip to Maggie's garden you promised me the summer."

A trip to the garden might divert his thoughts. If nothing else, it would spend some of the minutes that stood between him and Maggie. By the time he closed the cottage gate behind them, the cannie old woman's questions had him pouring out his grief at Maggie's absence.

"Then you must keep yourself busy during the day so you can get a guid night's sleep."

"I can't sleep, so I work most nights on the design for the boat." He rested his weight on his right leg.

"Then when do you sleep? And when do you eat? You're already losing weight and our Maggie isn't long gone. If you keep this up, you'll no' be fit to return to duty."

"You sound like John. I take a nap in the afternoon and I'm eating as much as I can. About all Flora cooks is mutton, which I detest."

"Mutton is it? That will never do. Our next lesson, I'll bring you some of those scones you like so much."

"As long as you don't sneak any mutton in. Or hensbane."

They spent a long time in the garden, Shep cavorting about chasing dragonflies while Elspeth told Rob the names of the flowers and bushes. She knew when they'd been planted, many with Maggie's help when she was only a wee lass.

What a phenomenal memory for someone her age.

She suddenly looked up and pointed with her walking stick

"Here comes Angus, and right on time."

Rob and the crofter exchanged greetings while Angus helped Elspeth onto the cart bench. "Thank ye." Rob squeezed her hand. "You've shared a part of Maggie's past I knew nothing about."

The high point of Rob's life occurred every other evening when John fetched the post from Alice Ross. He read Maggie's letters until he could quote each word from memory. He wrote every day, sometimes only a note, and other times a one- or two-page letter. He shared each physical milestone with her, like his graduation from crutches to two walking sticks, and gave accounts of his numerous ventures into her garden, including the one with Elspeth. He also wrote about Shep's progress.

You wouldn't know the pup. He's doubled in size and his herding instinct grows keener each day.

I watched an Oyster Catcher drop a shellfish onto one of those large rocks below the fell to break it open. That cannie bird devoured it in several bites and flew off, making a pik-pik-pik cry of victory. Angus tells me the marram grasses on the western strand bend and ripple in the winds and the girse is growing greener each day with the freshening rains.

How I long to inhale your sweet, warm-honey heather scent. Please take care, my precious Maggie. There are no words to describe how much I love and miss you.

My Dearest Rob,

Thank ye for your latest letter. It sounds like Shep is keeping you company, which is what I wanted so badly. I'm happy you and Elspeth took time in my garden, though it must look dismal with the weather so dreich. From your description, I could see the marram grasses, their yellow needles bending in the wind. I'd forgotten how delightful the Oyster Catchers sound.

I'm so kittled up to read you're using walking sticks. Please keep writing me about your progress. The air raids over London of late summer have no' slackened though the cloud cover is verra dense. I would love to tell you more but the censors would just blacken it out. I can tell you that my work helps keep me too busy to dwell on how much I love and miss you, but the nights I'm no' on duty are so dreary. Remember, my luve, "We'll Meet Again."

Rob put Vera Lynn's record on, but stopped it in the middle of the first song. It hurt too much without Maggie nestled in his arms.

"John, I feel guilty keeping you away from your work just to monitor my recovery."

The doctor chuckled. "Och, lad, I always try to spend three months here, from the middle of August to the middle of November. I travel so much and am so busy at the university and infirmary, I need time to do research and writing away from all of the duties I'm expected to perform."

"You're sure you're no' making excuses to be here because of me?"

"Ask Elspeth. I didn't make it at all last year because we were short-handed with all of the war-wounded, but this year they've added several locums—physicians who fill in for others—so I'm back to my usual routine."

Flora cooked and cleaned every day. Rob ate as much as he could, but he didn't relish her food the way he had Maggie's. It was all he could do to choke down a mouthful or two of the rank-tasting mutton. She was also reluctant to use the tightly rationed sugar and flour John provided, so she never made sweet scones or shortbread. There were times when the three scones Elspeth brought him every other day made up the bulk of his diet. As the days passed, his appetite dwindled until food became only a necessity.

His lessons with Elspeth continued. For a brief time every other day he became the old Rob, eagerly memorizing verb forms, language patterns, and vocabulary in the Gaelic. She always made a point to touch his hands or arms, and never left without hugging him tightly. The warmth of Maggie's hands pulled suddenly from his had left a frozen block of ice in his belly. He looked forward to Elspeth's warm touch even more than he did the lessons.

He devoured the books on boat-building John had brought, writing copious notes and drawing diagrams, often spending the entire night reading and thinking through problems. For the first time since arriving on Innisbraw, he drew the blackout curtains every night to block out the light from the lamp he kept burning in his room.

Bill Pointer, the son of the orphanage director in Newton, New Hampshire, sent an outdated copy of the boats used by the U.S. Coast Guard, exactly what Rob needed. His notebooks filled with ideas quickly piled up on the table he used as a desk.

The Royal National Lifeboat Institution's books disappointed him. The R.N.L.I. boats were too small and underpowered for the type of rescues he envisioned.

He incorporated everything he could remember about the British Navy's rescue boat, which had plucked him and his crew out from the English Channel the time they'd bailed out, with his notes on the United States Coast Guard. A clearer picture of the boat he wanted to design took shape.

After scanning every book, Rob realized he faced a serious problem. None of the books addressed how to build a modern, engine-propelled boat that would resist capsizing in high seas without using an inflatable bladder, which took up most of the aft deck. He mulled the problem over for days, praying for Divine help.

One night, he dreamed he was making a crash landing of his damaged B-17 into the English Channel. As the bomber neared the water, he braced for impact. None came. Instead, the B-17 slid through the water smoothly before coming to a gradual stop. He looked out the side windscreen at the left wing. Though submerged up to the engine cowlings, the plane didn't sink. Somehow, the air trapped in the lower half of the fuselage kept the B-17 afloat.

He woke with a start. Air pockets. Empty chambers, filled with nothing but air, built into the hull could stabilize a boat and keep it from capsizing, or even right it once it had.

He had fallen asleep at his table. He ground his fists against his stinging eyes and grabbed a drawing pad and pencil. The engine room he planned would take up some below-deck space, but putting the stretchers and medical equipment in a large cabin on deck left a lot of space inside a boat's hull. There had to be a way to balance and maximize the space. He sketched a possible design.

Darling Maggie, I think I'm getting closer to a design for an almost unsinkable rescue boat which should right herself even if she capsizes. I've been meeting with some of the fishermen, including Malcolm, Tormad, and Mark, getting all the information I can about their trawlers and the kinds of problems they encounter at sea.

'Tis the first week of October, and I reached another milestone. Today, I walked with just one stick. You should see Shep when I move too fast. He races around and stands in front of me, barking, and acting like he's taking silent commands from you. Pray God this war ends soon so you and I can be here to see the first sprigs of green in your garden. You can never know how much I long to hold you close and look into your violet-blue eyes.

Dearest Rob,

I'm so proud of you. One walking stick! How far you've come and in so little time. Please don't work too hard and remember to eat a lot of meat, for it builds muscle.

I finally found you a pair of sturdy walking shoes to take the place of your dress boots. They are military issue, but leather is so hard to come by and no one else had a size sixteen—American—in stock. I am sending them by post the day. I miss you so terribly. Only your being on Innisbraw brings me any peace of mind.

P.S. Of course, I'm communicating with Shep. How else can I make sure you don't over-do? Remember, I live for the time we can be together again.

*

My Dearest Maggie, I went to my first ceilidh last een at Alan and Ishbel MacRae's cottage. They had music—a young crofter who played a button box and sometimes a penny whistle and twa other crofters, one with a guitar and the other a piper.

The left leg is coming along much better. Next week, I may discard the stick and start walking on my own. I'll be wearing the shoes you sent. They're a perfect fit. I miss you more than I can ever convey with words. Take care, my luve.

P.S. Everyone sends their luve and prayers.

P.P.S. Please tell Shep I can go a little faster. He's driving me daft.

Chapter Forty-three

RAF airfield hospital, outskirts of London

Maggie hurried down the ancient manor staircase to the converted operating theatres and recovery rooms on the first floor. No time for a bath in the huge, ornate bathing room, just a splash of water to her face and a change into a fresh hospital dress. She signed in at the desk and rushed to a recovery room just in time to hold the door for orderlies pushing a patient on a trolley. She stood in the doorway while they transferred the patient to a bed.

"Last one of the day, Leftenant—a real Spitfire ace." One of the orderlies gave a tired grin, handing her a vitals chart. "Looks like they're working you to the bone."

"You too, Will. Staying over, are you?"

His grin widened, revealing a missing incisor. "Not me. This lad's on his way to the nearest pub for a pint of bitters. Ta-ra."

"Guid-bye to you." Maggie gazed down at the unconscious pilot. So young, but weren't they all? She stretched her aching back and rubbed her eyes. Six doubles in as many days was too much. If only they had more nurses. She checked his IV and blood catheters, making sure there was no swelling or seeping blood at the needle sites, then took his pulse, counted his respirations, and recorded the information on his vitals chart.

For his blood pressure, she palpated his inner arm to find the brachial artery and strapped the cuff around his upper arm. As she reached for her stethoscope, the strident wail of the air-raid siren warped into the night.

She gasped, hand flying to her throat. She couldn't leave her patient now. And his condition was too critical to wheel him down the ramp leading to the basement beneath the manor.

An orderly threw open the door—one of the Cockney lads. "Come on, Leftenant, you need to get out of 'ere!"

"I'll no' leave my patient! He just came from surgery."

"Cor blimey, I'll 'elp you push the bed, but we 'ave to move now!"

Maggie shook her head. "It won't fit through the doorway, and he's too critical. Just go!"

He shook his head and disappeared. Why did Will have to be off-duty when she needed him? He would never have left her alone.

The loud drone of a low-flying airplane filled the air and voices shouted when the siren dropped in pitch. She unlocked the bed's wheels and moved it into a corner, then raced to the linen shelf, gathered an armload of pillows, and piled them over her patient's body.

A violent explosion shook the building. Blood and saline bottles crashed to the floor.

Surely they were bombing the near-by airfield, no' the hospital! The ancient slate roof would melt like soft butter under a direct hit. She leaned across her patient, shielding his face with her body.

The light flickered and died.

The building shook as another blast followed, then another and another. Old emulsified plaster drifted from the ceiling like giant flakes of dirty snow.

The room filled with such a cacophony she put her hands over her ears.

"Help us, Faither!" she cried. "Please, please help us!"

Chapter Forty-four

Two days. No letters from Maggie.

Rob tried to ignore his anxiety.

Four days without a letter.

He sat on the entry bench, shivering in the stiff, bone-chilling wind. Why didn't she write? Was she sick? Had she been injured—or?

He groaned and rested his head in his hands. "Please, Heavenly Faither, please take care of my Maggie. I can't bear this waiting, not knowing how she is. Be with her, protect her, and ..." Sobs tore from his throat.

Shep's nails dug into his knee.

"You're a guid lad." Rob picked up the shivering pup and cradled him in his arms, burying his face in soft fur. "I'm sorry you're cold. I should have put you in my room last een."

A warm tongue slavered his chin.

He raised his face, staring into the cloud-shrouded night sky. "Lord, I'm begging You, be with my Maggie."

⁂

Angry black clouds wrestled the frigid morning wind as John hurried across the infirmary entry. Rob huddled on the bench, Shep in his arms. Surely, the lad had not spent the night outside? He clasped Rob's shoulder. "I know you're verra worried about Maggie. I'm certain 'tis just a mix-up at the military postal service."

Shep whined.

Rob, clad in his leather bomber jacket over a thin cotton Jacobite shirt, did not acknowledge John's presence.

"You didn't eat a bite of supper. You can't go on like this."

"Something's happened," Rob mumbled, "but I don't know what. I've prayed all night." He raised his head, eyes bloodshot, face haggard. "She's never missed a post." He rubbed the stubble on his chin. "Twa letters every-other-day since she left—and nowt for four days."

"I'll meet the *Sea Rouk* myself this een. I already have my staff looking into it, but they've found nowt so far. If a letter doesn't arrive the night, I'll radio my contact in the RAF for information about her hospital."

"They could have been bombed."

"Och, stop torturing yourself. There could be countless reasons for a delayed post."

John lowered Shep to the stone flags.

The pup shook himself vigorously before bounding off to the path.

"We have to trust our Lord in this. Go bathe yourself and shave while I make some tea and coffee. Flora's due any minute."

※

Three more days of agonizing waiting. Rob sat on his bed, forehead pressed into his palms. Was Maggie injured? Was she . . .no, he couldn't even think the word. Without his Maggie, there'd be no more dreams of the future, no laughter, no hope. A sudden mind picture halted the breath in his throat. Maggie in her uniform, her hand clasped in his, a shy smile on her lips. *The nearness of you.* He closed his eyes and allowed the music to sweep over him, to blot out his fear, to bring her so close his mouth filled with her taste. Warm-honey fragrance, tiny, trembling body, violet-blue eyes offering a glimpse of tomorrow. *The nearness of you.*

Shep nosed his hand and reality crushed him again. Despite all the sorrow he'd endured in life, nothing compared to this. Why had God deserted him now, after he'd spent months trying to understand and obey God's will? Had his occasional doubts deafened the Heavenly Father to his pleas?

Scriptures taunted him: "Fear not, for I am with you." *Then why haven't I heard from my Maggie?* "Let not your heart be troubled, neither let it be afraid." *I'm no' afraid, I'm terrified!* "He who fears has not been made perfect in love." *Och, is that why I'm in such agony?*

Shame drove him to his knees beside the bed. "Forgive me, Faither. I've blamed You for keeping me in the dark, when it's me who's the problem. If this is a test, I know I failed. My mind's in such a muddle, I can't think—only feel. And all I feel is fear. I know I'm no' the only one going through this. There must be thousands waiting to hear the fate of those they love. Strengthen each of us with knowing You're there, offering luve and words of comfort, no matter how long it takes for an answer. And please, please be with my Maggie."

An hour later, Rob trembled with relief when John trotted up the path, waving a letter in his hand. *Thank Ye, Lord. Thank Ye, thank Ye!* He snatched the proffered letter and limped over to the bench. Hands shaking, he tore open the envelope.

My Precious Rob, Please forgive me for no' writing but I've pulled ten straight doubles and fall into bed so exhausted, I can't even think. We had a bit of excitement here but I can't say owt because of the censors.

I'm so happy the shoes fit. My heart aches when I realize I won't be there to watch you take your first steps, but I rejoice that you'll soon be stepping out on your own.

I just spent an hour rereading your letters, though they're so worn, I can recite them word-for-word. I often find myself reliving the months since you came into my life. I have so much to look forward to, I can barely stand how slowly the time seems to crawl until you hold me again. I don't know why, but my mind has been filled with memories of the song we danced to when we met. "The Nearness of You." How I long for that to become reality. But our Lord has been so faithful. How I praise Him!

P.S. Don't try to dissuade Shep from keeping you in line. He's too smart to fool.

He read the letter a second time, his breath freezing when he came to the line about the "wee bit of excitement." He passed the letter to John. "I'm thinking I was right. They could have been bombed."

John read the letter before handing it back. "Och, could be they had some visiting dignitaries."

"But it might be more. Check it out, John, please. I've got to know."

※

By the time John finished going through his secret channels of information he was tempted to keep the results from Rob. After much thought he called Rob into his office the next morning.

"I want you to sit down and keep calm, for you've heard from Maggie and you know she's fine."

"I was right. They were bombed."

"No' really bombed. A German Heinkel bomber, trailing fire from its twa engines and carrying a full load of bombs, crashed into the ground only ninety-five metres from the hospital. The building received some damage from broken windows, flying metal, and a small fire on the ground floor, but 'tis already up and fully functional again." John sat back, rubbing his beard.

Rob pushed himself up. "But Maggie? You're certain she's no' hurt?"

"She was on the first storey, opposite where the bomber crashed. There were some patients shaken up, but no injuries."

※

Though Rob had known from the beginning Maggie could be in danger, he had pressed it to the back of his mind. Now, it tortured him. He even had a nightmare about her being trapped in rubble, pinned by a beam that had fallen across her hips, her body limp and lifeless, her face and hair covered with bits of plaster and splinters of wood.

He woke with a start, almost falling off the chair he used at his worktable. He buried his head in his hands, sobs shaking his shoulders.

Och, Heavenly Faither, please keep my Maggie safe. Now I know how she feels about me being killed. Quiet my heart, please, Lord. I couldn't live if owt happened to her.

※

A storm in the middle of October brought a second tragedy to Innisbraw. One of the island's fishing trawlers was lost at sea, all five hands perishing. The bell in the kirk steeple tolled the slow death knell. Rob, wearing his uniform, accompanied John. He now walked unaided and though limping, climbed the steps to the kirk entry without hesitation and joined the folk crowding into the sanctuary for the memorial service.

Seeing Hugh in the pulpit for the first time shamed him. Why had he put off attending kirk so long? John translated the words of the Gaelic he had not yet learned and the message, uplifting and reassuring, impressed Rob.

The minister ended his homily with a quotation from John 11:25. "I am the resurrection and the life. He who believes in Me, even though he dies, he shall live."

Rob's resolve to provide a local rescue boat strengthened.

My Precious Maggie,

I went to Kirk this Sabbath and was impressed with the practicality of the Word Hugh teaches, especially his lessons on how to incorporate what we learn into daily living. He has provided answers to many questions I've had for years. I never realized the Scriptures could have such a daily impact on our lives. What I once viewed as an optimistic outlook on the part of the folk of Innisbraw is really a daily practice of what they've learned. They're "casting their bread upon the waters" every day in the way they conduct their lives. What a marvelous revelation.

I walked down to Elspeth's the day. Of course, it was blowing hard and raining, but she had scones and a pottle of coffee waiting. What a blessed, blessed woman she is. I don't think I could have made it through these past weeks without her loving, practical words. I've come to view her as the grandmither I never had.

Keep yourself safe, my dearest Maggie. Always heed the siren quickly and remember above all else, I live for the time we're together again.

My Dearest Rob,

How comforting to know you have so many people bringing you strength. You could never have better friends or advisors than

Hugh and Elspeth. Faither has written to tell me you want to start running. Don't do too much, my darling. The ground can be treacherous after a hard rain. Remember, Shep is your guardian, so pay him heed.

The weather here is dreich and turning cold, and the work continues to be arduous, but I'm content in knowing you're on Innisbraw and among such warm friends. Please give them my luve, but keep most of it for yourself. I miss you so dreadfully.

⁂

Elspeth's concern for Rob's health grew daily. When she first began offering scones during his Gaelic lesson, he wolfed them down but as the weeks passed, he took only a few bites. His appetite for coffee, however, remained as high, if not higher. She never saw him without a mug in his hand, even after kirk services when Hugh opened the kirk hall for tea, coffee, and sweets to go with the socializing.

She must talk to John.

She cornered him after kirk, making certain Rob was nowhere near. "I'm worried about Rob. He's as thin as I've ever seen him and his eyes look dead."

John sighed, stroking his beard. "I've already talked to him about needing more sleep and eating more, but it's done no guid. He agrees and goes his own way, doing exactly what he's been doing since Maggie left—slaving away at the plans for that rescue boat and working to get fit enough to return to duty."

"It has to be Maggie's absence, for that's when all of this started. I've never seen twa young folk so smitten. I've prayed and prayed for something to spark that lad's appetite, but so far my prayers have no' been answered."

"Nor mine." John leaned against the wall. "Some men are just naturally thin and I'm thinking Rob's one of them. He has such broad shoulders and with all the sit-ups and weight-lifting he's doing, he's so heavily muscled 'tis easy to miss how gaunt he really is."

She started to respond, but John placed his finger to his lips.

Rob approached, his ever-present mug of coffee in his hand.

"What are you twa blethering about? You look like you've received bad news."

"Och, just the twists and turns life takes," John said. "I haven't heard from Maggie in almost a week, but I've fetched your post. How's she doing?"

Elspeth flinched at the shadow of pain blooming Rob's eyes. "She sounds fine, though I'm concerned about the danger she's in and she seems to be pulling a lot of doubles again."

"That's to be expected now the war is escalating on so many fronts." Elspeth rested her hand on Rob's arm. "Walk me to the refreshment table, lad. I could use a cup of tea and a scone and I never did like to eat alone."

"Sounds guid to me."

Delight at the idea of getting him to eat turned to despair when he refilled his coffee mug and made an excuse to leave.

"I need to ask Malcolm where he got the diesel engine for his boat."

Rob didn't spurn food deliberately. He never felt hungry. That block of ice had been consumed by the fire now burning in his belly. Working, on either the rescue boat or his legs, was the only way to put it out. He never slept at night, but napped at his table every afternoon for three or four hours, just enough to keep him going for another twenty-four hours.

He started running in earnest—not far at first—but he increased the distance every day, no matter the weather. His left leg strengthened until he could run up and down the rocks along the strand at the bottom of the fell without stumbling.

He worked on his design every night, often until long past dawn. Malcolm brought him a large roll of drafting paper and soft pencils—though rationing was so tight—and Rob began the final design. He wrote detailed specifications on the construction and kept a separate notebook for every piece of hardware needed, plus another for the equipment necessary for cutting and shaping the wood. Several times, he fell asleep at the table and awoke an hour later, berating himself for time wasted.

Now that he could get around well, he allowed himself a few days to explore the island, wanting to store up those mind-pictures he and Maggie had talked about. Shep at his side, he covered seldom-used paths on the western shore that led down to the Atlantic before jogging to that cove near Scaur Fell that had impressed him with its beauty. He slipped off his shoes and socks, rolled up his denims, and raced barefoot through the sand, whooping like a bairn when a sneaker wave wet him to the knees.

The fresh-water loch beckoned him and he spent over an hour circling its banks before the nearby peat bog caught his attention. He scrambled up the slope and studied the countless pits where generations of islanders had cast peat, amazed by how much of the broad bog still remained.

He climbed down the brae to the burn below the McGrath cottage where rains had swelled the placid water into a small river, almost covering some of the willows. He sat on a large rock and watched the tumbling, frothy water, certain that Maggie had often sat in that same spot, looking up at the slopes of Ben Innis before turning her gaze to the vast sky. Though he searched diligently, none of her footprints survived the wet autumn. Heart heavy, he left the burn and climbed the brae.

Shep enjoyed the hours they spent trotting along cottage-lined paths, barking at ranging chickens and exchanging wary sniffs with other dogs. Rob returned greetings in Scots or the Gaelic and stopped to talk to Katag MacLeod, who hailed him from her cottage doorway as he passed. She handed him wee Beasag, now a plump, sonsie lassie. His eyes burned with tears when she grabbed his nose and squealed.

When he checked out the large shed he intended to use for building the rescue boat he found it in even better shape than he had hoped. With a sturdy wooden floor and a large door on the harbor side that would be perfect when it came time to launch the boat, only the roof needed repairing.

The last hours of indulgence were spent climbing to the top of Ben Innis. The sun, only a faint white smear behind black, roiling clouds, offered no warmth as he reached the summit. He walked around the tall stones and looked out over all Innisbraw. Smoke from peat stoves and fireplaces curled around thatched roofs. The autumn rains had transformed closely-cropped cow and sheep pastures into a patchwork of lush green grass between old dry-stone dykes.

The ocean, wild and unfettered, surged from horizon to horizon, and above, the vast, endless sky filled the heavens. The wind off the sea played a haunting song around Ben Innis's stone sentinels—the same song he heard when flying a bi-plane. The music spoke to his soul as he studied the green, rocky land below, bounded on all sides by the sooking sea. If the Lord called him to Heaven when he returned to duty, he wanted to be buried right here. Kneeling, he rubbed Shep's ruff. "This is what home looks like." A husky whisper.

※

Rejuvenated from the change in routine, he returned to running every day, cutting his naps to a maximum of three hours. If it were raining, or even blowing and raining, he still ran until his A-2 jacket was soaked completely through with rain and sweat. Often exhausted, he forced himself to eat something, even a few bites, to keep John's lectures to a minimum. He drank at least one pot of coffee at supper.

※

One overcast day, he had an exceptionally good run and was still going strong when he rounded the corner where the path passed the harbour. He came to a sudden stop.

Four men were lifting a large sign high above the entrance to the howff.

"Paddy's Howff," he read aloud. He jogged in place for a few minutes, then slowed to a walk to cool his muscles. He strode across the path, ordered Shep to stay, and ducked his head to step inside.

A tall, well-built, young, red-headed man barked orders to several young lads who were scraping the sides of the bar down to bare wood. "I'll tan the daylights out of ye if ye scratch that wood, I will," he shouted. "Gently, gently, like you're caressin' a baby's bottom." He whirled about as Rob approached. "Well, if you're expectin' to be paid, you'd better get to work."

Rob grinned for the first time in weeks. This must be Paddy and from his heavy brogue, he was an Irisher. Rob stepped forward and extended his hand. "I never thought the Island Council would find somebody to take over this place," he said in English. "I'm Rob Savage and welcome to Innisbraw."

Paddy shook his hand briskly. "Paddy McDonald. You're a tall one, that you are. Sure you don't need a little silver to line your pocket? You won't even need a ladder to do the paintin' I need done."

"Sorry. I'm on medical leave from the Air Forces, but I'll soon be going back to duty in England."

"'Tis a cryin' shame. Well, if you'll excuse me, I'd better keep at this crew of mine before they forget what they're doin' and ruin that pretty wood. It's been nice meetin' you, Rob."

"Same here, Paddy. Guid luck with your new enterprise."

"'Tis thankin' ye I am."

Progress on Innisbraw, no matter how small. If the howff was a success, others might be encouraged to open businesses. He praised Shep for staying and whistled the dog to his side as he walked up the hill to the fell, spirits buoyed.

Chapter Forty-five

RAF airfield hospital, outskirts of London

The nursing supervisor confronted Maggie on her way down the stairs. "You're looking much too thin, Leftenant. I want you to eat a hearty dinner. We're having Bubble and Squeak today. Mashed potatoes and cabbage are both very healthy and filling." She shook her finger. "Remember, no excuses."

Maggie's stomach roiled. Another dinner fried in rancid oil. "Yes, ma'am." She brushed by her supervisor and hurried downward, soles squeaking on the waxed oaken steps. The ground floor at last. She ducked around a corner and made her way to the back door off the scullery, avoiding the noisy, crowded dining room.

Once outside, she stopped and looked around. No one in sight. She cut across the tall grass, blades bending beneath the weight of last night's rain. At last! Almost half an hour to spend alone.

Thank the Lord the nursing supervisor never took her meals with the nurses or orderlies. She didn't like deceiving her superior, but how could she eat when she worried so about Rob?

She wandered through a copse of trees, tights wet to the knees, chapped hands thrust deep into the pockets of her sweater. His last few letters had been so brief—no information about his progress, no news of their friends, no humorous anecdotes about Shep.

Only weekly posts from her father, Elspeth, and Hugh kept her from panicking. But they didn't answer one unsettling question. Why did she learn from others that Rob really could walk unassisted now? May soon start running?

He should have told her.

He wrote only about how much he missed holding her, hearing

her voice, inhaling her scent, looking into her violet-blue eyes, how no words in any language could express his love for her. Every note ended with an underlined admonition to heed the air raid siren immediately. Had news of the German bomber crashing so near the hospital been reported in the Edinburgh *Scotsman*? But even if it had, Rob didn't know where she was posted.

A tangled bed of ivy tripped her, but she continued to a copper beech tree she favoured for its shimmering, handful-of-new-minted-pence foliage. Now, only a few brown leaves clung to the branches. She leaned against the slick grey trunk, hugged herself to keep from shivering, and glanced at her watch. Only fifteen minutes before her dinner break ended. And she should allow time for a change of tights and shoes. Always such a regimented schedule.

Eyes closed, she rested her cheek against smooth bark. *Take care of my Rob, Faither. I miss him so dreadfully. He used to write long posts, filled with news about the island, our friends, and especially how well he was doing. Now his letters are just notes. I'm worried about him. Something is wrong.*

By the last week in October, Rob abandoned the entry bench where he and Maggie had spent so much time together. He climbed down the steep path to the strand at the base of Innis Fell and hunkered down beside a large rock, staring southeast toward London. He confessed his despair to the Lord. Countless couples worldwide had been apart far longer, but unlike most adults, he'd never known what it meant to love and have that love returned. His heart ached, the pain almost unbearable.

John grew more and more concerned about Rob. The lad drove himself relentlessly, sleeping little and eating far less than he should. Though his muscles were rock-hard, his clothes hung loose on his tall, thin frame. He never smiled or laughed, and his eyes looked empty—lost.

The doctor wrote to Maggie, asking her to request a leave.

Tell them your faither is ill, anything. I hate to resort to duplicity, but I'm worried about Rob. He's driving himself relentlessly, sleeping, and eating little. I don't want to frighten you, for he's no' really ill, but I'm afraid he will be if this continues. Please try to come home as soon as possible.

She replied by the next post.

I've requested compassionate leave. I've been told I can only have three days off, but no' 'til the end of my shift on the fifteenth of November. Pray for guid weather so Malcolm can take me home from Oban and please take care of my Rob. He writes over and over that I'm to take great care if I hear the siren. I'm worried sick about him.

⁂

The plans for the rescue boat almost complete, Rob focused on his return to duty. He could run the path around the island—over seventeen kilometres—and do a hundred sit-ups on the incline board, more than enough to pass any physical the doctor at Edenoaks might throw at him.

He asked John for a few minutes of his time. He needed that medical release signed.

"I would be remiss as your physician if I didn't remark on how much weight you've lost. Yes, your muscle mass has increased greatly, but you also need some fat on your body. You have none."

"Fat slows me down."

"Nonsense, fat gives you stamina. You must start eating more. I'll post your release when you put on a few pounds."

"A few pounds!"

"Aye. In the meantime, I suggest you write your commanding officer and inform him of your desire to return to duty. By the time the paperwork's done, we'll have a little more flesh on that tall frame of yours and you'll be ready."

Rob shook his hand. "Thank ye. I'll start eating more. Anything to ..." he choked up "... to get back to duty—and Maggie."

"Then, go ahead, lad, write your commander. But don't go running off yet. I have some news that might interest you."

"News? From Maggie?"

"No' this time." John stroked his short beard. "I just received a letter from that young constable on Skye. It seems there's to be no trial for Una after all. Several psychiatrists have examined her and all agree that she must be institutionalized before she does herself harm."

"She's that bad then?"

"Aye. According to the constable, she spends part of her time sitting in her cell rocking back and forth, as though holding a bairnie, and crooning lullabies in the Gaelic. The rest of the time she's tearing at her hair and clothing, and making the evil eye at the guards, screaming about revenge."

"Och, what a terrible, tormented soul. What could have driven her to such madness?"

"I've no idea, but I'm thinking she's been daft far longer than any of us realized."

"What makes you think that?"

"According to the constable, Una has no kin living at or around Portree or anywhere on the Isle of Skye. The Hunters have all passed and the Monroes immigrated to America before the war, including that auntie she wrote about in the note she left on her door. They sold the family home and land outside Portree to pay for their passage and set them up in business when they started their new lives. They do send Una silver every month, but that's been their only contact with her. She's been living in an imaginary world far longer than any of us ever knew."

Rob could only shake his head. A life destroyed by madness—what a waste.

John re-stacked papers on his desk. "Get busy with that letter to your commander."

Rob forced himself to eat more, hoping to hear from wing quickly. When General Wells did not reply after almost two weeks, he again went to John. "Since we don't have telephones here, I'm going to Oban with Malcolm on the morra to call General Wells."

"No need. I'll radio my office and have them put in a call to Wing Headquarters. General Wells may no longer be there."

John was informed that Brigadier General Thomas Wells had been transferred back to the States and that Major General Harlan Fielding replaced him. When Rob heard the general's name, he showed more animation than John had seen from him in weeks.

"Hal Fielding and I go way back." He paced the office. "He was my instructor at Flight School, plus multi-engine and P-47 training. You couldn't ask for a better man to command wing. I'll catch that ride with Malcolm so I can phone Hal at Edenoaks Hall. We got along verra well. I need to find out if he wants me back in command of the 396th."

"No' necessary. He assured my head nurse he's eagerly looking forward to your return. He's only waiting for my release. He also said something most puzzling."

Rob stopped in mid-stride. "What?"

"He said he was verra happy to hear you still remembered how to land a plane without your initial three bounces."

Rob grinned. "'Tis a private joke." He eyed John closely, grin fading. "Well? I've been eating more. Please sign that release and post it to him. I have to get back to duty."

"Has Maggie written you about her leave?"

"No! What leave?"

"She'll be here on the sixteenth. She has three days, so with travel time, she can only spend one full day here."

Why didn't Maggie mention a leave in one of her letters? Mebbe because of the censors. It didn't matter. His Maggie was coming home! "Then write that release. With luck, I can coordinate my return to duty to coincide with hers."

"I'll send it by the morra's post, though you're still too thin by far."

⁂

While Sim tied the *Sea Rouk's* mooring ropes to the bollards, Rob waited on the dock, fingering the wad of twenty-pound sterling notes in his pocket. If he could make this something routine, something done so many times, familiarity might take away his fear.

A vital mission and already turning on the IP, target almost in sight.

Alice Ross took the mailbag from Malcolm's outstretched hand. "No' verra heavy," she said, brushing by Rob on her way to the pier. "Anxious for a letter from Maggie? You know I have to sort the post before you can pick it up."

Rob ignored her teasing tone and hurried to help Malcolm lower the gangplank.

The skipper doffed his cap. "Thank ye. What brings you down here this een?"

"Need a few words with you—alone." No flak, no bandits. Target in sight.

"Get yourself on home, Sim, lad," Malcolm said. "Don't want your mither's supper getting cold."

Rob smiled his thanks. Time to open the bomb bay doors. "It could be a fool's errand with the tight rationing, but I'd like you to buy a wedding ring. I don't know Maggie's size, but it has to be small."

He'd said the words. Bombs away.

Malcolm pounded Rob's shoulder. "Wedding ring!" He snorted a laugh. "I wondered how long it would take you to make it official."

"I have to ask her first, but I need that ring if she says, 'Aye.'"

"I have a friend in Oban who collects auld jewelry. If he doesn't have anything, he'll know who does. As for size, let me fetch a piece of cord. I'll measure your finger and subtract several sizes."

Late the next morning, Rob sat in Hugh's chaumer, nursing a cup of the minister's notoriously bad coffee. The mission yesterday had been a direct hit. Should make him not sweat this one, but praying and thinking about it had kept him awake all night.

"You look tired." Hugh warmed himself in front of the fireplace. "You've lost too much weight to allow another fankle to disturb your sleep."

How did he know that? Hugh and Elspeth—nowt got by them.

"'Tisn't a fankle right now, but it could turn into one."

"Borrowing trouble again? I thought you beyond that."

Rob drained his cup, stalling for time. Not even to the IP yet and flak bloomed in his mind, clouding his thoughts. Who would refuse, Maggie or Hugh—or both?

Abort! Abort!

He couldn't abort. The entire war hinged on his next few words and he was about to drop a whole load too soon.

"I want you to marry Maggie and me when she comes home on leave."

No time for regretting his impatience, no time for worrying about Hugh being willing, no time for fearing Maggie might say it was too soon.

Hugh put his cup on the mantle and rushed to embrace Rob, wide smile revealing his answer. Not only was Hugh eager to perform the marriage ceremony, he also promised to see that all the arrangements were made in time.

Rob trotted up the path to the fell, tears of gratitude burning his sleep-deprived eyes.

One more mission—a milk run so easy he could do it blindfolded. He turned in at Elspeth's cottage and took the steps two at a time.

She greeted his news with a hug and young, vital eyes in a lined face. "Sit a moment while I fetch something." She returned with a large box. "Open it."

He raised the lid and lifted out a red and black tartan Hieland dress kilt, black jacket, vest and tie, ruffle-fronted white shirt, wide black belt, leather sporran, long white hose with plaid flashes, and a sgian dhu—a small, short-bladed, black-handled knife in a scabbard.

"For me?" Rob stared at it open-mouthed. "A kilt? For me?"

"'Tis tradition for the groom to wear the Highland dress. Since you've no tartan of your own, the ladies of the island wove one for you in the McGrath plaid. Maggie will wear her mither's plaid, of course, but you're one of us now. 'Tis only fitting you start your married life dressed for the occasion as custom demands."

Rob fingered the fine woolen garments as he placed them back in the box. "Hugh somehow got word to you I asked him to marry us the day after Maggie arrives."

"Och, Hugh's no' one to tell another's secrets."

"Then how did you know we were getting married—and long enough ago to get all this done?"

Again, those sparkling young eyes. "'Tis just another of our Lord's mysteries."

"I've never had such friends." Voice hoarse with tears. "How can I ever thank you?"

"By being happy. 'Tis all any of us want, is for our Rob and our Maggie to be happy."

He thanked the Lord all the way up to the infirmary. God's perfect plan was coming together. He needed only to write the final specifications for the rescue boat. And he was fit for duty. Would he never learn to leave things in God's hands?

He finished the specifications in two all-night sessions.

The following morning he walked down to Elspeth's for his last Gaelic lesson. Before he left her cottage, he rested his hands on her stooped shoulders and looked into her eyes. "There aren't words to express how grateful I am for all your luve and support."

"It's been a joy and privilege to spend time with you. You're the only student I've ever had who actually enjoyed learning the Gaelic. 'Tis a difficult language."

"Then save a place for me when we return. I still have a long way to go before I'm fluent."

"You know I will, lad."

"Will you write us, Elspeth, please? Both Maggie and I will answer—'tis a promise."

"Of course I'll write. How else will you know how your family on Innisbraw is doing?"

"Our family on Innisbraw—that sounds so guid."

Rob's reactivation orders came by special post the day before Maggie's impending arrival. He was to be at Edenoaks Air Base on November 20th where he would be required to pass a rigorous physical before once again taking command of the 396th. He called Shep and they went out for a long run in the rain. As they passed the pier, Rob slowed to a jog and reached into his pocket, pulling out a small velvet box. He stopped and opened it, studying the gold band nestled in blue satin. A Celtic love knot adorned the center of the band. Malcolm had chosen well.

Only one last obstacle.

※

John looked up when Rob walked into his office later that evening, a wide grin deepening his dimples.

"I need to ask you something." Rob took the chair opposite John's desk, fingers exploring the scarred armrests like a blind man reading Braille. "I'm a little new at this, so please bear with me."

"Och, what are you blethering about now?"

"I've never asked a man for permission to marry his daughter."

John leaned back in his chair. "What took you so long? Surely you didn't think I'd refuse."

"I wasn't certain."

John rose and stood over him, gripping his shoulder. "Lad, I've watched you mope about this place like a luve-sick bull seal, and I've seen you almost kill yourself trying to walk again. Any doubts I once had about you luving Maggie are long past. Of course, you have my blessing. I'm hoping it's the day after the morra so I can give her away properly."

"It is, if she says 'Aye.'"

"As if she'll refuse. Are you wearing that fine Hieland kilt the ladies made you?"

"You know about that?"

"How else could they have your measurements for a proper fit? I'm thinking almost every weaver on Innisbraw took part. 'Tis a guid thing they can dye, spin, and weave the cloth here, or with rationing so tight, there'd have been no kilt."

Rob's smile widened. "Thank you for all you've done. I'll do everything in my power to make Maggie happy. That's a promise I can give you whole-heartedly."

"I know you will, lad." His grip on Rob's shoulder tightened. "Just keep yourself alive."

After Rob left his office, John went to his knees beside his desk.

"Our Heavenly Faither, my heart is filled with both joy and fear. The joy comes from knowing my precious lass has found the lad who'll bring her the happiness she so richly deserves. But I fear Rob might be killed when he returns to duty. Look what he's already been through. Please, please, I implore You; see that lad through the rest of this terrible war. I've come to luve him like a son. And I cannot bear the thought of what will happen to Maggie if she loses her one true luve."

Rob took a long soak in the bathing tub. Relaxed, he hurried into the foyer, lifted a cushion from the sofa, and pulled out a sprig of heather he'd placed there the morning Maggie left.

In his room, he ordered Shep to the blanket in the corner and climbed into his bed for the first time in three months, certain he'd fall asleep in seconds. But mind-pictures of their last night together flooded his mind with bittersweet memories.

He brought the dried heather petals to his face and inhaled. No scent remained. He closed his eyes, remembering her fragrant hair and skin and how her tiny, warm body felt pressed close to his. He could see her violet-blue eyes soft with luve, feel her warm breath as she raised her lips to his.

"On the morra, luve," he whispered. "Only one more day."

Chapter Forty-six

Afraid to look, but needing to know, Rob peered out the window. Took a deep breath. No clouds marred the dusky blue dawn. It had been dreich and rainy for weeks, but the day of Maggie's return promised sunshine. A sign of God's blessing?

He spent a long time convincing Flora to give him a haircut. "I can't report back to duty with my hair over my collar. Maggie cut it before she left but that was almost three months ago. Just make sure 'tis verra short."

It took over an hour. When she finished shaving his neck and handed him a mirror, he let out a grunt of relief. "Perfect. You could open a business. You're that guid."

She blushed, rosy cheeks dimpling. "Och, quit your blethering. Every woman on Innisbraw cuts her own menfolk's hair."

He and Shep went for a long run in the afternoon. The pup must have sensed his master's excitement, for he pranced and frisked about, tail high over his back.

Rob bathed and shaved before putting on all of his uniform but the blouse. He spent the few minutes before Malcolm's boat was due at his worktable, rolling up one drawing and setting it aside.

He looked around the room. Images of Maggie flashed through his mind, stunning him with their clarity. Until last night he'd shut them out, unable to bear the hurt they brought. Now, he welcomed them. A surge of emotion choked him. Maggie—his bonnie, loving, exceptional lass—would soon be his to cherish forever. John's parting words of the night before echoed in his mind. "Just keep yourself alive."

He knelt beside his chair. "Heavenly Faither, I know I've a long way to go before I'm worthy of all You've done for me, but with Your help, I'll be the best husband and faither I can be.

Someday, I want to know You so well I consider you my verra best friend." He laced the fingers of both hands into a fist. "You know I'm no' afraid of dying, Faither, but I don't want my Maggie hurt. If it be Your perfect will, allow us to return and grow auld together here on Innisbraw with our eight bairns around us."

The sky darkened before he spotted the boat from the window of his room. He shrugged into his uniform blouse—fingers stumbling over the buttons like a bairn learning to dress himself—picked up the roll of drafting paper, and raced for the door, calling to John, "The *Sea Rouk's* about to enter the harbour!"

"I'll catch you up," John replied, "and I'll keep Shep here."

Rob ran down the path, heart beating so hard each breath demanded a conscious effort.

Elspeth waved from her porch. "Hurry," she called. "The tide's in-coming. They're almost at the dock."

His feet flew over the dirt path as he ran to the packing shed and placed the plans on a shelf inside the door.

He crossed to the pier. Sim was fastening the mooring lines.

Rob's heart lurched. Where was Maggie?

She stepped from Malcolm's shadow.

He sprinted toward the dock. "Maggie!" he shouted. "Maggie!"

Their eyes met.

"Rob!" She scrambled down the gangplank and broke into a run.

They collided in a tangle of grasping hands and flying tears.

He threw his arms around her and lifted her up. "Och, Maggie, my Maggie." He kissed her cheeks, her forehead, her pulsing throat.

"I'm home!" She hugged his shoulders. "I'm home, luve!"

Their lips touched. He devoured her sweet taste, chest heaving. "You're really home."

He lowered her, holding her tight. Needed to feel her close to him, needed to absorb her essence into his soul, needed to know this was no dream.

She looked up at him, cheeks wet. "I've been so worried about you, but you were running and look fit for duty." A smile surrounded her words with shimmering radiance.

"I report on the twentieth."

She turned her face up to his, their kiss long and filled with joy.

He lifted his head, gaze piercing hers. "Marry me, Maggie, lass. Marry me on the morra."

She closed her eyes for a moment. When she opened them, he read her answer in the love shining from her face. "Och, Rob, I'll marry you on the morra, or this een, or right now."

He caught her hands and twirled her around. "On the morra, at the kirk, at 1400." He stopped suddenly. Teetered on the brink. Plunged into the depths of her sea-blue eyes. Heaven must be like this. "Do you have any idea how fine you are to me?"

"Just as fine as you are to me." Eyes bright as stars in a summer night's sky.

He framed her face with his palms. "I'll luve you forever, my Maggie. Through our lives and throughout eternity, my luve will be there. Always." No panic at voicing his thoughts. No hiding from the truth. No groping for words. He kissed her again. Tenderly. Softly.

"Is there nowt left for your poor auld faither, lass?" John stood to one side, smile tilting his beard.

Maggie threw herself into his arms. "Och, Faither, how I've missed you! Why didn't you tell me Rob could run so fast?"

"The lad wanted to surprise you."

She kissed his cheek, laughing. "Then, I'll forgive you both, for I have a little surprise of my own. Look." She pointed toward the boat.

A tall, thin lad stood on the dock in front of the gangplank, wearing a self-conscious smile. He was clad in an ill-fitting tweed suit, with knobby wrist-bones prominent below too-short sleeves and pants at least three centimetres above his scuffed brogans. He looked so much like Maggie, Rob immediately realized who he was. Her brother.

"Calum, lad!" John rushed forward. The two hugged before John led him down the dock.

"Rob, I'd like you to meet my son, Calum. Lad, this is Rob Savage and come the morra he'll be Maggie's husband."

The lad had Maggie's black hair and blue eyes, but long arms and legs and big hands and feet presaged a large man in his future. He extended his hand, eyes downcast. "I'm pleased to meet you, sir," he said in perfect English.

"An awm prood tae meet in wi ye it lest," Rob replied in Scots.

The boy blinked and lowered his head. "Thank ye."

Maggie laughed. "Och, Calum, I told you Rob speaks Scots."

He shrugged. "Didna ken how well."

John picked up Maggie's bags. "Get your things, lad, and let's go home. Flora has a tasty supper ready."

⁂

Maggie ran her hands up and down Rob's ribs. "You're so thin you cannot have been eating enough. Your letters have been so brief I feared you were ill."

Those delightful dimples deepened as he took her into his arms. "I'm grand. And what right has the kettle calling the pot black. You've lost weight."

"No' much. As you know, hospital food is drearyful."

He nuzzled her neck. "On you come, I have something to show you."

When they reached the end of the pier, he led her across the side-path toward the packing shed.

"What can be over here?"

"Something I've been working on." He opened the shed door and led her inside.

"Are you planning to seduce me?" Her stomach flipped. How brazen!

"Don't put ideas in my head." He took the roll from the shelf. "Come back outside. 'Tis getting too dark to see much in here."

Well, in for a penny, in for a pound. She *would* have that private kiss.

"If you won't seduce me, I'm thinking I'll have to take the initiative." She stood on tiptoe. "Kiss me properly before I decide you don't luve me after all."

The roll hit the floor. He grabbed her. "You're going to be sorry you challenged me." A satisfied purr. He lowered his mouth to hers.

A long kiss.

Three months of longing and loneliness disappeared in minutes.

Shivers shook her body when their lips parted.

"Och, Maggie, lass, only a few more hours, and you'll be my wife. Then, watch out." A deep groan.

"That had better be a promise."

"It is that, lass. Och, it is that."

The yearning in his voice played a familiar melody in her soul. "Then show me what you've been working on."

He led her outside to a large rock and unrolled the sheet of paper. "This is a rendering of Innisbraw's Coastal Rescue boat, the *Maggie*."

She studied the detailed drawing, eyes tearing again. "Och, Rob, she's going to be so bonnie. I'm touched you chose to name her after me."

"She could have no other name."

"But she doesn't look a thing like Barra's lifeboat. How could you design something like this?"

"The design took a lot of hard work and prayer. I'm calling her a rescue boat, no' a lifeboat." He rolled up the plan. "We'd better hurry. Our Flora's been cooking all afternoon."

She sighed as she fingered his loose uniform blouse. So thin. "I'm going to have my work cut out for me putting some flesh back on your bones."

"'Twill be easy for you to do. But, I'm warning you, if I see one more piece of mutton, I'm going to mutiny."

※

Rob ate his words when Flora served the main course. Leg of mutton. His eyes lit on a jar of lemon curd Maggie brought from London. No one commented, but there were a few raised eyebrows when he slathered the sweet-sour sauce onto his meat.

John cornered Rob in the hall while Maggie helped Flora with the dishes. "Calum and I will be staying here at the infirmary for the night," he said. "No reason to start any more gossip."

He and Calum retired to their infirmary rooms early. Rob added an armful of peats to the fireplace and he and Maggie sat on the sofa, cuddled together beneath the knitted blanket while he answered her many questions.

"Are you going to give your crew medical training?"

"Absolutely, that's another way she'll differ from the lifeboats the R.N.L.I. certifies. What guid would it do to rescue someone only to lose them to a medical emergency?" He pulled the pins from her hair. "Enough talk, lass. You've been driving me daft all een." He spread her hair over her shoulders and buried his face in its fragrance before tipping her chin and lowering his lips to hers.

Maggie responded with all her heart.

He walked her to her room just before the turn of the night. "There's nowt I want more than to have you on my bed the night," he said, "but I don't trust myself, and you've had a long journey." He kissed her lips, then parted her hair so he could kiss the nape of that silken, fragrant neck. "Guid-night, my bonnie lass. I'll see you on the mornin."

"Och, I'll no' fix your breakfast if you're going to pick at your food the way you did this een."

Her earlobe begged to be nibbled. "Maggie, my luve, I promise to eat every bite of whatever it is you cook—as long as it isn't mutton. But right now, I need another of those wonderful kisses to tide me over."

"One more, then off to bed. It has been a long journey."

She tasted so guid, he almost lost the battle right then.

Why hurt her now when you've waited so long?

"Guid-night, my bonnie lass."

Emotions high, he thought he would lie awake for hours, but moments after he went to bed and thanked the Lord for his Maggie's safe return, he tumbled into sleep.

Maggie lay awake. She turned onto her side and hugged herself with delight. Could it really be true? In only a few hours, she and Rob would be husband and wife? "Thank Ye, Lord, for giving me a man with such honour and integrity," she breathed. "And please,

please protect him when he goes back to duty, for I cannot allow even the briefest thought of ... of what life would be like without him." She buried her face in her pillow, unwilling to allow such dark thoughts now.

She pictured him racing up the pier toward her, his long, healthy legs covering the distance in a few seconds, his soft hazel eyes filled with tears of love as he grabbed her up into his strong arms. She heard his husky voice in her ear. *Just a few more hours and you'll be my wife. Then watch out.*

"The morra's night, my luve," she whispered. "The morra's night."

~*~

Maggie baked scones for breakfast and they ate early, long before John or Calum awoke. Rob ate six scones and drank an entire pot of coffee. Though relieved to see him devour his food, it saddened her that he had eaten so little while she was away. Somehow, she'd have to arrange a posting closer to Edenoaks. Her man needed fattening.

No sun broke through the grey clouds and a cold wind battered the island. They bundled up in sweaters and jacket and walked across the top of the fell, her arm around his hips, him hugging her shoulder. Shep romped around them, brushing against Maggie's stocking-clad legs, blue eyes soft with welcome.

They stopped at a large, flat rock near the edge of the cliff. She settled into his lap, rejoicing at the beat of his heart against her cheek.

They looked deeply into one another's eyes and talked about how they filled the lonely hours they spent apart. They kissed deeply and often and clasped hands when their words faltered while trying to express how much they had yearned for this moment.

When they returned to the infirmary, Maggie prepared beef pasties and mashed tatties and neeps for a hearty dinner, while Rob sat at the kitchen table, watching. John and Calum rushed in late, out of breath, their cheeks lashed red from the wind.

"Sorry we're so late." John warmed his hands over the stove. "We've been for a walk around the island so Calum could visit his friends. Spending his summer holiday apprenticing on a trawler instead of coming home called for some explaining."

※

After she finished the dinner dishes, Maggie gave Rob a quick kiss and disappeared into her room. Rob bathed and shaved in the small bathing room. When he returned to his room, he eyed the Hieland dress outfit with trepidation. It'd better never get back to Group he married wearing a skirt.

John knocked on his door a little after 1300, dressed in an outfit identical to Rob's, except for the shape of the sporran. "I thought you might need a little instruction."

"Thank the Lord you're here. I don't know where to start."

"You begin with the hose and then the shirt."

Rob squirmed. "I've a question," he said after an uncomfortable silence. "I've heard things—I mean, there's the question of what to wear under the kilt."

John laughed and whispered into his ear.

Rob grinned, face flushing. "You're the expert." He put on the hose and pulled the shirt over his head. "Now what?"

"The kilt." After the kilt was buckled, he showed Rob how to pull the plaid flashes over the tops of his hose to hold them up, then picked up the small black-handled knife in its leather case. "You wear this in the top of your right hose." He tucked the knife into place. "Now, fasten the sporran chains and you're ready for your shoes, vest, and tie."

"This takes more effort than getting into full dress uniform at the Point."

After Rob knotted his tie, John helped him into the jacket. "Och, you're looking like a true Scotsman. Nobody would doubt it, seeing you now."

Fully dressed, Rob didn't feel nearly as uncomfortable as he'd feared. Only a small area from the middle of his knees to his hose, which came up over his calves, was exposed. "Well? Do I pass muster?"

Tears—tears!—sprang up in John's eyes. "You do that. Now, I'll get Calum and we'd best be off for the kirk. Maggie will need some privacy. You cannot see her 'til you're ready to take your vows."

Rob spent a long time with Shep, rubbing his ears and ruff and talking to him in the soft, deep voice the pup loved. "I couldn't have done it without you, lad. You kept me going when I wanted to give up. Don't worry, we'll both be back before long."

The dog leaned against Rob's legs, shivering and licking his master's chin and hands.

Rob choked back tears when he, John, and Calum left for the kirk.

Chapter Forty-seven

A sea of smiling faces greeted Rob when he stepped out of the small anteroom onto the dais at the front of the sanctuary. Men's and lads' hair slicked back with water or a dab of hoarded Brylcreem, women's neatly plaited and lasses' pulled back from their shining faces with colourful celluloid barrettes—all clad in their best Sabbath clothes.

Surely, everybody on Innisbraw had come to help him and Maggie celebrate their wedding day.

Holiday ribbons festooned the ends of the pews. Bees-wax candles flickered, transforming the richly coloured, woven threads of the altar cloth into strands of sparkling rubies, emeralds, and amethysts.

Rob inhaled the candle's warm, welcoming, fragrance.

Calum took his place at Rob's side, eyes downcast, studying his laced ghillies as if hoping they could transport him somewhere else with a silent plea. The pleats of his kilt quivered with the trembling of his knees.

Rob squeezed his elbow. "They're no' looking at you, lad. Relax."

Didn't help. He still shook. The shy lad must be overcome with embarrassment.

What was taking so long? Rob unclenched his hands and flexed his fingers. He took a deep breath and relaxed his shoulders.

Just like a bombing strike. Not much action until one neared the target. *Patience, Savage. This is the most important mission you'll ever fly.*

Hugh took his place before the altar, glasses reflecting the dancing candlelight, round cheeks red as winter apples. He wore a dark brown tweed suit, stiffly starched white shirt, and tightly woven, wide tie behind a too-snug tweed vest. Warm brown eyes flashed a twinkling message of kinship when his gaze met Rob's. He nodded to Sheila MacNab, the organist.

The pump organ wheezed the final note of a hymn. Sheila began the processional.

Rob's pulse stuttered.

The door at the back of the nave opened and everyone stood, craning their necks for a glimpse of the bride.

Maggie and John stepped slowly up the aisle.

She looked so bonnie Rob forgot to breathe.

A long light-blue and green plaid skirt swirled around her ankles and a pale blue sweater hugged her slim body, the lace points of the sleeves almost reaching her fingertips. A blue and green plaid sash draped over one shoulder, pinned above her breast with an ornate silver brooch where it crossed to the other side. A silver barrette held the sides of her shiny black hair high at the crown of her head, and curls cascaded over her shoulders and down past her waist, as soft candlelight danced on her fair skin.

He sucked in a deep breath. A wave of emotion threatened to sweep him off his feet.

Her violet-blue eyes caught his. With a radiant smile, she walked toward him, head held high.

His arms ached to hold her close. His Maggie, the lass who brought meaning to his life, the woman who would bear his bairns. *Bless this lass, Lord. Help me give her the happiness she deserves.*

Willing his legs not to betray him, he walked down the stairs to meet her.

John placed her hand on his arm and together, he and Maggie climbed the steps and faced Hugh.

※

Maggie glanced up at Rob. Och, he looked so braw in his McGrath kilt. The light caught the red and blonde in his hair and green flecks danced in his almost translucent hazel-brown eyes as their gazes met.

His arm trembled beneath her hand. Was he excited?

Surely no' as excited as she. This was the culmination of

childhood fantasies, grown-up hopes, dreams, and prayers. *Thank Ye, Lord, for my Rob. For his luve and bravery, even his impatience. You've given me the lad You prepared just for me. How I praise—*

"Before we begin," Hugh said in Scots, "you may wonder why all of our auld folk have been seated in the front rows at the left of the nave. I will be conducting this solemn ceremony in Scots so Rob can understand and Morag will be translating it into the Gaelic for those with no other language."

Rob's smile brought a bubble of delight to Maggie's throat.

"Dear folk of Innisbraw." Hugh raised his arms as if embracing the congregation. "In the names of Rob and Maggie, let me welcome you to this joyous occasion. I know you have come the day to celebrate with luving hearts and generosity of spirit. Rejoice with them and share their joy.

"Let us bow our heads for a moment of silent prayer as we beseech our Heavenly Faither to bless this most holy of unions."

Rob's warm hand engulfed Maggie's.

Her heart sang praises to a loving, faithful Faither. *Help me be the wife he deserves, Lord. Give me patience and wisdom. Watch over him when he goes on missions and give me Your faith when mine falters.*

"We offer these prayers in the name of your Son, our Savior, Jesus Christ. Amen." Hugh turned his gaze to her faither, who remained in the aisle. "Who gives this woman to be married to this man?"

"I do," John said, voice choked with tears.

***

Hugh watched John take his place beside Elspeth in the front pew.

What a wrenching moment this must be. *Gratitude that your daughter has found her true luve, and regret that she no longer belongs to you alone.*

He turned his attention to the beloved couple before him. "Rob and Maggie, at this very moment, our Heavenly Faither is present in your hearts. What began as a friendship in a hospital room during a terrible war is coming to fruition in a kirk on this wee island we all call home.

"These are difficult times, often grim times. They call for different words than I normally use. I have seen with my eyes, and felt in my heart the luve our Maggie and our Rob have for one another. Theirs will no' be an easy beginning for they are both dedicated to serving Scotland and America in this just war in which we are engaged."

His gaze swept the congregation. "Every day, our Maggie will give solace and care to our brave lads who are injured in battle. And every day, our Rob will fly deep into hostile territory to do all he can to end this horror. We must all do our parts and offer their names daily before the Throne of the Prince of Peace.

"And we must also remember that our blessed Savior, Jesus Christ, placed his seal of approval on the sanctity of marriage when He turned water into wine at a wedding feast in Cana."

He smiled at the young couple. "Robert James Savage, do you promise to cherish this lass, to honour her, to luve her as Christ luves the Church?"

"I do." Strong voice of a lad who knows he has found his perfect lass.

"Margaret Julia McGrath, do you promise to cherish this lad, to honour him, to luve him as the Church luves Christ?"

"I do." Trembling voice of a tender lass about to realize her dreams.

"Rob, you may place the ring on Maggie's finger, remembering its significance as you do, for the shape of the ring symbolizes the unending luve you offer her."

Calum handed the ring to Rob, fingers shaking.

"Please repeat after me. 'Maggie, with this ring I give myself to you completely, willingly sharing with you the bonds of marriage as a seal of our luve throughout eternity.'"

Rob repeated the words as he slipped the ring onto Maggie's finger. Such luve in his eyes.

"Maggie?"

She reached for Rob's hand.

Rob gazed at the ring in wonder as she slid it onto his finger. Wider, but a perfect match to hers, and a perfect fit. He owed the cannie skipper far more than he could ever repay with silver.

Hugh placed their right hands together and squeezed them between his palms. "'Tis with great joy I say, that in the name of God our Faither, I now pronounce you husband and wife. Rob, you may kiss your lass."

Rob gathered Maggie into his arms. "Forever and ever and ever," he whispered.

She nodded, tears slipping down her cheeks.

Lips so soft, so sweet.

Her heartbeat echoed through his body.

When he raised his head, her tear-streaked face filled him with such overwhelming luve, those sitting in the first few pews surely heard the sob he couldn't repress.

She was his. At last, Maggie was truly his!

The congregation, laughing and blethering, followed Rob and Maggie into the kirk hall.

"I'm going to show you around before 'tis too crowded to move." Maggie pulled Rob toward a table covered with plates of sweets. "Those are clootie dumplings—fruit-filled, steamed buns." She pointed. "And those are sair haidie—iced sponge cakes." A laugh tickled her throat as she hugged his arm. "Of course you recognize the shortbreads and scones."

"Och, I wish I was hungry. The folk must have used all their sugar coupons so we could have sweets."

"You're no' hungry?" No reason to mention she couldn't swallow a bite. She guided him to the next table. "Then I see something you've never turned down. Coffee."

His delightful dimples deepened. "Coffee? You just said the magic word."

She stirred honey and milk into her tea and watched him gulp his coffee, hoping he would finally realize how welcome he was on Innisbraw.

She also hoped he would be willing to leave early. Hens-flesh pricked her body.

Married.

And he had promised to carry her to their marriage bed.

She ducked her head to hide her burning cheeks.

He pointed to an army of bottles at the end of the table. "Looks like that Lucozade you made me drink at the Royal Infirmary."

She bumped his leg with her hip. Brazen again. But now, he was her husband. "'Tis skoosh, no' Lucozade.

"Skoosh?"

"Fizzy lemonade. 'Tis really a drink for women and bairns."

Cups empty, she led him through the crowd toward the opposite wall, their progress halted often by folk conveying their best wishes and vowing prayers for Rob's safety.

She stopped in front of a table piled high with gifts wrapped in bits of ironed, used paper or bleached muslin sacking. "This is the handsel table. These are all handmade gifts given by those who want to help us furnish our first home." Tears threatened. Such generosity from folk who had so little.

Rob squeezed her hand. "All those gifts and so much luve. I've never felt like I truly belonged until the day. Now I know what it feels like to have a home."

What a blessed, blessed day. He finally realized he belonged!

She fought more tears and tried a smile. "Och, you belong here and there's no escaping it. You're an Innisbraw lad now, and always will be."

The wheeze of a piper filling his bag and tootle of a whistle cut through the buzz of conversation.

Rob peered over the heads of the crowd. "That looks like that Irisher who bought the howff."

Maggie stood on tiptoe. "Och, I can't see over all the folk, but Flora told me somebody named Paddy and several musical lads on the island have been playing at the howff most eens."

John shouldered his way through the folk and tapped Rob's arm as the musicians launched into a rollicking tune. "That's the shamit reel. You're expected to dance the first tune with Maggie."

"But I don't know how."

"Och, you can dance, can't you?"

"Of course, but it has to be slow."

"I'll see what I can do."

After a few moments, the music changed to a slow, rhythmic tune. Rob blotted his forehead on his sleeve and grimaced. "Och, Maggie, I almost made an eejit of myself at our wedding ceilidh."

She swallowed a smile. "They'll assume your legs aren't up to a reel. On you come, luve, everybody's watching."

The crowd moved to the walls.

She stepped into Rob's arms, resting her cheek against his chest as they danced around the center of the room.

Memories of their first meeting flooded her mind—his huge hand so gentle on hers, his tall, strong body so close she trembled. His voice so deep, words so hesitant.

She shouldn't cry when everyone was watching.

He leaned over and whispered, "'Tis bonnie you are, Maggie lass."

The same words he'd spoken that night. Tears flowed.

As the evening progressed, Maggie showed him some of the Scottish dance steps. Considering himself too tall and ungainly he had never enjoyed dancing, but inspired to learn, he soon mastered a gliding strathspey. Other dancers guided him with soft whispers and hand signals every time he and Maggie separated.

When the dance ended, he ran a palm over his sweaty forehead. "That wasn't too bad, but that first tune they played scared me to death."

"Don't worry. We'll have lots of time to practice before we come back home."

"How long is this ceilidh going to last? 'Tis already"—he checked his watch—"gone 1900."

"'Twill most likely go on all night. It's been a long time since anybody's had owt to celebrate and those who've been guarding the shore need time for a wash-up before they come."

Rob's face fell.

"But we can leave any time we want."

"Now you tell me." He wiggled his eyebrows. "I hate to leave early, but I have a date with the bonniest lass on Innisbraw, and we have a boat to catch early on the mornin. If you're certain 'tis all right, I'd like to go soon." He held his breath.

Her pert nose wrinkled. "Is now soon enough?"

He nodded at the table laden with handsel gifts. "Shouldn't we thank the folk?"

"Morag will help Elspeth make a list of everything and pack it up for us and Faither can put it in the attic storeroom at the infirmary. They don't expect us to acknowledge their gifts now, or even use them 'til we have our own home."

"Our own home. I like the sound of that." He led her away from the dancers. "I'd like to build us a cottage when we get back, Maggie—a home of our own, for us and our eight bairns."

"I didn't think you'd ever get around to mentioning it."

"Och, lass, I've disappointed you again."

She laughed and grabbed his arm. "I'm teasing. Let's leave now, while that red-headed Irisher and his lads are taking a rest."

They made their way to the back wall where Elspeth, John, Hugh, and Calum visited.

"About to take your leave, are you?" Elspeth asked, faded blue eyes lit with an inner glow. "'Tis only fitting."

While the two women embraced, John pulled Rob aside. "I have a wee gift for the twa of you, but you won't be able to claim it until you reach Edenoaks."

"You shouldn't have gotten us owt, John. How can I ever repay you for all you've done?"

"This is no' something tangible, lad. I was able to twist a few arms and call in a few favors. Maggie will report for duty at the Edenoaks hospital on the twentieth of this month. One of the American nurses was most happy to trade duties with her. It will be a permanent posting."

"Och, John!" He clasped John's shoulder to keep from staggering. "You couldn't have done anything more wonderful. We'll be together."

"You can tell Maggie later when you're alone. You'll have the cottage the night."

"But you and Calum ..."

"Will stay at the infirmary. After all, you can't spend your marriage night in a hospital bed."

Rob squirmed. John's words, though sincere, were a bit too personal. "Thank ye."

"Then, it's time to take your leave. Though 'tis still blowing a cold wind, the rain has held off, so 'tis a nice night for a walk up the fell." He took a small hooded torch from his sporran. "Use this along the path. Angus is picking up Shep on his way home the night and will keep him until your return to Innisbraw. I'll see you at 0600. Malcolm must sail a bit after that if you're to make your train."

"Thank ye for everything." Rob pumped John's hand. "We'll be at the infirmary in plenty of time." He thumped Calum's shoulder. "And thank ye for standing up with me. I'd have felt the eejit all alone."

"It was nowt," the lad stammered, red staining his cheeks.

Maggie kissed her father's cheek, then Calum's, before embracing both Elspeth and Hugh. "Guid-night, dear friends. I'll no' say guid-bye, for we'll be back home soon."

Rob hugged Elspeth. "You've been the shining beacon of hope the entire time I've been here. Your prayers are the main reason I'm walking again."

She patted his chest. Just like their first meeting, her hand radiated warmth. "Take care of yourself, lad. We need you back once this terrible war is over."

"With you praying, I'll be back." He hugged her again and kissed her cheek. Tears filled his eyes—and hers—before he turned away.

He gripped Hugh's hand. "That was a grand ceremony. I can't thank you enough for your friendship and lessons in the Word."

Hugh smiled, eyes sparkling. "You're verra welcome. It's been my pleasure." He grasped Rob's hand tightly. "May the Lord guard and protect you, dear lad. Our fervent prayers are with you for your safe return."

Broken Wings

"Thank ye, and I mean that from the bottom of my heart."

Rob shook many hands as they made their way to the door, spending time with the MacDonalds and MacPhees, thanking them for the kindness and support. Mark and Susan Ferguson stopped them at the door with more hugs, handshakes, and promises of prayers.

He slipped into a woolen jacket John had loaned him, pulled Maggie's coat collar up around her ears, and they ducked quickly out the door so little light would escape. Once outside, he picked her up and whirled around. "On you come, Missus Savage. Mister Savage wants to show his wife how much he luves her."

Candlelight lit the tiny cottage bedroom with a warming glow as Maggie glided into the room wearing her white nightgown. Her hair glistened in the flickering light, spilling over her shoulders and down her slender back.

He stood by the blacked-out window and watched her approach, swelling heart threatening to crowd the air from his lungs. He held out his arms and she stepped into his embrace.

Their lips met, melted together, expressing a love too powerful to voice.

"My wife. My bonnie, bonnie wife. How I luve you."

"And I luve you, my husband." She hugged his hips. "Carry me to our bed, Rob. I feel like I've waited forever."

He picked her up and walked to the bed, pulled back the covers and laid her down before climbing in beside her. He looked down at her, awed. Maggie was his wife. *I want to remember this moment forever.*

Never alone again.

The Nearness of You.

The Lord, with his matchless grace, provided the one woman in the world meant to be his wife, his love, his everything. He kissed her forehead, cheeks, nibbled on her earlobes, and ran his lips over her throat.

When he unbuttoned her gown and helped her remove it, the love shining in her violet-blue eyes flooded his heart with intense joy.

Her soft fingers caressed his shoulders and moved over the mat of hair on his chest as he trailed his lips down her trembling neck, his movements slow and gentle.

No reason to hurry.

All the time in the world to show his Maggie how much he luved and treasured her.

Like the Selkie's crofter, he had forever and ever and ever.

The End

Acknowledgments

My father started my love affair with flying when he bought his first bi-plane in the 1920's and began barn-storming. My scrapbook contains an article from a Tillamook, Oregon, newspaper recounting Ben Hathaway cutting his engine to yell to his wife what time he'd be home for supper. And this book could never have been written without the help of my daughter, Valerie McDonald, and her husband, Jim McDonald, accomplished Air Guard, Air Force, and airline pilots. My thanks, too, to Kenneth Manley, who served as a Radio Operator on a B-17 in WWII and shared with me his experiences of having to bailout from 12,000 feet. Three of my cousins, Roland Heusser, Wayne Erskine and Delmar Erskine, served on B-17s and were among those who came home after the war.

Many people helped with the medical side of the story, most notably my nephew, Geoffrey West, an ER nurse, and Stephen Kornfeld, MD (love his infectious grin).

Patricia (Paddy) MacKinnon, of the Isle of Barra, Outer Hebrides, Scotland, took me under her wing and has become a life-long friend. Paddy was a goldmine of information and provided humorous idioms, a cosy bedroom with a view of North Harbour, gourmet dinners of fresh prawns and salmon, and the companionship of her flat-haired retriever, Josh, who kept me company on my walks across the "machair."

Christina Tarabochia, my editor and dear friend, has been a champion and a lifesaver. Thank ye, Christina.

Mary Hall and Jen Simons offered critiques, support, and a shoulder to cry on, even if their arms had to reach from the east to the west coast.

My son, Steve Price, provided my website. I am so grateful for his time and hard work.

History buffs will note that I have taken liberties with a few dates, including the introduction of P-47 fighters and B-17s into England, and Eisenhower's appointment to head SHAEF. All other facts are as accurate as I could make them, and any and all mistakes are mine alone.

A little hint: don't look for Innisbraw on a map of the Outer Hebrides. It is like *Brigadoon* and appears only in the misty glens and braes of this author's imagination.

Bio

Dianne fell in love with writing at the age of five. Because her father was a barnstorming pilot, she was bitten early by the "flying bug" as well. She attended the University of California, Santa Barbara and met and married the man God had prepared for her—an aeronautical engineer. After their five children were in school, she burned the midnight oil and wrote three novels, all published by Zebra Press. When her husband died only three years after he retired, she felt drawn to visit the Outer Hebrides Isles of Scotland, where her husband's clan (MacDonalds) and her own clan (Galbraiths) originated. Many yearly trips, gallons of tea, too little sleep, and a burst of insight birthed her *Thistle Series*.

PUBLISHER'S NOTE: Dianne, born August 1933, lived joyfully despite dealing with terminal cancer and died in August 2013, a mere week before the release date for the first book of this series, *Broken Wings*. Everyone involved with the production of this book and the next five has been blessed beyond measure to have known Dianne and be a part of giving readers a chance to meet Rob and Maggie and visit the beautiful, fictional isle of Innisbraw.

Leave a message for her family and sign up to hear the latest about her books at www.ashberrylane.com/dianneprice or www.facebook.com/authordianneprice.

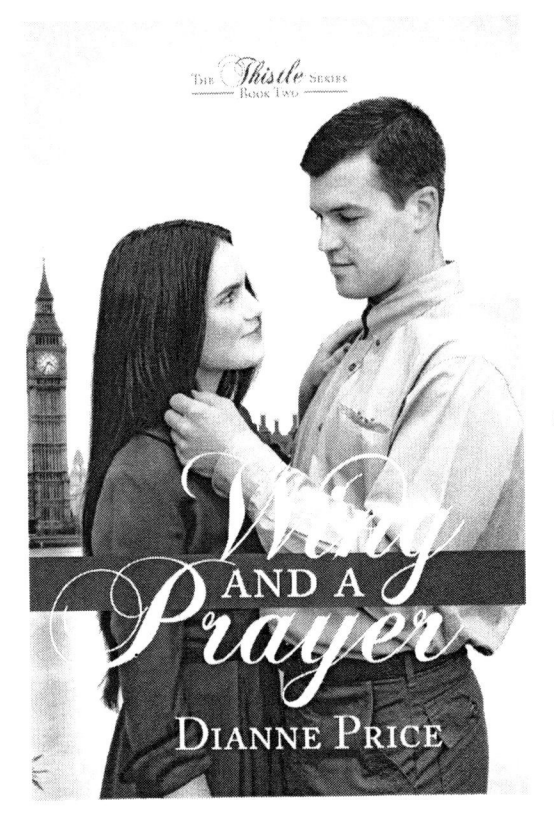

Coming Soon
Book Two of
The Thistle Series

Wing and a Prayer

DIANNE PRICE

Colonel Rob Savage is confronted by almost insurmountable difficulties when he returns to command the 396th Heavy Bomber Group at Edenoaks Air Base in England: low morale, bombs seldom on target, and damaged or destroyed Flying Fortresses which take far too long to replace. While Rob labors to make his group best in Wing again, his bride, Maggie Savage, an RAF nurse posted to the base, works long, exhausting hours, fearing for Rob's life every time he leads a bombing mission.

Can Rob and Maggie cleave to their faith in God through such hardships and trials? Can Innisbraw's folk survive constant poverty, heartache, and fear for their lads in service?

Glossary

All words are Scots, unless otherwise noted

aumrie: hutch or breakfront.

bairn: child.
bairnie: baby.
bannock: oat griddle bread, similar to English muffins.
bee skep: beehive.
blether: talk, visit. (In the plural, nonsense.)
Bonnie: beautiful.
braw: handsome, a pleasing sight.
bree: soup or broth.
breeks: pants or trousers.
buttery: biscuit made with butter.

cairt: cart pulled by a horse.
cannie: shrewd, expert, skillful, or lucky.
ceilidh: Gaelic (pronounced *kay-lee*), party with music, dancing, sharing of news.
chaumer: parlor or gathering room.
clothes-press: dresser for clothing or bedding.
coo: cow.
cor blimey: UK, exclamation originally meaning "God blind me."
crabbit: crabby, cranky.
croft: piece of land.
crofter: farmer, or one who owns a croft used for agriculture.
cuddy: small, shaggy horse, usually used to pull a cart.

daft: insane.
disremember: forget.
door flags: group of flat stones before door to a cottage.
dreich: dreary, dull, grey, usually describing weather.

eejit: idiot, fool.
een: evening, can be written e'en.

emulsion: UK, paint.
entry: porch, passage into house.

faither: father.
face flannel: UK, washcloth.
fankle: disorder, entanglement.
fash: worry, vex.
flag: piece of stone used as floor of a cottage.

ghillies: Gaelic, shoes worn with kilts, usually laced up over calf-high hose.
girse: grass.
gloaming: twilight.
grandmither: grandmother.
guid: (pronounced *gid*) good.

hoy: greeting.

incomer: outsider who comes to live on island.
IP: American Air Forces, Initial Point of bombing run.
Irisher: Irishman or woman.

jaw box: kitchen sink.

keek: look at, peek.
kirk: church.
kittled up: excited, enlivened.

machair: Gaelic (pronounced *ma-K-er*), alluvial plain, unique to Outer Hebrides.
mebbe: maybe.
medicaments: UK, medicine.
midden: dirty, mess, untidy place.
Minch: arm of the Atlantic between Outer Hebrides and Scotland.
mither: mother.
mufti: Universal, civilian clothes worn by someone who usually wears a uniform.

neeps: turnips.
no': not.
nowt: nothing.

owt: anything.

partan: common crab.
PDI: American Air Forces, Pilots Directional Indicator, used when bombing.
pishing doon: hard rain, usually used by men.
plomping doon: hard rain, usually used by women.
polis: police.

reekie: smelly, sometimes refers to smoke.

sark: shirt.
Siobhan: Gaelic (pronounced *Shi-vahn*), woman's name.

skirlie: recipe made with raw oats and chopped onions browned in meat fat.
slaiger: eating food carelessly.
slubber: slobber.
slutterie: slovenly.
snell: cold, if a wind, usually from the North.
strathspey: regal, gliding dance.

tatties: potatoes.
ta-ra: UK, good-bye.
the day: today.
tick: second of time.
turns: jobs or chores.
twa: two.

wedder lambs: lambs born prematurely.

yean: birthing of a lamb.

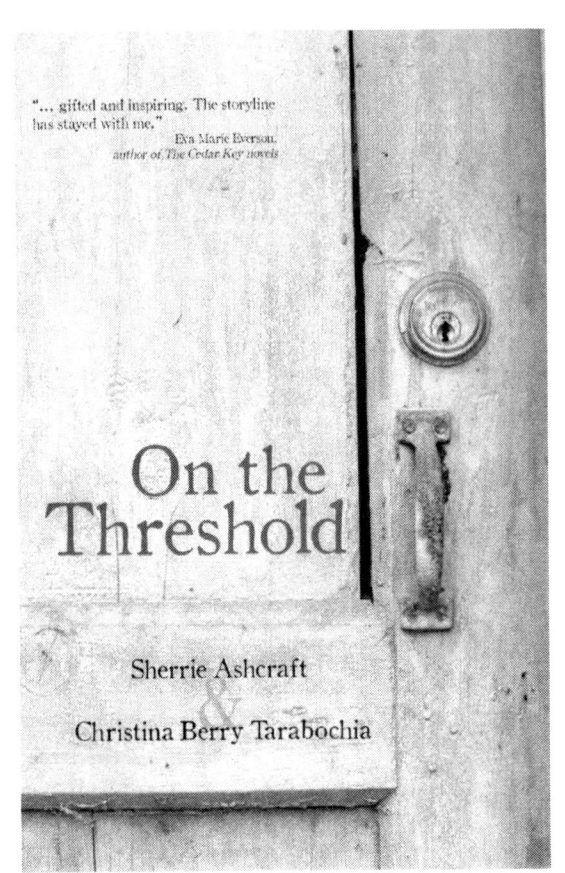

More from Ashberry Lane

"... gifted and inspiring. The storyline has stayed with me."
— Eva Marie Everson, author of The Cedar Key novels

On the Threshold

Sherrie Ashcraft
&
Christina Berry Tarabochia

Suzanne—a mother with a long-held secret. Tony—a police officer with something to prove. Beth—a daughter with a storybook future. When all they love is lost, what's worth living for?

Like a sandcastle buffeted by ocean waves, Suzanne's façade crumbles when her perfect life is swept away. Tragedy strikes and police officer Tony Barnett intersects with the lives of both women as he tries to discover the truth. Left adrift and drowning in guilt long ignored, Suzanne spirals downward into paralyzing depression. Beth, dealing with her own grief, must face the challenge of forgiveness. Can these two women learn to trust each other again? Will they find the power of God's grace in their lives?

CPSIA information can be obtained
at www.ICGtesting.com
Printed in the USA
FSOW01n2335030615
7594FS